THE SECRET COURTESAN

Published in 2026 by
She Writes Press, an imprint of The Stable Book Group

32 Court Street, Suite 2109
Brooklyn, NY 11201
https://shewritespress.com
Library of Congress Control Number: 2025918197
ISBN: 979-8-89636-064-3
eISBN: 979-8-89636-065-0

Interior Designer: Tabitha Lahr

Printed in the United States

THE SECRET COURTESAN

a novel

Kerry Chaput

SHE WRITES PRESS

This book is dedicated to all the
disobedient women history has erased.

Chapter One

DR. MIA HARDING

London, Current Day

Yes, I can feel you.

The same thought flies through my mind every morning when I arrive at the library's grand foyer and stare up at the sculpture that seems to ask who among us is more than a spectator. Thousands have never answered, walking past the smoothed Carrara marble and down these hallowed halls. An unnamed artist spent years refining every edge and striation, smoothing every crack into the form of a blindfolded woman kneeling at the feet of a powerful man. The beating heart of this sculpture connects with me in unsaid words. Created during a time of upheaval, of war and famine, the stone hums a message of power. Of survival. It asks, "Can you feel me?"

Leaded glass windows peek into the blustery inner courtyard. I graze my fingers across the Portland stone columns to feel a rush from all that this building has seen over the centuries.

By the time I arrive at my office, I've forgotten about the marble statue entirely. I've smoothed my pants and shaken my trench coat of misty drops and dried horse chestnut leaves, gathering my focus for what awaits.

The plaque at my door displays my credentials: Mia Harding, PhD, Visiting Researcher. Said plaque now reads—in red Sharpie and poor penmanship—Mia Harding, Expert in Wenches and Witches. It takes no time at all to sigh, roll my eyes, and rip the paper away. My colleagues' childish prank is somehow worse in red ink. At least have the balls to insult me in black.

"Good day, Dr. Harding." Dr. Byron's chipper young assistant appears at 8:00 a.m. on the dot, cappuccino in hand. Her boss sends her every day to pump me for information.

"Thank you." The first sip may well be the perfect vodka gimlet for how my brain awakens with a jolt of happiness. I remain rigid, keeping my thrill to myself. "You're very sweet." I should turn her away, but her eagerness is endearing. The kid has aspirations, just like I did years ago.

"My pleasure." She seems to float as she says this, her bright blue eyes lingering on mine. "Dr. Byron would like an update on his research." She glances over her shoulder. "Have you made a decision on the Armani statue?"

I've scoured the archives and picked apart Dr. Byron's research, desperate to silence that voice of doubt that's been with me from the moment I laid eyes on the now infamous statue. My mind tells me his work is satisfactory, yet my suspicions grow larger by the minute.

I break eye contact and take another long sip of coffee. I've avoided this question for weeks, but today is my last workday here. Friday. Three days until the expected announcement I'm not entirely sure I'm ready to give.

"He makes me ask," she blurts as her cheeks flush to bright pink.

"You're simply doing your job." Boy, do I understand her. More than she can know.

She nods and shakes off her embarrassment. "I admire you, Dr. Harding. Most historians would have swooped in, become chums with Dr. Byron's team, and signed the press release on day two. Not you. You're here to find the truth. Maybe even discover secrets?"

The good old boys club is alive and well in the art world. She's still young enough to believe there are renegades among us. Women who defy expectations, as if our moral compass is enough to rise above the bullshit. Before she can hit me with another compliment, I smile and grind the sexist note in my hand until it crinkles. I want her to leave, but some part of me wants to protect her. From what, I'm not sure.

She glances at the paper in my fist. "I'm sorry the museum staff hasn't been more welcoming."

"Well, you make up for that, don't you?" *Always compliment the ones who bring the good coffee.* So often, I've had to choke down the bitter remains of a carafe after the important players got their fill. "Besides, I'm used to the games."

"Games, Dr. Harding?"

Who am I to shatter her lovely glass snow globe? I suspect she believes truth and integrity are all that matter. "No one takes kindly to having their research questioned." Certainly not men with fancy degrees from places like Harvard and Oxford.

I'm eager to speak. To tell someone about my theory. For one brash moment, I consider admitting to this young woman why my heart won't let me close the door on this office just yet. One beat later, I remember all that's on the line. Not just a promotion. My credibility would be questioned, my intentions mocked. Besides, my damn intuition won't stand up against the world of facts. Unfortunately, with women's history, that's often all we have.

"I'm certain you'll find the answers you're looking for." Her smile reminds me of a younger me. Enthusiastic and naive. We share a nice moment of sisterhood. So much that she slips. "Have a good weekend, Mia." She startles in time to catch me bristle. She would never make that mistake with one of the male researchers. I'm not sure those men even have first names. They could have changed their forename to *Doctor* and I wouldn't be the least bit surprised. She gasps, pressing her fingertips to her lips. "I'm so sorry, Dr. Harding. I meant no disrespect."

"Say no more. It's fine." Despite my tailored blazers and perfected chignon, I'm afraid the real me finds her way through the sheen. A Burberry coat can only cover so much.

She breathes slowly, mortification written all over her face. "You're under tremendous pressure."

You mean how the fate of the most photographed statue in the world rests on my shoulders? If I discredit Byron's research, the entire art world will have my head on a platter. I'm under enough pressure to crack. "This needs to be done right."

"I understand."

She doesn't understand. This statue could change everything. I may be the only one who thinks there's more here.

An English family submitted an online inquiry for their little garden statue. Sotheby's hired Dr. Byron, who determined it's from a clandestine excavation years ago in a crumbling Venetian palazzo. The man has sensationalized *The Estasi* as our generation's version of King Tut's Tomb. My reputation as an expert on Italian Baroque art landed me the role of authenticator. Like an unsaid threat, everyone expects me to deliver.

"Remind Dr. Byron my deadline is Monday. He will have my findings then."

I shut the door without a glance back and slide my chair to the window. Most of the view is a brick wall, though a sliver of overcast light pokes through the corner.

I scroll Google news, reading only the headlines. The art community refers to Lucca Armani as "The Baroque Baddie," with stupid internet memes and everything. My name comes up enough times to make me wince. Inexperienced. A virtual nobody. A woman with an axe to grind.

My success is quiet, and no one has heard of me. I'm the woman behind the research, not the flashy name who attends New York art shows.

I go over everything in my frantic mind yet again.

The art world believes Armani statues are buried all over Venice.

I don't listen to online chatter or folklore. I follow the historical records, and the composite analysis and carbon dating indicate Armani. Some materials even match pieces found in his studio.

But the historical records only tell one side.

. . . Don't be emotional, Mia. No one will believe you.

Why not? History needs advocates to ask hard questions.

I'm not here to ask the hard questions though, am I? I'm here to authenticate this research, satisfy my boss, and release the statue whose value increases by the minute. Researchers await, ready to tear apart Venice, on the hunt for more erotic art.

A high-resolution photo of *The Estasi* is pinned to my corkboard. I don't need to go to Sotheby's again. I've seen her in person, and it only solidified my thoughts. The woman's face is twisted in ecstasy, as if mid-orgasm. One hand is on her nipple, the other between her legs. Dr. Byron insists the woman is Lucca's wife, Caterina.

Historical records suggest he hated her. Why the hell would he sculpt her with such deep passion?

Can you ignore everything you've felt?

What I want doesn't matter. Once I complete this assignment, I'll see the title of *curator* after my name and I can do some good, creating exhibitions of powerful feminine art the world wasn't ready for four hundred years ago.

According to Dr. Byron, Lucca could have buried his other taboo pieces, leaving a trail of sex-fueled art hidden for us to unearth. He's viewed as a wild, passionate artist who died in obscurity after a lifetime of unrequited love, having never again sculpted after this fine piece.

Blame the frigid woman, pity the tortured artist.

The same lies I've spent a career trying to undo. And they are most often *always* lies. But people love a story, even one that's fabricated.

My frustration begs for another hit of caffeine. That single shot just left me wanting more. Umbrella and trench coat in hand, I leave my tiny office to walk down the street to the nearest café, housed in an old cottage, with low beams and crooked windows. The history here always makes me swoon. Three days until I return to my sparse apartment where the all-white interior reflects the blinding LA sunshine.

Outside, as the rain patters a linen overhang, a familiar voice bellows.

Byron.

I eye the exit, force my feet to stand firm, and glance through the cracked door. He's holding court for his assistant researchers and a few colleagues. His jacket has elbow patches. Like a proper snob.

"Time is almost up, Dr. Byron. Think she'll sign the authentication?" an eager assistant asks.

"Of course she will," he says while rocking heels to toes. He smiles at a pretty young student who waves from a nearby table. "My research is impeccable, and she knows it."

I should leave. Turn away now before my confidence crumbles. Of course, I have no interest in doing so, hoping he gives me reason to question him. A man outside the circle catches my eye. He's dressed in a bright purple sweater. Off-puttingly purple. A researcher who's been on assignment until this week. I've noticed him but not *noticed* him like I do right now. He stares up at the trees instead of at Byron. Black glasses. A dimple on his chin. Not at all unhandsome.

"Miss Harding?" Byron scoffs. "Not who I expected to lecture me on Baroque artists."

"Because she's American?" the man in the purple sweater asks.

"Yes. And because she specializes in *women's history*." The way he says women sounds how hot oil spits. I specialize in all artists of the time, but the media caught wind of my undergraduate women's history degree and ran with it. I am now fodder for misogynists.

"Wenches and witches," an assistant sputters.

I lean on a familiar mantra. Smile through rage, breathe when you want to scream. You can't change the world by fighting every ridiculous man in your way.

"You're an ass, Byron," the not unhandsome man says. "The woman is just doing her job."

I like you already, Mr. Eggplant Sweater.

Byron growls like a feral animal. "I expected a dowdy nanny with warts. Instead, we're to have our research questioned by an unsmiling child who doesn't even dress appropriately." He lowers his volume to a young man beside him, though his voice still carries. "She's probably hiding a tail under those oversized trousers."

Purple sweater throws a tea bag at Dr. Byron's face. "Have your tea alone, you arse."

"What's the matter, Beckett?" the young man asks, eager to prove himself. "Got the hots for the visiting ice queen?"

"Sod off."

Beckett. *Must remember him.* He's coming this way. Shit. In a dizzy spin, I search the café. No way out, so I turn to face the coffee counter, pretending to read something on my phone, but a bright red late fee notice pops up in my email. I shove the phone back in my pocket and smooth the fine hairs at my neck under the chignon.

"Dr. Harding?"

I turn, feigning surprise. "Good morning—Dr. Beckett, is it?" Oh God, up close he glows like a luminist watercolor. I'm so caught by the light reflecting off his cheeks, I can't take in anything else.

He nods, then glances over his shoulder at the table of men outside. "I'm sorry they're so insufferable."

I nod once. As much as I want to praise him for his chivalry, I opt for safety. "Just ordered. Lovely winter morning."

He stares at me for a moment, a subtle grin forming smile lines like a diamond with the sharp cut of his jaw. "Dark, cold. The usual. But I suppose to a Californian, it all feels new."

"Yes." New and very alluring. "Excuse me," I clear my throat, "I've work to do." I say this just as he says, "Research calls," and we bang into each other like some sort of ridiculous romantic comedy. My face hits his chest, which smells of soft cedar cologne and soap, and he knocks his glasses askew with his own hand.

The waitress presents my cappuccino, and by the time I turn, Beckett has left the building and my heart patters with the memory of his presence.

Back in my office, I set to work. I remove my favorite notebook with its worn Los Angeles Community College emblem, a gift to myself after earning my AA degree many moons ago before racking up piles of student loan debt that will hang over me until I die. I stare at my notes as a knock disrupts me. I'm about to tell them to come in, but Byron helps himself inside my office with a disapproving scowl.

His eyes wander over my desk, then to the large bag at the foot of my chair. "Today is your last, yes? Announcement on Monday."

"I may need a bit more time," I say, clasped hands propped on my desk. Now that I've said it out loud, I'll have to follow through. My cheeks flush and I force a deep breath.

"More time?" He slips his hands into his pockets, jiggling change in one of them. "Is that really necessary?"

I consciously lower my shoulders and soften my voice. "The truth is always necessary, Dr. Byron."

He doesn't even try to hide his snarl. "I can't see why you'd question the data. Are you an expert in carbon dating now?"

"As much as you are." My practiced breathy voice works like a charm to disarm him.

He forces a smile. "You do seem very accomplished, for a twenty-something."

"I'm thirty-seven." *Not that it's any of your concern, you jerk.* "And I've worked very hard." Harder than he'll ever know.

"Almost forty?" He raises his eyebrows, more offended than impressed. "This is quite an opportunity for you."

This time, I don't force a smile through my rage. I don't move at all. He wants me to beg for his approval. I've had my fill of that nonsense. Soon enough, my title will outshine his.

A heavy, uncomfortable silence sucks all the air from my office. Despite several well-regarded articles on Baroque Italian artists and the find that launched my name in the art world, my status as a history expert still feels like a rigid pair of running shoes not yet broken in.

I force myself up from the desk. "Well, Dr. Byron. It's been a pleasure. But it's late and you should get home to your family." I open the door and cross one foot over the other. "I know you're eager for my findings, but I still have three days to work." He's also eager to hit the interview circuit. As for me, a fat bonus, promotion to gallery curator, and a newfound respect await if I sign the prepared statement. One measly signature.

"Right." He turns to face me, but looks over his shoulder at my office one more time. "Admit it. There's nothing to question here. Lucca Armani sculpted his wife Caterina and more of his art remains hidden in Venice, I'm certain of it."

And yet, he's powerless until I authenticate his research. His ego rests in my hands. The sudden realization bolsters my confidence.

He's nearly out of the office when he turns to me and winks. I didn't plan on losing my cool today, yet here I am, struggling to press the cork on my bottled rage as it expands inside me.

"Have a lovely evening, Doctor." I practically shove him out with the door. *Just click it shut and move on, Mia.* And then, against everything I've learned and perfected, a cheeky retort finds its way free. "And to satisfy curiosity, I bear no tail under these trousers. I wear them oversized so unprofessional men look at my eyes rather than my ass."

I shut the door with a soft hand, though I want to slam it.

~

The sun has set on another Friday. My authentication letter and press release land in my inbox just moments before I shut my laptop for the evening. All standard and expected, though the last sentence lingers like a bad taste.

I'll give orders to prepare your new office as soon as I receive the signed documents. —Dr. Wright.

Strings. There are always strings.

Once more, I stand at the foot of the marble statue with thoughts of time. Months or years a man chiseled and sanded because the world allowed him to indulge his creative soul. Someone commissioned him. Supported him. Promoted his notions of greatness.

"Dr. Harding, you normally don't leave this early."

My heart skips, but I remain collected, refusing to be upended by his black glasses and chin dimple. "I've lived in the archives for weeks, so tonight, I'm letting my hair down." I touch my bun and know returning to my flat for an early bedtime is no one's idea of letting loose.

"Brilliant," he says with a smile. "I'm sure you heard Dr. Byron this afternoon berating your, well, everything."

I lift my hand. "Thank you, Dr. Beckett, but I'm fine. I've been called every name you can imagine." My childhood nickname, Mia Trashy, rises to the surface, but I force her down with a shove. My trailer park days are over. "I did appreciate you throwing your tea bag at his face though."

"Dr. Byron may insult my choice of jumpers, but I won't stand for him disrespecting a colleague."

I look at his chest. His firm, round in all the right places chest. "Your jumper? I hadn't noticed."

"Please, you could see this from space." He swings his arms at his sides. "My niece picked it out. I promised to wear it, and I am a man of my word."

Mia, you're near the finish line. Don't do something stupid, like swoon over his adorable dimple and love for his niece. "Why today?"

"It's my birthday."

I click my heels together and dip my head, like a proper nerd. "Well, happy birthday, Dr. Beckett."

"You can call me Noah." His eyes sparkle. His hair falls somewhere between brown and red, while his lips flame a perfect bright pink. I stare at him a beat longer, avoiding the reality that threatens to suffocate me. The pause holds me hostage. I look for something to say but no words seem to appear, so I turn toward the door, and he blurts out, "Fancy a pint?"

The depths of his good looks rattle my brain, but I don't date professors or researchers. I only date non-academia types, and I do it very, very poorly. I check the clock ticking in the hallway.

"It's just a pint, Dr. Harding." He places his hand on his chest. "With a man in an embarrassing jumper."

Don't do it, Mia. No. Absolutely not. "Okay." *Good grief, I have no willpower.*

We walk a block to the closest pub, which is at least three hundred years old. The steep roof and cross gables suggest Queen Anne style, but the turret adds a delightfully gothic touch. I'll miss this. I love dating buildings from their architectural details.

Noah must notice my distraction. "Wait until you see the interior. Nottingham alabaster abounds." He opens the door and pulls out my chair as I curse myself for feeling a rush of heat in my belly when he smiles.

In a dark corner near a roaring fire, I decide the best approach is to focus on work. "What draws you to the Italian artists?"

He sips his Tennent's Lager. "I spent a summer in Florence and became one of those insufferable blokes who attended art lectures and droned on about da Vinci's inventions."

A summer in Florence. Must be nice. "Inspiration. I like it."

"What about you?"

I sip my stout to fill the thick silence. The truth seems appropriate here. "It was the opposite." Noah tilts his head. I could offer many Freudian theories as to why I long to prove women are strong and capable, but I stick to what he'll understand. "While you admired the Vitruvian Man, I focused on the Renaissance facts that made me want to scream. Like how women couldn't stand by windows, lest they inflame the carnal desires of men. Or how women were banned from wind instruments for how they'd twist their faces in unattractive ways."

He forces a swallow. "I don't remember learning that."

"Once I heard it, I couldn't unhear it."

This is about the time men's eyes glaze over. Feminism is a super-hot topic, generally landing me back home well before sexy time with a bag of Ruffles and a rewatch of *Downton Abbey*.

"I'm glad I didn't work on Byron's article," he says.

Solidarity. He's trying to connect with me. "Why is that?"

He shrugs. "Call it a hunch."

I crack my knuckles hidden in my lap. Nothing gets a historian hotter than a research scandal. "You know I can't talk, but I'd love to hear your thoughts."

He scratches his jaw, slow and deliberate. "All the internet hype around Armani." He shakes his head. "It would cloud my head, you know?"

Yes, I do know. Dr. Byron has always struck me as a megalomaniac, but even narcissists can perform accurate research. "I prefer the halls of obscurity to the Reddit history forums."

"Besides," Noah swirls his glass. "It's a mystery what happened to Armani when he cracked."

"And Caterina's disappearance was so—"

"Mysterious." Noah leans across the table with a disarming smile. He pushes his glasses up the bridge of his nose. "There's something else."

This is a history nerd's version of dirty talk. I raise my eyebrows and lean my weight forward as my heart pounds in my chest. "Do tell."

"It's not authenticated. Remnants of a letter from a seventeenth century Turkish prince discussed an Armani creation."

He's reaching. Is that what I'm doing? "Venice hosted plenty of powerful rulers, and one of them saw the statue. That's not too odd."

"Except." He shrugs his shoulders up high to his ears. "That creation had two torsos."

Our statue is broken on the back half. This theory is just far-fetched enough to be intriguing. "I'm gonna need another beer." I look over my shoulder, but Noah touches my arm.

His eyes sparkle, aflame with the fire's reflection. "That would mean *The Estasi*'s other torso has broken off and could be anywhere in Venice."

The nutty smell of dark ale wafts into the air as I roll the hourglass pint between my fingers. "Or the letter is nonsense." My cheeks burn, usually a sensation that indicates a rare find. *Must keep my wits sharp.* But that's very hard to do with his fingers still resting on my wrist.

"That's why Dr. Byron didn't include it." Noah tips his head sideways, slowly trailing his fingers away from me. "He didn't need to. There's no record of this ruler ever traveling to Venice. Besides, that prince dabbled in art and had a reputation for fabricating wild stories."

The clay was obviously broken, and the jagged edge that starts at the woman's hair shows damage. But it isn't obvious that there was another person carved behind her. Still, I can't let on that I also question everything about this statue. "And this alone makes you doubt Dr. Byron's research?"

"That and the man's galaxy-sized ego. He blathered on for talk shows and had a writeup in *The New York Times*. He shook Sir Elton John's hand for Christ's sake."

"He was in the spotlight for a hot minute there."

Noah removes his glasses, and I find his naked face quite adorable. "You're skeptical of his research," he says. "That's why you haven't published your conclusions yet."

I don't deny it. I don't agree either. Suspicion sat like a stone in my gut well before I took this assignment. Everything would be easier if I were wrong. Still, a strange comfort settles in my bones at the thought I may not be the only mistrusting one. "My job is to validate Dr. Byron's research, not comment on his ego." I rub the back of my neck and signal the waitress for another round. "Come Monday, the museum will release my findings, and I'll be on the red eye for Los Angeles." To a promotion that will pay for the late rent on my studio I just had to have in Venice Beach. I'm willing to ignore a hunch because of material things. Who am I?

His neck elongates like my neighbor's cat when it eyes a bird—on alert and slightly offended. "You can't sign that authentication."

I loosen a bobby pin from jabbing into the base of my head. "There's nothing to hold me back." Nothing that I can prove, anyway.

Noah slides his glasses back in place, then props his hands on his thighs. "So, let's find something."

"That's not how research is done," I say. But his wavy ginger hair makes me want to blow the lid off how things are done. *Tell him, Mia. You're dying to.*

"Listen, Byron's work is satisfactory. We both know it." He curls his knuckles against his cheek to conceal the conversation from any curious pubgoers. "What if we find something even bigger than anyone could imagine?"

Oh, how I long to say yes. I'm in no hurry to return home, filling my Amazon cart and listening to friends and lovers celebrate at the bistro outside my window. Initially, I considered the proximity to action a selling feature of the apartment, but their laughter has become one of the loneliest sounds imaginable. "Is this all to take down Byron?"

"I didn't get the Sotheby's contract, and I'm far more qualified than him." Noah leans back in his chair. In this light, his sweater almost looks a sexy crimson. "History has been scripted by men like Byron. When is it our turn for the spotlight?" He rocks on the back legs of his chair, then leans forward again onto the table. "I'm quiet and polite, and that never gets me anywhere. Let's explore unearthed secrets and ignored truths."

Talk dirty to me, Noah.

He checks his glasses for alignment, unwittingly mastering the sexy professor gaze. "Well, what do you think?"

I think I must overcome this annoying hesitation and jump at the chance to earn everything I've ever wanted. It's not as if I had a choice in the matter. He catches me spinning my pearl earring as I stall.

"Let me ask this." He stretches, extends his arms, and places his hands behind his head. "What if you didn't sign it today? What if you discovered cause to question Byron?"

There's no harm in indulging him. "Then I'd ask for more time to interview subjects and track his sources." Saying out loud what I've already secretly considered sends a chill up my neck. "The outcome of my assignment was implied and holding it up would put a target on my back. It would take one hell of a find to stop this train."

Noah throws on his jacket and tosses a few bills on the table. "We better start straight away, then."

He can't be serious. "You want to spend your birthday in the archives for the minuscule chance we'll discover something major in the next forty-eight hours?"

"Hell yeah, I do."

I'm two beers in, and Noah's excitement is infectious. Two more days. Maybe I'll finally quiet that questioning voice that threatens to upend my career. I toss my bag over my shoulder, suddenly unconcerned that my hair twist has come undone. "To the archives, Dr. Beckett."

Chapter Two

Venice, 1608

He twists my hair in his fist, and I part my lips in a well-rehearsed groan. It may as well be a yawn, though he will only ever see pleasure. I exist in two parts. The body a man sees, and the hidden longing for things just out of my reach.

"Tell me I am strong," Lord Marco begs between forceful grunts.

"Strong as a sword." *And rotten as a spoiled apple.* I purr against the clammy flesh of his shoulder as he drives into me.

The act comes easily, for I have learned a great many things under the sweating, thrusting bodies of men. How to expose their weakness and soothe their insecurities—how fragile their meager hearts. They soften their harsh edges against my curves and demand things too shameful for polite society. I always give in to them, for therein lies my only hope.

As a kept mistress, I've long ago swallowed the hunger for genuine desire. I must find pleasure elsewhere. In my patron's arms, I have always had one purpose: turn him into a god so I may partake in his rise to power. Tangled in their beds, I heal salted wounds and craft men into giants. Though Lord Marco could no more become a giant than he could a toad, and I do not choose my patrons. They choose me.

Lord Marco's body trembles. I time my cries of ecstasy like a well-crafted symphony, tapering off to a whistle of pleasure until he collapses in a softened heap. He breathes hot air onto my shoulder. A spent man is one least likely to fight. He knows what I want. "My love," I say, "tomorrow's celebration is fast approaching."

"Yes." He looks at me with sleepy eyes. "I cannot wait to drape you in jewels and disrobe you."

He cannot afford jewels. I force a laugh to appease him, though my heart races with anticipation. "Your guests love me."

"All of Venice adores you." He flops to his back and rubs his belly. "And you are mine." He smiles for only himself.

I roll to my side and stroke his hair. "A courtesan turns all things beautiful"—*even the horrid men we bed*—"through poetry and music and art." The last word leaves my mouth with a hitch. The title I do not dare utter out loud presses into my lips like a stolen kiss. *Artist.*

He slams his fist into the bed as he rises. "You must stop begging, Sofia. It's unattractive." He stands naked in front of the fire, positioning himself tall, like the king he deems himself to be.

"My paintings—"

"Your unsavory paintings would cause a scandal," he hisses.

In contrast to the predominant darkness of Venetian painters, my art is full of light, celebrating the strength of womanly figures. The beauty of a woman's power. Everything else represents us as bodies to be conquered—or worse—kept.

I roll out of bed and press my breasts into his shoulder. "What is scandalous about our bodies? You understand how these curves can heal sorrow and lift a man's soul to the heavens."

He taps his teeth together over and over, a most grating habit. "Then stay where you belong. In the bedchamber and decorating a room with your beautiful breasts." He traces my nipple with his finger. "Stop this art nonsense."

Three years I have begged, and three years I have been denied.

I can't bring myself to praise him. I'm afraid I may slap his cheek if I come anywhere near his sticky skin. He notices my hesitation and turns to face me. Even as he lengthens his spine, he stands no taller than my chin. A mushroom of a man next to my towering oak.

"Careful," he says. "You don't want to cross me."

I lick his lips but do not kiss him, watching with glee as he begins to desire me once again. I dress, tightening multiple layers until I can hardly breathe. My life was written in the stars years ago. Bed powerful men until I am discarded like a useless carcass, picked of its meat. Little does he know, I will never stop asking for what I want.

"Darling, we are nothing but skin and sex and hate." I add a slow sigh to soften him. "Tomorrow, we shall press our hateful bodies together once again."

Our routine remains a careful dance where I tiptoe between undying affection and casual disrespect, just as he likes. I do not bid him farewell as I leave.

A short walk from Marco's palazzo to my crumbling home allows me to bask in another glittering Venetian evening. A deep purple, starless sky hangs overhead. I arrive home with a sigh of relief. Another perk of the charade I play—freedom and money to live alone in blissful silence. By twenty-four, I've lived more lives than women twice my age shackled by marriage.

On my loggia, I listen to the canal lap water against stone. Most prostitutes long for the warm, naked flesh of a man and his gold coins. Not I. That is a feast in my world. The only cure for my longing is with a blank canvas. Paintbrushes. An easel. Art flows from my hands like a golden river, lighting my dark nights.

I untie my restricting bodice as my ribs expand. His voice haunts me. *"Stay where you belong."* I cannot tell if men have worsened with time or if I have grown less tolerant of their disrespect.

With a desperate fling of my arms, I throw my gown across the room. Oh, the things I've seen in the hidden world of men. Odd desires involving feet or blindfolds. Men who only wished to watch me pleasure other men. Once, a lover would only indulge in my body if I promised to slap him across his cheek until he screamed.

My silken nightgown scratches at my hot skin and I tear it away. Better. The shift lands crumpled on the pile with the rest of my garments. No more clothing. No more theater. Just me, a vision, and a breezy night to cool the fire on my skin.

As the moonlight casts shadows of violet, I drag paint into the shape of a woman. My naked body can move and stretch with the desires of my brush, its purpose, for once, not related to a man. Paint flies onto my stomach and legs. It splatters my hair in a glorious splash to remind me I'm alive. I am free.

The painting of a maiden takes shape from somewhere inside me. Brushstrokes become vengeful eyes and snarled lips.

Thoughts slice into my mind like a chisel as I paint. My prospects have dwindled as I age out of courtesan work. I've landed with a manipulative benefactor who derives pleasure from restricting my access to his perfectly untouched studio full of pristine Carrara marble and sandstone and clay. In a twisted cycle of sex and wits, I make him beg for what he wants, and he responds in kind.

I force my worries away with every streak of paint. Here, in my home, I am whole.

The hours progress toward sunrise, but I don't notice the color of the room or if my limbs ache. I may as well be dancing, or sculpting, or immersed underwater. Nothing matters while paint and pigment stain this hemp fiber with the emotions of my soul.

By the time I step back, breathless and on fire, dawn illuminates my creation. A woman, fury in her eyes and blood dripping from her teeth. Her murderous hands hold a man down after having sliced his neck. *The Vengeful Maiden* drips anger, and I love everything about her.

Marco pays just enough to house and clothe me while I barter and steal supplies. The hungry beast inside me must create art or I shall certainly die. I imagine life if Marco discarded me. My body would be deemed useless, my beauty a failure. The desperation of a homeless prostitute would be horror enough. Perhaps worse would be bearing an unreleased world of art inside me. Sacrifices must be made, and I offer my body at the altar of dreadful men.

For now, in this moment, I can breathe. And that is enough. I initial the lower corner with a trembling hand. *SR*. Sofia Rossi, artist, courtesan, and mad woman.

I drop the paintbrush to my feet. My body follows, and soon I'm fast asleep in a pool of paint and dreams.

Chapter Three

The library on a Friday evening is nothing new for me. Sharing space with a man who cares about something as much as I do? Well, that's undiscovered territory. Rain patters the tall old leaded windows as dim light flickers in the brewing storm. Like we're about to hold a seance.

We've been staring at the images of *The Estasi* for ten minutes in full silence under the low, filtered light of table lamps. This hall could rival Hogwarts, with its wood paneled ceilings and arched alcoves of faded books all around us, as if pages may begin flying off the shelves in a cloud of stardust.

"What do you see?" Noah asks.

"I think she's sitting against something."

He rests his arm over the back of his chair. "Do tell, Dr. Harding."

I lift one of the high-res photographs. "They say she would have been a standing statue in the garden, a depiction of his wife in the throes of an orgasm. But the way the skin folds at her waist, she's sitting."

"Perhaps against a second person," he says with a twinkle in his eye.

"Another thing." I show him a close-up of her face. "This. Her mouth and her eyes. Either the artist didn't know what ecstasy looks like—which is entirely possible—or they were aiming for something else."

"Color me intrigued." Noah rolls his chair closer.

"Okay, humor me." I face him. Our knees accidentally touch. My instinct is to pull away, but his lips twitch into an almost-smile, which feels even more intimate. I soften my legs against his.

Noah seems to have noticed me hesitate. He tilts his head until we meet eyes, his reassuring smile pulling me back in. "Prepped and ready to humor, Doctor."

I sidestep right past his charm. "Close your eyes." He does, and I resist the very real urge to kiss him. To cup his cheeks in my hands and breathe in his cologne. I shake away the desire. Must focus. "Imagine you're in the dark with a woman. Er, uh, or man?"

He peeks open one eye. "Woman." He closes it again.

"Yes." Me, biting back a smile. "You've wanted to touch her for weeks. She leans her mouth to the soft spot behind your ear. She kisses your neck while her hands slide up your torso." His face has changed. Intensified. "She runs her tongue along your jaw. She hungrily seeks out your mouth. Her kiss is full and soft. Her tongue slips through your barely parted lips." His mouth parts. "She straddles you and reaches her hand to your throbbing—"

Snap. My phone's camera startles him.

He throws open his eyes. "Did you just take a photo of me?"

"Yes."

"I feel oddly offended and aroused." He considers. "Equally."

I can't resist a tight-lipped smile. "I'm sorry, Dr. Beckett. But we all must sacrifice in the name of science and discovery. Stick with me, I have a point." I hand him my phone. "Here. Fair is fair."

"Shared mortification. I can get on board with this."

"One caveat. You don't want me aroused." My breath hitches. "You want me to fall in love." This may seem forward, but I need him to understand the depth to which I believe this. *The Estasi* drips with feminine energy. I can't explain it, so I'll have to make him feel it.

His eyes remain steady on mine, but he cracks the hint of a smile. "Challenge accepted. Close your eyes, Mia."

"No turning back now." I hesitate. My need for someone to understand my wild ideas suddenly feels dangerous. Too close to my real feelings.

"Eyes closed," he says. "Go on."

He swallows and clears his throat. His voice drops to a husky whisper. "Candlelight warms the room with amber light. You want him to touch you. Undress you while he stares in your eyes. He slides the dress strap down your shoulder and presses his lips on the curve above your collarbone. He pulls you close. Chest to chest, your breath heaves together. While his mouth explores your throat and neck, his hand reaches back to slide the clip from your hair. Locks fall free down your bare back. He loses his hands in your soft, honey brown hair as he whispers, 'You're perfection.'"

Snap.

I open my eyes and we share an intense moment as my heart thumps hard against my chest. So hard, the beat thrums in my ears. I expected him to make a terrible joke about boobs, but the man made my toes curl.

He breaks the silence, and between heavy breaths says, "Holy hell, why didn't I major in women's studies?"

"I didn't learn this in school, Mr. Purple Jumper. This is life." I pull out my phone and watch as he toggles between the images.

"They're different, but I'm unsure what I'm supposed to find," he says.

"Here." I point again to the mouth. "Your mouth is parted, but the face is taut. Pulled down and primal."

He looks between the image and me. "And in yours, it's a parted mouth but everything is elevated. Light."

"Yes. Being touched for lust versus touched for deep passion. They're different." Even in my very limited experience in relationships,

I know that much. Though my work demands sixty hours a week, I've managed a few unsatisfying romances over the years. Art admirers make great sexual partners, but romantic ones? Not so much.

He lifts the picture experts believe is Caterina. "She's in full passion. Love, even."

"Very good, Dr. Beckett. What do we know about their relationship?"

He runs his fingers through his thick, wavy hair that desperately needs a trim, as it keeps falling over his temples. "Lucca sculpted his wife in a moment of love and passion?" He catches himself. "Lucca and Caterina weren't in love. They were toxic at best."

"Like the sixteen-hundreds version of Johnny Depp and Amber Heard." I tilt my head and grin. "Give me a theory."

I don't want to say it. He'll think I'm ridiculous. Better to make him guess.

He taps his fingernails on the desk. "This face represents a woman who loved him."

"Maybe," I say with a shrug.

He twists his mouth to the side. "This is how he wished Caterina would look at him?"

"Doubtful." I lean back in my chair. "Come on, Dr. Beckett. Dig deep."

His blushed cheeks suggest frustration. The wind picks up. A gust sends a smattering of leaves onto the window and howls through the arches just outside. "If you have a hypothesis, why not just tell me?"

Because I'll sound like a fool. "Because this is more fun."

He releases a frustrated growl. Then he looks up. "Wait. This isn't a Lucca original."

Satisfaction blooms with the hope he may see what I see. "Closer."

The cadence of his voice quickens. "He commissioned an apprentice. He discovered another man sculpting his wife."

"Now you're just disappointing me." I cross my arms as he huffs.

Please see what I see. Please help me find a reason to say it aloud.

He slams his hands on the desk with a sweet, frustrated whine. "Okay. You said you learned to examine facial intricacies because of your life."

"Yes."

"Your life as a historian?" I don't respond. "As an American?" Now, I roll my eyes. "As a . . . a woman." He says the word not as a question, but with whispered declaration.

I feel exposed. Naked, almost. "Correct."

He shakes his head. "You think *The Estasi* was sculpted by a woman?"

Ah, the sweet sound of my theory said aloud. As if I'm not alone in a bubble about to burst. I shrug, downplaying my relief. "There were plenty of women artists of the time. Few made history books, of course." I search his eyes for signs of pity or horror. I see only intrigue and I can't stop myself. "Besides, there's a quality here we haven't seen in men's sculptures from that time. This woman reveals life. Not the mother archetype or the harlot, either. She looks how a woman feels."

He rubs his face with both hands and stares at me in disbelief. "This would be an enormous discovery."

"All off my hunch as a woman." The words deflate any bravado and bring the romantic air of the evening to a crashing halt.

"I see your conundrum. If you dig into this and you're wrong, you'll lose all credibility as a historical expert. But if you're onto something, you'll blow up several careers."

Including my own.

We're so close, wading in the shallow end of the danger pool. It's nice not to drown alone. "If we look at history from a different angle, we see different truths." I point to the images on my phone. "That's what they taught us in undergraduate women's studies."

He stares at the picture of me imagining his hands on my body. "The question now is who sculpted *The Estasi*?"

"I suspect our answer lies in the buried truth of women artists. No one thinks to look there."

He smiles. "Except another woman."

My cheeks flame with heat. "When you aren't part of the important conversations, you learn to read faces." I trace *The Estasi*'s profile with my pointer finger, purposely avoiding Noah's gaze.

"Are you not part of the conversations at your museum?"

I rub my eyes, pushing away tears. Board meetings where I served coffee and handed out papers. Days where I missed visiting artists while picking up Dr. Wright's prescriptions. Years I've paid my dues, writing his research, waiting for the opportunity that hovers at my fingertips right now. I'm so close to becoming lead curator. I'll have a voice, and I can highlight exhibits of my choosing. All I have to do is ignore that deep voice that knocks on my consciousness.

"I'll be leading the conversations after I authenticate this statue." All that stands in my way is every emotion that inhabits my body, and I can't shut them off. He doesn't need to understand. His career isn't on the line. "I hope you've had a nice birthday."

I gather my purse and move my thumb to delete the image on my phone, but Noah reaches his hand to stop me. "You can't leave now. The fun has just begun."

I tuck my phone in my purse. "It's ten o'clock. What, do you plan to sleep here?"

"I have a long list of Baroque artists to go through," he says. "It will take all night. Maybe through the weekend."

It's all so precarious. One scribble of my signature and this entire exciting ride ends. I return to Los Angeles as an empty sellout with a title. I'm beginning to question whether a promotion is worth all this.

"You'll never forgive yourself if you walk away now." Noah sighs.

He's right. My last chance to find the truth. My one opportunity to reward the women artists of history with recognition they never had. Girls who live in Venetian palaces and California trailer parks don't earn accolades; we have to fight for them. Standing up for what I believe may give me the chance to feel worthy of my title

Dr. Mia Harding. But rocking the boat on this would make me a target. Online mocking would be the least of my worries.

I close my eyes to bask in the moment before one's life changes. Long enough to exhale the doubts that prickle my eyes. Here I have a purpose. I feel the glimmer of the young woman with fire in her soul, ready to make her mark on the art world, before desire for money and status and a promotion changed everything. Suddenly, I'm once again the girl who entered college with a dream and a heart full of integrity.

I open my eyes, focused and ready. "Buckle up, Doctor. You're about to get an introduction to women's studies." I drop my purse on the table. "Here's your first lesson: Forget everything you know about history."

Chapter Four

Life as a courtesan brings art and music, education and status. Even women of nobility are forbidden from spaces where I roam freely. For all we are gifted, we also accept danger. Aging out of work long before we are ready, most of us will die from poverty or disease.

Tonight, I will push those thoughts down as I always do and convince Lord Marco to display *The Vengeful Maiden* for his guests. I've powdered my hair to his liking, oiled my skin with the heady scent of rose petals, and armored the fragility in my heart.

Strolling alone through the Rialto, I pass the desperate *cortigiana di lume*, lifting their skirts for any man with a lira in his pocket. My mother once flaunted her body on this bridge. Seeing my potential early on, she trained me in the ways of wooing men, promising me a better life where I could practice art and bask in fine linens and adoration while she tended to her wounds, slowly, painfully creeping toward her end. The looming threat of syphilis chips away at my courage nearly as often as the fear of dying alone.

I look the other way as I pass, unwilling to remember her that way. Under the citrine sunset and amid the water breaking on the banks of the Grand Canal, I recount my mother's words recited to me like the poem of my youth. *I am the entertainment, the beauty, and the passion in any room I enter.* I lift my chin. *I am art.*

With her reassuring voice in my head, I float with calm through alleyways and over bridges, past hollering gondoliers and whistling street merchants.

Time crushes down on me a little more every evening. Time is running out to make a name for myself as an artist. How do I change the minds of Venetians who only see me as an educated prostitute?

I lift my skirts and take a deep breath as I approach Lord Marco's palazzo. One might think I only satisfy the urges between his legs, but I also enlighten his mind and embody his passions. Tonight, I must break his will.

Servants open the door and nod to welcome me inside the palazzo I've come to know well. Lord Marco spends much of our time together weeping in my lap about the passions he will never experience. My burning need to slip into his studio is enough to set me on fire.

I enter the grand ballroom in a strut, waving my fan and lifting my chest. The crowd smiles and nods. Each man reaches for his mistress. Their wives appreciate us. We lift their sexual burden and stroke the emotional needs of their men. In return, we gain access to all things off limits to women of the Republic. Education, music, freedom. Tonight is a gathering for celebration. And celebrate we shall.

Lord Marco wraps his arm around mine. "Hello, my love." He kisses my hand and I smile. His nose practically rests between my breasts. The other men paw at their courtesans, but Marco knows how I bristle when over-touched. "I've hidden a trinket for you somewhere in the palazzo. Black pearls." He lifts to his toes to bite the air next to my ear. "I shall watch you search for them and drape them over your naked breasts tonight."

A defiant move, as sumptuary laws forbid courtesans from wearing pearls around their necks. Marco does love his little games.

The evening is full of celebration and drink, platters of food, and music. Courtesans play harp and read their poetry as I look on. Several girls dance. Their lean frames and soft arms resemble clouds passing through a meadow.

His words still linger from yesterday like a bite of stale bread, soaking my mouth dry. I had my painting delivered this morning, defying his orders.

Marco tugs at the gold braiding at my waist. "Come, see my new piece."

We enter the grand entrance hall, a tiled masterpiece built specifically to display his treasures. With curved alcoves at every level and an opening in the roof like a frescoed cavern to the stars, Marco's palazzo shines with natural light. His guests linger. They admire the sculptures, the gilded paintings, and the tall courtesan on his arm.

"Here she is," Marco says, leaning on his cane, which he does not require but believes makes him appear intelligent.

I examine the piece. How uninspired. Yet another ridiculous depiction of a woman as a motherly sack of flesh, reclined and revealing her breasts and womb as if begging the closest man to plant his seed.

"The lines," Marco says, tapping the tile floor next to her. "Sensuous and plump, like a pheasant ripe for the plucking."

It takes every bit of strength in my body not to roll my eyes. Oh, pathetic Marco. He understands little about perspective and color and light, though he desperately wishes he did. Three years ago, he chose me for my curvaceous body and eye for all things artistic. He loves the notion of art yet forbids me to have a hand in its creation.

"Where will you fit her?" I ask. "There is no room for another reclined mother-to-be."

He sneers at me over his shoulder, twisting his head in an unnatural spin. "This woman represents lust and love."

She represents man's view of us as empty, useless, and hungry for a master. Even her face appears both begging for sex and dead inside. Like most art created by men. Any acidic thoughts remain silent. A necessity to my survival. "Yes, Lord Marco. Correct as always." I lift the string of pearls coiled at her feet. "These are gorgeous."

His cheeks flush. His chest expands before my eyes. The only thing I am more skilled at than painting is acting. Behind the stairwell, I glimpse the corner of my painting, thrown on the ground in haste, next to a mop bucket.

Though rage swells against my insides like a tide, all Lord Marco sees is my flirtatious smile. "I believe it's time to retire." I lower my voice into a whispered, breathy tone. "You can recount your conquests from the comfort of our bed." I pull him away from the art display and that horrid sculpture, up the winding staircase to our shared bedchamber. Thus begins our nightly ritual.

On our way to his bedchamber, we pass his studio. The door, always shut, hums to me. She begs me to slip inside her forgotten walls and grasp the unused tools to create. I only disobeyed his rules once, and once was enough.

I undress him while singing. I remove his clothing slowly, meticulously, while I run soft fingers over his body until he moans. Marco owns me, yet while he's naked he becomes fragile glass in my hand. He closes his eyes, arms outstretched, waiting for direction from me. "Sit," I demand.

I bend to my knees and lower his breeches so Lord Marco can revel in the sensation of being tall. I often imagine his gangly fingers wrapping around my neck, wishing to rid the world of me. Thankfully, he desires me too much. He lowers the pearls over my neck, gawking at his possessions. I remain small and curl at his feet yet force a firm voice. "Have you been naughty, my love? Tell me who you have touched in my absence."

He looks down at me, waiting for my show of jealousy in this ridiculous game we play. "Three women this week. One prostitute whose breasts devoured me whole."

I shove him back to the bed and press my hand to his neck. "Your body is mine."

"Harder," he says.

I squeeze ever so subtly against his thready muscles until he bursts into tears. "I'm a filthy man, my love. Please allow me to repent."

Something twisted lies in his need to recount his conquests. He curls in my lap on the luxurious bed, where I tease fingers through his speckled black and white hair as he weeps against my belly. Dark needs rule his mind, requiring this ritual of confession before he mounts me.

Four women this week who have bedded countless others each. Pustules and peeling skin enter my mind once again, but I force down a shudder. I prepare myself for his confession, where he relives, in detail, every moment with women of Venice before he will find his way between my thighs.

He curls in my lap like a child and leans his head against my hand. "I've done something terrible." He drags his pointy finger in a line along my hip bone.

This is not part of our usual routine, which sends alarm through me. I cover his naked body with a sheet. "You have a heart the size of the moon." Lies froth to my mouth with such ease, I wonder where I ever lost myself. What moment did I finally fade away to become the curated image of a siren?

His face twists as the room shifts, my power disappearing like wind.

"Sofia, I've lost a great deal of my fortune."

No money means I'm the first casualty. My mind spins over what this means for my future. "How?"

He throws his face again onto my belly, arms wrapped around my hips. He mutters into my skin, "Too many favors bought, it seems."

Perhaps another soulless statue wasn't the best choice, you selfish man. "You mustn't worry, dear Marco." I stroke the shallow depression of his temple as my mind tumbles with thoughts of homelessness and disease.

He sits up, face to face with me, frustration burning in his eyes. "Many things will change."

My stomach tightens yet I remain soft in the eyes and mouth. "You cannot pay me any longer. Is that what you're trying to say?" I pull the sheet over my naked body, but he instantly lowers it.

"I need you." He leans his cheeks to my breasts and kisses them with a sort of frantic hunger. As if my bosom may restore all he has lost.

"You can no longer have me." I had been so close to breaking him, I could taste victory. If another patron allows me one last commission, how many years would I waste convincing him to buy me clay? I don't have that sort of time.

"You are the most beautiful courtesan in all of Venice. Every patrician fought for their chance to bed you, and these last three years you have been all mine." He rubs his knuckles along my cheek. "I've made arrangements."

I swallow against the thickness in my throat. "Arrangements?"

He speaks to my nipples. "I've sold you."

Sold like goods to feed his hunger for motherly statues. Handed off to another demanding man who owns papers that list me as an asset. A thing. "You don't own me, and neither does anyone else."

His lips curl into thin lines. "You're already twenty-four. I did you a favor. No one wants an aging, used courtesan."

Used. I stand and begin to dress, hiding my offense under a cloak of coldness. "Imagine me naked with another man, Lord Marco."

"I refuse to picture it." He stands with a grunt, grabbing his cane to force his posture taller. "This loss devastates me, for I once had it all."

I would never dare to dream of having it all. I turn to face the fire as the flames warm my neck and arms. Another patron. Another palazzo and another man's needs to fulfill with rules and boundaries I must follow. More ignorance to contend with.

Forced once again. "Who is he?"

Marco walks up behind me, grabbing my pelvis in his firm hands. He presses his forehead to my mid-back as his fingers curl into my hip bones. "Your new benefactor is Lucca Armani."

A hint of excitement bursts in my chest. "The artist?"

"Yes." Marco groans the word, reaching his hand for my breast, but I throw his hand from my body.

"I am no longer yours, Lord Marco. This body now belongs to Signore Armani." A new man, even an artistic one, is yet another shackle for my limbs. Another weight around my ankles and hand around my neck.

"You owe me a thank you," he says, lips tightened into a straight line. "I could have left you to rot."

"That is exactly what you've done." He's sold my body without a thought to the human who lives inside. These monsters toss me from one cage to another and expect me not to sharpen my claws. "In spite of you, I will thrive. Your penance is an empty bed with no goddess to stroke you. You may now stroke yourself."

I storm out of his bedchamber, ready to scream. This will be my last commission. My last chance to become the artist who lives in this body. Before death erases me forever.

Chapter Five

The worry of presenting myself to Lucca Armani can only be quelled by art, and I've painted myself into a slumber again. As I wake under my easel to a bright morning, I sigh at the thought of readying myself for the day, and for a new life.

Fury and desperation exploded onto the canvas last night. Once home in my studio, staring at my last palmful of lire, my gown became too heavy to manage and my mind too wild to contain. I stare up at the result. A half-finished form of a woman reclined in a golden gondola.

In a few hours, I become property of a man I've never met. After years of hard work, I convinced Marco to pay for my studio. Will Signore Armani be so kind? Doubtful. I must present myself like a shining jewel to the artist rarely seen outside the walls of his palazzo. And so I wash and dress as if a knife presses against my throat.

I can do this. With over a dozen patrons and hundreds of admirers over the years, I don't question my abilities. I understand men down to their very core. How each wishes to be stroked and held. A parted mouth and an intense gaze send them to their knees every time. Just where I like them.

I tuck my hair behind my ear, crunching the dried paint between my fingers. "Gondola woman, you may never be seen, but you are lovely."

This painting, as all others created from my hand, releases me from the fiery damage of secret rage I carry in my heart.

I lower to a chair near the window where the morning breeze cools my face. A basin of water warms in the sunshine, its bowl colored from years of pigments like the interior of a mussel shell. I dunk a scrap of linen in the water and wipe paint from my cheeks and hair.

Using the rippling water's reflection, I scrub a particularly difficult patch of black pigment in the curve of my ear. "Lucca Armani," I say to the wind. His name rolls around, leaving a sweet taste on my tongue as images of polished marble fill my mind.

I scrub myself clean until my skin glows red, and I cover myself with a crisp shift.

Mother warned me. Every day of my life, her lecture remained the same. For a woman without wealth or land or a father, I had one directive: Become a goddess. Touch a wealthy man with my grace and leave him wanting more. I agreed to this life before I knew better and stayed out of necessity. Though through it all, I've held on for the promise of another title: Sofia Rossi, famous Venetian artist.

"They will leave you. Some might hurt you," my mother would say. "But your smile and beauty will ensure protection." With lessons on potions to prevent babies and clothing to make my breasts mound like ripe fruit, her lasting and only gift was to make me wanted.

It's the reason I'm not abused and penniless in a brothel right now.

I scarcely maintained this studio though Marco threatened to yank it away at every turn. What will happen to this blissful retreat? What will happen to me?

From my loggia over the narrow canal at the western edge of the Castello, I welcome the warmth of another day and decide which gown might please Signore Armani. For that is all that matters now.

~

His home rises tall from behind the gates, with an air of solitude. Every Venetian gossips about Caterina Armani, the demanding patrician trading favors in the background of every celebration. Yet I care only about her husband, a man who hasn't been seen outside these walls in years. I've seduced men of many backgrounds, yet never an artist. The breeze chills my skin, which suddenly feels fragile and cool. I have one impression, and must make him want to devour me.

A side garden borders the Grand Canal, shaded with magnolia and fig trees that reach toward a surprising domed roof. I stare at his door for so long, sweat beads on my neck. Today, the sun shines luminescent gold, lighting the imperfections in the marble façade where blackened stains creep from the cracks.

Forcing the lump in my throat back down, I present myself to the servant at the entrance. "Lord Marco sent me."

The young man nods, though without hiding his scrutiny. Marco's name frequently elicits scowls and grimaces. "Follow me."

I lift my skirts and take in the expanse of the gallery. Noble tapestries, silk drapes and gilded leather, cornices dipped in gold. A quiet darkness blankets the palazzo, its halls still and cool with shutters closed tight.

The servant leads me up a winding flight of stairs to the dome, which seems separate from the house. "Stand there." I move to a patch of sunlight where my skin appears to shimmer. I rubbed my skin with violet and rose oils to ensure a supple glow.

"Signore." The man clears his throat. "Your gift has arrived."

Gift? I could slap Lord Marco.

The servant disappears. Similar to the rest of the house, the dome is dark, with dyed linen blackening every corner. Paint colors the floor as flicks of powdered pigment float in slivers of sunlight from one exposed window.

Footsteps.

A man's voice says, "Lord Marco didn't want to lose you."

Then he shouldn't have spent all his money. I scan the room, packed with canvas and sculptures in various stages of completion, but I can't find the source of the smooth voice. Artists are temperamental, and every word must be thought through first. "I am here for you, signore."

A paintbrush handle taps against an easel somewhere in the darkness. Through shadows, a man appears. Unkempt hair and a straggly beard. Thick shoulders. As he nears, his bright blue eyes come into focus, so vibrant they distract my usual focus. Hooded by heavy lids, their corners hang like faded wisteria dangling from the vine near the end of spring. His lost expression turns my insides soft. Sympathy does nothing to help me succeed in this situation.

He steps close and examines my body. His breath smells of wine and wood. I suppose he chews on his brushes. A terrible habit. "You are more beautiful than he described."

I don't want his mind or his fingers to wander. I must leave him wanting me. Addicted to the thought of me. This performance has rules, and I must abide. "Such passion in these pieces."

He leans against the wall and watches, mouth parted. "Your passion precedes you."

"I excel at acting."

He laughs, deep and loud, so rough he coughs. "Tell me more, Sofia." He follows me through the dome like a shadow.

"My purpose is to please my patrons, Signore Armani. And I do a fine job."

His eyes trail down my breasts and hips before he steps back, shoulders angled away from me. "Lord Marco promised you could help me. As if such a thing exists."

Intriguing. He's fractured and lost. Possibly even humble. I cross my hands at my hips. "I can help any man become who they wish to be."

A long moment of silence compresses the space between us. He turns toward a sculpture of a faceless woman. "Here." He breathes into my hair and points to the bust. "What is wrong with this form?"

With one glance I can see desperation in his eyes. He needs words of affirmation. An unspoken rule of my life is that no man ever wants the truth. He wants the illusion and the dream to hold in his earthly hands. "Nothing."

His lips touch my ear. "Lies."

I force myself not to pull away. Not to stutter with fear. I need this contract, and he must see me as the embodiment of art, inspiration, and passion. Burning at the core of my worry is the dismissal every benefactor has had for my love of sculpting. Unladylike muscles might bulge. They've all rejected the notion of a woman with limestone dust in her hair.

But this man understands the power of the artist's soul.

I run my fingers down the marble shoulders, around the curve of the statue's breast. "The proportions are perfect. The curves are sensuous." *Take a risk, Sofia.* My stomach aches with regret before I say a word, yet his eyes magically coax something deeper from me. "She is faceless because you cannot picture love while you sculpt. You create from anger and pain."

Lucca tilts his head and steps in front of me with a deep grunt. "Young courtesans are fickle. They laugh too much. Experienced courtesans close their eyes when they should be open and force expressions of lust, donned like a mask for every man they touch." He twists his robe around his fingers until they appear violet. "Which are you?"

He knows very well which I am. I break eye contact, afraid he may discover this experienced courtesan's secrets.

He pulls my gaze back toward him with a finger underneath my chin. "Empty groans and thrusts will land you in the streets, for I do not want a hollow vessel to make me further despise living."

I will turn his existence into a kingdom where he reigns in power. Where confidence swells in his chest and his body becomes a gift to the world. His threat still hangs in the air, a blade touching my flesh as a warning. "I am more than a hollow vessel, signore. I am an artist." My response is angrier than I intend, but he has already cracked my glass armor.

I wait to see if he will punish me for disrespect.

He paces, arms clasped behind his back. "Wealthy patricians have discarded me," he says. "In their eyes, I am worthless."

I understand the pain of being dismissed. "Is this why you haven't emerged from your palazzo in years? Are you afraid of criticism?"

First, he considers me, as if to size up how much I deserve the truth. He motions to his multiple unfinished projects. "That is accurate."

I nod in solidarity with this fragile artist who begs for approval. "I can help with that."

He stands behind me and places my hand on a terra-cotta form of a maiden holding a bowl of fruit. He runs my hand along her smoothed arm and fingers. "If you pretend to adore me, I will feel it and act accordingly."

I drop my arms and face him, needing to pull away from his touch before he accuses me of doing exactly what I am here to do: play the part of a woman in love when I have never been one. He cannot expect me to reveal my true thoughts, that his graying beard makes me shiver. He's at least twice my age. I've been with worse, but my tolerance for the older gaze shrivels by the second.

Sensing my resistance, he drops a cloth over the sculpture we just touched. "Everyone looks through me, as if I am soulless. My wife needs me to be"—his eyes shine with tears—"someone else."

He hasn't approved me yet. His cheeks are hollow and his skin ashen in the slice of sunlight. I listen for the cadence of his breath, the way his chest falls with every exhale. I suddenly see the man behind the beard and force down my resistance. "You need me to help you feel again."

His brows pinch together. "Yes."

The dark room suddenly makes sense. The city outside is an onslaught of clanging wares and laughing peasants. Songs from violas and lutes fill the night sky. The things I love about Venice make the world intolerable for him. With this, I presume the emotions that arise with art have become intolerable as well.

"I live a numb existence, signora."

He needs more than any man I've met. I cannot create a god until I find the man hiding inside. "You wish to have my body and mind, my passion and creativity."

He inhales, eyes closed, head tilted back. "I wish to have all of you. Suck the art from your very being until love blossoms in my heart."

I squeeze the pleats in my gown hard enough to tremble my entire arm. This man is desperate. For the first time, I worry I might fail.

He seems to smile at my discomfort, so I steady my arms at my sides. He reaches into a velvet bag.

I'm skilled at seduction, how to arch my back and twist my face. How to shower a man with adoring gazes. But I do not love them. I *never* love them.

He lifts a necklace. Glowing emeralds on a gold chain with an oval diamond large enough to stir a gasp. He dangles it over my breasts. "We shall be artists together."

Did I hear him correctly? I don't dare react, turning the words over in my mind to imagine my time in this dome as more than a prostitute. "How do you know I have any talent?"

"I don't. Though your creative passion is a sign of hope." He lowers the smooth gems over my neck. "I will have a notary draw up papers. A contract between myself and the woman who will turn my face once again toward the light."

His thready voice drips with unease.

He lifts my hand to his mouth, closing his eyes for a soft kiss. "Sofia." He holds up one finger. "Do not fail me as everyone else has."

His request is too much. Too offensive. "I've never been in love," I say, breathing a little easier once the admission leaves my lips.

"Perhaps, neither have I." He smiles through the heavy cloak of facial hair. "But with sculpture and paint, we can ignite heat between our bodies. Maybe that will feel like love."

Everything I've dreamed of, but only if I open my heart and bleed. I can say with certainty that I will never love Lucca. I buried the desire for intimacy years ago, when Mother taught me how to daydream through every irritating thrust.

He admires the necklace draped around my tense neck. "I will prepare your quarters and ensure the staff is prepared for your arrival."

"My quarters?" He'd have access to me day and night. My studio is freedom, a rarity for Venetian women. I've always been sought after enough that I've negotiated some semblance of freedom. But now I'm an aging, used courtesan. "My studio, signore."

He considers. "Marco paid for your studio? I see. I will pay the rent for the time being, but you are my muse. We cannot accomplish all we need to unless you are close."

"I'm very grateful." I want to sleep there, but his expression makes clear this is not open for discussion. I dare to ask the question that burns inside me like an eternal flame. "May I sculpt with you, signore?"

"Lord Marco did not approve of clay and stone, I hear."

My face remains stoic and light, though inside, I wince hard enough to tighten my ribs until they sting. "No man has approved. Art distracts me from their affections."

The one time Marco discovered me touching his chisels, he slapped me and paraded me around to every servant, pointing to my reddened cheek with a warning. Lord Marco does not tolerate disobedience, and the only one in his home to produce art would be him.

He's never produced a single thing.

Lucca leans toward me, a youthful gaze surrounded by heavy skin and wisps of gray at his temples. "We may fail, Sofia." He motions to the studio. "Welcome to my darkness."

An endless supply of easels and soft clay. Pots of paint and pigments in every color imaginable. Red chalk and metalpoint. Black and red veined marble slabs. My heart thunders in my chest, possibility bubbling.

"All I ask for is your soul," he says.

That may be the one thing I am unable to give.

"Prepare to arrive in two days' time," he says.

"Your wife, signore?"

His eyes darken like the night of a slivered moon. "Yes, she approved this arrangement." He leads me to the door. "Caterina requires me to make art and money. I can do neither until you fix what is broken in this wasted world of mine."

Every man I've disrobed for has viewed me as a conquest. Lucca Armani is the first one to see me as a healer. I bow, lifting my eyes to him with a subtle smile. Deep below my assets of flesh and beauty lives a terrified girl who may be as broken as the man she's tasked with healing.

Chapter Six

Two in the morning in the library lounge. Eerie quiet smothers us as old wood creaks like arthritic bones. Amid empty takeaway containers and the scent of bitter coffee, we collapse in the realization that we have nothing more than we did five hours ago. The documents on female artists prove lean and unhelpful, just as they've always been. As my time here dwindles to its last hours, all I can do is share what I believe in hopes that something will direct me forward.

"There are plenty of women painters," Noah says. "Longhi and Fontana. Sirani. La Tintoretta. Perhaps they secretly sculpted?"

"No." I review the facts. "The carbon dating indicates the sculpture was created between 1600 and 1612. The powerful woman narrative matches Artemisia Gentileschi but she's not known to have sculpted. Properzia de' Rossi did marble work more than one hundred years earlier."

Noah rubs his eyes. "There's a reason Dr. Byron feels so secure. Nothing from the artists of the time contradicts his findings."

"Yet." I lean back in my chair, staring blankly at the table of documents.

"What are you thinking?" he asks.

Against all logical reasoning, I want to tell Noah everything. "Laws prevented women from studying art and anatomy. They couldn't apprentice or obtain materials."

He slides the pile of scribbled papers away. "If *The Estasi* was sculpted by a woman no one has heard of, then Italy had one of the only Baroque female sculptors and history all but forgot her." His face twists into a confused grimace.

A hesitant smile tugs at my lips. "That's been my theory since I laid eyes on her."

"Wait. You sat here with me for five hours while I figured this out?" he says. "Why didn't you just tell me?"

"Now, where's the fun in that?" I'm playing coy, but now that this is out, I can never turn back. I've been too afraid to face this impossible decision. "Besides, this night was exciting." More exhilarating than anything I've felt in years. My heart patters into my throat when I notice his thick, messy hair.

Looking into his eyes is all too much, so I busy myself clearing containers that earlier held curry noodles and fish and chips.

Noah sighs with the slightest huff. "You're leaving?"

"It's the middle of the night, Dr. Beckett. You're exhausted and I need to review the statement for Monday." *Stay logical, Mia. You still have a job to do.*

Once the remnants of the night have been cleared and the papers filed away in their proper drawers, Noah and I awkwardly face each other. I tighten my coat as he rocks back on his heels.

"Thank you for indulging me," I say.

His fallen face shouldn't disappoint me as much as it does. "I'll walk you home."

"That's very nice, but no need."

He reaches for the door and motions me through. "Not a word about it. I won't be able to sleep unless I know you made it home safely."

Concern. For me. He doesn't see me as an uptight researcher, but a woman who doesn't like to go home. "That would be nice."

We huddle under my umbrella, his arm solid next to mine. The heat from his body makes me want to lean against his chest, to curl together by a roaring fire and pretend Monday isn't fast approaching. The pattering rain lifts a mossy, earthy smell from the ground with every step we take. Back home in California, the warm air makes it easy to live in solitude. Here, the cold and the layers of clothes make my body hunger for closeness.

"This is me." I point to a sad building primarily used for graduate students. "Happy birthday, Dr. Beckett."

I want to stay here, in the stale espresso and fading cologne of his purple jumper. But I'll be on a plane two days from now, dealing with the aftermath of this trip. I'll accept a promotion and acknowledge that my feelings mean nothing without proof. *The Estasi* is whatever the collective deems her to be.

With mystery dancing in his eyes, he says, "You wanted me to go through the process of questioning everything we think we know. I can imagine how scared you are of blowing everything up."

I pause to take in his intense gaze—which is sexy as hell. "There's nothing to blow up. We didn't find anything."

"There must be proof somewhere. Think of all the people lost to time."

"That's called women's history. The records will disappoint you every time." I unlock the door and already miss his body next to mine.

"But now I believe it too." Noah's hands are in his pockets, his arms tight and shoulders up to his ears. He backs away slowly, his bright smile shining and glossy. "We simply need to find something Byron missed."

I appreciate his commitment to the truth. I lost mine along the way, somewhere between student loans and an apartment with heated floors close to Sunset Boulevard. In its place sits a black hole of regret. "Good night, Dr. Beckett."

Back in my furnished flat that's been home for two months, the air feels thin and empty. I crank up the heat and run myself a bath. Once I slip in up to my neck, the hot, soapy water warms my chilled bones. In my mind, I replay Noah's smiling face and nerdy charm over and over like a record to feel that thrill again.

If I provide reason to question Byron's research, the world will hate me for ruining the fantasy crafted for them. My boss may pull my promotion. Not to mention the *carabinieri*. The Italian government's art squad will never allow me to work again if I play a part in *The Estasi* landing in research exile for decades. This statue belongs in Venice. I'm just not certain we're working with the truth here.

Though I play with the notion of grandeur in my head, I can't bring myself to throw away two decades of hard work, at least not without rock solid proof.

I drain the bath and slide into pajamas, braid my hair and moisturize my face, then stare at the bedside table. Every night of my adult life has ended with me journaling. Tonight, I'm distracted.

Why is it still so cold in here? A familiar sensation grips me. I've always been able to hear and feel things, though I've shoved that ability so far down, I didn't know it still existed. That statue at the museum entrance reminds me daily how historical objects speak to me. Sometimes it's magic and other times it's a nuisance, but my senses are never wrong.

I can't sleep. The air is different. The silence creeps me out.

I need to make research notes. Like scribbles of a madwoman, I relay my deepest, darkest emotions to the pages—lonely ramblings about love and work and the looming threat of middle-age. Inside the journal, I always tuck a strip of fabric into the spine of my latest page as if to bury it away from sight, a faded purple remnant from a cotton blanket of my childhood. I'm not sure why I keep it, as its presence fills me with more anxiety than joy. Maybe that's why.

I pull out the drawer but stop mid-reach when I notice something off.

The fabric hangs slightly out of the page. Never once have I ever not tucked it perfectly into the spine.

I shiver and shut the drawer quietly. I look around the room but I find nothing but cold, hard silence.

Chapter Seven

Today I move into my new space and my new world. I shut the door to my studio while swallowing the fear that won't subside. I will have no escape at the Armanis'. No life outside the hairy man who pays for my body.

Women aren't permitted to own a home, and certainly not without a man to live with. Another benefit of courtesan life. This studio has been my sanctuary, a home to indulge in my artistic dreams. I plan to return with money, connections, and a portfolio of sellable art, though reality tempers my hope, whispering that I may lose this place along with everything else.

I don't look back at my balcony overlooking the tiny canal as I might burst into tears. There is no way out, so I walk toward the dome with shoulders high and gaze fixed firmly ahead. I must be Armani's lover, his muse, and his confidante. His everything.

Sometimes it feels as if all this power locks me in an even tighter cage.

Over several bridges and through snaking alleyways, I walk toward Palazzo Armani on the Grand Canal. I stroll past the bobbing gondolas on the shining blue water and savor the life I may not enjoy for some time. Not until I've proven myself to the despondent artist. Wealthy patrician women would never dare walk alone, and they certainly wouldn't run their fingertips along the stone and lift their faces to the warm sunshine. Alas, I am not a patrician. I am not even a woman by Venice's standards. Sofia Rossi is a courtesan, first and only.

I arrive at the dome by noon. Servants greet me at the gate, with only deliveries arriving by this door. Anyone of wealth and importance presents themselves at the water entrance. They lead me toward my new quarters, through the hallway I walked through three days prior. Today, the drapes are pulled back, letting in the light.

Inside my suite, there are layers of rich satin, carved bedposts, and walnut chests stained by vibrant pigments. The room's cornices shine with gold. Tapestries and mirrors line the walls, and thick rugs soften my steps.

"This is all for me?" A padded, gilded cage to disappear in.

The servant bows. "Yes, Signora Rossi. You are welcome to rest and explore the garden. Master Armani will send for you as he wishes."

Once I'm alone, I inspect the gowns and jewelry in the wardrobe. A harp and violin sit near the window that overlooks a canal. The silence in this cavernous room grips me like a fist.

Free to wander, the servant said. The entryway glitters. From the frescoed walls to the tiled floors of polished, precious stones, the grand entrance swallows me in extravagance. Through the arches into the courtyard, I notice red porphyry roundels embedded in the walls, a rare sign of extreme wealth.

Past potted palms and ornate statues of kings and Greek gods, I step through a breezy walkway. Topiaries, sculptures, and tufts of overflowing herbs fill the sizable garden, and I bask in the golden amber light under the warm afternoon sun.

By evening, I've walked the palazzo and the grounds, explored the various harps and pianos, and noted the vast number of paintings in the house—none of which are by Armani. A table is set for one in the dining room.

A servant appears from the doorway. "For you, signora."

"I eat alone?"

He pulls out my chair, and I proceed to eat an extravagant meal of stew and bread, rice with peas, and even a fruit biscuit with wine. So much luxury tasted in solitude.

At nighttime, the warm wind laps through my window and I dress for bed. A nightshirt and robe cover me in silken threads, meant to slip me into ease and desire.

I drift to sleep. A servant appears at my bedside in the dark of night. I nearly scream, but he steps back. "Apologies, signora. The master requests your presence."

"Now?"

He opens the door and waits.

I reach to dress, but the servant says, "Not needed, signora."

I tighten my robe and follow him up the winding turret stairs to the dome. Once inside the candlelit room, I search for Signore Armani. "I'm here," I announce.

A door opens in a dark corner. He emerges into the flickering light, hand out. "Come."

I approach, but his eyes aren't on me. He has turned and pours two goblets of wine.

"This is my sleeping room," he says, still unconcerned with my face, my eyes, my needs.

A giant bed crowds the middle of the room. Glass lines the peak of the dome overhead, a direct view to the heavens. He hands me a goblet filled with ruby red wine.

He called for a companion, and this is my role to fill. I try not to glance at the domed studio full of supplies where we could be sculpting. "Did you want me to join your bed, signore?"

His flattened eyes don't twitch. "No."

A far more definitive answer than I'd expected. "What can I do for you?" I lower my voice into a soft purr, whispery yet sharp. "Tell me what you need."

He drinks from his goblet, and he finally examines my face. "I am lonely."

"I can help with that." I step closer. Mother taught me years ago how to force down notions of resistance or revulsion. I must view his touch as the key to everything I want. I tilt my head and examine his eyes. Somehow both full like the sky and hauntingly empty.

I run my hand through his hair, but he grabs my wrist. "I do not want your touch. Not yet."

I drop my hand. "I see." Too eager. I remind myself Lucca requires a connection. He needs to be seen and heard.

He drops his head. "I want passion. I want life to flow through my fingers once again. Empty touch only causes more pain."

Plenty of men fight their demons in bed with me. Together we slay the dragons that burn them with fire and topple the giants who crush their souls. Lucca asks for something different. I must crawl inside the darkness with him. "When did your passion disappear?"

He faces a dark window. The candlelight casts his long, warped reflection on the glass. "Was it ever here?"

Lord Marco's needs were easy to decipher. Most men's are. Make them believe they are larger than the moon and more powerful than Zeus. Signore Armani's tortured soul seems to hold his emotions prisoner. Dark and broken. Injecting him with power won't heal his wounds. This man begs for something soft, which turns my body rigid. "Would you like to sit together, in silence?"

"Yes." His voice rings with hope, childlike in its tone.

The warm night drifts through the cracked windows and onto my neck. Enough time passes that I begin to nod toward sleep. My body falls against the bed, unable to stop slumber from taking me.

He wakes me with a whisper. "Look at the sky, Sofia."

I turn onto my back. We lay next to each other without touching and stare at the twinkling sky through the glass overhead.

"It's beautiful." No pretense, no lies. For this moment, I am honest. Perhaps, for the first time with a patron, my limbs turn languid, my mind at peace in this quiet space.

"When I lie here, I want to paint," he says. "I want to sculpt. I want to taste the joy of art and life and a beautiful woman.

Until I sit up and face the daylight. That is when all the hunger disappears."

"Then let us watch the stars and dream of the day when life gifts us the strength to truly live." The back of my hand brushes his, and he does not recoil.

He sighs, and somewhere in the early morning, we fall asleep.

~

I wake with the hot sun beating on my skin. Red heat creeps into my neck and cheeks as I open my eyes to look for Lucca, my body rested from my night under the stars.

Someone stands over me.

I don't gasp or move to cover my exposed breast where my gown has fallen over my shoulder.

The woman breathes heavily, her rigid chest rising and falling like a skeleton puppet. "Sofia Rossi," she says with a growl.

"Yes." I sit up and stretch, pulling my sleeping gown over my exposed chest. "Signora Armani."

She is tall and regal. Her gold hair is so sleek I ponder if she oils her tresses. Her green eyes trail over my face as if they have fingernails, while her stare locks me frozen in place, shift gathered in my fist.

"I expect great things from you," she says.

The smattering of freckles across her nose is so strangely innocent, they disrupt my thoughts. A dizzying whimsy to her otherwise stone-like features. "I hope I will satisfy your family's needs, signora."

She glances at me from the corner of her eyes. "Lucca is emotional. He has not completed a commission in over two years." She faces me. "I brought you here to fix him."

"Brought me? Lord Marco told me he arranged for this."

"I'm certain he thought so."

Her skin is as smooth as candle wax. Her gown shimmers in the morning light, colors of deep blue I've never seen before. "He needs time," I say.

She stares at my mouth long enough to make me flinch. "I no longer care what he needs."

The heat turns me shaky, and I struggle to catch my breath. *And that is part of the problem*, I yearn to say. "I understand."

"You seem to be quite popular with the men of the Republic." She puffs out her lips as she says this, her gaze unwavering from my mouth.

"I am a prized courtesan. I deliver what men desire."

She runs her gaze over my neck as her jaw pulses with gritted teeth. "Make him the artist he's capable of being." Her tone is so cold and rigid, I shrink in place. "You will deliver what I demand, not what my husband wants."

She turns to walk away, gliding her hands down the soft lines of her gown. I already understand what's expected. In this home, she is the power, the money, and the thumping heart. "Why did you choose me, signora?"

"As you said, you are Venice's most coveted courtesan." She pulls her shoulders back and lifts her chin. "Enjoy it now, signora. For one day soon, your beauty will fade, and your age will ruin you."

She wants me desperate and compliant. Why, I don't know. "Until then, I belong to this house." I soften my voice, growing small right before her eyes.

She lifts a paintbrush long dry of paint and pigment. "Lucca's talent cannot be wasted alone in this attic. I married him for his prospects." She drops the brush to the floor. "A beautiful courtesan always brings him to life. At least enough to start a commission. Perhaps you will help him finish one."

I imagine Lucca, used for his talents and admonished for his failures. It's no surprise he's fallen out of passion. "Thank you for your trust."

"Do not thank me, girl. This is business." She wipes her hands of dried yellow paint flakes. "In three days' time, you will accompany him to Palazzo Pietro. Woo them all with your voice and your body. Convince the Republic that Lucca Armani has returned in full virility. I will make certain Lucca's bedchamber is prepared when you return."

"He is not ready to bed me, signora."

She takes a deep, impatient breath. "I already told you. You are not to concern yourself with what he needs."

With great focus, I keep unease from creeping to my face or my body. I've never taken orders from the lady of the house and certainly never slept next to a man who didn't desire my body.

"Welcome to the dome, Sofia. Here, there may be only one queen."

Behind Caterina, a glossy, pristine hunk of alabaster begs to be cut and molded into something magnificent. In the morning light, rough frescoes come to life along the base of the walls. Potentially grand scenes await, unfinished.

I raise my eyes to her rigid, tall figure. "At your service, your majesty."

Chapter Eight

A knock jars me awake. Terrified of every noise, I didn't fall asleep until sunrise. The clock reads eleven through my foggy eyes. The sky is a deep gray, and the trees rattle outside my window. I turn on my side and slide the bedside drawer open. The memory of the misplaced fabric sends shocks through my body. If someone has been in my flat, I need to discover who, and fast.

Another knock.

Shit.

That could be anyone. I tiptoe across the apartment and lean into the door to listen, for what, I don't know. The only people to visit my apartment in Los Angeles are food delivery drivers.

"Dr. Harding?"

"Beckett?" I crack open the door to find his chipper, smiling face and a perfectly boring beige jumper. He's holding two coffees, and rain drips from his hair down his temples, spotting his glasses with tiny droplets.

"Cuppa?" he asks.

I lean toward the mirror on the wall and wince at the sight. Gone are the perfect chignon and pearl earrings and with them, any semblance of professionalism. "Yes." The smell hits my nose, and I no longer care that I look like a Muppet. "Come in."

"I'm sorry I woke you. You must be tired."

I do my best to slick back my hair, aware that it's no use. "Were you up as late as I was?" I open the door wide and hand him a kitchen towel to dry the raindrops that moisten his temples.

"I couldn't sleep." He sits on the couch and reaches into his jacket. He pulls out a folded paper. "I found something."

If he's discovered something questionable, I'll need to come forward with it. My integrity is already dangling by a thread, but he could have a once in a lifetime find. "I'm listening."

He unfolds a paper with scribbles and smooths it out on the table. "I kept thinking about Armani and Caterina, wondering how we could get a glimpse into their marriage, to prove he wouldn't have sculpted a love cast of her."

"A love cast?" A laugh catches in my throat, and his cheeks flush red.

"There isn't much out there." He looks up at me. "Are you going to sit?"

"Oh, yes." I lower to the chair far away from him, pulling my robe tight to cover my chest, and glance at a passerby on the street below. "Go on."

"Armani went dark for years. I found a record of commissions, and complaints of uncompleted work. Then, nothing. Researchers assume he stopped making art, and that's when he lost his money and palazzo, and Caterina left him."

"You realize I have actually read the documents." I force myself to ignore the pit in my stomach and shove down the urge to search the flat for anything amiss.

"Of course you have." He slides the paper toward me. "You told me to look at the women who didn't make it into history, so I did."

I place down my coffee and lift the paper. "It's a list of names." I recognize them all. "Venetian courtesans."

"Yes." He smiles as he pushes up his glasses. "At least the ones we know of."

My body tingles despite my warnings against it. "I've seen the tax record. None of the courtesans stood out."

"I got to thinking about Armani and the money he married into with Caterina. He would have been wealthy enough to have a courtesan."

My heart races. A courtesan would have access to everything about him. His body, his private moments, his every waking thought. "And?"

"A fire destroyed tax records in San Marco for those years. So, I searched his name along with the nobility of Venice. Armani was reclusive, but in 1608, briefly, he appeared in the registry of benefactors, but with no woman after his name."

"You did all this while I slept?" I feel my promotion slipping through my fingers as Noah pushes his way to the truth.

"Oh, I haven't slept." He gets up and paces around the couch. "Too much to do."

I haven't pulled an all-night research session since graduate school.

"I figured he did some sort of tax evasion, marking that he paid for a courtesan, without actually having one. There's no record of a courtesan in his home." He nods once with emphasis. "I searched any primary source I could find for mention of Armani." His breath catches with a smile. "I found one."

"Go on."

"An Englishman from Somerset recounted his travels through Venice in a journal, most of which became published work. I combed through his notes that didn't make it into the final volume."

"I'm familiar with it. He stayed with the British Ambassador to Venice."

"Yes." He points to me, an infectious fire in his eyes. "His English host accompanied him to several events. I cross-referenced all three men and found this." He removes a paper from the folder and hands it to me.

I read Noah's scribbled notes aloud.

"'Our young friend seems enamored with the glory of Venice. He was especially taken with our artistic beauties. What is not to adore? The dancing women in contract with patricians have intrigued me since my first night here in Venice. It was the most elusive of courtesans who caught his eye, with her luscious black curls and bright blue eyes. Her ribbon of teardrop pearls braided through her hair. Yet, she did not look away from her troubled artist and his demanding wife. I suspect the doge's commission has driven the poor artist mad.'"

Noah's eyes widen as large as mine. He nods with a smile.

I sift through data from the records. "He never completed that commission. At least, it isn't listed in the registry from the palace. The dates line up. This has to be in reference to Armani." I scan the words again. "The courtesan and *her* troubled artist."

Noah leans against the wall and crosses his arms. "Armani had a courtesan."

"How did I miss this?" *Oh God, how did I miss this.*

He holds up his hand, as if to halt me from beating myself up. Too late. "This wasn't in the archives. I called a friend who keeps a record of unconfirmed artifacts."

Of course, wealthy friends with expensive hobbies to the rescue. I scan the list of names. "But which one?"

The usual winter mist has turned to a rain dump outside, obscuring the view out my front window. "That, I'll need your help with."

I scan both pages of Noah's notes. "Courtesans paid taxes. They were heavily regulated. Why is there no record?" I meet his gaze. "Who the hell is she?"

"Certainly this is enough to halt the announcement, yes? A courtesan would change everything. Someone with intimate knowledge of his art and his relationship to Caterina."

These things always play out the same. An emotional woman desperate for relevance. The press would tear me apart. It wouldn't be the first time our museum threw an assistant to the wolves. "This isn't enough."

Noah nods. "We have forty-eight hours to find her before—" He clears his throat. "Before you leave for Los Angeles and my life once again becomes purple jumpers and solo nights in the pub."

I sense those days are gone. I yearn to tell him about my journal, but fear he'll dismiss me as irrational. Maybe I'm making a big deal out of nothing. I notice my robe has fallen open, exposing my terrible nightwear. An oversized JPGM T-shirt and sweats. "I have to shower. And put on some acceptable clothing."

"I quite like the collegiate pajamas."

"This isn't a college. It's from the Getty Museum. I spend every Sunday wandering the exhibits, then hike Topanga and grab a green juice." I do so alone, cursing my impossible boss, but that's beside the point.

"Hmm, yes. I have no idea what you're referring to. That was a lot of American thrown at me at one time." He gathers his things. "Dress warm. The weather is miserable."

I reach for his arm, unable to imagine being here alone. "Will you stay? Wait for me while I get ready?"

He responds with a stunned, yet satisfied gaze. "Of course." He lowers his satchel to the coffee table. "Is something wrong?"

Several possible answers roll around in my mind, competing for the chance to be blurted out. Do I tell him someone has been in my flat?

"Do you believe we can sense things we can't see?" I ask. He nods without judgment, so the truth wiggles its way to the surface. I look out the window, then I lean my mouth to his ear. "I think I'm being followed."

Chapter Nine

Three days into my stay, Caterina has traveled to Padua for the week, leaving the house calm but very empty. I meet Lucca in his dome for evening poetry and stargazing. We don't touch. He rarely looks at me, and I wake in the mornings to an empty bed. I enjoy every moment of Lucca's quiet dance but know Caterina will return and expect an improvement. I have only a few hours to convince Lucca to accompany me to his first celebration in years.

The servants roll the harp out to the salon at my request. Today, I pluck the strings for an hour while I stare out the windows to a warm golden afternoon, thinking of the ten blank canvases that sit in the dome, waiting to fulfill their destiny. I hope to coax Lucca downstairs with my music, but he doesn't appear.

"Signora." I pause my music to find a servant, head bowed. "Signora Armani left word. You may take the gondola tonight to Palazzo Pietro for the ball."

I push the chair with the back of my legs as I stand. I can't make him leave the dome, let alone attend a celebration.

The servant turns away, mumbling about proper clothing being sent over promptly.

The tight, musicless room doesn't breathe. Bowls of ripe fruit top gold-painted credenzas, and a round table of oiled walnut wood reflects the low midday sun. Colors and sheen light up the salon, yet all I feel is the dull ache in my chest.

I creak open the door to the dome, stepping over a silver platter of untouched food. Curtains are drawn, and Lucca groans, tossing a paintbrush into the air over his head before catching the handle and throwing it again.

"I have not called for you," he says, his voice flat and lifeless.

"No, you haven't." I consider leaving him, but Caterina is the one I must please, so I walk toward him slowly. "Pietro is hosting a dinner tonight. Your wife would like us to attend."

He slides the paintbrush across the floor. After a grumble, he turns his head toward me. "Caterina is impossible."

Among other undesirable traits. I lower to my knees facing him though he ignores me, more interested in the uninspired ceiling. "Are you imagining the stars?"

"All I see is darkness."

I reach for his hand. At first, he recoils, but I attempt again, and he remains still. "You can see darkness at a dinner party too."

His eyes lock onto mine. I nearly slide away, but he laughs. I've yet to see the man's upturned lips, let alone his teeth, and the sight is shocking. "You are no Caterina, beautiful one."

"Thank goodness for that." My needs rest right here in his vulnerability. Keep him here. Soften him by softening yourself. "Do you love her?"

"Caterina? I admire her. Appreciate her." He tilts his head. "I fear her. But there is no love."

Our hands still touch. His are splayed over his stomach and mine rest on top. "Your hands are smooth." I examine his palm. "Elegant."

He has not pulled away. Somewhere in the depths of his pain, he needs touch. They always do.

I lower to the ground in a side sit and bring his palm to my cheek. "What do you feel when you touch me?"

"Darkness."

I know only one way to control him. I tuck my mouth into his palm and kiss his skin. He closes his eyes. I run his hand along my neck and let a gasp escape as I trace a line down my sternum. Again, he hasn't pulled away.

His hand remains soft, perfectly cupped around the curve of my breast. Finally, he sighs. A crack of light into the darkness. I untie my bodice and slip his hand inside my gown. His warm hand slides against the lower weight of my breast. Eyes closed, he massages me gently, rhythmically.

"Blackness is less likely to devour you while touching a beautiful woman, signore. You might even glimpse the stars." I twirl his hair around my finger then bounce it free.

"I am no fool. Your task is to make me paint and sculpt."

"True." I run my hand down his face and slip my thumb into his mouth. He responds as every other man does. He suckles and licks. "We both have needs."

He opens his eyes. "What are your needs, Sofia?"

I glance through the crack in the drapes toward the amber sunshine. His touch may as well be water or air. I feel nothing, just as I always do. But I am a skilled performer. "I need you to want me."

For want brings life, and life brings art.

He continues stroking my breast. "Not enough. Tell me what you really want."

I believe my body may be made of iron, and my heart of stone. All the passion I pour into men is nothing more than a fable I've read about in faraway lands. I drip passion from an utterly dead soul. He knows a lie. "I need power."

My heart races when I say the honest words I've held close all these years. He needs me to shiver in vulnerability just as he does.

He moves his hand from under my breast to flat against my chest. My heart beats against his palm. Thump. Thump.

"Those who crave power never have enough," he says.

"That is a problem I would love to have."

His lips tug at a smile. He draws little circles on my collarbone then taps in place. "Yes. I will go with you."

His hand rises and falls with each of my breaths. "Why?"

"Because you may be filled with more darkness than I, beautiful one."

~

Caterina's team of lady's maids fluff and tighten so many layers of silk around my body, the weight nearly knocks me to my knees. They decorate me with sapphires and gold chains, with ribbons of pearls tucked into an elaborate hairstyle. With a dab of some red paste to my cheeks and lips, the women lift me and shove me out the door.

I wait in the back garden, glimpsing the canal through arches as the sun lowers into a fiery blaze across the horizon.

The gondolier steps one foot on land with a sly grin. "I do not belong to you," I say with intended harshness.

He clears his throat and notes Lucca approach from the back door. I turn, surprised he has shown. His beard is combed, at least.

He slides his hand around my waist, squinting at the bright sun. "Sofia, let us find you some power."

Lucca helps me into the gondola with a soft hand steadying mine. His face appears younger in the daylight. His eyes wide and alert give hope for his state of mind. I smile at him and only him, already preparing to shed my clothes for him tonight. Once I feel his bare chest against mine, I will rule his desires. And desires are the essence of all men.

"Sofia," he whispers, "do not think I'm fooled by your luscious breasts and pouting mouth. You do not crave me."

He's making certain I understand he sees through my advances. "Why did you return my touch earlier?"

He bites my earlobe once, careful and soft. "You want power. And I want to give it to you."

The gondola stops against the foot of the Ponte della Paglia as we wait for our turn at the water entrance. Near the Doge's Palace, Palazzo Pietro sits just two over from Lord Marco's little castle on the Grand Canal. A row of wealth in competition for the most elaborate façade and the most beautiful women.

A servant welcomes us inside a room of jeweled mirrors. Together, we step through the tiled hallway and up the grand staircase to the salon. With gleaming terrazzo floors and Murano glass chandeliers, dazzling light seems to bounce around us like stars, while silk wall panels in cyan and vermillion give the room a sense of celebration. Laughter and harpsichord notes fill the palazzo with life, causing me to examine Lucca for any signs of retreat. He remains close, but does not hesitate to lead me into the grand hall.

Lord Marco never could ascend to this level of patrician status. They shunned the odd man with his riddles and his obscene art collection. Not even I have stepped foot in these grand palaces, and Lucca seems to enjoy my awe.

A trio of coveted courtesans dance with fans. Lucca slides his hand from my hip and vanishes, as if he has soaked into the walls. I'm left to fend off stares by patricians imagining which way they would flip me around if I were naked. Some recognize me from the parties Marco hosted. Others smile and wink, communicating how my body pleases them.

My figure is second only to control as my greatest asset.

A man appears beside me, his ruffled collar so tight his face appears purple. "Good evening, signora."

I nod politely, with a firm air of coldness.

"Signore Armani is a lucky man." He eyes the dancers. "We'd all thought him dead."

"He is far from dead, as you can see." I am not interested in wasting my time with gossip. "He is full of passion in his art studio—and elsewhere."

The man looks aroused, poor thing. So easy to manipulate,

they are. I completely ignore the man who will do nothing for us and step aside to scan the room for the most important patricians to target. Through the smiles and mouths hanging open, I catch eyes with a young man without the slightest smile. He stares at me with eyes like still water—a fountain left ignored and stagnant.

His expression unnerves me enough that I glance away. When I turn back, he is still staring. Heavy eyebrows and dark, rich eyes. The lines of his cheekbones could carve marble.

I've been staring long enough, and he hasn't the decency to smile or leer or even lick his lips. Lucca is nowhere in sight, so I find fresh air on the balcony. I gather myself under the arcade, in the façade that faces the Grand Canal. Candles flicker and reflect along the water. The air smells of tallow and honeyed spice from the lilies in marble urns at my feet and a bell rings nearby in Piazza San Marco, signaling the workers may return home.

Despite my confidence that I am the most beautiful woman in every room, unease still ripples through my belly. I must sell a healed version of Lucca. I'm peddling a lie.

"Your makeup doesn't suit you."

I turn toward the voice that borders on a growl. The man who doesn't smile. I realize my hand grips the stone railing hard enough to ache, so I force my muscles to relax. "Thank you for your thoughtful insight, signore." I roll my eyes. Such an obvious sign of disrespect, still, he steps closer.

"I only mean that your face needs no embellishments. Though I know your status demands jewelry and silk heavy enough to drown you in a canal."

His face doesn't move, yet I find myself smiling. "You aren't impressed with me, are you, signore?"

"My opinion of you matters little."

"How true." I straighten my skirts and glance over his shoulder as if searching for someone.

"Signore Armani is off in a room somewhere, hoping you will chase after him."

My gaze runs down his body and back up to his firm jaw. His brown eyes are dark enough to pass for charcoal. "I am here for only Signore Armani. When I smile, it is for him."

He leans against the railing on his forearms as if he owns the city. Perhaps he does. "Do those words work to convince him or you?" He turns, looking straight through me.

His audacity flames rage through my chest. "No one needs convincing, signore." At least, not the true me who hides deep inside, lost to the light. I slide my hands to my waist and inhale to puff my breasts like summer fruit.

He slides his fingers through his dark hair to push the locks away from his forehead. "Your patrons see only a beautiful body."

That is what they pay for. He stares as if he sees inside the closed casket of my soul. He cannot. No one can. "Who cares of such trivialities when I can control the minds of men?" *Have I spoken with enough conviction for him to believe me?*

He opens the door and steps back. "Someday, signora, perhaps a man will see past your beauty."

"Certainly not tonight." I walk past him without acknowledgment, though his gaze burns hot against my backside. I dare glance back, shocked to find his intense gaze at my eyes and not the curve of my buttocks.

Back in the salon, Lucca wraps his hands around my waist from behind. "You appear flushed." He whispers in my ear. "Where have you been?"

"Jealous?" I ask with an unintended spark of frustration.

He breathes heat against my neck. "Intrigued." I try to turn but he forcefully holds my hips in place. "I've done as you've asked tonight. Paraded around smiling, cloaked in lies. Now you must play my game."

I simply love when men give me orders. I force a girlish voice. "Game, signore?"

"You turn cold at my touch, Sofia." He wraps his arm around my stomach and pulls me tight against him, hard enough to cause my heart to thump into my throat. I force a calm expression as all men in the room seem to watch me. "I will bed you when you make me feel wanted," he says.

He still will not allow me to face him.

"If you want control and freedom and access to every medium of art you could desire, you will teach me how to experience passion in the depths of my soul." He loosens his hold and intertwines his fingers through mine. "What makes your thighs quiver, Sofia?"

Much as I fight every screaming voice inside my head that tells me to turn and face Lucca, I collapse under his grip. I search the room. When my gaze once again connects with the dark man who followed me to the balcony, my breathing quickens, for I know exactly what would make my thighs quiver, and it isn't Lucca Armani.

Chapter Ten

Gloom shrouds the museum's library from the blustery day outside. Now that we're settled into the quiet of a Saturday morning at the museum with its low table lights and protective walls, he finally leans across the table and it's clear we're here for more than courtesan research. Noah wants to *know* me, and beyond all reason, I want the same.

"We're alone," he says. "Now tell me, what's going on?"

How to explain? I feel things. He'd never understand my odd sensations and glimpses into things that aren't there. Energy in houses and whispers of objects.

"You'll think it's all in my head, but I'm certain it isn't." I rub my wrist then crack my knuckles. "I keep a journal in my bedside drawer to document my life. It's a nightly ritual that helps me sleep."

"Okay." He leans back against his chair, waiting for me to elaborate.

"Inside, I keep a strip of fabric. A stupid memento that goes everywhere I travel. I have an obsessive need to tuck it deep in the spine as a bookmark." I can't help but look over my shoulder. "Last night, I reached for my journal. The strip of fabric was hanging loose, half out the side. I didn't leave it like that."

He jerks forward ever so subtly, whispering, "You think someone's been in your flat?"

I swallow my frustration. "I know it sounds crazy. But I felt it. The room was off. Someone had been there."

He rubs his eyes then adjusts his glasses. "Byron?" he mouths.

I shrug, holding my shoulders at my ears. "Maybe?"

Noah clasps his hands behind his head and stretches. "We're talking about a researcher who throws a fit if his espresso is less than the ideal temperature. Could he really break into a woman's flat?"

Embarrassment lands with a burst in the back of my eyes as I fight the urge to tear up. "Someone was in my place, Dr. Beckett."

He nods. "I believe you."

"Let's just finish what you started, okay?" I reach for the registry of courtesans at the turn of the seventeenth century, forcing down every bit of fear.

We split the registry and review the names aloud, talking out reasons why each woman couldn't be Armani's mistress. Years don't match. Contracted to another patrician at the time. After a few hours, only a handful of names are left. Of those, most have light brown or blond curls, the fashion of the time. Even fewer display blue eyes or were important enough to wear a hairstyle with teardrop pearls.

"Once we find his courtesan, then what?" I ask. "We aren't going to find anything worthwhile by tomorrow." I slide the binders away, realizing how ridiculous we've been.

He mirrors me as I stand. "Don't give up. There's something here. I know there is."

"I'm going to pack up my office." I walk away but Noah follows, knocking over a chair to catch up with me.

"We're onto something, Dr. Harding." He keeps his voice low, like a whisper-shout. Once close, he speaks soft enough for only me to hear. "Why are you fighting this so hard?"

He's so close, my body overrides my senses. "Too much is at risk here, okay? It's not just my reputation at stake."

"Tell me what's going on."

I examine the paneled ceiling and tall windows of this historic hall. His eager gaze is too much to fight. "I took this job aware that something didn't match up. I took it because—" I gather my thoughts, then decide I'm too tired. "I'm so far in debt I'm close to homelessness. I have no family, and friends are sparse. Dr. Wright promised me a promotion and a huge bonus. He wants the press for the museum and threatened to fire me if I refused this project."

"Shite."

"Yeah. He knows everyone. Without his reference, my future in the art world is dead." I rub my eyes until they sting. "This assignment should have been straightforward. My future wasn't supposed to come at the expense of everything I thought I stood for. Spend two months in England and prove what everyone else already believed."

"Until I came along to push you." He reaches for my hand as we walk. "Mia, if we see it, others will too."

The empty hall seems to hum as we pass closed doors. It's early and most researchers won't be in today, yet the air flickers with energy, like someone unseen stands beside us. His expression flattens.

"Dr. Harding." Noah's eyes widen as he looks over my shoulder. "Did you leave your office door ajar?"

There's no need to look as I remember. "No. I locked it."

"The nighttime caretaker?" he asks.

Something is very wrong. My shoulder presses against Noah's as we near my office. We push the door open with a creak, and I flip on the lights.

I examine my desk, nothing amiss. Inside the drawers, paper and pens are just as I left them. I sigh, then open the curtains on the window to lift the unease in this room. Someone has been here, and it wasn't for emptying the wastebasket.

He slides my notebook toward him. "What is LACC?"

"The Brits don't love an acronym quite like Americans do." I force a smile. "Community college. I worked three terrible jobs to pay my way through classes and hardly slept for two years but it earned me a scholarship to a university. It may not be Harvard or Oxford, but it was mine."

"Very impressive, Dr. Harding. My parents paid my way through Cambridge. I don't think I appreciated it at the time."

"Try working as a maid at a seedy hotel. That will make you appreciate everything in life."

He runs his fingers along the binder and flips it open.

"Come on," I tell him. "Let's get out of here." I wait at the door, but he's frozen in place. "Dr. Beckett?"

He looks up at me, face flat and pale.

"What is it?"

"Someone left you a note," he says.

He turns the folder upside down so I can read it. I step hesitantly toward the desk and catch Noah's face before I dare glance down, noting the shimmering fear pooled in his eyes.

The note has six words. "Approve the Armani research. We're watching."

Chapter Eleven

Lucca held me like a doll all last night. His hands pawed at me like an animal guarding its food while staring at dancers with an uninspired gaze. But in the gondola, he ignored me, and once we returned home late into the night, he walked away with only a few words. "Make me desire you, Sofia."

This morning, I consider my options for tapping into his hidden world of passion as none of my usual approaches have done a thing. Impossible man.

The image of the young man on the balcony consumes my thoughts. I never discovered who he was, though I caught him staring at me all evening. He sat across from me at dinner, sneaking glances at my neck and eyes. Like a shadow, he moved through the party without interacting. Without a word to anyone but me.

My body warmed when I looked at him. All of it confuses me. I remind my foolish whims that love means nothing in our world. I've given my body to the man with the largest bag of riches. That is the only truth allowed in the life of a courtesan where I am a lover of men and seller of skin. Mother told me that once your heart has a voice, it will snuff your power.

Servants surround me, carrying trunks. Caterina has returned.

I slip into my quarters and clean up. A fresh powdering of my hair and face, a spritz of perfume on my neck, and rouge on my cheeks. She greets me in the salon, where she lounges like an artist's model near the fireplace. "My husband remains useless, I see."

"He attended the celebration, as you asked."

She motions for the chair near the window. "Sit."

I obey but remain tall and rigid, my hands folded in my lap. I won't reveal a word of Lucca's resistance to my advances.

"We must prove to Lucca that his art will move people." She walks over to me and runs her fingers along my jaw. "Feed him the nonsense he requires." Her hand remains on my skin, twirling her fingers along my chin. I recoil and she laughs.

"What Lucca needs takes time," I tell her.

She stands over me, blocking the sun from my face. "You are a paid liar. Stop pretending as if you care for him."

A servant opens the door. "Announcing Signore Antonio Bruni."

I stand and straighten my skirts, adept at immediately turning frustration into demure attentiveness.

"Signore. What a pleasant surprise." Caterina welcomes the man inside. It's the man with the serious face and intensely dark eyes from last night. The man who warms my body with his gaze. He knows Caterina. I repeat his name in my mind over and over like a song. *Antonio Bruni.*

He steps into our salon and presses his heels together with a slight bow. His gaze crawls over to me then back to Caterina. "My apologies for arriving unannounced."

"You are welcome anytime. Please." She gestures to the largest chair in the room.

His intensity could halt time. I blink slowly, forcing a controlled breath. He stares at me without a word, without one twitch of emotion.

"This is Signora Rossi," Caterina says with such contempt, she practically spits. "What can I help you with, Signore Bruni?"

His dismissive wave flicks in Caterina's direction. "You may leave us." He doesn't look away, and the room fades to black around his frame.

"Pardon?" Caterina chokes on a forced laugh.

He finally turns to her. "There's a matter to discuss with Signora Rossi, and I would like privacy. May we walk in the garden?"

"I don't see what could require such inappropriate discussions."

He ignores Caterina's resistance and presents his arm, which I take—reminders that he is merely a man and not some apparition from my dreams. Servants open the doors to the garden. The odd sensation of a racing heart knocks against my chest, turning me woozy, as if he were wine and I've drunk too much.

We walk arm in arm to the balmy afternoon, under the waxy greenery of a magnolia tree, where I yank my arm away. "Why are you here?"

He shakes the loose waves of black hair from over his eye. "For you, signora."

Power lies in the fervor of our convictions. The ability to demand silence in your heart and obedience in the face. "I told you, I am wholly Lucca's."

A grin tugs at the corner of his lips. "I need something from Signore Armani." He glances over his shoulder and back at me. "And I always get what I want."

"What a privilege."

He smiles fully now, and it changes his entire face. "Signora Rossi, you've been called to fix the man of the palazzo, have you not?"

"I'm not certain anyone needs fixing, Signore Bruni."

"You offer him anything he wishes, yes?"

I lift my skirts with tightened fists. "Why must you be so intolerable? It's obvious you despise what I do and have no regard for the sacrifices a woman must make." I swoosh my skirts aside and face the view of the canal. *Silly woman, Sofia. Never let your temper control your voice.* His handsome face threatens to topple everything I've built.

"I don't despise you." He steps next to me and together we watch the subtle waves lap against the dock through the arches. "Quite the opposite." Though I feel him stare at my neck, I don't dare acknowledge it.

There is power in the words he doesn't say, which is why I haven't turned away just yet. "This conversation is dangerous. I suggest you speak the truth before I stomp on your foot."

"As signora wishes." He bows. "The doge wishes to display a painting in his palazzo. I'm here to commission an Armani original. Something surprising and challenging."

"The Doge of Venice wants his work?" This elaborate ruse is about a commission. I should have guessed. "Perhaps you should speak with the artist."

"There is no artist without you." His eyes soften. "I know the truth. You must teach signore how to bleed onto canvas again. Caterina will make certain you do."

Caterina need not say the words for me to understand the consequences. If I fail Lucca, she'll ruin any future contracts. Besides, my time in this business is limited. "I already live under their threat; I don't need yours too."

"There is no threat, signora. Only admiration. Perhaps a touch of jealousy." His cheeks redden. "Please, call me Antonio."

His eyes. The way his voice softens when he looks at me. I see him. Not the vague outline of his presence, but every smile line near his mouth and the luscious curves of his upper lip. How shadows of facial hair outline his wide jaw. I've dared allow a crack in my stone walls with this one look. His gaze pierces down through my very core, and this one moment could ruin me.

"You could have spoken to the Armanis. Instead, you came to convince me with your sweet smile."

He straightens his shoulders, his cheeks turning from rosy to crimson. "You think my smile sweet?"

No, I will not respond to that. I turn away once more and we've practically begun to dance as he follows my movements, swooshing and turning in this shaded garden, under the saffron glow of afternoon light.

"Like everyone," he says, "I merely want Armani to sculpt again. The doge wishes to display a secular presence at the entrance to his palace, a symbol that we are humans in charge of our own destiny. We are not at the mercy of the papacy."

Using lust and skin to defy the pope. Interesting choice. "How do you benefit from all this?"

"I'm an art dealer. I trade and barter for the most powerful among us. A large commission awaits me when Signore Armani delivers."

Antonio deals in art and power, working behind closed doors in transactions of whispers and gold. Now I understand. "You could have told the Armanis yourself. Why involve me?"

He looks to the sky and takes a deep breath of heady air scented by rosemary. "You are the one with the power here, signora. If you are half as entrancing in private as you are in front of a party, I have no doubt you could convince any man to catch the stars."

My heart swells with a shot of pain through its center. My desires cleave in two; I wish he would both disappear immediately and grab me with his rough hands and presumably soft touch.

"I am a courtesan, not a magician," I say.

"You appear to deal in both body and soul." He checks the sun's position in the sky. "I'd put my faith in that over anything else." He steps past me.

I don't want him to go. "My given name is Sofia." If he can be dangerous, so can I.

"Sofia." Again, with that softness. His voice both purrs and growls. He nods, his angular cheeks pulled taut by a smile. "I must confess, my interest is only partially in the artwork." He controls his voice into a whisper. "By hiring Armani, I have given myself the opportunity to see you once more. Forgive me for risking your employment. It will not happen again."

He walks away toward the center courtyard. "Signore?" I call.

"Yes?"

Perhaps it's lust, or intrigue, or sheer stupidity, but a new emotion has exploded inside that little crack that now fills with warmth. I want to live in it. Bathe in it. I suddenly understand how Lucca won't settle for less than all of me. "I do hope it won't be the last of your visits."

He dips his head ever so subtly. "I'll make certain of it."

~

Lucca summoned me once again in the middle of the night. I present myself in my sleeping clothes as he stares at a canvas painted in round, obscure shapes.

"You called for me?" I ask.

After a prolonged silence, he says, "You promised the doge I would paint for him."

"I made no such promise." I glide three steps closer, dropping my shoulder and lifting my eyes. "Though I believe you can complete this important commission."

"You are not in a position to determine that, signora." He drops his paintbrush to his side with collapsed shoulders. "You have yet to make me crave the light."

"I am but a woman, signore. No more capable of life than you." I walk up behind him and run my hand through his hair. He leans back, closing his eyes to savor my touch. "Perhaps we can light a fire together."

He stills. Something I've said intrigues him. "Together."

"Yes." I continue to muss his hair and caress his scalp. "I will sit in darkness with you until we both can breathe."

"I watched you with Signore Bruni in the garden." He pulls from my touch and turns to face me. Eye to eye. "Even the mention of him shows your softness. Your one mar of bruised flesh that weakens your resolve."

Correct. On all points. I cannot lie, for he will retreat like a snail in its shell. "He intrigues me."

He smiles in response to my candor. "You feel something new with him. Something dangerous."

All I can manage is to look away, focusing on the mess of his canvas.

Lucca reaches for my neck, gliding his fingers from chin to chest with a feather soft ripple. "Your beauty shines through when you are soft." He hooks his finger around my robe and slides the fabric over my shoulder to expose my skin. "I am not angry you want another man." His eyes flick up to mine. "Quite the opposite."

As Lucca lays a kiss on the curve of my shoulder, I suspect he is attracted to my fear. Much as I want to scream and push him away, there exists only one requirement for me. Desires must be swallowed.

"I may die having never felt love."

My admission thins his armor. His lips part. I remove his robe, allowing my fingers to trail across his skin with incredible restraint. Twenty-five years my senior, yet he seems almost childlike in his mannerisms.

I untie his smock and kiss his chest. "Do you want me now?" I ask, biting his skin with clear restraint.

"Nearly." He holds my chin and pulls me up to face him. "You feel tenuous. Like you could slide away any moment. And it sparks something inside me."

There is no *me* to slide away. "I'm right here, signore."

He releases my chin. I don't dare move. He could change in an instant. "I want to want you."

"I've never met a man who did not want to touch me."

"Who said anything about touch? You are beautiful, Sofia. A goddess I could sculpt." He turns to examine the beginnings of his painting in swirled hues of erratic lines.

I must make him reach for me. I hate what I'm about to do. "I fear not only love." A burst of life hits his eyes. "I want to sculpt figures that make people weep. I want to be remembered though my life dictates that I will die young, alone, and insignificant."

I tighten my robe, tears bursting to my eyes. Lucca grabs my hands to stop me from covering up. He slides the fabric to the floor, his eyes dissecting my naked figure.

"We both fear that which lives inside us. That our greatest moments will die inside the darkness we must live in." He wipes the tears from my cheeks. Tears that make me want to cower. As I cover my breasts with my arm, he holds my hand. His eyes appear glassy too. "May I touch you now?"

"Yes."

He points to the window. "Stand there, in the moonlight."

I do as he asks. When I lean to kiss him, he presses his finger to my lips. "No. I fear your kiss may erase this moment." I suspect his excitement feels like crawling on ice in the dark. "Show me your beauty."

His orders seem to me to be expressions of desperation. Cries garbled inside harsh words. I stand tall. Naked and unafraid. Then, I remember my old ways won't work here and drop my shoulders, hating how I allow vulnerability to take over.

He removes his smock. We face each other, examining our bodies from afar.

"Place your hand between your legs." I follow his commands. "Touch yourself." I do as he asks. "This is how I envision this painting. Rapture, intrigue, and beauty."

My body doesn't shudder in response to my touch, yet my face tells a different story through groans and whimpers. My flesh swells under my fingers though no heat rises in my belly. Detached arousal.

"Do you want to sculpt now?" I ask, perhaps too eager.

"No." He steps close and runs his fingers along my stomach. "Turn around."

I follow orders and lean my free hand against the window.

I've won my first conquest. He now wants my body. Even if he cannot stand to look at my face. A jolt of power hits my core when I think of how I broke him. Now my panting is real, releasing the heat that builds under my skin. As he enters me, he grunts and huffs, sounding more angry than aroused.

Anger and passion live in unison. I've won this battle but have many more to come.

Movement near my reflection in the window catches my eye.

As Lucca growls, I shake with the rhythm of him. And in the corner, in the darkness, Caterina watches his every thrust.

Chapter Twelve

As we pace the research viewing room, I mumble about safety and fear and just wanting to be back in my little apartment in Venice Beach where no one cared about my research or about me at all. Today feels like a test. Like my fate rests on one moment. Do I act on suspicion, knowing I can never turn back, or do I willingly ignore the voice in my head?

"He's desperate to keep his title as Armani expert, but I doubt Dr. Byron is capable of this," I say.

Noah slides his glasses back into place. "You don't deserve to feel unsafe for simply doing your job."

I try to pinpoint the moment I lost my way. There is no one moment, only a collection of questionable choices. The wind grows in force, howling just outside the windows. The lights flicker but remain on.

"I'm tired of being pushed around," I say to the slate clouds and bare trees. "I've spent my career tolerating people who degrade me. My museum director calls me 'Legs' and fills my time running his errands. Dr. Byron joked that I must have a tail underneath my oversized pants. Don't you think I want to wear fitted clothes?"

All my years of quiet acceptance and belief in an eventual reward suddenly sound incredibly naive. I've trusted the notion of fairness and hard work, committing my life to a world that never owed me a thing. I wonder if Dr. Wright ever intended to follow through with this promotion. Who else could fetch his favorite Americano *and* write his research papers?

Noah's look of confusion brings me back to earth. "Dr. Byron made those jokes because he's afraid of you."

"He may not be the only one."

"What are you saying?"

I thud into the nearest chair and pull over the fattest pile of documents. "Someone knows more than we do. Whoever broke into my space is looking for answers. If there is something out there, I need to find it or I'll be marked incompetent. A complete failure." I smooth the hair at my part and check my bun. "We're going to find this courtesan before morning light, and we're going to discover the truth of *The Estasi*. If anyone is going to derail my career, it may as well be me."

He hesitantly slides into the chair next to me. "I like this side of you, Doctor."

I glance at him before gently opening the next file.

"There's no need for slim trousers when yours look perfectly beautiful." He fumbles with his hands, rubbing them together and placing them on his thighs just as I look over at him. "Unless you want slim trousers, in which case, fuck Dr. Byron."

"Indeed."

~

By dusk, we've exhausted all resources and ourselves. We lay our heads on our folded arms and mumble to each other about the last gasps of our somewhat lucid minds. The clock ticks away in the corner, like a fading heartbeat about to flatline.

"Damn that fire for destroying the tax records," I say.

"It seems a little too coincidental."

I perk up. "Go on."

"The fires in the Doge's Palace were frequent and devastating. That's not a surprise. But to have select files go missing? Some survived those years while others, like anything that mentioned Lucca's art and this elusive courtesan, went up in flames. Supposedly."

"That does seem odd."

We wash our hands for the tenth time this evening. Noah disappears down an aisle with the cart and returns with a binder titled 1605. "The doge had begun to stand up to the pope, and popes don't like that sort of thing." He flips pages gently, landing on a letter from a minister.

> *I fear our Lord the Doge has wandered down a dangerous path. He has commissioned secular works to display at the palace, in direct defiance of the papacy. The doge has chosen the one artist who shows little interest in Venice life, sending an intermediary to track his progress. His trust of outsiders may be our undoing.*

"The most interesting thing about that letter is the word *intermediary*."

"Agreed," he says. "I've always had my eye on Antonio Bruni."

"Oh yes, the art dealer of the time. Tell me more."

"He was a wild card. A sort of art dealer for patricians who refused the rules of court and made a scene at Carnival one year."

This piques my interest. "What kind of scene?"

"The only record we have is some scene he created in St. Mark's Square. He commandeered a merchant's gondola, captured a masked woman, and passed out pissed drunk. If someone knew about this statue, it was Bruni."

"And the woman he took with him?"

We both sit tall and jump to action. We hurry down the aisle that ends in December 1605 and turn the corner to find January 1606.

"Which year?" I ask.

He scratches his forehead, probably sifting through the file folders in his mind. "1609, I think."

Down the most drab, boring aisles imaginable, an adventure starts to brew. Thousands of documents tucked away, forgotten, and potentially holding incredible secrets. The air buzzes with electric heat. We trace the numbers labeled floor to ceiling until we both point to winter 1609 at the same time. We each take a side of the crumbling book, place the file in the cart, and roll it to the nearest table, sensing there might be some monumental answer between these pages.

Over the years, I've learned that big revelations and shifts in my world happen in my body before they reveal themselves. I sensed my UCLA acceptance letter was in the mailbox before I even opened the door. I felt the morning my mother would die. The world felt sucked dry and empty. I knew when I walked into my apartment last night that someone had been there. And I know right now that what's in these pages will alter our lives.

"You ready?" he asks.

I answer with a firm nod, because, despite my fear, I feel more alive than I ever have. Women throughout history have been buried and forgotten, and we could bring one of them to the surface. I can change this one thing.

Even if it means losing a promotion that may never have been real.

"I'm ready."

Inside the binder are remnants of documents long shredded by time. Faded ink and thinned paper leave little in the way of facts. We scan each page, silently searching for the big moment.

That moment arrives on page twenty-one. "'A recount of the Carnival theater,'" Noah says.

We read through every pained word using the available transcription translated into English, but many words are missing.

"Doge. Celebration. Music and dance." I follow along with my finger.

"Looks like several hooded men fought near the Grand Canal. One abducted a woman during the masquerade. He mentions an art dealer. Bruni?" Noah suggests.

I turn the page. "Woman. Torn from a man in a black robe and gold mask."

Noah audibly gasps. "Masked woman screams. Her cape falls, revealing thick black curls."

"Black curls." Pressure builds in my temples. "Golden blond was the fashion of Renaissance Italy. Dark curls were rare."

"This doesn't sound like theater," Noah says. "It sounds like someone made the woman disappear."

We hover our hands over the document. With shared shock and hope, we look into each other's eyes.

"Why was an art dealer abducting Armani's courtesan?" I can nearly feel Noah's heart thump in time to mine. "And who the hell was she?"

"There's only one reason someone would have burned all records of her." A chill zips up my spine. "She was too important."

The lights flicker again, but then turn black.

Across the room, papers shuffle and crinkle. I instinctively shift my body toward Noah's. His chest is warm and solid, and his breathing warms my cheek in the dark. When the lights turn back on, the sound is gone, and I'm gripping his sweater while he holds me tight.

He looks down through his thick black glasses but neither of us let go. "I don't know who she is," he says, "but we need to find out."

"How?"

"We go where the answers are." He smiles that dopey, adorable grin of his. "We go to Venice."

We're out of time to discover a three-hundred-year-old secret. The email waits in my inbox for a signature, teasing me with money and a title. All that aside, adrenaline surges through my veins, and the hint of a groundbreaking discovery tugs at my heart. My life could go up in flames for this, but what good are a promotion and status when this heat and excitement tease the adventure of a lifetime?

With thoughts racing, I force myself to say, "Let's find some answers."

Chapter Thirteen

Four nights since Lucca finally bedded me. Four nights since Caterina stood watch while her husband grunted his way through six minutes that seemed neither passionate nor enjoyable. And four nights of lying awake, allowing Antonio's smile to consume my thoughts like a ball of sun burned into my memory.

I'm lucky, I tell myself. Minimal work with Lucca, a quiet palazzo in which to make music and dream. Mother would be proud. A patrician's house and all its finery. And it means nothing until Lucca invites me to make art.

Lucca has agreed to meet me in the garden where I gather my best effort to keep him in the sunshine. Under the shade of a fig tree, I stroke his cheek. "You've made such progress, signore."

He no longer pulls away from my touch, yet he doesn't respond to it either. "I have done as everyone wishes. I attend the parties and strip naked for you. And still the darkness lives inside me, devouring any notions of art."

"Would you like me to recite a poem? Perhaps sing you a song?"

"No." His voice lightens and fades away with the breeze.

I hope my naked form may someday break his melancholy. He seems impervious to my sexual charms, only caring of my ugly, hidden weaknesses. His may be the strangest fetish I've encountered. I reach for his hand and lead him under the arches where we are protected from the midday heat.

His shoulders droop. "You have yet to inspire me."

This man can identify a lie before the words leave my mouth, and I consider my options. I cup his cheeks in my palms. "I want us to make art that sings."

Finally, he smiles. "Desperation glows in your cheeks."

I slide my hands from his face. Of course I'm desperate. A locked studio awaits and lust for this hairy man is the only key.

"I quite like your insecurity, Sofia. Let us walk the merchant stalls to find the perfect clay."

Although I hate that he finds me desperate, I come alive at the prospect of sculpture. I loop his arm in mine as we walk through the courtyard and out the gates. Venice bounces with life, the air somehow full of wonder and adventure. Laughter fills the space between friends, while touching hands connect quiet lovers.

"Signore, have you considered your painting for the doge?"

"Pfft," he says. "The man never appreciates my work. This must be a ploy by Caterina to coax the art from my bowels."

Or Antonio orchestrated this entire endeavor so we all get as we wish. "Maybe it is."

"And maybe I will catch the stars in my eyes under a black night." He resists my touch yet again as his gaze wanders toward home.

"You promised me clay." Still unsure, I decide to step fully into all he needs. "I will talk of my darkest thoughts until I sob helplessly in your lap if you allow me to sculpt for you."

His eyes dance with a flicker of life. "I want to watch you sculpt naked by candlelight. Your body dripped in jewels." He wipes his brow then repositions his velvet hat.

I could no more use jewels than I could a pet tiger, but he craves my naked form. Progress. "Yes. Drape me in jewels, signore."

He considers each shop, from glass to precious stones, even flashing a smile at the little game. "Call me Lucca." He creeps toward the shops while I exhale a sigh of relief.

I lean against the curve of an arch as the sun warms my skin. Gondoliers sing at the helm of their elongated boats, carrying patricians on gem-colored pillows. As the boat glides under my feet, I lean over the railing to watch the water ripple like two hands orchestrating music.

"Signore Armani seems to have come alive."

Antonio's smooth, controlled voice turns me breathless. I've recounted his every word in my mind since I last saw him. By the time I dare turn to see him leaning against the balustrade, I've forgotten my own harsh orders to forget him.

And then he smiles.

"He is quite well, signore." I peer over my shoulder, hoping to steal a few moments before Lucca returns.

"The doge will be pleased. He's asked for weekly updates on his commission."

Golden flecks dapple his dark eyes. I glance away before they render me helpless. "The lady of the house can provide you with the details you require."

"I'd much rather hear from you." He taunts me with his flirtatious voice. "You are the woman with answers."

My heart thumps and swells, growing larger in my tightened chest. I turn, setting my gaze straight upon him. "I need time." I hope Antonio understands without me saying the words. Lucca is as fragile as cracked porcelain.

He moves close enough to warm my cheek. "You have brought him to life already, and you alone can help him complete his first commission in years."

"You expect much from a simple courtesan."

His body nearly touches mine though he stares at the canal. "Nothing about you is simple."

I remind myself not to believe his compliments. He needs this commission. I fear it is too late, and my body already craves him the way I long for the sun's warmth. "You should take a courtesan. We make magic." I don't know why I suggest something so awful. Perhaps I want to imagine a world where I am his.

He considers my suggestion. "Never."

"Why wouldn't you want to be the man who commands a beautiful woman's body?"

"I wish to be the man she pictures in her quiet moments." He looks down at me, his cheekbones glistening gold in the light. "The man who crawls inside her heart to alter it forever."

He wants deep, everlasting love. A fable if there ever was one.

"Even more than that." He steps away, leaving a cavern of evaporated heat between our bodies. "I want to love her with the breath of a thousand lives." A slow, almost imperceptible inhale stutters through his chest. "If such a woman exists."

A waft of warm spice-tinged air floats across my lips, carrying earthy tones of cinnamon and cloves from the spice shop nearby. I inhale winter spices and orange flower wax Antonio must use on his hair. As the turquoise canal glitters behind his tall frame, I lose all manner of responsibility and lean close, chest to chest.

Antonio steps to the side, nearly shoving me away while looking over my shoulder.

I step out from behind the pillar as Lucca appears, smiling. "I have found you something luminescent." He peers behind the pillar to find Antonio.

"Signore Armani." Antonio does not cower. He lifts his chin and smiles.

I open my mouth to speak but Lucca places his finger on my lips. "No, Sofia. I need nothing from you but your promise to wear my gift." He hands me a velvet cinched bag. He forgot the clay.

If Antonio bristles, he does not show it.

"Shall we host a celebration tomorrow?" Lucca's surprising burst of life unnerves me. "We will provide an early look at my work. And we both can admire her beauty."

It is unclear whether he refers to his art piece or me.

Antonio doesn't share even a speck of a glance with me. "I'd be honored, signore."

"Splendid. We will send you notice with the details." Lucca turns me away. He maintains a firm grip on my waist, forbidding any glance over my shoulder.

"You do not have a work in progress," I remind him.

"Ah, well, let me string these pearls over your delicate neck and we will create something magnificent." These men do love to risk my safety by breaking laws. Lucca smiles, a twisted change from his somber mood just moments ago. He stops walking and leans his mouth to my ear. "Your need for him excites me."

I focus on the glistening water for fear that I might cry. I may ache for Antonio, but he can never be mine. Lucca need not remind me that I am his powerless servant in body and mind.

~

Dressed in my shift, hair tumbling over my shoulders, I step inside the dome under a black as olive night. Lucca beckons me to the window with a curl of his finger.

He presses his chest to my back and buries his nose in my hair. "Rose water?" he whispers.

"Yes. Will you truly host a party in my honor?" I twirl my fingers in a circle on the glass to feel something cool on this hot night.

"I truly will."

The heavy night sits on my chest. "We must create something by tomorrow evening."

He spins me around and presses me against the window. He lifts my hand to the wall and grasps my fingers between his. "I am ready to make art, Sofia. With you."

I lean to kiss his neck, but he pulls away with a grin of firmly gritted teeth, and a stare like lightning. "How can I help when you won't allow me to touch you?"

He drops his arms yet still holds my hand. He leads me to a strip of linen on the ground, held in place by rocks in the four corners. "Here."

"What is this?" I ask.

"This is where I begin to see color again."

His vague directions and moods shifting with the candlelight leave me ready to scream. Of course, I don't display anything but awe.

He stares at my shoulder. My neck. He reaches for my waist, gathering my shift in his balled fist.

I search every corner and patch of darkness.

"Caterina is not here. She does love to watch my conquests. No," he says, "this night is for us."

I undress. I drop my shift to the floor and step to the side. Lucca undresses as well. He points to the palette of colors he's prepared. "Paint for me." His orders hold no softness, no love. They are orders to the very core of their words. He dips his finger in a mound of midnight blue pigment. A line of shocking color follows his finger from my sternum to my pelvis. He reaches into the velvet bag with his stained fingers and lowers a string of bright white pearls over my neck, winding twice so they sit close to my throat.

He wipes the pigment on my chest. "Like a snowflake on velvet." His voice drops as hunger rises in his eyes. "Make me something inspiring."

I bend down to the floor, resting on my knees. With my fingers, I draw big, sweeping lines and shaded figures in deep, inky black. My middle finger dips in gold dust and colors the lines with a hint of gilding. Lucca watches me move and slather my hands in pigments of earth and heaven.

I move wildly and dredge myself in color. Lucca kneels behind me, his hand pressed into the paint on top of mine. His warm body hugs mine. His firm legs wrap around me, and we become like a snail and its shell, unable to distinguish one from the other.

His breath heavy in my ear, he says, "Antonio."

It takes every speck of power in me not to stiffen.

"You look at him with eyes that should be mine." He squeezes my ribs in an embrace of vigor while breathing heavily in my ear. "He has your obsession. Your desire for someone you cannot have turns something on inside me."

"Lucca—"

"Shh, my pretty one. Let me feel your pain." He presses his pelvis into mine. "Tell me how you want him."

I cannot. I will not. "Look." I turn his face down so he must absorb my painting. Two figures dipped in gold, wrapped in a naked embrace. I press against his naked body. "I paint for you and no one else."

"You paint anger, my beautiful one."

Images of Antonio's lips hold my mind captive. A mouth I want on my neck and breasts. I paint rage because love is too great a pain to bear. I grab Lucca's buttocks in my firm grip. "It is the ugliest part of me."

"No." He moves my hand to his cockerel. "Sadness brews under the anger." He leans his head back, his eyes lost in the darkness of his thoughts. "You are lonely and empty. You wish it were his body you devour."

He has let me in. Lucca found a way to feel something.

My one hand strokes him until he moans, while the other grips his hair and tugs. "Antonio makes my body pulse with heat." Flashes of this exact moment but with Antonio in my hands, in my bed—they make the flesh between my legs throb. "Oh, but how I want his tongue inside me."

Lucca releases a strangled, breathy cry of ecstasy and collapses against the blue-stained pearls on my chest.

Naked, color splashed across my arms and trunk, I've never felt more like a whore.

Chapter Fourteen

Three hours ago, a very confident me rallied for adventure. I agreed to this while sleep-deprived and hopped up on the promise of a historical chase. The Mia of this morning stands side by side with Noah on a Paddington Station platform, wondering what the hell I've gotten myself into.

"You look worried." Noah places his suitcase down at his feet.

"Venice? We're nearly out of time." A rush of people fills the concourse, moving past me like a bee swarm. "I can't believe I agreed to this." *Just get on the plane, Mia.*

After my declaration at the archives, we hurried to my apartment, where I packed and Noah kept watch. I didn't stop to consider the fallout of openly defying my deadline from the museum. If I thought too hard about it, I'd chicken out, sign a document I don't agree with, and stew in the deep regret that comes with a decision made from fear. I should know. It's how I've lived for years.

"If we have any hope of finding the dark-haired courtesan dragged from Carnival by Antonio Bruni, it will be by walking Venetian streets and scouring the city's records."

Damn him. I can't resist a romantic walk through an Italian archive. "Okay." I grab my cell phone and check the time. Eight.

"Train leaves in five," Noah says.

"Time to destroy my career." I dial my supervisor. While the phone rings, I look around the station as a chill snakes up my neck. He answers in two rings.

"Mia!" His eager voice almost makes me cave.

"Dr. Wright, I'm sorry to disturb you. I know it's late in California."

"Not a problem. We've all been waiting to hear your findings. The donors are lined up and eager to get the ball rolling. We're ready for a multi-city excavation. Venice, Verona. Anywhere Lucca Armani touched is fair game. Just waiting for your authentication."

I can't bring myself to speak. A giant dig will cost buckets of money. None of this sits right with me.

"Where are you headed?" he asks nervously.

My right eye twitches. "I never said I was traveling."

"The noise behind you. I'd recognize the sounds of a London Tube station anywhere."

"Oh." I glance at Noah, searching for something in his face to remind me I'm not simply following a hunch. "The thing is, Dr. Wright, I may have discovered something."

A noise disrupts the background of the call, like a scratched record on a turntable.

"I see," he says, not as surprised as I would have imagined.

A pause so heavy fills the line, I consider telling him it was a silly joke. Everything is fine, the statue was created by Armani, and a city-wide search should unearth dozens more rare masterpieces. That last part seems to be of utmost importance to Wright.

Louder than my insecurity is the memory of how my heart thumped while reading that letter from 1609 Carnival. How my skin lit up with the inexplicable awareness that we're onto something big.

"I need more time, Dr. Wright."

"More time with Dr. Byron's research won't reveal much of anything. The two months we gave you was enough to validate his research."

Another tactic. "His research is consistent with the accepted view that *The Estasi* is an Armani. His research is not the concern."

"What is the concern, Mia?" His patronizing tone sets my cheeks aflame.

He's impatient. Agitated. He wants to start hitting the PR hard. Money is ready to flow through international channels to discover the next big thing. Sex and art combine to make one sensationalized discovery, with my boss at the helm.

I'm out for something else. A raven-haired courtesan in a Carnival mask forcefully dragged from the celebration and erased from history. The image bites at me hard enough that I can't turn away.

"Current assumptions about the piece might be wrong."

The scratching noise ticks up. I pull the phone from my ear then listen for his response.

"This is not what we discussed, Mia."

"This is my job." Control your voice, calm his anger. "Dr. Wright, I might be onto something that would be even more exciting than a garden of erotic Armani art."

Noah taps my arm and flashes me an urgent gaze. I walk with him slower than is necessary. I'll be told in the next sixty seconds to return to Los Angeles and take the damn promotion.

"Mia," he growls, "sign the documents."

"I—" I ponder what to say without giving up the treasure Noah and I hold. Without building up hopes of something I'm incapable of proving. We approach platform seven as a voice overhead announces that the Paddington to Heathrow train leaves in one minute. Near the entrance three cars down, two men in black jackets stand near each other, but look in opposite directions. They're both on the phone and their anticipatory looks catch my attention. As if waiting for bad news. They distract me for a second. "I don't think Armani sculpted *The Estasi*."

I hadn't intended to blow up my career in less than ten words. Noah's eyes grow wide. I consider my options. What if they go through with a giant excavation? Maybe there is a garden of erotic art buried for hundreds of years. Does it matter how those statues come to light? Or who sculpted them?

But of course it matters. Maybe more than anything else in my whole life.

"Mia, listen to me." Dr. Wright lowers his voice as if speaking to a child. "We've made a deal with the Italian government. This would become a groundbreaking search. Any unearthed artifacts will spend one year at a special show right here in Los Angeles, celebrating the historian who made it all happen. Then the statue moves on to the Uffizi. Do you understand what you could disrupt right now?"

"I do."

"You're the most level-headed researcher we have."

"You mean the most compliant." He couldn't take this commission—conflict of interest—so he chose the eager assistant he could manipulate. One of the men in black flicks a glance at us and it unnerves me enough that I grab Noah's sleeve.

"Mia, come on," Noah whispers.

He drags me onto the train, but not before I stare at those two men while saying to Dr. Wright, "I won't validate Dr. Byron's research. I need another week, and I promise I'll have something for you."

"Don't be foolish. I promised the media a statement."

Scratching and static disrupt my call and both men narrow their focus on us.

Noah tugs my arm again, but I meet eyes with the men in suits, phones to their ears, walking toward me.

"Tell the media I'm still searching for the truth." I don't wait for Wright's response before hanging up.

Noah finally yanks me back as the door slams shut. A beep sends the train rolling from the station. The train chugs forward, and I press myself to the windows as those two men watch the windows flick by from the platform.

My phone rings again but I switch it to silent.

"What was that?" Noah asks.

"That was the sound of me murdering my career." The men are out of sight, and I slide into the closest seat. Noah joins me. "Did you see those guys in suits?"

Noah shakes his head. "Will they authorize the excavation anyway?"

"They can't. Not until Sotheby's releases that statue back to Venice."

"You're pretty important." He snickers.

I rub my knuckles hard enough to sting. "Quite the opposite. I'm the director's lackey. He convinced me I'd make a name for myself under his tutelage. But all I do is write his articles and run his stupid errands."

I swallow, pondering how to lie to Noah, but the truth has been eating its way through me for months now.

He tilts his head. "You're an internationally renowned expert in Italian art. Why do you care what he thinks?"

Oh, how I don't want to tell him the truth. My mind races with excuses, but I fear I've run out of options. "I took out a credit card in my boss's name." It sounds even worse out loud.

"Holy shit, Mia."

"I know." I shrug, tears stinging my eyes. "It was to charge all his damn errands. I don't have money to pay for things like his tee time and car detailing until he reimburses me. I was too embarrassed to admit that, so I used his information to open a card in his name. One day, I bounced a check for groceries. Then my electric bill got shut off three days before payday. I tried to make payments but it got away from me. Before I knew it, I'd maxed out his card with my living expenses. He found out and agreed not to fire me. He's even offered me a promotion after this Armani assignment."

"Bloody miserable situation. He knew you'd be indebted to him." Noah grimaces in that charming, British way of his. "It took quite a bit of courage to take this leap with me."

"My apartment and this job are all I have, and I'm about to lose both. I've never really belonged anywhere." I bite my lip for one quick second, then force confidence. "Turns out it wasn't enough to make me ignore the shame I'd live with if I didn't at least try to find the truth of this statue."

Noah grasps my fingers with a light touch. "We can do both. We can find the history of *The Estasi*, and what happened to this disappearing courtesan. Everybody wins."

"Unless we find nothing." I shake my head. "You don't hate me for what I did?"

"I think you're trying to do the right thing, just like the rest of us. Your boss took advantage of you."

"I'm fully at risk of losing my entire life. And possibly facing fraud charges. Why are you doing this, Noah?"

He hasn't let go of my hand. "Besides the fact that a break this big could only help my career?" He looks down, rolling my fingers in his and tracing the lines in my palm. "Because my life has been predictable and boring, and because I hate Dr. Byron and his smug insults and those stupid elbow patches on his blazers." His fingers move along my wrist and rub the inside of my forearm. "Because you just called me Noah, not Dr. Beckett."

My entire body erupts in chills as he rubs my arm. "Okay, *Noah*." I like the feel of that on my tongue. Intimate and soft. "Are you willing to go on an adventure that could destroy both our careers?"

"*Andiamo*, Mia."

Chapter Fifteen

A party in my honor. Lucca has spent all night and day in the dome working on his wall frescoes. For no one but him, they portray scenes of lounging women by streams and basking in sunlight. Caterina has the servants in a whirling frenzy of cooking and decorating. Roses, violets, and olive branches have been plucked from the garden and arranged in tall glass vases on every table of the palazzo. Seamstresses have prodded my waistline for hours as lady's maids swept my hair into a crown of curls sewn with gold threads.

And here I wait. Before I can seduce Lucca again, he must give approval.

"Don't you look lovely?" Caterina steps inside my chamber, eyeing me like a hungry cat. "My servants have dressed you magnificently." She stands behind me and we both stare at my reflection. She sighs with pity at my hair. "My ladies tell me you refused to do anything about this hair of yours."

"I love my dark tresses. Lucca says they cascade like black velvet."

Her lips puff as her tongue presses to the front of her teeth. "Gold is the preferred color, Sofia. You look sickly."

I am unwilling to lie in the sun with my hair soaked in lemon juice and horse urine merely to appease the need of our city state to keep women docile. That nonsense should be left for the noblewomen. "I attract attention, just as a good courtesan should do."

Caterina lifts the chain of Lucca's gift over my head. Gold filigree with inlaid emeralds, to match my gown with marigold accents. A symbol of love to help Lucca fall into my arms. Green to create the allure Caterina so desperately wants but will never have.

The necklace drapes my chest like cording on a pillow.

"Perfect," she says.

"May I see Lucca now?"

Caterina flicks her fingers a few times. "He is not well, Sofia. I hope this party will cure him of ill humor." She rests her hands on my shoulders with a touch so light, my body shivers against the heavy weight of this layered silk gown. "Your intense eyes and womanly figure will certainly help coax him toward painting again. Even your pouting lips serve to remind him of life."

Her hands still rest on my shoulders. I yank away and face her. "Lucca is improving. He worked on the commission into the morning hours." We created together, though I wouldn't dare say that.

"Do not push me, child. I control this palazzo and everyone in it. Including you." Her eyes have turned stormy, prepared to send lightning through the darkness.

Lucca needs the vulnerability this woman is incapable of giving. Caterina thrives on power that can only exist by Lucca's art, and I seem to break myself into pieces for the hope of Lucca's teaching and connections. We live in a tangled mess of love and desire where no one can survive without the needs of another.

I step closer, smelling Caterina's nauseating bergamot perfume. "I do not protest when you watch us sheepishly from the shadows. Most courtesans would cower with a wife's eyes on their every curve. I can tell Lucca responds to your voyeurism, so I allow it. I have more sway with him than you might realize."

Caterina's face flattens. Her lips tighten like the tulips in the garden that coil at nightfall. "Lucca manipulates you. He does not dare do the same for me."

Her words send a shot through my core. How correct she is. "I am here to help him make art, and that is what I will do. As soon as you approve my appearance."

Caterina laughs, easy and loudly. She fluffs her skirts and stares me straight in the eyes. "You look every bit as sensual as you need to. Now parade your bosom for the crowds so they may see what we pay for." She walks past me in tiny, careful steps, her chopines clunking against the wood floor.

I am more than a body. I am the dream men wish to fall asleep with. Without blond hair, without platformed shoes, and without the burden of marriage, my power rests in my ability to sell that lie until my patron gives me everything I deserve.

~

The evening glitters. Starlight rains onto the candlelit garden and lily-filled fountains. Jasmine blooms perfume the night air as women pluck buds to tuck in their twisted hairstyles. Not one person in this palazzo can sense my aching disappointment at one man's absence.

I've smiled and caressed cheeks for hours, dipping my shoulders to reveal the curve of my breasts at just the right moment, commanding every moment of this evening like a maestro. Seduction is like breathing, something I do without thought, repetitively and with ease. We retire to the courtyard and garden, while every patrician in Venice celebrates with enough wine to dull their senses. Mine remain sharp as an unused pin, ready to reveal our creation to Signore Bruni, should he ever arrive.

Courtesans decorate the garden like sprinkled sugar. Tucked in every corner, they play harp and read poetry, dance, and sing. Beautiful women who read and create art, whose education lifts them to a status higher than most patricians. The view fills me with pride.

Lucca sips his wine next to the veined marble of a fountain, lost in the view of the stars above. Caterina holds court with the royal ladies, and I find a quiet spot behind a topiary where the sea laps against the steps of the palazzo.

"Your celebration is beautiful," a voice says.

I swallow a gasp, recognizing Antonio's low rumble. The night has finally begun. "Thank you."

"They wish to display you like a fine piece of jewelry. I'm certain you can't do that alone in the shadows." He stands arm to arm next to me.

"I've paraded myself around this night for hours, and now I will enjoy the quiet of a warm evening."

"I enjoy the sight of you not on a man's arm."

With a deep breath, I turn my body toward his. His cheeks shine under the silver moonlight and his lips puff like crimson clouds. I merely want to admire his quiet strength. His handsomeness. "None of this is me, signore. I am lost so far beneath the depths of tangible flesh and silkworm threads, I'm unsure she exists anymore."

His mouth tugs into a slight smile. He reaches for my cheek and brushes my skin ever so subtly with the back of his finger. "You are more than flesh and silk, Sofia. You rival the light from the moon."

Obligations seem so far away while his hand rests on my cheek. I've forgotten the Armanis and commissioned art and this heavy necklace hugging my neck a little too tightly. In a moment of pure stupidity, I reach my hand for him and press his palm to my cheek, hungry for more touch. More chills. More Antonio.

I risk everything by allowing him to touch me. I am not his, after all. My flesh and desires belong solely to the lord and lady of the house. I am but a necklace of jewels to be donned, shining for the patrons lucky enough to glimpse me. I am not, by anyone's standards, a human.

And then I remember how Lucca exposes my desire to make himself virile, and suddenly the heavens couldn't stop me from sharing this moment with Antonio.

He caresses my neck with both hands. His thumbs draw long lines on the underside of my chin while his fingertips press into the dips along my shoulders. I sink into his touch, which isn't lustful or controlling or ravenous. His touch eagerly searches for me beneath the layers, beyond the designation of courtesan.

Tears crest my eyes. Eager and desperate, my heart threatens to burst. Fragile. Soft. It's all too much, and I pull away to catch my breath, which seems buried so deep in my chest I may never recover.

He reaches for me again. "Sofia, please."

"No." I rub my cheek and stare at his chest. I will not allow myself to look in his eyes. If Lucca discovers I've touched another man, my aspirations for selling art would disappear before they ever had a chance to take off.

"I'm sorry," he says. "I shouldn't have done that."

"No, you shouldn't have." I want him. My body aches for his touch now, and I cannot release that want as its claws grip my every muscle. "You can't touch me again."

"I would never want to ruin your livelihood." He slides his feet across the gravel closer yet still an appropriate distance. "If you wish me to never touch you again, I will obey." I finally look up at him, his gaze once again holding me. "Though I will spend every minute not touching you remembering how you felt when I did."

What am I willing to risk? The way he looks at me makes me question everything.

"Sofia?" Caterina's caterwauls focus us both. Antonio slips away as I curse my flushed skin and woozy head.

"Here, signora."

"You're flushed. Are you unwell?"

I force a nod. "No."

"Lucca has summoned you. Come along." She leads me, her head held high and shoulders firm. Such confidence, yet I wonder if anyone has ever caused her to falter. She motions to a servant. "Fetch Signore Bruni. Bring him to the dome." Caterina opens the door to Lucca's studio without the slightest hesitation. "We're here."

Our creation, though nowhere near complete, shows signs of brilliance. I created the outlines and helped with shading. Lucca brought emotion to the canvas as only he can do. A woman standing over a man, both lost in desperate longing for what they cannot have.

Lucca emerges, clouded eyes red from drink. "Ah, my ladies." He looks at us both. Examines our bodies. Caterina's slender frame and slick tresses, and my curves and unwieldy hair. He places one hand on her cheek, the other on mine. His fingers slowly glide down our necks and rest over our beating hearts.

Caterina turns to watch my reaction, but I have eyes for only Lucca. She flicks his hand away. "Don't be so brooding, Lucca."

He stares at his hand on my bosom with unmistakable sorrow. I place my palm over his knuckles as our hands move up and down with each breath. Lucca pulls away from me and balls his fist just as Antonio enters the dome.

"This is your studio, signore?" Antonio does not look in my direction, which turns me into a sorrowful mess now too. I could curse myself for such weakness.

Caterina swings her skirts to the middle of the men. "Lucca, please. Show us." Her voice whines with anticipation.

Lucca's eyes dart between myself and Antonio. He is no fool. He uses his artist's perception to evaluate words that are not said. As we stand in front of a covered easel, worry creeps up my limbs. Tight tension mixes with hidden passions and secrets that cling to the air like smoke.

Lucca removes the color-dappled linen to reveal our masterpiece in the making, filled with cerulean and gold, but marred with large bands of black paint covering their stunning faces.

I swallow against the pomegranate-sized lump in my throat, but still, I can't form words. He ruined our beautiful work to live the part of the tortured artist. Fool.

"What is this?" Caterina asks.

"Truth." He faces Antonio. "While I lay naked and panting with Sofia, her fingers dove into pigment and swirled shapes. I caressed her hair and her supple skin, while she formed a breathtaking scene of anger and greed."

Antonio knows my body belongs to Lucca, though he need not hear my patron recount the details of our awkward, clunky encounters. Or worse, the passionate ones where Lucca indulges my fantasies of the handsome art dealer.

Lucca twirls his hand in the air as if nothing matters. "I could not tolerate such beauty in the world, so I covered it with darkness. This painting is for us and no one else."

Caterina throws an open pot of paint across the room. "You fool."

"We will make more." He lifts his hand toward me. "Won't we, my lovely?"

Silence and shock leave the only sounds a sizzling candle wick and murmurs of a dwindling celebration outside.

Antonio rubs his hands together. "What am I to tell the doge, signore?"

"That I will present art on my time, not yours."

Caterina trembles, her mouth rigid, hands held like claws. She takes two steps toward me. "You were meant to fix him, not turn him rabid."

"Oh, Caterina," Lucca says. "She has stirred in me feelings of rage and jealousy. Passion now grows from my body, knowing she hurts as deeply as I do."

Antonio does not react. He merely nods and says, "Signore Armani, this is your last opportunity to fix your damaged reputation. Either produce as the doge asked, or you will never work in the Republic again."

Antonio disappears with only a swift glance of pity at me. Caterina grabs a knife and slashes a slow, precise line through the canvas from corner to corner without even a wince from Lucca. He never cared about this painting. He only wished to hurt us all.

"Lucca, you are worthless." Caterina drops the knife with a clang and walks past me, leaving a draft of icy air.

"Go ahead," Lucca says with a wisp of satisfaction. "Leave me. I know you want to."

Right now, his art does nothing but stir bile in my throat. He may threaten everything I create with him. I cannot tolerate sharing space with him. "You make me want to hurt you with such fervor that I sicken myself."

He closes his eyes, hand to his chest. "And now I want you more."

I storm out of the dome, ready to set something on fire. I follow Antonio's steps that echo through the winding stairwell. On the main floor, I glimpse him duck outside, into the breezy evening. I race to catch him, stumbling over rocks and pebbles. Just as he steps inside his gondola, he sees me.

I stop at the edge of the steps, tears covering my eyes like a watery sheen.

"Signora?" he asks, a confused but hopeful lift in his voice.

I've teetered forward, weight on my toes, but pull back when I glance at the dome. My breath whistles in my ears. Somehow, through my thumping heart, I say, "Take me with you."

Without hesitation, he holds out his hand. "Always."

The night is bright and balmy. As I settle into the plush cushions and run my hand along the garland of olive leaves, I wonder why he hasn't spoken.

"Take me to my studio in the Castello."

"As signora wishes." Antonio does not look back. He slowly guides one oar through the dark waters of the Grand Canal, dipping left at the edge of the golden row of palazzos and into narrower canals that shimmer still with moonlight.

"I'm sorry," I finally say. "For what, I'm not sure. Their behavior bewilders me every hour of the day and night, but you have now been introduced to their madness."

Antonio guides the gondola to a halt near my old neighborhood, helping me to the stone pathway. "Their madness does not concern me." He releases my hand, careful to give me space and stay true to his promise.

"You barely looked at me as you fled the dome."

"I hoped you would follow me, away from the distaste of that painting, and into a quiet moment. Just as we have right now."

I could stay here all night and swim in his gaze, but I must find my own art pieces that could allow me an escape from the horrors of the Armani home. I lift my skirts and hurry through the alleyways, over the footbridge, and up the steps to my home, Antonio quietly following.

My door is splintered, hanging on its hinges.

I push it open to find a gutted house. Furniture remnants sprinkle the corners, and dust gathers around my footsteps on the wood floor. "I've been too trusting."

"Has someone broken in?" Antonio picks up a strip of discarded canvas.

"Lucca promised he would pay rent. It appears that changed."

Antonio steps past me. "The Armanis always get what they want."

I rush to my studio. Empty, save for remnants of my torn paintings and cracked clay sculptures. I run my hand along the dried pigments thick and cracked on the walls. "They destroyed everything. My paintings."

"Was this your studio?" Antonio asks.

"Yes. Before they owned me." When I shut my eyes, I see Lucca's pleasure at my pain.

Antonio lifts a torn canvas with a section of a woman's face. A naked courtesan with roses in her hair. "Your work is stunning."

The Vengeful Maiden is gone.

Gone.

I'm desperate to throw myself into his arms and weep. I don't, of course.

He lifts his hand toward my waist but stops himself. "I'm sorry, Sofia."

"All I wanted was a life where I could sell my work rather than my body." I spin to take in the last view of my home. "I can't let go."

"Let go of this studio if you must, but never your dreams."

Antonio guides me back to the gondola and steers the boat back toward the dome. We don't speak yet again, absorbing the silent Venetian night. Antonio stops early, for privacy from prying eyes in Palazzo Armani.

"Be careful." Antonio slips under the canopy in the center of the gondola where he reclines, hands behind his head, and stares out to the watery view ahead.

With a glance up the alley, I imagine begging for Lucca's affection though I don't want it. I was once a girl who gave my body for the promise of something bigger. Who admired the women with art in their lives. And then I watched courtesans just like me fall sick, pregnant, and forgotten. Mother died alone while I bedded a paying customer. My friend's body transformed into boils and her teeth fell out as payment for her life of freedom.

Nothing is as it once seemed, and memories sit on my heart like lemon on a wound.

"I hope you find all you are searching for," he says.

With tears in my eyes, I turn back to the canopy, duck underneath, and kneel at Antonio's side. He remains frozen, but turns to look at me, his hands still behind his head.

"Sofia."

I softly hold his cheeks in my hands and press my lips to his with such a quiet breath that he sighs. He doesn't reach for me, but he returns my kiss. Nothing has ever turned me upside down like the feel of this moment. His sweet breath and perfumed lilies on the evening air. The way my soul begs to be set free, and my body wants to curl helplessly in his lap.

As our lips part, his mouth shifts into the suggestion of a smile. "You may touch me whenever you wish, signora."

I pull away, crawling out from under the canopy. Under the sparkling night, I look at him, place my hand over my heart, and dip my head into a nod.

I shall dream of that all night, Antonio.

Chapter Sixteen

By the time we arrive in Venice, Noah and I have discussed every detail of Armani and his secret courtesan. We spent the flight sharing details of our lives: Noah's days at Cambridge and his childhood in Windsor, and mine in a Northridge mobile home with wood paneled interior. We're armed with questions and the need to find this breakthrough before my terrible choices come back to bite me. I casually mention that someone might have tapped my phone call with Dr. Wright.

"Who would have access to a wiretap?" Noah asks as he lifts our bags into a water taxi.

I point to the boat. "Certainly, there's a cheaper way to get there?"

"This will take us right to our hotel." Noah arranged everything on his phone before we left London. I offered to help pay but my sob story may have triggered his savior complex. I've never met a man without one. My ex-boyfriends are proof of that.

We are the only ones inside the enclosed taxi with the driver up front, yet I'm still concerned about privacy, so I lower my voice as we settle in. "Those men I saw at Paddington? I think they were listening to my call and following us."

The boat sputters as we leave the dock.

"Do you think they were the ones sneaking around your flat?" he asks.

"Maybe. This is much larger than Dr. Byron's research." The boat picks up speed as the murky water froths around us. Noah leans his shoulder to mine. "Why would someone stalk me just to find out about some historical research?"

He shrugs. "Eccentric rich investors with too much time on their hands?"

"Those kinds want recognition. Only two types of investors I've seen who buy and trade behind closed doors: philanthropists or thieves."

"I doubt philanthropists are tapping your calls."

Money and power turn ordinary people into hungry monsters. The art world is filled with them. There seems to be no gray area between status seekers and struggling art lovers.

The open waters narrow as our speed slows and the boat tuts through a canal. White poles wrapped in red ribbons jut from the water's surface like candy canes without the curve. Faded bricks and arched Verona Marble announce our arrival to somewhere special. As we pass under a bridge barely tall enough to fit the boat, I lean out the window as salty droplets of water spray my face.

We pass sleek black gondolas rocking side to side, through the watery roads, past domed rooftops and intricate terraces. I lean my arms over the side of the boat to take it all in.

"Have you never been here?" Noah asks.

"The closest I've been to Venice was my big discovery at an excavation outside Rome." That one dig I assisted with years ago made me someone. The crew discovered the partial form of a woman's face, and I fought everyone to identify it as a Luisa Roldán. At first they laughed at the notion of a female Spanish artist leaving work in Rome, but after further research, they all had to admit I was right.

"A Baroque art historian who's never stepped foot on Venetian stone?" He laughs, charmed by the idea. "Adorable."

"I spent a year in graduate school at a museum in Florence. No time or money to travel. I was too busy in the research halls."

"I believe I've holidayed here more times than I can count."

Something in his flippant words drives a spike right through my gut. "Well, when you're a kid who grew up next door to a strip club and had to work three jobs to pay for school, a holiday in Venice isn't high on your list."

His face flattens. "I'm sorry, I didn't think—"

"It's fine." It's not fine and I want to shrink into a tiny ball. I've been face to face with enough snobbery in my career to fill a stadium, but Mia Trashy will always be with me. I've learned that most wealthy patrons of the arts are insufferable assholes.

We don't speak for the remainder of the ride.

Later, we step onto the platform of a grand hotel, something that can only be described as fantastical.

"What is this?" I ask.

"Oh, I'm sorry, Mia. What a prat I've been." He reaches for the luggage from the driver and pays his tip. "I didn't think about how ostentatious this might be. We can find a quaint pensione instead."

"Like hell we will." I grab his sleeve and pull him toward the entrance. "I want Nutella pastries in bed, served on a real silver platter."

I may be grounded in the dirt of my youth, but modern-day Mia has developed an affinity for shiny things.

Walls paneled in champagne-colored silk frame a columned fireplace capped with carved angels. The speckled marble staircase seems to hug what once was the exterior of a grand Renaissance palace, complete with gothic lancet arches. Three stories above, a ceiling of stained glass floods the foyer with light, and wispy palm fronds dangle over the balconies with verdant bursts of softness.

I snap my gawking mouth shut as we approach the counter. At the sight of us, the man quickly transitions from Italian to English.

"I've reserved two rooms. The name is Dr. Noah Beckett."

"Um." I grab his sleeve again. "I thought we'd share a room?"

"Oh?" His eyes widen.

I turn so the clerk can't see my mouth. "After my apartment got ransacked? No way am I sleeping alone."

"I can cancel one room, if you'd like." The clerk smiles.

"Yes, thank you," I say, noticing Noah's attempt to hide a grin.

We complete check-in and walk arm in arm down the hallway that's been dipped in gold. Even the ceiling's patterned tiles reflect light from the crystal chandeliers of Murano glass. The stairwells practically beg for a chorus of dancers to descend over their carpeted steps.

With the old-fashioned key, Noah clicks the door open to a room with sky blue velvet drapes, a bar full of liquor and crystal, and a terrace overlooking the Grand Canal.

"I realize now that this might have been overly indulgent," Noah says as he slips his hands in his pockets.

I pour two glasses of some sort of hard liquor and hand him one. "Okay, are you some sort of secret royalty or something?"

"No." He sips the amber liquid. "Old money, as you Americans call it. If it were up to my parents, I would be running the estate, playing tennis, and sipping brandy with the town's most eligible women."

"Sounds dreadful."

"The estate provides plenty, but I enjoy work. And silence. And I prefer history to real people." He shrugs, forcing down another sip. "But I'm sorry. I like nice things."

His apology is like a tic. Still, it's not his fault I can't pay my bills. "You don't need to apologize for having money."

"Sometimes I feel that yes, I must."

I throw back the liquor in one fierce, hot gulp. The alcohol warms a trail down my throat and into my stomach. "You can fall in love with a rich man just as easily as you can a poor man." I slam my glass on the bar. "That's what my grandmother used to say."

"And which have you fallen in love with?" he asks.

"Neither." I throw my crossbody purse over my shoulder. "I fell in love with myself."

~

The Armani residence has been restored and turned into a museum after the internet deemed him the next historical figure of significance. At the courtyard, girls pose for selfies, some taking the erotic position of *The Estasi*. All this hype started with renovations two years ago and went into fever pitch after Byron's published research.

"I never understood the intrigue with him," Noah says.

"I think it's the portrayal of a brooding romantic. Unrequited love, buried art. Besides, it's this statue that stirs something in us. She makes history come alive."

We enter through two giant carved wood doors into another palazzo that forces my eyes up and my mouth agape. Refurbished frescoes, gilded ceilings, walls of four-hundred-year-old leather, and red terrazzo floors.

Noah buys two tickets and curls a map in his hand. We step past the photo ops and paintings of what Armani and Caterina may have looked like, knowing those are fabricated and a sneaky grab for tourists' money.

We pass a long display case of items discovered around the mansion. A restored emerald necklace, strands of pearls, chipped and discolored with time.

Noah reads the sign. "When Caterina disappeared in 1609, Lucca Armani appears to have moved to Tuscany and never again produced a portrait or a sculpture, while a powerful patrician took over this palazzo before it fell into disrepair. This is when we believe *The Estasi* was stolen in the night by thieves."

We step through the arcade and into the open courtyard, where the sun warms my face. "Imagine the balls they had here," I say. "Gowns of silk and men in feathered hats." I can nearly hear the whisper of its memories as they brush against my cheek. My neck erupts with chills as a wisp of wind flutters against my arm.

A line gathers at the glass doors to the garden—the assumed burial site of the famed statue of a woman in the throes of passion, the likes of which the world has never seen. The place where *The Estasi* was born.

"Remember when images flooded the internet?" Noah asks.

"The art community hated the name social media gave her. *The Ecstasy*. So juvenile and unsophisticated."

Other than one slivered opening, thick plastic lines the garden's perimeter, blocking out nosy tourists and eager historians. Noah examines the fabricated drawing of Lucca Armani. "He was a nobody when this all came out. A few pieces over varied mediums. A flailing artist who couldn't complete a commission then disappeared from the historical record."

"Social media lifted him to the level of Bernini. It's like the internet sculpted him, their chosen one, curating an image the world could rally behind. A struggling man who buried his erotic masterpieces, ruined by shame and failure."

"We do love a comeback story." Noah leads me through the main floor of the palazzo, over polished tiles that seem to vibrate under my feet. The world is obsessed with a couple who walked these same floors four hundred years ago. I remain obsessed with the woman no one cared to remember.

A large room tucked into the north side of the palazzo kicks off the tour. A bedchamber for family or guests, the sign reads—though we know better. This room would have been fit for a courtesan.

"To think, this elusive woman could have lived here," I say. "She would have slept and dressed here." I peer out the textured windows to the canal below. "Dreamed from this window."

"What do we know about courtesans?" Noah asks.

Oh, I love this game. Discovering the hidden stories we don't find in history books or museums flips some sort of excitement switch inside me. "Highly educated and talented in the arts. Beautiful. Young. Charming as Venice itself. This woman had long black curls, was presumably abducted by the art dealer for some

Carnival theater, and was so alluring that onlookers wrote about her in their diary."

Noah leans against the wall next to me, his head turned toward me with a grin. "What don't we know?"

"Why there's no record of her. Was she abducted by Antonio Bruni? Where did she disappear to?" I push away from the wall with a gasp. Ideas burst into my mind. Was *The Estasi* the courtesan? Was he madly in love with this woman? Was she an artist? "His studio may have answers."

Noah reaches for my hand right as I move toward the door. For better or worse, we're in this together.

Up the winding staircase, the tourists mingle left down a hallway, but we go right through a set of heavy doors and come to a screeching halt at a construction sign. "No entry," Noah says. "Damn."

I shake the doors to find them locked. Thick, clouded plastic sheets block the view through the partially deconstructed wall. Quiet memories knock on the door from the other side, enticing me to come listen. "I have to get in there, Noah."

I've not felt moved by whispers this much in years. They've mostly faded until recently.

I freeze as footsteps echo in the corridor. My eyes dart around. There must be cameras on our every move. A man appears, looking out over the rim of his glasses. "This area is off limits. Please follow me." He leads us back down the staircase. I glance over my shoulder to the doorway, desperate to run back and crash my way inside.

That door leads to the dome that was Lucca's studio.

He leaves us in the gift shop surrounded by keychains of "Baroque Baddie" and magnets depicting *The Estasi* with the quote LA VITA È BELLA. "Be on your way now," the man says. "Thank you for your patronage."

Noah sneers at the gift shop. "They sell chocolates in the shape of *The Estasi*'s breasts! Get me out of here."

As we approach the gates, I grab Noah's sweater at his waist. "Look."

We stare at the scaffold-covered dome, and dumpsters that fill the grounds. Noah shoots me a look of complete disbelief. "You must be joking. You'll get us arrested."

"I'm already on my way to prison unless I find something to save me. Now, you can stand watch down here, or you can climb that scaffold and stand in the middle of Lucca Armani's art studio like a total badass."

He puffs his chest. "I have never been a badass."

"I highly recommend it."

We stroll the grounds as if we're taking pictures. Just two giddy tourists fangirling over the Baroque Baddie. I find two cameras at the entrance and another near the gate to the garden. I slip between them and climb the first platform of the scaffold, just as I used to sneak into the movie theater as a kid.

Noah follows, but not before murmuring a "bloody hell."

The scaffold is sturdier than I imagined, so we climb through the exposed patches to the next level, using the ladders on the framing. By the third platform, the view of Venice takes shape, with a rippling sea of tangerine rooftops. Noah collapses, back against the curved stone wall. "I can't make it another four levels."

Thankfully, there's no breeze, but the sun beats down on our foreheads. "Sure you can. Come on." I lift him by the arm and climb to the next landing, helping him slide to his stomach. Below, a man announces something in Italian.

"He's coming up," I whisper.

Noah grunts but agrees to move. I glance over the side to see work boots shift along the lower platform. He's carrying a bucket, thank goodness, otherwise he'd be on our heels already. We slide as quietly as we can manage, trying to time our moves so we avoid his eyeline at each open square. I suspect that Noah's heart is beating so loudly it could rattle the framing.

The man speaks again in Italian, his hand flying. "He's seen us," Noah says, his face pale white.

I peer through the opening between the slats to see him staring up at my feet, hand slicing the air, yelling something I can't decipher.

"Shit." I drag Noah up the last wrung and through the opening to the dome. We tumble inside and lock the shutter. The man continues to yell, banging on the wood.

"We only have a few minutes," I say.

The dome is empty, yet full of energy and life. Painted walls in various states of repair show figures of royalty, canals and gondolas, bare-breasted women holding books by streams. Like Renaissance doodling. Noah takes pictures, slowly spinning in a circle, while I enter a side room with a glass paneled ceiling. My skin erupts in goosebumps, noting a chill in this space despite the light beating through into a splash of sunshine around my feet.

"Come on, Lucca. Tell me something." I run my hands along the plaster walls and stained-glass window. His energy is everywhere. I feel him. Or, what I imagine to be him. I also sense someone feminine. Maybe Caterina? Or perhaps his courtesan. I know in that instant, this was his bedchamber. This room exudes rest and trust. Breathless, I allow the whispers into my mind. It's been years since I've dared listen to the things I hear. He lay here watching the stars at night through the glass opening of the dome. He created masterpieces right here in his mind before crafting them in his studio.

It's as if their spirits stand right next to me, frozen in time. Feeling the dead is like coming home.

"Hurry," Noah says with a squeal. "Someone's thumping up the stairs."

"Quiet. I need one more minute."

"Seriously, Mia?" He growls but does as I ask.

I close my eyes and hope something settles in my heart. This room has stories to tell. I sense a cavity. A dark extension of this room, like fingers spreading from a palm. I run my hands along the wall again, knocking lightly to hear any change in tone. Thick, deep. Over and over. Then . . . hollow.

"Mia, what are we going to do? They'll be here any second!"

I paw at the wood detailing that covers the bottom half of the room. "Help me."

"What are we looking for, a portal to another universe?"

"Stop being so dramatic. I'm looking for a—" *Click.*

We stare at each other in wonder. A slab of wood opens to reveal a tunnel.

"No," Noah says. "I despise heights and small spaces." He stares into the black, musty cavern that smells of mildew, his hands and head shaking. "Nope. No way."

The door to the dome rattles open, and we hear voices. I press the flashlight on my phone. "It's the only way out."

We climb in and clasp the door shut behind us, grateful to see that the tunnel opens up to be quite wide. Candle wax has dripped along the walls and stone floor for hundreds of years, creating a bumpy, hardened texture like stalactites in an underground cave. The dust burns my eyes.

We hurry down the corridor, down the narrow, spiral staircase, and arrive at a wall. "Okay," I say. "This has to open up somewhere." We run our hands along what appears to be a wood door with no handle.

Noah panics, slamming the door with his palms. "I've changed my mind. I don't want adventure anymore. I am not a badass." He presses his back to the tunnel wall, gasping for breath.

I place my hand on his chest, the beam of light from my phone illuminating his worried face. "Trust me?"

Begrudgingly, he forces a nod.

After a few minutes pawing around, I finally find a lip on the top of the door and pull enough to slide it ajar. Noah reaches for the handle on the half-sized door, which appears to stick but creaks its way inch by inch.

"What is this, *Alice in Wonderland*?" I kneel behind Noah to the height of this pint-sized door, when something catches the light from my camera. While Noah works with the handle, I reach behind the hinge to a burrowed-out area of stone where something glimmers. I lift the delicate ring of gold, such a pristine shimmer of gilded light among this dank forgotten tunnel. I lift it just as Noah manages to open the door. The image of the ring appears in my palm for a brief second before Noah yanks me forward.

I slip it into the tiny pocket in my jeans before I have the good sense to put back this incredible find. Just as the lock clicks open, adrenaline surges through my hands. What hidden gem awaits? We burst through into blinding light.

"The courtesan room?" I ask in shock.

We've crawled through the miniature door into the wardrobe, back to the bedchamber downstairs. Nothing magical. Workers enter the tunnel, so Noah slams the door shut. Two elderly tourists watch us—who thankfully don't have phone cameras at the ready. On our way out of the palazzo, I rip a swath of plastic from the worksite to cover our heads.

Noah and I run toward the street, heads covered, with a secret piece of historic jewelry warming my pocket.

We discard the plastic before turning a corner and slowing to a stroll. Playing the part of tourists for CCTV, we link arms and walk over bridges and along narrow canals, our shaking breath filling the silence when we're unable to speak.

"Shite," Noah manages.

We make our way back to the hotel unimpeded, convinced all of Venice will come for us any moment. First, we exchange bewildered glances, then we collapse in relief.

Noah scours the internet for news of the Palazzo Armani intruders. "It's a miracle," he says. "They decided we were two Lucca-obsessed tourists eager for an Instagram-worthy reel. We aren't the first to storm the palazzo."

"Oh, good."

I bite my bottom lip, and Noah shoots me a sideways glance. "Oh no. What haven't you told me?"

How to explain the treasure in my pocket? I've long obsessed over the idea that houses have souls and trinkets hold someone's wishes. That all humans across time are tethered to some invisible web of togetherness. How to explain I might summon answers from this golden jewelry hidden in time?

I reach into my pocket and place the ring on the glass dish on the coffee table, where it clangs like a golden bell.

"What is that?" Noah leans down to examine the find. "Please tell me you did not add theft to our trespassing offenses?"

I lean down on the opposite side of the table, both of us staring at the gold circle with an etched figure. A tiny cameo of a woman's profile carved into a deep blue stone, with luscious curls and full lips. She practically sings to me.

"At least we now know what the courtesan looked like," I say. "It's her. I know it is. Do you see what I see?"

He's removed his glasses and now pinches the bridge of his nose, breathing heavily. "I can't look."

I place my chin on the table, supported by my fist. "She's the same woman from *The Estasi*. The figure isn't Caterina. It's the courtesan. Noah, we found her." This moment makes all the risk worth it. Like a hidden trail in time just for us.

Noah wipes sweat from his brow and forces a gaze at the delicate ring. "Why did you take it?"

"Because this woman will speak to me just as Lucca's ghost did in his chamber, and I couldn't leave her alone in the dark or risk returning there again." I don't wait for his questioning response before announcing, "You wanted an adventure, Noah."

He tilts his head, frustration spread across his face. "You use my first name to soften me. That is an unfair advantage."

"Women must use all their charms if they wish to get anything done." Perhaps I'm already influenced by this woman, the secret courtesan.

Chapter Seventeen

This morning, a servant appears at my door. "Signora requests your presence in her chambers."

Barely awake, I rub my eyes and squint. "Why this early?"

But he has already gone.

Two days ago, my lips tasted Antonio's, and I haven't been the same since. I long to touch him again. I don't know what I'll do when Lucca's bony hands seek my breasts to ease his ridiculous notions that art should be sacred and secret between us.

Dressed in my most simple, moveable gown, I arrive at Caterina's door. I've never seen her quarters, nor do I want to. I prefer distance between our worlds, with only Lucca between us. Memories of my ransacked studio fill my head with a white-hot anger.

A servant allows me into the hallway to Caterina's quarters. We pass two empty rooms, and he opens double doors with a motion for me to enter.

Caterina reclines in her bed in only her shift, a young man nibbling at her ear. "Sofia," she growls. "I've been wanting a moment alone with you."

"We are not alone, signora."

"Oh, him?" She grabs the man's hair and guides him to kiss her neck and shoulder. "He is none of your concern."

"You called for me?"

She closes her eyes and moans, and I turn to face the window into the shaded area of the garden.

"Come now, Sofia. You aren't shy about such things. You bed my husband and paint naked in his studio, bodies knocking together with moans loud enough to wake the dead."

I withhold a shudder at the mention of bedding Lucca. While I want to scream when he touches me, I care for him in a pitying way. Sorrow fills me like wine in a carafe, despite how I hate his manipulation.

"You're running out of time." Caterina's voice does not shift in tone despite the sucking noises from the young man.

"That painting was beautiful. He ruined everything."

"I do not wish to speak to your hair, Sofia. Turn around."

I spin around, disgusted to find her shift around her waist, the man devouring her breasts. "Sex does not offend me, signora," I say, directing my gaze away from the two. "Disrespect does."

As I approach her door, she stops me with one word. "Traitor."

My body stiffens from head to feet. "What are you inferring?"

"Well, that is something to discuss to my face, not my door."

By the time I've turned once again, the man has disappeared under Caterina's sheet and is now lost between her legs.

"Why do you wish me to watch you bed a prostitute?"

She gasps. "I am a powerful, passionate woman, and I crave riches that only my inept husband can fulfill, but our bodies can fix all the hurt, can't they?" Her breath turns rapid, her eyes closed.

"Lucca is mad," I say with force.

Caterina opens her eyes and extends her hand to me. "We're all mad. Now force him to finish this painting or I'll ruin more than your studio."

Threats won't frighten me. I am already on the path to ruin. I consider asking if Lucca knew she ruined my studio and demolished my art, though I suppose it doesn't matter.

I storm out of her bedchamber, leaving a fading trail of gasps and groans. I stop briefly to peek in a door left ajar, a bare room with no furniture and drapes blocking out the sunlight.

Once I step inside and my eyes adjust, I see paints and pigments, canvases and figures obscured by cloth. Sculptures fill the corners. Dust and shavings make the room reminiscent of the woods, with a fatty backdrop odor of linseed oil.

Caterina lets out a roar, and I stomp back to my quarters to rid myself of her offensive behavior. After pacing the room, I clean and dress myself, pin my hair, and spray my neck with rosewater.

Just as I tuck coins in my pocket, a tiny stone raps at my window. Again, another tap. I open the window to find Antonio, his finger to his mouth to instruct me to remain silent.

Without hesitation, I click the window shut and stride out of the palazzo, through the courtyard, and out of sight. Antonio turns the corner. His eyes brighten when he sees me, and I take a deep breath to slow my heartbeat as it thrashes against my chest.

"Sofia," he says.

"Have you come to whisk me away?" I ask playfully.

"Come with me." He glances over my shoulder.

"I am not a child. If you want me to follow you, you must tell me more."

Antonio drops his head with a sigh. "Very well. I have something for you, though I'm uncertain how you will respond."

Caterina's threat sits on my tongue as bitter as dandelions. I glance back at the palazzo, considering what may happen if Caterina discovers my time with Antonio. With Lucca destroying everything we make, I crave something that is mine.

"Where is this thing you have for me?" I ask.

"My home."

Excitement shoots through my chest, but I do not show it. "Take me."

Antonio leads me through the busy streets, sweeping past merchants and maids as I follow behind. We pretend to walk separately though he glances back to catch my eye. Deep in San Marco, we step through a door to a modest two-story home without a garden or servant's quarters or balconies.

"This is your home?" I ask.

"I do not live by the rules of patricians, Sofia." He allows me inside, and down the hall to a sitting room with one corner window. Faded chairs sit positioned in the light. "Wealth makes monsters where men should reside."

He's so unassuming. So deeply decisive in his attempts at humanity. "Wealth as an enemy?" I say. "I've never heard such a thing."

His wide eyes and warmed cheeks make me believe his convictions.

"You look upon me with a strange gaze."

He straightens his posture.

Warm sunlight fills my core with pressured heat, like a firm embrace of goodness. "Signore Bruni, you confuse me. In the most delightful way."

His eyes smile, brightening with a hint of happiness. "I work with patricians, though I do not care for their life." He swings his arm in a gesture of bewilderment. "The jewels and the gold. The courtesans and the lies. All of it is nonsense."

I step closer to him, our chests nearly touching. "I am a courtesan. Do you assume me to be nonsense?"

"I assume you to be a woman whose passion has never fully been realized."

"You are correct, signore." Those words bubble up from the depths of me with such ease, such certainty, I must brace myself on the wall. "There are passions I have yet to feel."

"Come." He shows me to the second floor where a towering, vacant hallway opens to two rooms, one on each side of the windows. He points to the left. "That is my bedchamber." He turns the handle of the door on the right. "And this is my gift to you."

He opens the door to a flood of sunlight. Windows stretch floor to ceiling. I run my fingers along the untouched easel and the boar bristles of a paintbrush. The cool slab of marble chills my skin as I run my palm over its smooth surface. A table of trowels and picks and gouges beam with potential, waiting to shape the hunk of marble into something beautiful.

"Antonio?" I fight back tears.

He steps out from the burst of sunlight into an illuminated space. "I saw the look in your eyes when you discovered your studio had been destroyed. The way you gaze upon the sculptures in Lucca's studio. You are more than a courtesan. I should have seen it before. You are an artist who must create."

"This studio is too much." I emotionally release the images I've already conjured of sculpting into the night as Antonio watches. I dare not dream too big nor hope too strong. "You should save this for someone else. Someone you can share a life with."

He turns to stare at the birds who swoop past the studio's window. "I want to share moments with you, Sofia. I cannot offer what you have with the Armanis. But I want you here. Close to me."

I lift a small slab of Carrara, hold it to the light to watch the colors bloom in the sunlight. "Please understand." I place the marble back on the table and turn Antonio to face me. "Caterina owns me as one owns a commissioned statue. They've signed a contract and have paid taxes on me. I'm registered with the Republic as *cortigiana oneste*, and that is all I will ever be."

"You were always more."

How to explain to a man who only knows freedom in a world built for his every need. "I've been shaped and sanded, molded into the likeness that pleases the eyes and hearts of men. Somewhere in the making of a goddess, a power has erupted. If only the world saw who I truly am." Antonio shifts his gaze, but I hold his chin in my hands and turn him to face me. "I remain locked in a decorated cage, any notions of love having been beaten out of me."

"They hurt you?"

"Sometimes." I don't wince or blink. "Until I teach them how beauty lies in softness."

He touches my hand, slowly gliding it away from his chin. "And Lucca?"

"Lucca is unwell. We created something of such beauty, the images took my breath away. And he ruined our work. My work. All because I fight his persistent need to break me."

Another woman might never notice how a man's chest collapses a little deeper with every exhale when they speak of love. "I've seen how he looks at you," he says.

"He's desperate for me to crumble. He wants me to fall so deeply into pain that we both drown." I step closer still, lifting my hand to his mouth, softly pressing my fingertips to the slope above his upper lip. "We are capable of brilliance, but like every sacrifice, glory webs with pain. His touch leaves me empty and sick."

Antonio glances down at my hand then back at my eyes.

"I want you to touch me now," I whisper.

"Once I allow myself to enjoy the curves of your body, the swell of your lips, and the silken threads of your hair, I fear I will never recover when you leave me alone and return to another's bed."

"Why build me a studio then?" I run my fingers along his chin and neck, my mouth begging for his.

"You are always welcome. Here you are safe to create and sleep, rest and stare in wonder."

I've never uttered a word of my deep, burning desire to sculpt, yet he built me a studio. "Please kiss me." I lean toward him, but he pulls away.

He rubs his face until crimson streaks line his skin. "Caterina will destroy you if you don't help fulfill this commission."

"I am aware of my prison, Antonio. You need not remind me."

"This is why I built you this room. To release you from your prison." He paces, arms folded across his chest. "What am I to do, Sofia? You have me in a hold by your eyes and the way you move. I long to kiss you and hold you until the sun rises, and again until it sets." His jaw pulses while he catches his breath. "Yet you live in another's home. You touch another's skin and loop your arm around another man's elbow in the presence of our city. I'm not certain my heart can take the pain, and still I want you."

I step away from the gorgeous studio and all its potential as tears gather in my eyes. "Thank you for this incredible gift." My chest tightens. Squeezed and gripped by the reality before me. "I must return home before Caterina finds me gone." As I reach the doorway, my wants threaten to overtake me.

Antonio follows. "I will be here. Always."

I close my eyes as tears flood my lids and spill onto my cheeks. Without turning back to him, I say, "Antonio, please understand. I've pressed my naked body to dozens of men, yet I've never really been touched."

Tossing in my bedsheets on this stifling evening, sleep has finally found me through wicked night terrors and hovering doom that claws its way into my head. I cannot forget Antonio, and long to run back to his studio and beg him to take me in his arms. If only I were brave.

Nightmares hold me like the devil, arms pinned at my sides.

I drag my eyes open to see a figure standing over me. Lean arms. The scent of roses. I will myself to say her name, acknowledge her presence where she should not be. But I cannot form words, so I lay still in the dark, pretending to sleep.

Caterina watches me for ten long minutes before disappearing from view. I expect to see her figure slink out the doorway under the sliver of moonlight, but she disappears into the wall of my wardrobe like an apparition.

Vivid dreams of fire drag me back to sleep as if warning of things to come.

Chapter Eighteen

Noah paces the room, biting his thumbnail and flicking glances at the tiny cameo ring. "Tell me again," he says.

"I told you. I found it in the tunnel, on the door hinge."

"And then you put it in your pocket."

"Yes."

His eyes roll back, and he wobbles ever so slightly before collapsing to the nearest chair.

I kneel on the floor in front of him. "Noah, look at me." He reluctantly lifts his gaze. "This ring can help find her."

"Well, at least your reason isn't total nonsense."

"Please, listen." I touch his hand long enough to disrupt his freakout. "Houses whisper to me. Not literally, of course, but somehow, they speak, and I listen."

Noah swallows with a pained grimace.

"I'm not psychic, I simply feel the past. That passageway appeared when I asked the dome to speak to me, and I knew I had to run out of the palazzo with that ring."

"Why not just ask the ghosts for answers?"

"I don't talk to the dead, Noah."

"Because *that* would be madness?"

I grasp his hands in mine and squeeze tight. "Nobody believes me, which is why I don't talk about how museums and libraries speak to me. Among artifacts and words, loneliness fades."

He looks down at my hands then back to my eyes. "I believe you."

"This ring will speak to me. Somehow, she will help us find the truth." I stand and collect myself.

After a firm swipe at his brow, he forces his head upright. "There's an Armani display at the Palazzo Ducale. Should we try there?"

"Okay." I place the ring on my left middle finger. "A perfect fit."

"Mia, what happened to that reserved historian who arrived in London a mere two months ago?"

"Deep down, below the perfectly smoothed bun and stern face, rests the girl I've spent a lifetime covering up. She's always gotten me in trouble, yet I come back to her time and time again, to let her ruin me."

"You, who now steals artifacts and isn't afraid to crawl into a hidden tunnel?"

"I've always been resourceful." Young Mia was sneaky while grown-up Mia learned to be smart. "I'll do just about anything to find the overlooked, secret parts of the world I've never been allowed in." I'll even throw away the life I tried to build with status, coworkers, money, and a social life. Each enticing moment that passes here in Venice makes me realize I was never very good at any of it.

Venice has set up an Armani exhibition at the Doge's Palace. We examine the pieces relating to Armani: paintings of Venetian landscapes and bustling city life of the Renaissance; oil on canvas of merchants selling their wares; the Verona countryside and standard religious images on display next to marble sculptures of mythology.

"They're all from before 1600," Noah says.

"Armani was born in Verona in 1560 and his earliest work appears around 1572. A twelve-year-old artist must have been overwhelmed."

Recounting facts out loud soothes my weary soul. "Can you imagine being successful at such a young age? It's no wonder he disappeared from the world by the time he hit fifty."

Noah examines a bronze sculpture of Aphrodite, one of Armani's few completed works. "Nothing here has that salacious look of *The Estasi*."

"He could have grown as an artist," I say.

He cocks his head. "Certainly you aren't on board with Byron's research findings now?"

I sometimes forget how different the world looks for men. "To prove anything, I must be armed with answers on every possible scenario. I'll have to defend this theory with my fingernails and teeth."

"That's life in the archives, baby," he says with a sweet smile.

We move to the section that details Lucca's personal life—nothing we don't already know. He seemed to resent his status as noble artist and rarely completed his commissions. He married Caterina at thirty years old, at which time his art ran dry. They never produced children, and the record goes dark until his death in a village in Tuscany a decade after Caterina's disappearance.

"What do you see?" Noah asks.

"Lucca disappeared. He died somewhere in the Tuscan Hills, alone and desperate, while Caterina vanished into thin air. Don't you find that odd?"

"What I find more intriguing is the day they were last seen together." Noah points to the date the Armanis were last seen, then scrolls through his phone to an image of the letter detailing the stolen courtesan. "Same date the woman with black curls disappeared on a gondola. February 10, 1609."

"That can't be a coincidence." The way my skin tingles makes me forget Dr. Wright could be drawing up fraud charges against me at this very moment.

Noah checks that his glasses are straight. "Imagine, all those Venetians in black, covered by hooded robes and colorful masks.

If you wanted to get away with a crime, Carnival would be a perfect place to do it. Make the crowd imagine you're putting on a show."

The doge's artist, his wife, and a secret courtesan all disappear from Venice on the same night. An erotic statue appears four hundred years later in the artist's garden. "Why didn't Antonio disappear?"

"The details of the time claim Lucca Armani died of a broken heart," Noah says.

"Venetians loved to romanticize anything they didn't understand. A broken heart doesn't take you out. That particular torture ensures you live in the hell that is your failures."

Noah's brow tightens. He opens his mouth to say something but shakes it away. "If the records won't give us this courtesan, let's start with Antonio Bruni."

"Let's talk facts," I say.

Noah removes a notepad and pen and begins to scribble. "Antonio Bruni, born in Venice 1582. Scoundrel. Linked to many women and had his hand in every art sale of the time."

As Noah details everything about Antonio, I scan the room with the unnerving sensation we're being watched. Tourists and onlookers fill the room, taking selfies and reading the signs below Armani artifacts. No men in suits this time.

"Noah, am I paranoid, or does that woman with large black sunglasses look out of place?"

He pretends to admire a limewood statue of a horse but glances to his left where a woman lingers nearby. Young, alone, and wearing shades inside. Her sleek black pantsuit doesn't match the sensible outfit of every other tourist here.

"Yeah, it's odd."

The woman turns to glance at us. She lowers her sunglasses, meets our gaze, and slides them up again.

"What the hell," I mutter, my eyes so wide they sting.

Noah slides next to me so our arms touch. "Did she just try to tell us something?"

She lifts her head and walks straight for us. I widen my stance, worried she knows about the stolen ring in my pocket. She bumps into my arm then stops at my side, bends down, and comes up holding a folded paper. "I believe you dropped this." Her thick Italian accent sends gripping panic through my legs.

Once she disappears, I unfold the paper.

"What does it say?" Noah watches her fade away into the crowd.

"'The stairwell behind Café Dolce. Four p.m. today. I have something you'll want to see.'"

Noah tightens his lips. "This is how movies begin. And they all end with us in a chase for our lives. I feel like Robert Langdon chasing the Illuminati."

I slip the note in my pocket and try to connect the dots with the men in London, someone in my flat, and now this woman watching our every move.

"We aren't going to meet her, are we?"

"You wanted adventure. Four o'clock. We have two hours to kill. I hear Nutella gelato is to die for."

"That is far too many murder references for my liking." Noah's eyes could roll out of his head. "First a stolen ring, now a secret rendezvous with an Italian stranger?"

"I need answers." The shady side of adventure lights up my insides, making me realize I've been trying to survive in the dark.

Chapter Nineteen

Café Dolce. Four o'clock. Tourists swarm the plaza, fighting for their selfie-worthy bistro seats with cones of gelato and demitasses of espresso. Behind the line of impatient, sweating youngsters, we stand on the bottom step of a stone staircase, ready to risk our safety for a piece of this Armani puzzle.

"This woman followed us," Noah says. "She watched us and lured us here. Do you get the feeling we're about to step into something we can't escape?"

"We already have."

The woman appears. Her black bob shines like the hair of a ballroom dancer. She walks toward us, dipping her giant glasses down so she meets our eyes, then walks past, motioning for us to follow.

The ring sits in my pocket like a hot coal.

She unlocks a gate then a door around the backside of the building and waits for us to join her inside. Noah growls, looking back at the safety of giggling American college students.

"I won't hurt you," she says.

"Encouraging," he scoffs.

Once inside, she closes and locks the door behind us. A wet mildew smell seems to rest in the walls. Chunks of stone lay scattered on the floor of this once basic kitchen. She leads us up the stairs with a few rooms off a main hallway. Empty. Long ignored.

"This way." Her spine remains rigid, even climbing stairs.

Once on the third level, the whispers begin. As if souls rise from the trusses and plaster, plump up like droplets to the air once again, and drip onto my shoulders and arms. I grab Noah's sleeve, but my eyes don't leave the doorway at the end of the hall.

"That one," I say. "That room."

The woman looks at me. "Yes."

As we near the doorway, the energy grabs hold. My palms sweat, and my forehead tightens. "Where are we?"

"This is Antonio Bruni's art studio. This was his house."

I feel him. He was passionate and a bit unrealistic. This home is filled with romantic notions and broken hearts. We're one step closer.

Noah shakes his head. "The city's art dealer lived in this basic home nowhere near the Grand Canal? I don't believe it."

My fingers slide from his sleeve to his hand. When he turns to me, I nod once to confirm that yes, this was an art studio. Pressure builds at my temples as visions of candlelight and paint and laughter grab hold, pulling my feet down with a grounding ease.

"You've entered a dangerous game here," she says. "There are powers at play well above what you can handle. You should authenticate *The Estasi*."

"How do you know all this?"

"The details are of no consequence to you." She walks across the room to a chest of drawers, her ballet flats as quiet as fine sandpaper. She removes a box and hands it to me. "Open."

Noah recoils, as if the bubonic plague might live inside this palm-sized box and rise from the dead for our weary modern souls. My intrigue wins over fear in these situations, so I lift the lid. A teardrop pendant of silver and ivory, and a carved likeness to the same woman on the ring. Only this one isn't a profile. In this one, she stares, straight on.

"We found this pendant buried in the floorboards," she tells us.

"You haven't handed it over to the authorities," Noah says.

"No, Noah," I say. "They need something to bribe us with." Everything in our world is trade and power.

"You're smart, Dr. Harding, just as Dr. Wright suggested."

What the hell is Dr. Wright doing speaking with these thieves?

She looks around the room and out the window to the café below. "Sign the authentication, and you may keep that. You seemed quite interested in Antonio Bruni back at the palace museum."

"You're not?" I ask, fully aware that she would care very much that I found a ring in a hidden passageway from Lucca's domed art studio. All those attempts to remain ethical, yet here we are, facing a bribe. "I don't want this."

I try to hand her back the box, but she smiles and turns away. "The future of our art world rests in your hands, Mia."

They know Bruni commissioned Lucca. What else do they know, and what are they hiding? "Even more reason why I cannot do what I came here to do unless I follow the leads we've been finding." All I can do now is buy time and hope to find the truth before these people do something drastic.

"Careful where such discoveries may lead."

"Are you threatening me?"

"No. I'm reminding you who is watching."

Noah peeks under the box lid again. "Maybe we'll go to the authorities."

"Our reach goes far and wide. You never know who at the *polizia* works for us. Besides, I'm sure they'd be interested in your credit card scheme." She places her sunglasses on.

"*Ciao*."

She leaves us staring at each other over the cameo pendant. Another image of whom I'm certain must be the lost courtesan in all her glory.

Once we hear the door downstairs click shut, Noah clutches his stomach. "What the hell was that?"

"That was my warning. This just got very complicated."

Noah rubs his temples. "If the art world discovers *The Estasi* is a real Armani and there may be more under foot in Venice, the *carabinieri* will have complete control. Why would this thieving group of criminals want the police in charge?"

My brain hurts. I'm stuck between a fraud charge and the impossible truth. "I know one thing." The souls of the room evaporate back into their stones, and I can breathe again. "This courtesan holds answers. And we're going to find them."

Chapter Twenty

Another ball this evening. Another tedious night of gambling and dance with Lucca's hands gripped to me like tree roots. Since Caterina watched me sleep several nights ago, I've been on edge, ready for an attack at any moment. Luckily, she's been gone, anywhere she pleases, and Lucca has not summoned me once. The quiet leaves long, painful hours to conjure Antonio's hands and lips. Pangs of desire strike me with such intensity, I have no air to breathe. He is the man I dress for this afternoon, hoping he will attend this celebration at Lord Marco's palazzo and whisk me away from this terrible game I play.

I wait by the garden, warming myself by the afternoon light. Finally, the days have cooled, and the weight of this glorious red velvet ensemble becomes mildly manageable. The women who dressed me made sure to remark on the saturated color, as this hue is only obtained by crushing cochineal insects. This knowledge dampens my interest in wearing such things.

"Sofia." Lucca's voice may as well be drowning in a barrel of oil for how he drags his words.

"Lucca."

Our exchange is a lilting echo of sighs and strangled words. "I have not forgiven you," I say.

"That piece was ours. A creation forged between the heat of our bodies. It seemed dangerous to reveal to anyone, let alone the two people who hold our future." His forehead crinkles like a marionette string attempting to hold up his eyelids. "I'm sorry."

"You don't have to be insufferable."

He tilts his head. "I wasn't aware I had a choice."

Despite my hurt, I still see a fragile man who cannot tolerate his own brilliance. "You are Lucca Armani. You may choose to be anything you wish."

He rubs his freshly trimmed beard and sighs. "I wish art rose to my fingertips with ease and did not leave a hole in my heart." His jaw pulses. He twists my emotions and pummels my confidence to find the art inside us both. I hate that I understand him. "To the gondola."

He escorts me through the garden and to the platform over the canal. Our gondolier nods, clearly surprised Lucca has left the dome. Again, he does not glance at me, but as we pass the wealthiest corner of the Grand Canal, he reaches his hand back, resting it on my thigh.

A deep, reactive flinch attempts to surface as I stare at his fingers. I've dreamed of Antonio's hand on my leg for days.

As we arrive at the palazzo nestled between the glittering wealth of San Marco and the modest homes of the Castello, a familiar unease presses against my abdomen.

Once inside the water entrance, Lucca forces a smile, his arm tightening around my elbow. All I can think as we smile to every patrician here is how many poor insects have been crushed to make their gowns. Slits along their sleeves allow for the silk underneath to pucker through, showing even more wealth, like a competition. Who among us wears the most expensive undergarments?

Lucca leans close to my ear, as he loves to do while attending these celebrations. "I must say, you decorate the evening like starlight."

His words, like poetry, are not meant for me. I can tell by the hum in his voice. The faraway thirst for something he cannot have. He wants to taste my love despite not loving me. All the man knows is marriage with an unfeeling broomstick in a game of *love me until it hurts*. I smile though I cannot swallow the ache in my throat that Antonio is nowhere to be found.

Strings plucked on lutes and harps match with the blare of horns to fill the ballroom with a lively, almost obscene spectacle. Lucca closes his eyes to listen to the notes, to feel them in his bones. "Marriage to Caterina is like sleeping with a tiger. The constant threat of her claws and teeth ripping me into strips of flesh fills me with excitement. Will she touch me softly or devour me whole?"

Lucca is worse off than I imagined.

"Tonight, we will forget about Caterina."

I stop scanning the room for Antonio and turn face to face with Lucca. "I can give you affection and tangle in passion as we did while painting the other evening. However, if you destroy something I create ever again, I will gouge your eye out with my fingernail."

I mean every word. I pity this poor man, yet I loathe for him to have power over me. Much as I hate to admit it, my heart pounds when our fingers wrestle through pigments together on a blank easel. I am not his muse. He is mine.

"Ah, but there lies my predicament. I cannot control my rage, Sofia."

As I lean toward him, hungry to shake him into sensibility, a horn blares.

"Good evening, friends. Please welcome our guest of honor. Lord Marco!"

"Guest of honor in his own home," I mutter. "The man is intolerable."

The crowd parts. We step to the sides of the ballroom, lining his path with smiling faces, fluffed skirts, and bowed heads. His gown must be even heavier than my own. Silk brocade held in place by belts of gold, covered by an ermine-rimmed cape and draped in strands of pearls. He doesn't have the funds for such a show. At least, he never has before.

After Lord Marco passes in his grand parade to the corner of the ballroom, Lucca leans his body into mine and whispers, "He gives the courtesans a challenge for most luxuriously decorated bosom."

To my surprise, I stifle a laugh. "I did not know you could be humorous, signore."

"I am many things, wrapped in a cloak of darkness." The slightest glimmer twinkles in his dark eyes. "Dance with me." Smile through the rage. Give the man anything he wants.

He escorts me to the dance floor with surprising confidence. A balletto. Up and down with grace, we move in surprising ease.

Side by side, arms raised into a cross, we watch each other. A strange connection exists between us. There's a complete lack of love and lust, yet in his eyes I see possibility. A relationship born of a common vision.

"What do you want from me, Sofia?"

I slow, unable to dance through this question. "You know what I want."

He wraps his hand around my waist. Standing on the outskirts of the mirrored room, laughter rolls past us. "And I am the man to provide. How did I end up here?" He waves his hand, flicking his fingers toward the trays of sugared grapes and brandied pears. "I am not your average patrician. I belong in a cottage outside Verona, painting landscapes of golden fields."

"Sculpture." I say the word like a poem.

His eyelids drop, almost seductively. "You bury too much of yourself under a cover of beauty and sex and intrigue. I do believe you have the darkness too. And that, my dear, will make you a fantastic sculptress."

He spins me forward so I'm facing the room. His hands curve around my hips in a slow crawl. He whispers in my ear. "Do you see him? The man who makes you want to cut yourself open and bleed out all the fear?"

Lucca can see truth. He can feel my lies. "No, I don't see him."

"Ah." Lucca kisses my neck, right here in front of the dancers and the servants. None seem to notice us. He runs his lips and tongue behind my ear, down my neck and shoulder.

"Why do you ask about another man while tasting my skin?" I ask.

"You taste like sugared violets." He sucks on my earlobe. "When you think of him, you grow hungry and soft. Open."

I yank away. "You speak of Antonio to watch me swoon. You use the emotions I am denied by law so you may feel my love?"

"You love him?"

"I said no such thing." I thrust his hands from my waist.

He examines my lips, a wicked smile cast across his face. "There is your passion. It makes me want to ravage you. Right here in this ballroom for everyone to see."

How this man can incite my sympathy and rage in the same breath.

"Greetings, fellow patricians!" One of Marco's servants raises gloved hands and motions for the music to halt. "We have a special treat for you tonight. Perhaps, a little game."

Women ooh, hands to their mouth. I do not like games. Certainly not the sort invented by Marco.

Lucca whispers to me, "Your disdain for me excites me more than you know."

Women are prisoners in this life. Relegated to the property of men we do not choose, or we are sinners and whores. I cannot help but think the system they created has damaged them beyond repair.

"We have commissioned a line of masks and capes for Carnival of top quality. Our Lord the Doge has approved their release. The fine patricians of this ballroom will be the first to trial the garments."

The wealthiest among us prepare for months to ensure they drip with money at our yearly celebration.

The great doors open with a bang as an entire staff enters, black velvet gowns draped over their arms, carrying platters of plaster masks painted gold and decorated with gems and feathers.

"Tonight, we celebrate intrigue and adventure," Lord Marco says. "Our sumptuous Venetian lifestyle shall be tasted drop by drop. Welcome to my little game."

Perhaps Marco lied about losing his wealth or he lives as a pauper inside the shell of a performer. I'm grateful that this night will not end with him crying in my bosom.

Every person in the ballroom dons a costume. My mask is bright blue with gold trim. The eyes glimmer with purple pigment that reflects the light, painted in an elaborate swirl across one eye and around the cheek. All masks remain open over the mouth, so we may drink and eat, and speak our seductive words.

"Tonight," the servant says to a room of elaborate colors against bodies shrouded in black, "we shall dance for thrill. We shall woo each other and turn the evening into a dream. While no rose water eggs will be thrown, there will be one special egg for one lucky patrician."

Ovi odoriferi are a favorite of young men of the city, casting their symbol of affection at houses with beautiful young women. I've come to loathe the eggshells under my boots in the months of Carnival. But tonight, the suggestion of a special egg piques my interest.

Lucca senses my intrigue and reaches for my hand.

"A special golden egg hides in someone's pocket tonight. Look around. Could it be the noble to your left? Your right?"

The room glances in all directions, eliciting bursts of laughter. "A local artist created this egg especially for tonight. Hand painted with a crimson velvet interior. You must dance and celebrate. One person carries with them tonight a symbol of Venice, the Most Serene Republic. The holder may be a woman, or they may be a man. So, my friends, dance in merriment and seek the magic egg, for one attendee will soon win a palmful of gold."

Lucca spins me until my chest presses against his. "Let us dance, fair one, for I will soon lose you in this theater of gaiety."

Music begins once again as Lucca lifts and spins me into the reverie of excited, drunk nobles who cast their rigidity aside for one wickedly enticing night.

The orchestra ignites. A cello, mandolin, and viola jump to life, showering the palazzo's mirrored ballroom with light and vibrant trills. Protected by capes and masks, guests seem to float across the dance floor, their usual restraint traded for hysteria.

Once we switch partners and switch again and again, we all spin in dizzying joy. Some reach for pockets and pat hips to delighted squeals while others reach for hair to seek out the special egg. Lucca leaves me and finds himself a flowing goblet of wine.

Credenzas adorned with glittering sugar sculptures line the dining hall, where dancers go to fill their bellies with roasted boar and velvety wine. Groups disperse throughout the mansion. One glimpse of Lucca felt like a dream, as several people don a mask similar to his.

I curtsy to the servant at the credenza, grateful to quench my thirsty tongue. Glasses as flat and wide as a saucer of hand-blown Cristallo require the utmost concentration. As is customary, I grasp the delicate stem with three fingers as the cupbearer holds a candle under the rim.

"As beautiful as a freshly cut ruby," I tell him.

I normally sip the wine, trained by my mother for effortless elegance, to drink from a flat glass without spilling a drop. But tonight, *tonight*, this entire palazzo has thrown convention to the stars. In one giant gulp, I drain the shallow pool of scarlet liquid until it burns my throat and flushes my cheeks.

"On an evening such as this," a man says to me, "imagination may come to life."

"I believe you're right, signore." I spin and dance through the palazzo halls, grazing my hand across others' palms. Several sneak away behind a screen while silk skirts tangle with greedy hands.

Smeared red lips stain chins and women of all stations sit on men's laps, lifting soft, doughy bosoms to their exposed lips.

The masks and robes offer a sense of protection and danger, allowing all in attendance tonight freedom to bathe in forbidden waters. Men look on as their wives lose themselves in a sea of fingertips and lips. Some nobles share an illicit moment with another man cloaked in hidden black velvet without so much as a second glance from the others.

I slip by unnoticed. While hands reach for my arm or my neck, I twirl out of their touch, to enjoy the scene of debauchery from afar.

Marco remains at the head of his ballroom, basking in the glow of his extravagant display, solidifying his place among the noble and wealthy.

I pass by the salon, eyeing a party of lifted skirts in search of a treasure. I duck into a forgotten sitting room, though I know this palace's secrets. Against a frescoed wall, I lean my head back, grazing my fingers over the ground stone mixed with lime, pigmented to resemble Marco's favorite fables.

Suddenly, a hand reaches along my stomach from behind a tapestry. His skin is soft. His scent familiar. "Antonio."

His fingers crawl along my arm and up my neck to grab hold of my cheek. Just as I consider tasting his fingers with my tongue, he grasps my hand and pulls me into the darkness.

Breathless, I search the dark. "Antonio?"

A candle appears, and another and another. He lights the dozens of candles in this stunning room of painted stars and moons with gilded columns and arches over the windows of moonlight.

"How did you find this place?"

"I know every secret in Venice." He turns to face me, silhouetted by the amber glimmer from candlelight.

"My favorite room in the palazzo. Marco never comes here, stating the devil lives in these walls. You knew I would seek refuge in this quiet, mystical space."

"*Shh.*" He touches my lips. "We have one forbidden night together, Sofia. How will we spend these hours?"

"The hidden door behind a tapestry could lead to danger," I say. "Here we could commune with the dead or perform sorcery, and the party will know nothing of our adventures."

"There is only one danger I'm interested in."

My heart pounds as warmth spreads between my legs like I've never felt. A flash of worry pangs my stomach. A courtesan never indulges their desires. It is a good thing I am an artist first, and a courtesan second.

He presses his hips to mine but does not touch me. "You instructed me to walk away, yet I cannot inhale one breath of life without hoping for your body against mine."

The space between us pulses with heat. "Have you been here all night, dancing among us with your mask and cape?"

"I've watched. I have touched no one, hoping to find a moment alone with the only one I wish to dance with."

I reach for his neck, my hands cupping his rough, stubbled skin. "I told you to leave me because I thought I could devote myself to my patron. Give over my body to a man who paws at me and directs me as he wishes. Since you have arrived in my life, I can no longer tolerate anyone's touch but yours." I wrap him in a firm, almost feral embrace.

My mouth searches for his, our masks clunking together until my lips hover on his. His breath warms my skin, but he still has not touched me. I grab him, pressing into a kiss that ignites my soul with fire in my belly and on my tongue—in all parts that beg for his touch. He kisses me with hunger and need, yet his hands do not move from his sides. Our tongues twirl and caress, my mouth exploring the ripe plum of his flesh.

I rip his mask away, then mine, needing his skin all over mine in every way. "Touch me, Antonio." I kiss his neck as a whine escapes. "Undress me and love me."

He lifts me by the waist, carries me to the wall and presses me against the cold, frescoed plaster. "As signora wishes."

He tears at my bodice with the precision of a freshly sharpened blade, stopping to grab my hair and devour me in kisses. I drop my arms to my sides, too heated and lightheaded to remember life without his touch. Afraid I might ignite, I remove my gown and drop my shift to expose my breast. I lead his mouth to my nipple, where he explores with his tongue. I heave so deeply that each exhale escapes with a groan.

He steps away to remove his clothing, untying his breeches and lifting his shirt over his head as his thick, glistening arms move like a dance. I wait for him, one breast exposed, curls dangling in my eyes, my legs spread and hungry for his body.

He walks to me slowly, making me beg for his touch. He unties the front of my shift with his teeth, masterfully removing my final layer with a swipe of his tongue along my shoulder, my sides. My belly.

As his tongue reaches between my legs, I wrap my knee around his shoulder, crying for more of him. He twirls his tongue as my knees grow weak and I arch my back. After a cry of unfiltered ecstasy, I fall weak, but he rises and catches me, carrying me to the chaise, where he moves my hips and slides inside me, kissing my neck. He tosses me over the top of him as he sits wide legged. I straddle him, tightening my thighs against his hips as I roll my pelvis. Our eyes lock, and together, we moan and kiss, tears dripping together along our chins.

In exhausted sighs, I wrap my legs and arms around his torso, our moist bodies tangling like braids unwoven and waving free in a sunny spring afternoon.

I hold him. He holds me. I stare into his eyes as the world shifts. I can never again feel another's touch as I've felt his. He was right. I will never recover.

I nod off on Antonio's chest against his beating heart.

"Do not sleep yet, my love." He kisses my temple with the softness of a breeze.

"Do you plan to ravage me again before we rejoin the spectacle downstairs?"

"Yes. Though that is not why I want you awake."

Lost in a haze of warmth, I kiss the depression behind his collarbone and rub my lips back and forth, lingering on the taste of his skin. "Why then?"

He reaches into his clothing and presents to me a fist. "For you."

I turn over his hand and peel back his fingers. Inside, he holds a delicate golden egg.

Chapter Twenty-One

Two hours after our secret trip to Antonio Bruni's crumbling palazzo, we dine at a lively trattoria, poring over all that remains hidden.

"We know what this courtesan looks like. Or we assume we do." I dive into the most luscious risotto I've ever tasted. The day's events have awakened a deep hunger to taste this adventure to its fullest.

"These Italian criminals want you to authenticate *The Estasi* so they can search for more Armanis. If you don't, they'll report you to the police and paint you as a liar and thief."

Every fruity sip of wine bathes my taste buds between the tart lemon of the risotto. I am already too deep in this to let their threats stop me. "They're probably still following us."

Noah rubs his temples while examining the glass grape clusters that hang from thick wood beams over our heads. "I noticed something."

I place my spoon down and lean forward. "What?"

"She said that was Bruni's art studio."

"Yeah."

"I've read a fair amount on Antonio. There's no record of him ever attempting art. He merely sold and traded to patricians. He never hired an apprentice or trained with a master."

Salty sea air flows through the open doors, carried on a wave of sunshine. "It's so beautiful here, maybe he was inspired but never managed to make anything."

"Maybe. Doubtful."

I tap the side of my wine glass. "These people somehow own a key to Bruni's house, which means they've tracked his connection to Armani." After a few glugs of wine, I take a breath, focusing while I put the pieces together. "Antonio connected artists with the nobility, right? He could have convinced the doge to hire Armani, and that's how Antonio met this courtesan?"

"That would make sense."

"The doge's commission seems to have ruined him. Did he buckle under the pressure of such an important commission? Even if Lucca finished it, it's never been found."

Another lost piece hidden in history's closed fists.

Noah waves for the check. "It seems this group didn't find any worthwhile clues while chasing Bruni's life."

"Do you think we can?"

He shrugs. "You felt something in that room. I saw it on your face."

"I feel things all the time. Like this restaurant. It's joy and family, like hundreds of years of celebrations. Our hotel gives off serious drama vibes. Pretty sure some shady shit went down before it was a hotel." I shut my eyes with a reminder of my eccentricities. "I don't care if you think me strange."

Noah places his hand on mine. "We are all strange. I think you're fairly amazing. On all accounts."

"Moments like this make me glad I took this risk."

He smiles, brushing my hand with his thumb.

My carafe of wine and Noah's touch make the room hazy at its edges. With the faraway music floating on the briny air, my thoughts turn swoony. I clear my throat. "Bruni's studio held passion. Someone fell deeply in love in that room."

I consider kissing him, right here in this busy, romantic, fuzzy room, until the server returns to hand us our bill and we pull away from each other. I can't get too carried away when there's a job to do.

Noah nods to the server. He looks at me and says, "It can't be that hard to find a secret seventeenth century courtesan."

The server puffs out a breath. "She isn't here."

I turn to look over each of my shoulders. "A four-hundred-year-old courtesan? No, I wouldn't suppose she is."

"Funny American." He smiles. "Gabriella, of course."

"Who is Gabriella?" Noah asks.

"The one who sells antiques at the market. She is . . . *pazzo*." I'm unsure how this word translates, but I can infer by the way he motions to his temple.

"I think you misunderstand," Noah says. "We're researchers, looking for information on a courtesan from the early sixteen hundreds."

"*Sì*."

"And this Gabriella," I ask. "She can help us?"

One firm nod suggests he is growing exasperated with us. "She sells things. Silly things. But you know"—his voice raises high, and sing-songy like a soprano—"the tourists, they love her."

I'm fairly certain I'll regret this. "They buy courtesan antiques from her?"

"*Pft*." This seems to be a favorite word of Italians. "You want trinkets to bring back to America."

"Where is this Gabriella?" Noah asks.

"Upstairs." He points to the beams and glass grapes that dangle above his head. "Her customers visit us day and night. Her trinkets are—" He lifts his hands to his ears, wobbles his head, and grimaces. "But business is always welcome."

Noah hands him a pile of euros, and the man tucks them in his apron before carrying on to the next table.

We step outside and search for a stairwell, which we find along the canal. "She sells trinkets," I say. "I doubt she has anything worthwhile for us."

"Yes, but what are the chances we eat at this trattoria, served by that man who pointed us straight to a courtesan expert?"

"I suppose it can't hurt."

We climb the stairs and knock on the door, assuming we will find nothing and move along with our evening. A woman throws open the door. She wears giant, round black glasses. Her curly gray hair is gathered in a high ponytail, and a white and yellow cockatoo bobs up and down on her shoulder.

"We, uh, we hear you have things related to Italian courtesans?" I ask.

She straightens up. "Oh, yes! I didn't expect anyone, but come in. Come in." She tears through her apartment, throwing blankets and pillows around as if her goods rest between her couch cushions.

Noah whispers, "This could be a mistake."

"Here!" She lifts a key from the side table and uses it to unlock a giant trunk in the corner of her living room. "We have many antiques. Here!" She holds out a polished stone in her palm. "Proconnesian marble. Used in a palazzo that housed *two* courtesans!"

I shake my head.

"That is fine." She digs around in the pile more and comes up again with a sliver of wood. "Ah. Very special. Was once a piece of a courtesan's violin. Imagine her playing for a ball, dressed in layers of flowing emerald silk." When we don't respond, she tosses it in the trunk and pulls out a plastic necklace. "Exact replica of a gold necklace worn by a very special courtesan."

"I'm sorry, signora," Noah says. "We aren't here to buy anything."

Her neck seems to elongate. She shuts and locks her trunk of random items. I see why the server referred to them as trinkets. "Why waste my time?" The bird seems to squint at us.

"We are researchers," Noah says, "looking for information on a courtesan who lived around 1600."

"Go to a museum, ah?" She leads us to her door.

"Sorry to bother you," Noah says.

I notice her walls. Knockoff paintings of Renaissance women and miniatures of famous courtesan Veronica Franco. She's obviously an enthusiast. "Why do they intrigue you, signora?"

She looks over her shoulder at her mismatched collection. "They deserve honor. Respect. They were more than prostitutes. They were artists and composers. Highly educated, brilliant women revered by society. They should have their own museum. Their rightful place in history."

"I agree."

Suddenly, her wild eyes don't seem so manic.

I reach into my pocket, despite a terrified head shake from Noah. "Have you anything to say about this?" I open my palm to show her the pendant cameo.

Her mouth falls open. She examines the pendant, then looks up at me. "Where did you get this?"

A dangerous bribe from a dangerous woman, this pendant could lead me to answers, but I don't plan on keeping it or bending under their threats. "It was a gift."

She tugs us both away from the door and looks out the window. "That is a dangerous gift."

This city drips with secrets. I get the feeling everyone here knows more than they let on. "You can call me Mia. And this is Noah."

"Mia, this cameo is important. Renaissance or Baroque." She scrutinizes it, shifting the carving toward the light. "Who gave her to you?"

Something in her love for courtesans makes me trust her. "Someone who's following us. We don't know her name."

She draws the curtains and places her bird in its cage. Her voice drops to a whisper. "What does she want from you?"

Noah grabs my arm. "We should be going, Gabriella. Thank you for your time."

She holds up her hand. "I have no interest in stealing this pendant, though you should rid yourself of it right away."

"What, is it haunted or something?" Noah fidgets, his nervous laugh bubbling out of him.

"Haunted? Ridiculous Englishman." She waves us to follow her through her kitchen. "I once had many beautiful antiques. Items museums discarded, and things I found around the city. *They* threaten me and take anything of interest. I am left with wood slivers and stones." She throws up her hands.

"Who are *they*?" I ask.

She narrows her eyes and considers us both. "You have something they want. Give it to them."

Purposefully evasive. I'm running out of time for subtlety. "They want me to authenticate an Armani statue."

"*The Estasi*?" She retracts, her spine suddenly taking shape. "You are the woman from California. You'd be wise to do it. Now."

"I can't. There's so much still undiscovered. We think this woman is a courtesan, but she isn't in the historical record. If we can find her, we can discover why an erotic statue was buried in Armani's Garden."

She glances at Noah, her nose crinkled. "You don't talk much?"

"No."

"Just as well. Men ruin things." She dips her head, pausing to gauge our reactions. She focuses on me, and I don't waver. "There was a courtesan, I believe."

Finally, a lead. "Who was she?"

She points to the cameo. "Her. This woman was Bruni's lover. A dangerous act for a courtesan, no?"

Noah and I exchange glances as if to say, *We knew it.* I follow her lead. "Because her body would have belonged to her patron."

Noah's eyes widen. "Especially dangerous if her patron was Lucca Armani."

The tingle of a researcher's spine rarely ignites, but my skin is alight with all the details clicking into place.

"Of course, I can't be certain," she says. "It is just a guess. I've studied these women. Read everything. There is no proof Bruni's lover belonged to Armani, and yet, it would all make sense, wouldn't it?"

The worry that's been with me since London rises to the surface. "Why are these people following us?"

"Oh, dear. You don't see it?" She tightens the shawl around her shoulders. "This family supplies art to the Mafia."

Chapter Twenty-Two

Lucca's work is complete. He has spent the last week painting, feverishly pacing and muttering, working at all hours, yet allowing me to sculpt clay in complete silence. Today, we will attend an unveiling at the Doge's Palace, but I can only think of one thing.

Antonio. I have not seen him since our rendezvous in the palazzo's secret room. I've spent every second of that time dreaming of his hands and mouth, touching myself at night when I think of him. His entire being has absorbed into me, and I fear I've done what I never knew I could.

I've fallen in love.

"Your cheeks have flushed," Caterina says as I enter the lounge. I've caught her more than once watching me sleep. Something in her stare makes me imagine how I might die.

I cannot use the excuse of warmth as the light breeze necessitates a fire today. "I am simply tired."

Her servant positions her fur while Caterina's eyes remain on my face. "Leave me," she directs the woman. As she walks toward me, she seems to grow taller. "Has he managed not to ruin everything?"

I must bite back what I want to say and choose my words very carefully. "He has completed the commission." Whether he has ruined it with black paint, I do not know.

Caterina, ever the sly fox, licks her lips. "What must it be like to move in that body? To hold power over a man's will to live?"

Many people, both men and women, have admired me in the eight years I've worked as a courtesan. I've always appreciated the attention. None has been so defiant as Caterina. So intrusive. "It is why you called me here, no?"

Lucca arrives in the lounge, his face flat. His eyes glisten against the cloudy afternoon as he reaches for my arm. "To the palace."

We take the gondola, which has been decorated with colorful pillows and tassels. I place my hand on Lucca's knee. "The doge will love your work."

A smile crosses his lips that almost makes me believe we are friends. This painting is nowhere near his greatest ability. I suspect he knows that. After months of melancholy and being swallowed by the dark recesses of his mind, at least he has completed something. I've been too preoccupied with Antonio to help him search for magic.

At the entrance to Palazzo Ducale, we enter under arches to a reception in the courtyard. Lucca's painting sits under a silk cover in the center of the Istrian stone arcade. Patricians fill the courtyard while Lucca paces quietly.

I link my arm through his. "They will love you."

With a strained laugh he says, "No, they will never love me."

"Do you care?"

"It is what Caterina wants." He holds my arm tight against his body. "The doge has paid his commission, and I have broken the invisible forces that stop me from creating. I hope I can tolerate this benign pile of paint on display with my name."

A servant appears, hands behind his back. "Our Lord the Doge welcomes you to the reveal of his commissioned work by Signore Armani."

Caterina claps, scanning the crowd for the most eager admirer.

Antonio appears at the edge of the arcade, watching on as his commission comes to fruition. My body lifts at the sight of him, my stomach tightening to hold my heart inside my chest. Lucca watches me stare at Antonio in a strange little triangle of longing.

Lucca whispers, "This will not end well for any of us." He drops his arm and laces his fingers through mine. Before I can inquire what he means by that, palace officials have ordered the silk cover removed.

I keep my eyes on Lucca as the room grumbles between sparse applause. Lucca's eyes remain steady on a cracked edge of stone at his feet while Caterina tilts her head to examine the painting.

I presume the onlookers know nothing of art, but the soulless form of the Venetian Lion surrounded by soldiers and a setting sun does nothing to stir anyone. It has been done many times before.

"Uninspired," Caterina whispers. "This is not enough, Lucca."

Lucca does not respond. I search for Antonio, but he has disappeared into the palace.

She growls in his ear, "I will leave you. I will take my money and my wealth if you do not do as I ask. Would you like to become penniless, with no art and no luxury? Die a pauper?"

"I completed a commission."

She turns to me as the crowd pretends to admire the painting that will surely look amateur next to the inspired pieces at the palace. "And you. I'll send you back to the streets to die a blistery death alone, in tattered threads." Her threats ignite my guilt and squeeze hard enough to make me remember my mother, who died exactly like this. "Make him the great artist he could be, you useless wench." She gathers her smooth demeanor. "Now, come celebrate your commission and pretend you aren't a failure." She walks away, seemingly taller than ever.

Lucca strains to breathe. I find tenderness for him, sorrow for the way his wife abuses him. "You purposely completed something unimaginative. You're protecting your art from her."

"I enjoy my darkness. For it is the only thing I trust."

We stroll to the wild palazzo just west of San Marco Square where a celebration keeps music and dancing as a nightly affair, where men and their courtesans gamble their gold coins and end in one of numerous beds.

I search the room for the man who sets my soul and body on fire. The rules of high society lessen as the night wears on, as wine flows and dance becomes a chance to press bodies against one another. Lucca begs to return home, yet Caterina shoves him back every time he nears the door.

Though my body begs for Antonio's touch, I force myself to gaze upon Lucca. We have spent endless hours writhing together, painting and sharing moments of private creation. I touch his face. "We can be scared together. Paint and sculpt and face the dangerous world as one." Surprisingly, I mean every word.

He smiles with such innocence, but a courtesan has pulled him away with a screeching laugh to dance in the middle of their admiration circle.

"Signora, please come with me." I turn to find a servant waiting at the doorway. When I don't move, he nods. "Your presence is requested."

Caterina dances with a young patrician, and I take my moment and slip out the doorway to the terrace of shadows over the moonlit water of the Grand Canal.

Antonio steps out from behind an arch. "I've missed you."

My heart rate quickens, knowing he's near. I push down my fear and worry, thinking only of his hands on me. "I've ached for you."

He hooks his finger gently under my chin and lifts my gaze to his. "Your eyes make me a fool, for I forget everything when you're near," he says.

The Armanis could ruin him if they discovered our secret.

He leans into me. His kiss lights up my insides with a fire that shouldn't exist. A fire that rages through all sense of reason and control. His hand slides around my waist. When he squeezes my hips and pulls me close, I gasp with want and desire. "Risk is a choice, and I choose you."

"Then let it be so." He kisses my neck, and I grab a fistful of his dark hair in my grip.

His mouth hovers near mine, his warm, sweet breath bathing my lips in hunger. "I will steal joy where I can in hidden moments."

I press his back into the stone wall and kiss him, satisfying the cravings I've held between gritted teeth for a week. I run my fingers through his hair and scratch his neck and taste his tongue. It reminds me of sweet vanilla on a baked custard.

My mind cannot grab hold of thoughts, my body overwhelmed by the heat rising on my skin. "You could lose everything," I say, desperate to be convinced otherwise. Luscious lips and strong hands destroy my sensibility.

"Then let me lose. I will have gained a chance at love."

My head aches and my body has run away into a dreamlike state where there are no consequences. Breathless, I rest my hands on his chest. "You have ruined touch for me, Antonio. I have never felt the burning need I do when I'm with you, and I cannot possibly live a day of this life without this feeling."

He spins me around and kisses me hard. Fervently. He leads me up the stairs to the *altana*. Under the covered terrace, I grasp the railing to catch my breath. Antonio wraps his arms around my stomach from behind. He kisses my neck and presses his pelvis into me. Slowly, with controlled breath, he drags his hand over my breast, hugging me with his body as I watch the stars glitter in the deep purple sky.

He gathers my skirts and slides his hand from my knee, up my thigh, and between my legs.

"What are you doing?" I ask playfully.

"Showing you how your delight feeds my soul." His fingers strum my pleasure spot, eliciting an aching, hot swell that will surely kill me. I spread my legs and reach behind to grab hold of his hair.

The silver canal shimmers under the giant moon as dots of celestial magic twinkle above. I do nothing but welcome his touch and admire the glittering view as the cool air rustles a gentle hand through my hair.

Antonio uses two fingers, masterfully turning me to liquid, and then to silent screams. I grab hold of the smooth limestone railing and grip hard until the explosion inside me lowers to a simmer and I fall back against him, chest heaving and knees shaking.

I turn to face him, my vision dewy and heart full. One more deep kiss helps me hold onto this dream while I can. Once my head steadies, I lead him down the winding staircase where we glimpse a small fire hidden behind the Doge's Palace. Someone has set Lucca's painting on fire. And I couldn't be happier.

"Take me away from this place," I say.

A smile as soft as it is confident serves as a promise I can hold onto. "As signora wishes."

~

Antonio returned home last night while I slipped back into the reception to celebrate Lucca. While I smiled for the crowd, I whispered in his ear. "Did you set the painting ablaze?" He nodded once with the response, "Trash does not deserve to hang in a palace."

We returned home in silence, but Caterina slapped him the moment we walked in. She carried on berating the poor man. I reached for Lucca but he pushed me away. "Go to bed, my love."

I drifted to sleep under midnight quiet. My body once again mine and my heart about to burst, I held Antonio's smile close and imagined our future. In the light of early morning, my slumber fades as the gauzy darkness seems to rock me awake.

I turn on my side with a sigh, hoping to gaze into the courtyard, but the bedsheets block my view. When I smash them down, my hand hits something firm. I recoil with a gasp.

"Hello, Sofia."

I jump out of bed and grab the nearest candle, its wick burned black after the long hours of night. When I hold it close, I can see that I am not dreaming. Caterina is in my bed.

"Leave my bedchamber at once."

She lifts her head and rests on her elbow, shrugging playfully. "You looked so lonely."

The warm, loving touch of Antonio has faded, replaced with the disgust of being watched. "Leave me."

She uncovers herself and stretches at the bedside. "Calm yourself. Nothing happened. I simply wanted to be close to you. I admire you." Her voice lowers to a long eerie hum.

"Last night you called me a wench."

She sighs. "Lucca made love to me. He is virile again. The painting was a disaster. They all found the burned remains, chattering about his madness. But he is alive again. He can create now."

She seems breathless. Wanting. "Lucca will not allow this. I will tell him everything."

"Please." She covers herself with a robe and approaches me. "I own that poor man."

"You do not own me." I believe this in the depths of my bones, yet my voice still wavers.

"What must it feel like to make every man in a room hungry for you? Even in my youngest years of beauty, I was invisible. But not you. No, no." She reaches to touch my hair, but I pull away. "I watched your little tryst with Signore Bruni on the terrace. I want that passion."

She watched us moan and touch. I feel sick. No woman of nobility would dare keep watch over her husband's courtesan. Then again, no courtesan would dare spread her legs for a lover that wasn't a paying customer. "Has the evening turned you unwell?"

She laughs like the monster she is. "I know the look of love when I see it, Sofia. You want Signore Bruni to sweep you away to a quiet life where love and affection are yours forever. That will never exist for you, Sofia. We have art to make right here."

"We have been making art."

"Wrong." That one word seems to snap away my confidence like pollen in a stiff wind. "Lucca's passion still waits for your magic. I feel it too when I am near you. I'm intrigued that I both despise you and want to touch you."

"This body is not for you." Wax drips off the candle and onto the space between my thumb and forefinger. The heat stings then quickly fades.

"You may no longer see Signore Bruni. He distracts you from your purpose." She smooths her hair in place. "Lucca has found his muse, and I finally have the payout from my ten-year investment in him. Don't think I will let you free until his art makes us the wealthiest couple in all of Venice."

"Will it ever be enough?" I ask, peeling away the cooled wax. "Or must I become your prisoner, ready to rub your husband's naked body at your command?"

"Only through Carnival, Sofia. Merchants from all over the world will be in attendance. I've invited them all to a special celebration, where my husband's erotic, pleasurable artwork will shock and transform them. May as well capitalize on his reputation of madness and your talent for sensual art. Once we survive the dinner and art show, you are free to run wild with Antonio. I do not want you basking in our riches."

I know better than to trust anything Caterina says, but I can't risk her hurting either one of us. How long will I need to stay away from Antonio and how often must I give my body to Lucca? "Erotic?"

"Scandalous and illicit is what I want. You have five months to fix him after that embarrassment with the doge. Will your love wait for you? If you do not follow my rules, I will have you arrested for breaking our contract and your lover stripped of his livelihood. Do as I ask, and you will find freedom after the evening of February 10."

"All of this for money?"

She drops her robe to expose her naked shoulder. "It is always about power, beautiful one." She trails her hands along my neck. "You may be a whore, but I want to own you like my husband does."

I lift her hand and crush her fingers in my fist until she winces. "Touch me again and I will not help either of you. He cannot make art without me, Caterina. Do not anger me."

She backs away, her lips parted in disgusting want. "Fine." She covers herself with her robe. "I need money more than I need your body. Beauty may have eluded me, but being ignored by men has given me intense strength. If you cross me, I will make certain you do not live to see your next birthday."

Antonio will wait for me at his home all day, but I will never show. I will be held prisoner by Caterina Armani, assisting her husband in crafting something forbidden.

Lucca creates art when he is inspired and passionate. As I release my own desires, I remind my body that touch will be difficult. Feigning passion may now be impossible.

Caterina opens my wardrobe and slides a panel to the side. "We start now," she says. "Come. Your secret passage for easy access to Lucca. He's waiting for you."

With whispers of Antonio's touch on my skin, I follow Caterina upstairs, where I will undress her husband and paint in the nude as she watches. I will sculpt with Lucca as we both live out our prison terms with his evil, twisted wife.

Chapter Twenty-Three

In our hotel room, which overflows with pasta, focaccia, dipping oils, empty espresso cups, and a half-drunk bottle of Brunello, one might think we were on a lover's holiday. But my focus remains solely on this elusive woman with the black curls. "How did Armani have a courtesan who slipped through the historical record?"

Noah slumps back in his chair with a partially drained glass of wine. "A courtesan who was brave enough to take a lover of her choice. Perhaps even the man who sold her patron's art."

"She had dark curls. Her lover may have set fire to the records then swept her away on a gondola in some sort of theater to cover their secrets." I scratch my temple, noting the tiny hairs from my bun that now pull at my scalp. "Okay, so we don't know much."

"And the ones chasing us are connected to art criminals." His grimace reminds me how deep we're in already.

A fleeting moment of doubt grabs hold, and I consider authenticating the statue. Until I remember Dr. Wright. He spoke to the people threatening us. He's in on this.

"We've scoured the online databases, pulled out all our resources this afternoon to find information, and still, we have nothing more than the bird lady reminding us the Italian mob might like our heads on a platter." I rub my eyes so hard they sting.

"Have you noticed everyone is obsessed with Lucca Armani, but rarely discusses Caterina?" he ponders. "And he may have had a courtesan who disappeared, yet no one cares to ask."

"Welcome to history, Noah. Where women were only present to serve their men and didn't do things like speak or have opinions. They didn't exist at all."

"That's not true."

"Of course it isn't." I guzzle back the remaining inky-colored wine until my throat burns and I'm forced to catch my breath. "But that is what we all remember, and we take it as truth."

When Noah removes his glasses, I consider reaching across to touch his smooth cheek, but thankfully I haven't had enough wine to dull my obsessive brain.

"I don't believe they can disappear altogether," he says. "Not these women."

"Maybe the courtesan didn't want to be remembered. But Caterina? She had money and status. It's well documented she married below her station with Lucca. You'd think she would have entire novels written about her." I reach back to rearrange my bun, loosening the tight strands underneath.

"Pull up the ancestry again." Noah clinks his glass against the table.

We've kept a list of resources of interest. I read the names. "The usual suspects. Armani's cousins, nephews, and nieces, and their descendants. Caterina's family mostly died in the plague around 1630. Since they had no children, that's all there is."

"Someone knows something." He takes the laptop and types, hunched over the keyboard in total commitment. His glasses back on in all his scholarly sexiness, I taste a dollop of regret that sits on my tongue.

"Noah?"

He grunts a response.

"I put myself in danger long ago. There's no way out for me, but you didn't ask for any of this."

He looks over the top of his laptop, resting his chin on the narrow ledge of the screen. "I may not have asked for it, but I'm in it now, Dr. Harding. And we do this together. *Capisce*?"

"Sure. We do this together."

Another hour rolls by in silence as we scour our notes and sip the last drop of wine, so rich with tannins I could chew it.

Noah sits up with a start, dropping his feet from the table, thudding flat on the floor. "There's an anonymous writer posting serialized fiction about Armani, writing snippets of life in Lucca's household."

"That's no surprise. Did you see that ridiculous gift shop at his house? People do crazy things to feel close to this guy."

"Yeah, but this one mentions black curls and a cameo pendant."

Blood rushes to my head on a wave of endorphins. "No one knows about that pendant but us and this family who's after us."

"After today, Gabriella knows too." He spins the computer to face me. "This post was put up an hour after we left her house."

"Wicked woman!" I stand and throw my purse over my shoulder.

"Wait." He keeps typing, his eyes narrowed on the screen. "This blog is posted under the screen name CourtLover21. That name suggests the royal court but really, she's speaking of courtesans. She's clever, I'll give her that."

"That name is familiar." I squeeze in the chair next to him even though there's no room for me. I commandeer the laptop and pull up an online database of family trees created using DNA tracking software with a focus on Renaissance Italy. People do this for fun to see if they're related to Lucca Armani. And most waste their hundred dollars to find out they aren't Italian at all. "There." I point to the screen.

"CourtLover21." We follow the line back four hundred years to the name that leaps off the screen. Noah nudges my thigh. "Bird Lady is a descendant of Antonio Bruni."

"That's unexpected," I say.

"That's not all." Noah toggles back to the simple blog with no description other than one sentence on the homepage:

The secret courtesan will not be forgotten.

~

As the sun lowers, casting a marigold glow over the Adriatic, two slightly drunk researchers hopped up on a taste of adventure go in search of the bird lady with answers. We've found more leads with her than in the research, making me glad we came to Venice. I hope I don't live to regret it.

Though I want to bang on her door, Noah holds me back, gently rapping his knuckles and peeking through her window. "It's dark in there," he says. "I think she's gone."

"Dammit." I slump against the wall, arms crossed in utter disappointment.

He tugs on my sleeve and shoots me a smile of resignation. I follow him down the flight of stairs where the café bustles and the city awakens from siesta.

"She knows more than she's letting on." I drag him around the back of her apartment and tuck into an alcove across the street. "And we need information if we're going to cross the Mafia."

Noah grimaces at the mention. "I'm not sure what we'll get from her. She's completely mad," he says. "And obviously untrustworthy."

It takes less than ten minutes before we spot her locking her kitchen door. A baseball cap and sunglasses change her appearance, and the weekender in her hand suggests more than a trip to the market.

"She's wearing trainers," Noah says with raised eyebrows. "She's ready to run."

Silently, we follow her as she winds through alleys, keeping her head low. Though she continues to glance over her shoulder, we remain far enough back to blend with the tourists.

"What exactly do we want from her?" he asks.

"She's related to Antonio and knows about this courtesan. Maybe she has family information she's not telling us."

We dip through the maze of alleys and bridges that is Venice, threading through strolling tourists and colored umbrellas. The warm, yeasty aroma of baked bread lingers as bakeries and cafés yawn awake for their evening hours.

On the outskirts of the city where canals turn to pavement and tourists disappear completely, Gabriella unlocks a wooden door in a stucco wall and hurries to a broken-down car. I lead Noah to the side of the courtyard, under an olive tree, where the wall is short enough to hop over.

Gabriella drops her bag in the dirt, her hands shaking as she searches for the key, muttering what I assume to be Italian swear words. We walk around the back of a garage. I press my hand to Noah's chest and push myself forward, stepping between Gabriella and the car. She drops her keys and holds her flattened palm against her chest. "*Mamma mìa.*"

"Tell us what you know." Impatience rises from deep in my belly. We're running out of time.

She lifts her keys and searches the trees and courtyard. "Leave me alone."

"We found you online. We know that Antonio Bruni is your fifteen-times-great-grandfather and that you write some little fan fiction about his lover, the courtesan, and this story included a cameo pendant." I step forward, the threat of the Mafia nipping at my heels. I'm intimidating a lonely woman for keeping secrets while I hold a stolen ring in my jeans pocket. Irony at its best.

Noah steps in. "We want answers, just like you."

She tightens her cap and glasses. "They saw you leave my house. They watch me, you know. And now they watch you."

"Why do they care about Antonio Bruni?" Noah asks, pressing his hand into my arm to remind me to shut up.

"They care about one thing. Money." She shoves us aside, flops into the car, and throws her bag in the passenger seat. She turns the ignition but it only sputters. After a reluctant drop of her forehead on the steering wheel, she turns to look at us. "They don't care about Antonio Bruni. Only that his life may somehow lead them to Lucca Armani's hidden art."

I flick a glance at Noah. "Do you really think there are more statues buried or is this all nonsense?"

"They find treasures every day in this town. But *The Estasi* is the only piece that fills the gap in Armani's life. Unearthing that carving, this woman of ecstasy, ignited the world's desire for more." She squints against the sun, searching my face for, what, reassurance? Trust? "Antonio Bruni peddled art all through this city," she says. "He knew something of *The Estasi*. He had to."

"And this criminal family?" I ask. "Why do they watch you?" Despite my best efforts, agitation bleeds from my pores.

The woman snarls. "My grandmother kept a token." She wrings her hands together, still eyeing a way out of this. "Handed down with a story."

I force myself to focus. They're probably following us right now.

"For hundreds of years, the women in my family have kept a special, uh, how you Americans say, heirloom?"

I nod, Noah shifting closer as we hang on her every word.

"It is said to hold secrets. Spells." Her eyes dance as her lips purse into a smile.

"What is it?" I ask.

She leans forward and with exaggerated pronunciation whispers, "A golden egg."

"Oh, yes," Noah spits, "the well-researched Renaissance egg that casts spells."

"You have heard of it?" she asks, her head turned.

"No, I haven't heard of a magic egg! I follow the rules of logic and research. We're wasting our time." Noah grabs my sleeve, but Gabriella stops him.

"Legend says that Antonio Bruni gifted this egg to his youngest daughter. A heavy egg made of gold that opened with a hinge.

This represented the great love of his life." We have both leaned in close now. "A courtesan."

"What did the daughter do with this egg?" I ask, much to Noah's chagrin.

"She gifted it to her daughter and asked that the courtesan's memory be preserved. A piece of Venezia's history it was our duty to protect. And with it, came this message." She dips her head, eyes darting in each direction before settling on our gaze. "Antonio Bruni loved a woman who splashed stars across the sky and filled the ocean with tides of passion. Whoever opens that egg will fall madly in love."

"Oh, great." Noah looks to the sun and bites his lip. "More nonsense."

"Okay, I admit we're now listening to an ancient game of telephone, but it's very romantic."

Gabriella sits tall, exhaling into a deep, sad sigh. "This family wants our egg. I don't know where it is."

"Lies." Noah has lost all patience.

"What do you mean lies?" Gabriella continues to rattle off something in Italian, but I pull her attention back to me. With a sigh, she focuses. "I saw it as a child. My grandmother showed me. She hid it somewhere, and when she died unexpectedly, no one in the family has recovered it. The mob family doesn't believe me either, Signore Englishman, which is why they harangue a poor old lady."

"Is that why you collect trinkets?" I ask. "Hoping someday you'll find the egg?"

She shrugs. "I have had no luck."

"Why the silly short stories?" Noah asks.

"It's how I communicate without being tracked. Thousands of fan sites appeared online after the Armani frenzy the past few years. I share information with my cousins as I find it, so these Mafia types don't steal everything I have." She exhales, her eyes dropping to the dirt at my feet. "This is our family history."

She flops in the car and turns the key again, holding it until the engine coughs to life.

I lean forward, hanging on the open door. "I want to discover the truth behind *The Estasi*. We both know nothing is as it seems."

She considers me. "The Mafia wants art. This search may unearth dozens more artifacts, which will be shuffled around to different countries."

"International laws handling artifacts are muddy, at best," Noah adds. "Art gets lost and stolen far too easily that way."

"Yes." She revs the sorry engine a few times to keep it alive. "The sooner you authenticate, the sooner they can pilfer someone else's finds."

"Do you believe there is more buried art?"

"There is always buried treasure in Italy." She shrugs in that very Italian, dismissive way. "I believe the courtesan's memory is here, in this city. Somewhere."

"You care for her." Though I know little more than a few details of her life, I care too.

"Of course I do." She pulls the door shut and points at us out the window. "Careful, signora. This family has eyes everywhere."

Including in my London flat and at Paddington Station.

She motions to Noah to open the gate for her. "Can you give me anything else?" I beg. "Anything?"

She waits for Noah to clear her path and taps her fingers on the steering wheel, considering her options. "The courtesan with the black curls died in the upheaval of the 1609 Carnival. She was important, despite what history tells you."

Oh, God. She died. That theater could have been her last moments. It doesn't sound like Bruni killed her, so who did? "All women are more than we are remembered for," I say.

She rolls the car forward, but the brake lights flicker, and she leans out the window once more. "Her name was Sofia. You won't find that in the records."

"Thank you."

"Just remember, Dr. Harding, the closer you get to answers, the harder they will fight to silence you."

~

Noah and I discuss every detail on the walk back to the hotel. Though he is skeptical, I convince him to follow Gabriella's lead. We have a name. *Sofia.* She died, and we owe it to her to discover the truth. We may have risked our careers and put our lives on the line, but this ring in my pocket burns with secrets, and I can't imagine turning back now. I can tell from Noah's excited eyes that he can't either.

Back in the hotel lobby, the man at the desk signals us over. "You have a note, signora."

He slides an envelope to me and motions for the privacy phone in the corner.

Noah glances around then leads me to the fireplace, where no one is in earshot. As I tear open the envelope, my stomach seizes. What if this is a threat? How long can I go on fighting this?

Before I unfold the note, I turn to Noah. "We all want the artifacts. Every one of us. I'm afraid if I give in, this incredible art will end up in the wrong hands, and certainly for the wrong reasons."

"I don't think you can control what happens. All we can do is find the truth."

I slip my finger between the folds, and with a sigh, I open to read the words, *Call me. NOW.*

I feel the grimace spread across my face. "My boss." I've had my phone turned off since I left London.

We head to the black privacy booth in the corner, where businessmen, shady characters, and eager art historians know they have a secure line. I dial Dr. Wright's phone and touch Noah's hand for support.

He doesn't even say hello. "Jesus Christ, Mia. You took off to Italy while I've been cleaning up your mess. What the hell were you thinking?"

"Cleaning up *my* mess?" The audacity of this guy. "I'm being followed, did you know that? They've tapped my phone and threatened me. How far into this are you, Dr. Wright?"

"What's gotten into you?"

Noah's big brown eyes turn doughy. Soft and worried, like an emoji.

"I know you're in on this scandal." Silence, just as I'd expected. "I'm so tired. 'Be a good girl, Mia, and authenticate this research. Be compliant or I'll report you for fraud. Put yourself at risk so we can have a big fucking payout.' Who cares if it lands me a stalker and threats to my life?"

"Calm down." His voice is low, his words spoken between monosyllabic grunts.

"Nothing good ever came from telling a woman to calm down."

"We all know this is an Armani, Mia. We've drafted a press release and all you have to do is sign it. You can come home. Your promotion is still on the table."

This man is nothing but lies. I reach into my pocket and pull out the cameo ring. I twirl it in my fingers and examine the profile. Soft cheeks. Wide eyes, full lips. She has a name. Her story is just beginning to form. I can't turn away now.

"I have a lead on something major."

He growls. "What lead?"

All my ideas fly around in my mind. I sift through emotions to find facts. A pendant from an art dealer's house with a woman carved in agate, a subtle womanly expression in *The Estasi's* face, a skin tingle in Armani's dome, and the name Sofia given to me by a bird lady. A fucking *golden egg* with a spell.

Oh my god, I've fallen into a fable. I can't tell him any of this.

Yet Sofia is now real for me. She's formed in my mind with a tightness in her brow and a longing smile, like a hidden figure in the forgotten dust of history, pleading for me to find her. If I don't, I'm as bad as the people I'm fighting.

"I've spent my entire life being responsible. Stay quiet, smile politely, agree often." I exhale long enough to puff my lips. "I lost myself long ago trying to become one of you. I studied my ass off and worked three jobs and ate food from neighborhood pantries while begging for my place in every single classroom and scholarship and museum. I was so busy being grateful, I forgot to be proud."

Noah swallows with an audible gulp.

"I may go down in flames for this, Dr. Wright, but I'm going to follow this lead wherever it takes me."

"I'll have you taken off the project."

A light laugh bubbles from my lips and I know. Nothing will be the same ever again. "If you could, you wouldn't be on this call with me right now. I'll report you for conflict of interest and reveal your bribe. Oh, and don't call me Mia. My name is Dr. Harding."

By the time I slam the phone on the receiver, Noah's eyes have grown wide enough to wrinkle his forehead. "That's one way to handle it."

I remove the ring from my pocket. "We know her name now." The gold band reflects glittering sconce light from the diamond-shaped glass above us. "Sofia the courtesan. It's like she's been waiting all this time as a ghost of Venice, hoping her secrets will find their way to the surface."

"What happens if Sofia turns out to be only a courtesan with no secrets to whisper? What if *The Estasi* was an Armani original this entire time?"

Somehow, I know he doesn't believe this. He's testing me. Strengthening my resolve. "Then we will have lost our jobs and credibility for nothing. But we'll have the truth, and the art world will be better for it." I tuck the ring back in my pocket, patting it once to ensure the ridges feel secure. "But I'm not wrong."

He hooks his finger around mine, swinging subtly back and forth. "Gone is the quiet expert on wenches and witches."

"This ring. I've been feeling it for the past two days. She was more than a model for *The Estasi*. I think she was the artist."

Chapter Twenty-Four

One week, two unfinished paintings, and endless hours of coddling, all with a massive hole in my heart. Now that I've broken down, Lucca is more attracted to me than ever.

Antonio has stormed through the doors of our palazzo more than once, but Caterina always wins. She locks me in my suite, tells Antonio I am ill, and places guards outside my door. I don't fight it. Antonio was always an impossible hope.

As night descends once more, I open my wardrobe with one lit candle, and step into the dark tunnel. Drafty air seems to lift my hair from my shoulders. Up the tilted stairs and through the darkness, I emerge once again in the dome, Lucca waiting for me at the window.

"Come here." He extends his hand to me. I place the dish on the windowsill and run my fingers through his hair. "You are so beautiful by the soft candlelight," he says.

"Have you been sleeping?"

"Yes. During the afternoon hours." He runs his tongue along my collarbone. My body remains still as it always does. A lifeless act of one body part on another. He sighs heavy and deep into the skin of my sternum. "Lie with me?"

I take his hand and lead him to the bedchamber under a glass view to the sky. A September chill disrupts the warm night, but I lower my robe and untie my shift, letting the cloth fall to the ground. I withhold a shiver as he undresses. His naked body is stronger than it has been. I feel it when he presses his stomach to mine. I count the way the moonlight seems to flicker through the window, as if winking. *Uno, due, uno, due.*

I bite back tears, angry with myself for allowing emotions to seep into my work. Lucca pulls back, his brow furrowed in concern. Without a word, he lifts my robe, wraps my exposed shoulders, and tucks my hair behind my ears.

We lower to the bed as he tucks my cheek into his chest and wraps his arms around me. His skin is warm next to mine.

"We are so similar," Lucca says. "We long for a life we cannot have. And love that will never be."

I'm not convinced he is capable of love.

I sit up and stare down at him, my hair in wild loose locks around my shoulders. "The studio awaits." I run my hand along his cheek and jaw, forcing affection. I hold his hand. Kiss his wrist. His eyes light with anticipation. I tolerate his touch in bed, but when tangled over a lump of clay, I find him exhilarating. His genius bleeds through his hands and into my work.

I unwrap my robe and let him stare. He examines my curves. I pull him to sit. With gentle hands, I press his palms to my breasts as he fondles and caresses them, as if examining their shape and mystic beauty. A spell cast over men's eyes and hearts, but it is only to get what I want.

"Help me make a masterpiece," I say with an earnest plea. Passion swirls in the air. Something wild but grounded, carried on the evening wind.

We make art.

I stand and drop my robe, no longer feeling teary. Confidence pumps through my blood, hungry to taste something Antonio cannot give me—the full-throated heat of creation. Lucca's touch brings my work to life.

We stand in the silver light of approaching autumn, staring at each other. Heat between us, our bodies prepare for magic.

"We do not need love to create, Lucca." I follow the lines of his chest, his abdominals. His hips and lean thighs. His manhood on display like a carving from antiquity. "You are beautiful too," I say. "Your body is strong. Full of life with art ready to burst through your fingertips."

His breathing quickens. His cheeks flush.

Together, we knead a roll of clay, reddish brown from the earth and soft in our hands. Our shoulders and hips touch as we roll together forward and back.

Ecstasy is about more than touch. It lies in creating. Rising art from the depths of one's soul. Love means shared pain between two people. For me, love remains an unwinnable war.

I position myself on a chair between two candelabras, my back arched and hair thrown back. Lucca kneads the clay to free it of bubbles as I study every curve in my reflection, committing the vision to memory.

Suddenly, a chilled, bony hand presses into my back, and another stabilizes my shoulder, forcing me into an unnatural curve, straining my hips and spine curvature. "Like this."

Caterina has her hands on me. Lucca does not react, but watches with intrigue as I stiffen. Caterina places my hand on my breast, the other relaxed over my thigh. She parts my lips, dipping her finger ever so slightly into my mouth.

Once behind me, she stares at Lucca, who molds and presses his hands to warm the clay.

Her fingers trail along my waist and belly. I wince but wait for her to retreat to the corner and watch. She seems to kneel behind me as she buries her face in my hair. She kisses my low back with her rigid lips, then crawls her way up my spine to my ear as I turn rigid, afraid to disrupt Lucca's interest in sculpting. "Make something sinful."

I resist her touch, but I hold this position and think of Antonio's hands on every part of me. His eyes on mine. I long to forget him. Force his face from every corner of my mind, but with my body twisted in passion and heat, he is all I can see.

Caterina strokes Lucca's hair, which he laps up like a cat in the sunshine.

Hours pass as we shape and mold and Caterina falls asleep in the bed. He presses my fingers as we carve as one and he shows me where to shade and how to build a round form. My body aches with fiery pain, but Lucca caresses my hair and feeds me wine.

"We can't stop," I whisper. "We finish this tonight."

"But you're uncomfortable."

I have never, not for one day of my life, not been uncomfortable. I press my hand to his chest. "This is our time. I want to finish."

Fueled by the fury of art that lives deep inside us, I manage to listen to his every teaching and feel his creation move through me. We complete a beautiful, emotional piece. A recreation of myself with Antonio's memory resting on my heart.

As dusk sprinkles its way into the dome, Lucca motions me over, breathless and wild-eyed.

Though I have never been formally trained, I've spent my life studying the human form. My curls are buoyant and my eyes, though closed, shine with life. I've shaded feminine subtlety into Lucca's display of a woman who does not exist. I move to smooth out the eyelids.

He stops caressing me, pulling my stained hand gently from the clay. "No more."

"She isn't complete."

"They are never complete, not to us." He guides me back and instructs that I close my eyes. I listen. "Know when to let go. You can mold the magic right out of a piece. Now, look."

I drag my eyes open against heavy lids. "Lucca." His name is all I can manage. I tighten my robe over my body, searching for a moment of comfort. We've injected power and lust, strength and enchantment. It's how I choose to see myself.

The lure of the courtesan is her otherworldly charm. We turn an ethereal dream into a body a man can touch and hold. Not entirely unlike sculpture.

Lucca weeps. He feels life again, and it is all because of me.

Caterina stumbles out, hopeful to see the result of her prodding and manipulation. "Yes." We stare at the clay figure, merely a model for a larger work, in complete awe and admiration.

Perhaps our hands made this, or possibly, the stars themselves dusted our fingertips and possessed us with the power to create.

Caterina lays her hand on my hip with a sensual stroke. "I want more."

Not only does she not arouse me, but her disrespect flames my anger. I am not a lowly prostitute who allows anyone access. "I am not yours to touch. This body is not a vase you purchased or wine you wish to gulp."

Her eyes grow cold. "Your resistance only makes me want you more."

For power only. My body represents something to be conquered and ruined.

My limbs, aching and fatigued, beg for a reprieve. "I will rest now, and when I awake, we will make something magnificent. And you will not watch. You will not touch me or lay your horrid lips upon my flesh. You will languish away in your quarters with only the love of prostitutes to quench your loneliness."

Caterina stiffens her lips in disgust, her eyes narrowing with the fire of displeasure.

"Our art is ours."

Lucca sighs in relief, like I am his protector. Perhaps I am.

"I cannot perform while you stare at me. You disgust me."

She seems to wilt, stung but furious that she needs me. She runs her hand along our sculpture and while locking eyes with me, she shoves the piece to the ground. It both shatters and disfigures, having dried in places and still warm in some.

I stifle a scream, though Lucca stares, unmoving.

Caterina reaches her hand to cup Lucca's buttocks as he still stands naked in front of us. "You both belong to me. As does everything you make."

~

Sleep has stolen me for an entire day.

Darkness greets me as I wake, but thankfully, so has an empty bed. My body hums. Art still courses through me, tapping its fingers in my gut like a pulse. I hate her for ruining my work, but more than that, I cannot turn away from what I am capable of.

Saturated in both dreamy confusion and fiery motivation, I force myself to dress in a simple gown, hair loosely piled in braids around the crown of my head, thirsty for paint or clay or the slice of a chisel against limewood.

Thirsty to create. Hungry for Antonio.

One guard always sits outside my door. I glimpse another at my window outside. My only choice is the wardrobe. Through the darkness and up the tilted stairwell, I listen for any sign of activity in the dome. It is deathly silent, so I slide the door open to the bedchamber. Here, I stare at the stars, wondering what will happen to Lucca after Carnival. What will happen to me. Will this dome stand for another hundred years, and will my art live on?

From the window of the studio, the grand magnolia tree beckons me with her long twisty limbs. I open the window and the ground seems to wave below. The thought of staring at my silent walls for another night is enough to convince me to fly. Despite my skirts, I manage to balance on a thick branch, and slide my feet toward the trunk. I sit first, then hang from another branch, reconsidering my current choices. Then I let go.

I fall in a heap to the packed dirt beneath the magnolia, right under Caterina's window, which is cracked open to release the smoke from her fireplace.

"No, darling," Caterina says. "I hate her."

A garbled voice gives me pause. A man's voice, for certain. But higher than Lucca's. He sounds as if he is underwater, too far from the window to hear.

Caterina sighs, wistful, like a song. Completely unlike her. "Antonio has made her fall in love. Fools, the both of them. Can you imagine when she discovers his lies? His stolen collection of art?"

My entire body lifts with the mention of him then just as quickly collapses at the suggestion he's lied to me. I lean my ear close to the open window to listen for the man's response.

"A resistive wench who disregards order," he says.

I finally place his voice and it leaves me queasy.

Caterina makes a tsk sound. "Bruni could ruin everything. We must deal with him."

I force myself to peek through the window, where my suspicions prove correct. Lying naked, curled in Caterina's lap, is Lord Marco.

"She thinks she is an artist?" Marco says with a dismissive laugh. "She never could contain her childish whims."

Whims. As if being an artist isn't in the very makeup of my being.

I crawl away into the shadows of night, through the garden, past the topiaries, and along the crushed rock path to the lapping water of the canal. Pushing off in the small boat used for supplies, I have one thing on my mind.

~

The night is dark but young, bursting with possibility. I quietly make my way through Antonio's kitchen window. The floorboards creak. Silver shadows cast their light in the hall. I arrive at Antonio's room. Bare chested, his wild loose hair cascades over his pillow. The fireplace flickers a deep orange hue over his shining cheekbones.

The world quiets. His closed eyes and heavy breathing settle my frenzied heart. He shifts when I sit on the bed next to his hip, but he doesn't wake, so I watch him sleep until calm spreads through my body. I've watched dozens of men sleep. Most often I count breaths and twitches to determine when I can slide from their grasp. Tonight, I hold seconds as if they are gold in my hands.

I press my palm to his stomach, spreading out my fingers over his ridges and ropy muscles and soft skin. As I glide up his chest, he drags his eyes awake. He doesn't speak, but his heartbeat quickens under my palm. *Thunk. Thunk.* He lays his hand over mine where we hold still, and I stare into his glassy, soft eyes.

I crawl my fingers up his neck and over the crest of his chin, letting my fingertips feel the softness of his lips. Perhaps he is lying to me. Right now, I need his touch. My hunger leaves no room for anger.

He presses up where we sit face to face. Without moving his gaze, he unpins my hair and loosens my braids. He rests his fingers on my neck, waiting for me to kiss him. I lean forward, but he still waits.

"Kiss me," I say, a twinge of desperation in my voice.

He slides his hands against my cheeks. Presses his lips to mine and fuels the part of me that only wakes with his touch. Like a private ritual for only our bodies to share. His fingers slide through my hair and cradle my head as his tongue caresses mine, waking me from my lifelong slumber.

"I'm trapped," I say. "I want you too much."

Antonio fiddles with a loose hem on his bedsheet. When he looks up, he inhales deeply. "I love you."

From deep in my mind, my mother's words rise to my mouth. "'Love is weak, and ambition is dangerous.'" I loosen my gown and remove my jewels, piling my fine clothes on the floor. "My mother told me those words. The madam who trained me reinforced them." As I stand in my shift on this autumn night, I fumble with the anger that sits in my palms and on my chest. I find it hard to breathe when I think of myself at twelve, eager and proud and hungry for my own life.

If Antonio is hurt, he doesn't show it. "I'm afraid too."

Like a tether as I float away, his words help me find a home. I lower next to him and hold a firm grasp on his arm. "I feel nothing but power when men touch me. Their fingers are air, their breath mist. They have always been nothing. Then you." Tears sting the backs of my eyes. "You make my courtesan life intolerable."

"Can we leave this life together?" he asks.

I climb atop him, knees on either side of his thighs. "I want nothing more than to live in your arms for eternity."

Antonio grips my hips while looking up to kiss me. "We will save each other." He kisses my neck and breasts, pulling my hips into his with a firm thrust.

"They will try to ruin us both."

"Let them try."

If only love was enough. If they damage his livelihood, we will die in the streets. An idea forms in my mind. "Carnival brings investors, and Caterina will host an art display for the wealthiest of them."

His eyes dance with intrigue. "What do you have in mind?"

"My pieces belong there. The sale of a few can fund our new life. If investors will buy a woman's work."

"Is this what you want?"

"My patrons have dismissed my art. I may sing and dance and recite poems to arouse them. But it is time I produce work for me."

Antonio twirls me off him, presses me into the bed and kisses me. As my mind swims, he stands, whisking me up and lifting me in his arms. He carries me to the studio, knocking the door open with his hip. He places me on the floor, turns me to face the room, and whispers in my ear. "Make your own fire, my love, and leave the weak men in ashes at your feet."

In the window, balancing on the sill, our gold-plated copper egg reflects the light. Marco had the egg commissioned by an artist in Rome, and Antonio stole it from a man's pocket in the festivities that night. The flicker of light reminds me how far Antonio will reach for my love.

He steps away, a draft filling the space where he pressed against me. I turn to watch him retreat through the door. "Antonio, do you steal art?"

"Only from men who deserve it."

That is every man. "The answer is yes, then?"

"Yes." He flashes me a smile and a wink. "Wake me when you're done."

He asks me to trust his intentions. I am not sure how to summon that emotion.

Possibility hums in the studio. Blank canvases and barrels of clay wrapped in wet linen. A black night, candlelight, and hours until I must return. While Antonio sleeps, I will carve something magnificent with my own hands, no Lucca in sight.

Chapter Twenty-Five

A woman named Sofia has captivated me. All I have is her likeness on a tiny ring and a pendant, and a theory about her life. Yet, she's found a way into my life and rests on my shoulders like an invisible shawl. As I wake this morning, I roll onto my side to watch Noah sleep. No glasses, mussed hair.

I slip out of bed, wash my face, and brush my teeth, grateful for a full night of rest. I watch him in the mirror, sleeping soundly after a night of nothing more than subtle hand holding. It was perfection.

Noah gave me the password for his computer, so I start up the laptop to begin research. A notification pops up for a new email. While trying to close the notification, I accidentally open his inbox. Shit. I don't want to—

When I see Dr. Byron's name, all sense of personal space and boundaries flies out of my inquisitive head. What is he doing in Noah's email? Subject: Mia.

I click on that bad boy without one flick of hesitation.

Dr. Beckett,

I've sent word to the staff of your "family emergency." You will safely have one week to find the information we both need. Mia Harding is a menace, and I'm very grateful for

your help with this situation. Your reward has been initiated, and I await news of your findings. We will both be better off when this ridiculous chase in Venice proves fruitless, and Mia Harding's credentials are revoked.
Sincerely,
Dr. Byron

His reward? I peer over the laptop to see Noah stir, so I mark the email unread and shut the screen quietly, but full of so much rage I could smash this thing into pieces. No one can touch my credentials while I'm working on this, and Wright wouldn't dare fire me. It would be considered coercion.

Noah held my hand all night. Our touch felt *real.*

Noah could steal my research, convincing Byron he's here to keep me in line. Am I everyone's scapegoat? But his smile. Have I been wrong this entire time?

I wait on the balcony, watching the morning explode in orange sunshine over a glistening blue canal. Tile rooftops and flower boxes in windows overflowing with fuchsia petunias. It's no wonder courtesans ruled Venice. It's easy to fall in love here.

Noah steps into the warm sun carrying a silver tray of tiny espresso cups on saucers, Nutella bread, and a bowl of bright red strawberries. "I ordered breakfast." He sets down the tray on the bistro table and leans across the balcony next to me with a dopey smile.

"What?" I ask.

"Nothing. The light just . . ." He clears his throat. "You're beautiful."

Right now, this all seems real. As if he hasn't turned against me to help Dr. Byron. I want him to look at me like this and never stop. "Thank you."

I join him at the table, trying to decipher how I missed his lies. Where in his face does he hold secrets I can't read? I rarely miss these things.

"Is something wrong?" he asks.

I consider my answer. "Just concerned."

"Yeah, you and me both." He sips his espresso and lifts his face to the light.

I check that my bun hasn't come loose, smoothing my hair at its part. My hand finds its way to my pearl earring, twisting it between my fingers to buy time. When I look into his eyes, I still see the Noah who holds my hand and fights for truth.

"Is your family worried about you?" he asks.

I shrug. "I don't have any family."

I stop fiddling with my earring and my hair, and I throw back the shot of espresso like it's Patrón. The coffee burns my throat and instantly sets my stomach seizing, but the flavor lingers like warm spice on my tongue.

"Oh." His voice doesn't ring of pity like I expect it to. "You've mentioned your grandmother before."

"She's been gone a long time. My dad paid for the trailer and occasionally brought home fast food. He died a few years ago. Heart attack."

"And your mother?"

"Died when I was five." He doesn't hurl another question at me, and the silence literally hurts. Like a toothache from a rotting nerve. "I knew that morning when I woke something terrible had happened. I sat in front of the TV, rubbing my blankie on my cheek."

That blankie remnant still serves as a bookmark for my nightly journals. I can't imagine why I want to remember that morning or the sour smell from an unwashed blanket from Goodwill with some other kid's name embroidered near its hem. Maybe that's exactly why. A reminder of how far I've come.

"My dad told me while I watched *Dennis the Menace* that Mama died from bad medicine," I tell him.

"Medicine." He's trying to remain open-minded and present. I can see it in his face. He knows nothing of the place I came from.

"Drugs."

One nod. No real reaction, which nearly brings me to tears.

"She was an artist." I blurt out the words, shot from some soft, needy place inside me. "Not a real one, I guess."

"What kind of artist isn't real?" Noah seems to shrink himself, turning his presence opaque as if every word might spook me like an alley cat.

"She drew on everything. Cardboard, envelopes from debt collectors. Furniture. She etched a painting on my headboard of a fairy and toadstools." That toothache spreads like an infection to that sweet spot of trauma I return to over and over again. So painful I wince, but those bruises of the soul, for me, hold the beauty of things forgotten. "Once, she wrapped an old T-shirt around a cereal box with a hair tie and water colored with my dried paint tray."

"Did you study art history to feel closer to her?"

"Looks like someone took undergrad psychology." Like the snap of an elastic hair tie, my soft, squishy memory disappears under a reactive cover. "Sorry. No. Some rich girl in high school bragged about majoring in art history. It sounded so worldly and important. Nothing that ever came from a trailer park."

Noah glances at my hand, as if considering touching me. Reminding me I'm good now. Pretty and successful. I dress the part. Maybe one day I'll believe it.

"Now I'm Dr. Harding," I say with forced resolve, "who wears pearl earrings and shops at Nordstrom." My confidence falls. "And who can't afford the life she's spent years building."

"What do you want?"

Somehow, I know exactly what he means. "I want the fight they all burned out of me. I was smart and principled, but one day I turned around to find a voiceless girl with a sterile life and too many handbags."

Noah nods in understanding. "I think it takes decades to find the person we used to be before the world broke us." He closes his eyes and turns his face to the sun. "My posh parents wanted my nose out of a book. I was to socialize when all I wanted was to escape."

"That's sad."

He reaches for my hand, but I cross my arms as his email pops into my mind. "Where do we search for answers today?"

I try not to notice how he tightens his fist in embarrassment after I recoil. "I called in some favors last night," he says. *Yep, you sure did.* "We're going where the answers are. The archives."

~

The Venice State Archive is built in an old Franciscan monastery. With its chipped terra-cotta walls and water stains, no one could tell this crumbling building protects sixty thousand volumes of important documents. I know. I've been stalking this place online for clues since they have refused all our attempts at contact. The Italian government is notoriously shady, and we can never be sure who is connected to whom.

"*Buongiorno,*" Noah says, with a far deeper voice than usual. He speaks in Italian, pointing to me and nodding with confidence. I don't want to believe he isn't who I thought.

The man lifts an old-school phone and speaks to someone briefly before slamming the receiver down. He motions for us to wait.

Noah wraps his arm around me, whispering, "Just go along with me, okay?"

"This sounds dangerous."

The man returns, asks for our identification, and widens his eyes when I look at Noah, who nudges me to go on. I hold my passport between my thumb and forefinger, hesitant to leave a trail of our snooping.

"Go on, it's fine."

It's not fine, Noah. You could be walking me right into the same trap as my lying boss. Am I really going to ignore Noah's double crossing with the Mafia on our heels?

"Paolo is waiting," Noah says.

"Who the hell is Paolo?" I whisper.

The man sighs, not bothering to withhold his irritation, so I hand him my passport. He makes his notes and documents our presence while a tight tingling crawls up my spine. He places our passports in a locked drawer and presses a button. After a loud beep, the door behind him thuds, and he holds it open.

We step through, down a long corridor lined with books. Whispers hum to life on all sides, like a river of rushing water. I shut my eyes, unwilling to hear anyone's story that isn't connected to Sofia. In the large rotund reading room, a man pushes away from the archway he leans on. "Greetings, friends. My name is Paolo."

His English is perfect, but his accent is thick and rolling, like the golden Sabine Hills. Noah shakes his hand, as do I, though I can't imagine what Paolo must think of me.

"Come," he says. "I've prepared a collection for you." Paolo opens a door to the archives, with rows and rows of a temperature-controlled vault. He hands us each white gloves. "Here. This is what we have on Lucca Armani."

We stare at the volumes protected by Venice authorities and hidden from public view. Dr. Byron would have been here and combed through these with the help of Paolo, no doubt. Why have they hidden this from us until now?

He unfolds giant binders laminated over parchment and flattened scrolls. Images of paintings and drawings and taxation lists for Renaissance Venice. He stops at the rough charcoal drawing of a woman, similar to her position in *The Estasi*.

"This was found in Armani's studio. Drawn roughly around 1600, we think this sketch was the precursor to the statue found in his garden." His voice is sturdy and smooth.

Only a portion of the sketch remains, but her face is clearly visible. The woman with the swath of silk over her breasts is the same woman from the cameo. In full color and come to life right in front of us.

"This drawing was found in a recovered stash of unclaimed art in a refurbished palazzo. It's being archived as we speak and will have a full reveal at next year's exhibit." He compares the sketch and a picture of *The Estasi* side by side. "Authenticated for the years 1600 to 1610. Still think this wasn't Lucca Armani?"

Noah places his hand on my knee under the table. I can only hope it's a show of solidarity and not sympathy. I'm not ready to give up yet.

Paolo folds his arms. "I do not like Dr. Byron. He is, how do you say, pompous?"

"Yes, that's an accurate description." My eyes don't leave the painting.

"But I see no reason to doubt his research findings."

Tears well in my eyes. This may be the image of Sofia, but this sketch feels masculine. My head is a mess. Noah may be lying to me, and I can't seem to distinguish between the truth and a lie. Maybe Lucca carved his courtesan and I've been chasing a stupid dream this entire time. "This woman isn't Caterina," I say, pointing to who I know to be Sofia. The profile of her eye, nose, and flowing mane of curls remains visible.

"Correct. She is too young. Most likely a woman from his imagination. No one of significance." He clears his throat. "I will leave you two. I'll be right outside." A glass wall separates us from an office and I'm certain there are cameras on us. Paolo steps outside and scrolls his phone.

"No one of significance," I mutter. "Lost to the murky waters of the canals, Sofia's memory remains nothing but a washed away image of a lustful woman."

"Maybe that's all this woman was," Noah says, seeming to instantly regret this admission. "I mean, she could have been only his lover and not an artist."

"I know enough to say with certainty she was much more than that."

Noah slides his hand from mine, but I flip through the pages of documents. I don't look at him. "You told Byron you were here to put me in my place."

"Oh." His loud exhale serves as its own answer. "I assume you saw my email. I was going to tell you." He lowers to a frantic whisper. "How else could I get us in here?"

"Lies." I keep flipping the pages, noting the highlights of Lucca's life, perfectly curated to prove that his art reigns supreme and that history failed his greatness. Page after page of sketches and unfinished paintings.

"Truth." He grits his teeth. "I'm just as disappointed as you to find this. The world's obsession with Lucca Armani is all hype. I would love to see a woman behind his name burst to the surface and take all the credit."

I search the documents, unwilling to believe I was wrong this entire time. If I can't trust my instincts, what else do I have? "Why did I fight this so hard?" A list of courtesans in 1605 reveals nothing. I flip the page and examine 1606. Nothing.

"You wanted to believe," Noah says. "History is full of hidden truths. In the larger picture, we know nothing about anything, and maybe—just maybe—we could have rewritten the rules."

"People like us rarely get to do that." I sigh, running my fingers along the pages, when my heart thuds to a halt in my chest. 1607 courtesans. At the bottom of the list is a little name, nearly smudged out. "There."

"Sofia Rossi."

"Do you think that's her?" Noah reads the Italian script. "Taxes paid, benefactor Lord Marco." He squints. "Is that his name? One moniker, like Prince?"

"Why wouldn't anyone research these names? She's right there." My breath deepens into an aching realization that no one cared to look. Her name is right there.

Noah exhales slowly, as if blowing out a candle. "Mentioned in only one year and barely readable. That's strange."

I flip back to the sketch of Sofia in a chair. I examine the lines. The shadows. Something vaguely familiar takes shape. "Noah, do you remember those images when we were kids? A scramble of squares, but when you stare at it long enough, a 3-D image comes to life? A figure would pop off the page."

"Must have been an American thing."

I see it. Like a flashlight shining from the page. "I can't believe I was so wrong," I announce louder than is necessary. I throw myself into his embrace, breathing heavy into his neck.

He holds me, a sheepish grin tugging at his cheek. "What are you doing?"

"I don't want anyone to hear me." I wrap my arms around him, pressing my mouth to his ear. "Look closely at the images. I see something."

By the time I let go, Noah's glasses are askew, and his cheeks have blushed to hot pink. He clears his throat and looks again. I pretend to close the binder but use the cover as a shield between myself and the camera in the ceiling. I trace the lines of the woman's body, which forms the shape of two letters with the curve of her back, the extension of her leg.

SR.

Noah places his hand on the back of the binder and matches my intense gaze. He wraps his hand around my neck and whispers at my earlobe. "No way Lucca did that."

Armed with a name, an image, and renewed confidence, we hold hands to leave the archives. Sofia Rossi was an artist, and she created these sketches of herself. I'm certain of it.

We remove our gloves, prepared to walk out with our heads hung low, but Paolo throws open the door. "There's been a development."

Noah and I exchange glances.

"They drained the Severo Canal." He takes a deep breath, eyes alight. "A sculpture arose from the muck. It seems to be another Armani."

Chapter Twenty-Six

Three months have passed with the same routine: create with Lucca through the night, sleep under guard watch during the day, and slip out through a window whenever possible to Antonio's arms, where my soul comes alive.

Caterina no longer watches us sculpt in the nude. I've warned Lucca that I'll shove a paintbrush in her eye if she steps foot in our space again. "We will create beauty, and I cannot do that while her ugly eyes are upon me," I told him.

Lucca derives some sort of deranged pleasure from our fighting. The more fervor I hate Caterina with, the more passionate our creations become—and the deeper Lucca tumbles into his art. His motivations matter little to me, as long as we keep creating and he continues teaching me. For all his faults, he's a breathtakingly brilliant artist.

"Darling," Lucca says to me, brushing my hair as I sketch our next sculpture. "Do you hear them?"

"Hear who?" I'm lost in the sound of charcoal on parchment, moving through lines that seem to appear from an otherworldly place.

"Our art," he says. "Our creations seem to speak, don't they?"

"Yes." Only an artist would understand this. "I hear them."

He collapses against my naked back, cheek pressed to my spine. "Two months until Caterina's dinner. Two months until you will leave me."

I stop sketching. My hands and fingernails are black with charcoal soot. I turn to face Lucca, who kneels behind me. "We will always be one, Lucca. Our work will stand together, forever connecting us as one."

While still placating him, perhaps, those words are the truth. We create something magical. He sees it. We both feel it.

He forces a smile, his hand rested on my cheek. "You've breathed life into every one of these pieces. Our love has created these."

My stomach seizes. *Love.* Men read my adoration as love, so I've always been able to simulate it. Now I know what love is, and it isn't this.

"Bed me," he says.

We've only touched and created art in the nude over these few months. I can handle the fondling and the caressing. Even the occasional kiss. This body is his by law, but Antonio's by heart.

"We have more work to do." I turn to hide my near tears, frantic to pull away. I consider options for how to stop where this moment is heading.

He brushes my hair aside. He runs his hands along my waist and hips, pressing into my back with a heat I've not felt from him before.

"Please," I beg. "We must keep creating."

He runs his hands over my entire body. I arch my back, not from passion, but to create space between his body and mine. With force, he pulls me back to him. I search the room for something to grab, but I see only clay and my trembling hands.

I shove his arm from my stomach, but he resists, still slobbering on me with his pathetic lips and eager touch. "Lucca, stop." I wriggle and push away, panic rising into my throat.

Lucca knocks a jar of currant-colored pigment to the ground with his elbow. He holds me so tight that I can't resist. "Lucca, please." I'm begging now, something I've never done. "This isn't you."

He shoves me against the wall, my arms pinned to my side and my cheek pressed to the rough plaster.

Tears well in my eyes. "Stop." With one word, I tell him he will pay for his defiance.

Lucca freezes. He rests his cheek against my back, whimpering as his chest heaves between sobs. "I want to feel love."

"Nothing about this is love."

He loosens his grip and stumbles back.

I reach for my robe and turn to face him, heart still thudding against my ribs.

He rubs his hand over his face as he begins to sob. "I'm sorry." His breath catches and he collapses in a heap. "I am horrid."

I don't move, too afraid to step any closer. "The past few weeks have been wonderful. We create and touch. You've come alive with these sculptures. Why fall apart now?" I can't say what I yearn for as he owns my body and my words.

"You control me." He falls to his knees, begging at my waist. "I cannot do this without you, and I am not the man I once was."

"What man is that?"

"Powerful. Intensely passionate."

Tender Lucca still resides somewhere in the monster before me. "Your softness is your power." Yet all his beauty has disappeared in the quiet of this night. I walk near him though keep distance between us. "We all lose ourselves along the way, don't we?" I wrap his robe around his shoulders.

His arms crossed, he pulls the silk tight against him. "I'm afraid, Sofia. I sometimes want to devour you to become the passionate lover and the artist I've never been. Without you, I am nothing."

"Your talent is unmatched. What restrains you is fear. Fulfilling the expectations of every patrician in Venice is impossible when you will not love yourself."

"I hate myself because of the life I've created with Caterina. We've used our hate to build a twisted world of greed. When I am soft, she pities me. Pity is for the weak."

Against my inner voice screaming to leave him, I find myself reaching for his hand. "You are tender and emotional. You need more kindness, not less."

"My fall into darkness has left my wife with nothing but seething hate. I need her money to survive."

"There is no surviving if you continue to hurt me."

He nods, eyes reddened, wincing as I mention hurting me. He drops his eyes to where I cover my body from his view. "Go."

"What?"

"Go now. Leave me before I become the monster we all know I am capable of." He stands and stumbles toward me. He grabs my arms. "I release you. Go to Antonio. Live a life of passion and art where the voices don't hurt."

His hysteria worsens by the second. I now fear being close to him. As he twitches and rubs his ear, I consider how very unwell he must be. Still, I need him on my side to access Caterina's buyers. "Look at me."

"Please, Sofia. Leave." He screams, an anguished cry that startles me. Then he reaches for his whittling tools.

"Lucca, no." My hands lift in a protective wall, prepared to fight whoever he becomes next. The sharp metal blade glistens in the candlelight.

While staring at me with doe-like, mournful eyes, he presses the blade to his arm and glides the tip through his flesh, down his forearm, and through the center of his palm. His skin blossoms open like a bloody flower, and we both stare at the slice in terrified shock.

"I no longer deserve to make art."

Darkness has enveloped us both, and any hope of my love escaping unscathed has been purged out of me, seeping into the floor with Lucca's blood.

Chapter Twenty-Seven

Another potential Armani rising from the earth underneath the Floating City. Like ghosts in a misty cemetery, these statues seem to merge in a collective exhale as history rises from graves. Perhaps they have unfinished business here in the mortal world.

A sea of people flock to the location as tourists have posted the shocking moment on social media. In the frenzy of an entire city racing to a muddy canal, I lose Noah and Paolo. Being buried in squealing twenty-somethings readying their phones turns my panic meter to ten. As locals join the crowd, the cacophony of voices reaches piercing levels. I push people back with my forearms, trying to gulp air and steady my heart rate.

Historians prefer books to people and silence to pretty much anything else. My feet still move, though I can't feel my legs. The odor of bodies and perfume and lip gloss seems stronger than usual. It's all I can smell. Hyperventilation kicks in. My vision blurs. I tighten my hands into fists and prepare to thrash my way to clear air.

A hand grabs my arm and yanks me to the side. I gain my footing and shove the person to the ground. "Oh shit. Noah?"

He stands and wipes his hands on his pants. "Are you okay? I yelled your name, but you didn't hear me."

I lean against the wall to catch my breath. "Yeah. Sorry about that."

He reaches for my shoulder, his head tilted in sympathy. "Are you okay?"

"I don't like crowds." Feeling returns to my legs, but I can't move quite yet. I reach for him, grateful for something familiar. He wraps me in a hug, his soft cotton T-shirt cool against my skin. I considered him my enemy a few hours ago. It's hard to tell who's on my side these days.

He looks down, his face mere inches from mine. "Better?"

I nod. He holds my hand, and with a smile tugs me toward the unearthed statue, but I resist. "Don't you want to see?" he asks.

"Are you trying to prove me wrong?"

His arm softens but our hands still touch.

"You promised to help Dr. Byron. You turned on me."

"I got us into the archives. I'm sorry I lied."

My jaw stings as it tightens. Paolo appears, motioning us to follow. After an intense glance at Noah, we follow Paolo past the gathering crowds. He flashes his badge as police allow us through, into the dried gulch between buildings, past rusted gondolas resting along the stone foundation.

"No one knows for sure," Paolo says in a breathless hurry. "It would be a miracle, no?"

We arrive at a protected circle where a statue stands roughly five feet tall. We move around the authorities, all blocking the statue from view.

Paolo speaks to a man in Italian with flying hands and a loud voice. "A city worker rinsed her off before we could create a proper retrieval. Amateurs."

Her.

Paolo pushes through, and Noah and I follow. In the middle of a drained canal, resting atop layers of sludge, a stone statue of a woman takes our collective breath away. She is tall, naked, and seems to heave with power. Curls flow to her waist. One arm lifted with her hand resting behind her neck, her leg extended with toe pointed. A snake coils around her wrist and between her legs, slithered and curved to the ground at her feet.

Her face is the woman from the cameo. Sofia Rossi. Tingles flutter across my arms. She's here, face to face with me. And she's left us another clue. "You see it?"

"Yeah." Noah wraps his arms around me and whispers. "SR."

I imagine what I might say if we were alone. I'd say that Sofia Rossi must be buried all over this city. History and man have tried to bury her but like any great woman, she's found a way to rise.

"I don't think you're wrong about these statues," Noah whispers. "You might be the only one who's right."

On the closest balcony, a figure appears. The woman from the elusive Italian family with the black bob and deep red lipstick glares straight at us.

Chapter Twenty-Eight

By the time I arrive at Antonio's, I'm heaving for breath and can't rid myself of Lucca's filleted arm. Every scenario crashes through my mind, including Caterina dragging me back to the dome by my hair. This is my one chance to escape, and I can't let it slip through my fingers.

Antonio soothes my worry as soon as he opens the door, and I crash into his arms. "Has something happened?" he asks, his cheek warm against my forehead.

I pull back, unable to hide my worry. "Lucca released me. He told me to run away with you, and then he slashed his arm open. The blood and the meaty flesh didn't seem real."

Antonio's mouth drops open. "Why would he do such a thing?"

I push past him, up the stairs to pace the hallway. Antonio leans against the doorway to the studio, waiting for me to explain.

"Caterina has pushed him too far. He's gone wild." Somehow, the stomping back and forth keeps me thinking and planning how to get us both out of this. Lucca grabbed me. Only now can I feel the fear of his arms pinning me down. "Lucca threatened me."

Antonio stands straight, gritting his teeth.

"Nothing happened. He handed me my freedom." I stop at the window to notice the bright night sky illuminated like candlelight over a bluebell flower. "Caterina will be furious. I fear freedom has always been an illusion."

"Let's leave tonight." He steps into the window next to me, fingers grazing my cheek. "We can escape and never look back."

I walk into my art studio, with paintings and sketches and sculptures in various states of creation. The room smells of wood shavings and oil, the scent of creativity. "Leave this?"

"Leave it all," he says.

His romanticism, while endearing, is pure foolishness. Leave my life's work for what, the promise of undying affection? That is a fable. "Tell me your secrets. Even the dark ones."

He runs his hand through his thick, dark hair. "The pieces we admire at court and on display around the royal houses of our city are often not what they seem."

"Things are rarely as they seem. Go on."

"I acquire art for patricians. And for some outside of Venice. Those men who are not wealthy or powerful enough to commission an artist but wish to own something beautiful and unique."

"I don't yet hear a scandal."

"Have you heard of Carlo Bianci? Lorenzo Conti?"

"Yes. I've heard they live in the countryside. Bianci's oil paintings are superb."

Antonio picks up a paintbrush, twirls it in the air, and catches it by the handle. "Those fascinating artists are a ruse. They do not exist."

I swipe the brush from his hand and tap it against my thigh. "Who are they then?"

"I commission artists that are unknown. They will never crawl out of obscurity, so I fetch them at a fair price. What's a little false name when everyone is happy?"

"Forced anonymity is horrendous. Who would agree to this?" Realization hits me and I slam the brush onto the table. "Say the part you don't want me to know."

"Those who make the art are women." He waits for my reaction, but I don't react.

"You steal from women who have already had everything taken from them, and you present their work under a false name for a fraction of the price." I repeat the situation with a hollow voice, more to myself than him. "You steal and you lie."

"No one is stealing. I pay them." He says with authority. "Women artists aren't taken seriously. They're deemed too weak and fragile and should not be dirtying their clothes or lifting heavy tools. I give them an opportunity to work as artists, something the Republic would never allow."

"You are hardly a hero in this, Antonio." I rub my temples, pacing through darkness. "You contribute to the world viewing us as undeserving of money or power or even recognition. You help to shackle us."

"Would you prefer I ignore them?"

How can he justify this? He's contributing to every restraint I've ever known. "I'd prefer you sell them under their own names."

"I tried!" He pounds his fist in the air, then drops his arms to his side. "No one bought them, and I was laughed out of court."

I approach him, stand tall, and jut my chin toward him. "I was sold into prostitution by my mother, who died shortly thereafter from syphilis. Twenty years spreading her legs for men. I would have a grand life, according to her. An honest courtesan with education and money. Because the only hope I have is to sell my body for fine linens and gold coins, while burying any dreams that have developed in my heart. Do not bore me with your hardship, Signore Bruni, I live every day with the burden of womanhood."

Antonio drops his head. "I'm sorry."

Midnight silence spreads through the house, but this room glows with possibility. I run my fingers over the tools he has gifted me. The canvases he has provided. "Are you planning to steal from me?"

"You know I would never do such a thing."

Yes, I do know. Deep in my gut, in that place where intuition lives. That voice that whispers like an echo in a well assures me Antonio speaks the truth, or at least he means to.

"Time will move on, years will pass, and we will both die. Yet, I want the world to recognize my name as a great Venetian artist." Something releases in me as I say these words aloud. Speaking my deepest desires into the intensity of the night. "I can think of nothing sadder than for my life to end with my only contribution attached to a man's name."

Antonio slides over to me, shuffling his shoes along the gritty floor and running his fingers through my hair. "Make your art, my love. We will make sure history remembers the name Sofia Rossi."

I lean my cheek into his hand, both furious I cannot make this happen on my own and grateful for his kind love. "The Armanis own me. They've probably already sent the authorities to arrest me."

"I have one more secret," he whispers. "I believe we have more power than you realize."

"Why is that?"

"One of my artists requests to remain anonymous. And her name is Caterina Armani."

What should soften my fear merely ignites a new flame of worry. Caterina knows all our secrets.

Chapter Twenty-Nine

The investigation has stopped during siesta hours. Paolo hosts us for an afternoon meal and espresso at his apartment near the archives. His cool demeanor convinces me he knows secrets, and I'm not leaving until he admits to them.

"Another Armani," Paolo says, leaning back in his chair. "Do you believe now?"

His question is directed at me, but I still glance at Noah. "Believe what, exactly?" I ask.

"We're trying to discover works from a great Baroque artist we know little about. All the data suggests Lucca Armani carved these sculptures. I've shown you what we have at the archives, and that statue we saw today is the same woman from his painting. What more do you need?"

We're working to discover a different Baroque artist too. One no one seems to care about.

Noah nods so subtly, I barely catch it. A hidden conversation between the two of us. A subtle nudge to speak up.

"Paolo," I say, eyes focused on his, "our differences are obvious. You want these finds credited to Armani, and I want the truth."

"And you believe those are different things?"

I scan the bright orange rooftops, as a burst of sunlight radiates from this entire island. "I don't know."

Paolo puffs his lips then narrows his eyes. "There is no evidence another artist could have created such masterpieces. Why do you still question us?"

"Confirmation bias."

He mutters something in Italian, flipping his hand toward Noah as if he's tossing a ball into the air.

"She's right," Noah says. "You all want this fable to be true. Venice is the center of Armani-mania."

"I have integrity, signore."

Since we're sitting in his home, I suspect that's true. "I know you do," I say. "I'm talking about your deep belief in the magic of research. A story untold, and a rare find that changes the course of history. We all want that."

He scoffs, clearly still offended.

"We don't know much of anything, do we?" Noah smiles and warmth spreads over my cheeks. "We look for clues that will reinforce what we think we know, which really is nothing."

"Exactly." I catch his eyes and break into a smile. "The early 1600s. We're stepping out of the Renaissance. The Catholic Church is losing control to those pesky Protestants. Art that wasn't based in Catholic worship would have been dangerous. You don't think the artist could have secretly produced them then buried the evidence to save themselves?"

"That is just as likely as our theory that Lucca Armani produced dozens of sculptures in one year. We think he buried most to preserve them. The Council of Ten ruled the streets with secret informants and hidden agendas. They arrested Armani at the 1609 Carnival."

Every detail of this man's life has been scrutinized and studied, yet that record has never been released. Excitement bursts in my chest. "How do you know he was arrested?"

Paolo clears his throat and adjusts his collar. "Certain aspects of the archives are not available to everyone."

Noah slides his demitasse to the center of the table, tapping the tiny porcelain cup against its saucer. "Were they available to Dr. Byron?"

Silence spreads over the room, riding on a balmy, saltwater breeze through the open doors. "No."

I knew he had secrets. His heavy, pinched brow suggests he has a conscience too.

Noah's hands spread across the table, his cheeks heating to a bright red. "If you want Dr. Harding to authenticate anything, you better start talking."

"The records have one mention of Lucca appearing in the Piombi. Secret lead-lined cells above the torture rooms of the Doge's Palace reserved for special political prisoners of the council. February 10, 1609, is the last mention of him until his death years later in Siena."

Noah flicks a glance at me. There's that date again. "Why keep that secret?" I ask.

"They directed me."

Adrenaline shoots through my limbs like buckshot. Everyone's at risk here.

"They?" Noah asks.

Paolo pinches the bridge of his nose. "Today's find complicates everything."

He's begging to talk. I can feel it. "Paolo, you don't owe me anything, but I've risked my entire life for this."

He stands, paces the room, and closes the patio doors. "It was only meant to be *The Estasi*," he whispers. "Prove Lucca Armani sculpted the piece, match it to the restored sketches, and I'm free. Now there's another statue. I agreed because it was a rare find. An Armani original. Then the internet grabbed hold, and the whole thing spiraled out of control."

"What are you saying, Paolo?" I ask, fairly certain I already understand.

"I took a bribe. Five hundred thousand euros." He doubles over as the veins in his neck bulge. This could end his career and land him in prison. "It happens all the time. *The Estasi* is an Armani—I'd bet my hands on it—and I didn't see any good from sharing details of his arrest and potential torture after Carnival. Hiding the details was meant to speed up the authentication."

I want to pity him, but I'm too angry. "This alone falsifies the research, Paolo."

"Dr. Byron saw what he needed to see. Had the world not grown Armani-obsessed, no one would have questioned anything. You wouldn't be here, and I wouldn't be facing another threat."

"Who's threatening you?" Noah asks.

"The same ones who follow you."

"We're missing something," I say. "If I authenticate *The Estasi*, they will have to fight the government for her." I rub my cheeks to loosen the tension at my jaw. "If I don't authenticate it, it won't stop them from showcasing the statue. The world doesn't care. They're already invested in this story."

"With this country's corruption, there's always more than we can see," Paolo says. "This recent statue adds more for them to want. Each piece is worth millions."

Noah growls. "They want to steal the Armanis and sell them on the black market."

This was our theory, but now I'm not sure. "With the entire world watching?" Nothing about this seems right.

"No, this makes perfect sense." Noah paces. "These criminals play by international rules to get art back in their hands. The revenue is just a cover-up. Remember what I told you about laws and stolen art across countries? I bet these statues will disappear before they ever arrive at the Uffizi."

All these facts make sense. It's logical and tracks with high-end art theft. It would make sense why they bribed us with jewelry and Paolo with cash. They convinced my boss to ignore ethics and put me at risk. They intimidate me into authenticating so they can get control over the piece once again. Why, then, do I still feel like we know nothing?

"Go public," Paolo says. "I dug us into a hole I cannot climb out of. Do what you must, Dr. Harding."

"If I call this now, any potential discovery stops. I'll be vilified, even if I've done the right thing." And no one will know the truth about Sofia Rossi and why every statue credited to him bears her initials.

Paolo's phone vibrates on the table. We all look at the screen, lit up with a text message. Paolo rubs his face from his eyes down to his chin before reaching for the phone. We wait for any word, any response that indicates what direction we should take next.

Paolo swipes to read then locks eyes with me. "Well, Dr. Harding, you're in a predicament. Initial thoughts support the serpent statue as another Armani."

Of course they do. "This doesn't change a thing for me."

"You have two days," Paolo says. "Authenticate *The Estasi*, publicly state support for the serpent statue and a full-scale excavation—draining all the canals in Venice and anywhere Armani ever touched."

"They texted you a threat meant for me?" I pull out my bun and scratch my scalp as a headache has begun to pound at the base of my head.

His phone buzzes again. Paolo opens the text, then looks up at me.

"What does it say?" Noah asks.

He licks his lips, which suddenly appear dry. "'Dr. Harding should put her hair back up. Don't get too comfortable.'"

I stare out the glass doors and wonder where they're watching us from and what motives they still have hidden. Exactly how much danger am I in?

Chapter Thirty

Day and night, I sketch, paint, and carve limewood into figures—passionate, sensual women with power in their eyes, and men who symbolize my love for Antonio. I pull inspiration from Lucca, hearing him in my ear as I sculpt. He could be dead, slipped away in a pool of blood and haunting thoughts. I sleep little and make love while I can. Caterina has already threatened Antonio, and I know I'm next in her sights.

"Your figures are dangerously erotic," Antonio says to me under the amber flicker of candlelight. We've spent the evening naked in the studio, surrounded by creativity and passion. He smooths my wild hair from my face. "The patricians at court would burst into flames from shock if they saw these."

"Yes, they would."

"You could be arrested," he says. "Why take such a risk?"

I stretch and wrap myself in the blanket, my body finally satiated by his touch. "These figures live inside me, demanding release."

He kisses my arm, soft and sweet. "I've watched powerful men search for art to validate their position and prove their worth. I've seen men hide pieces away, so they alone know of their existence. And I have seen women risk everything to create works they will never be given credit for. I don't understand."

"It's why Lucca has gone mad. To hold something in your hands born only from your soul gives purpose to life. I feel as if I was put here on earth to create. Sprinkled with strength and misery, and a touch of stardust, my life's destiny has always been something grand." The pewter gleam of twilight fills the sky. "And without art, my being is hollow and useless."

Antonio tightens the blanket around my shoulders and kisses me. "I promise to protect you and everything you create, for the rest of our days."

As light drips into our studio, the magic of night seems to leak away through the floorboards. "How long until Caterina yanks me from this perfect little life?"

"There's no telling." Antonio agreed to fetch twice the price on any works she brings him in the next month, pending she leaves me alone. "Can we please talk of escape?"

We stare at my current work: a partial likeness of Antonio holding me in a naked embrace. She has potential and is nowhere near completion.

"You will never be free here, Sofia."

"If I let the Armanis dictate my life, I will never know freedom at all. Besides, these pieces, once finished, can buy us a new life."

"And if they don't?"

I've always known there is a chance I will never sell a piece as Sofia Rossi. "Then you may break my heart and sell them under a false name."

He scoots behind me and wraps me in his embrace, his heavy sigh on my cheek like another comforting reminder that he is human and not some impenetrable patrician like the rest of the men of the Republic. We both stare at my sculpture.

"This is us in heaven on earth, yes?"

I nod.

"As long as we are together and you can create, what does it matter where we are?"

The lines of my sculpture seem to sing. This one is special. The rare image that forms in my hand how I sensed it in my mind. "As a courtesan, I create perception and build a world on the shoulders of men. I enjoy the power of molding greatness." I exhale as I stare at my work. She is beauty, but with a fatal flaw. I have not become the artist I could be with training. "I failed Lucca, and my vision suffered." I reach behind to run my fingers through his loosened bronze hair.

"Perhaps you should let him falter." When I don't respond, Antonio pulls my arm away and twists me to face him. "You should be the artist history remembers."

"That is what I'm trying to be."

"You do not need him, Sofia. Your work can stand alone now. Look at this. She is stunning."

"I could be exiled or imprisoned if this all goes wrong. Lewd sculptures by a woman, even a courtesan, are grounds for trying me for witchcraft. I risk more than my pride with this plan."

"Or you could become the greatest Venetian artist of all time."

I bite my lip but tears still gather in my lids. "What must it be like to live with no barriers? You are free to dream without restriction while I have only ever envisioned my greatest achievement through the success of men who bed me."

He gently tugs one of my curls taut, then lets it bounce upon release. "I care little how anyone remembers me. I care only that you will love me with every breath left in your body. We will risk everything, and if we fall apart, we do so together."

I've never before felt this heat that burns in my chest. A lover who supports my dreams and fights my demons while handing me a sharpened sword. For once, someone stands behind me without their hands on my throat. "You keep Caterina in line, and I will work on Lucca. He must produce art with me, and together we will force these buyers to hand us coins. I suspect Lucca needs an escape too."

"Someday, Sofia, women will commission the same for their

art. One step is better than nothing when changing the world overnight is impossible."

My tears finally overflow, streaming down my cheeks, for this is the first moment I have ever dared to admit the aspirations in my heart.

~

Finally leaving my safe cavern in Antonio's studio, I travel at night across San Marco on foot, arriving at Palazzo Armani. It's midnight, my best chance at reaching Lucca without Caterina. I tiptoe across the street, walk around the side of the house, and open the gate along the canal. I tuck my skirt between my legs and into the hem at my waist. Back up the magnolia tree I swung down to flee not two weeks ago, ready to deliver a message. If I get my way, Lucca will follow my plan step by step.

Climbing up proves much more of a challenge. A branch snags my hair and rips my sleeve, but I manage to reach the window of the dome to find Lucca on his back, staring at the ceiling, eyes wild and arm a mass of mangled flesh.

I open the window and step through, expecting a grand greeting. Instead, Lucca merely sighs. "What are you doing here?" he asks.

I don't respond. I make my way to him, and lower to the floor, meeting his eyes.

Lucca reaches for my cheek with his good hand. "I am nothing without you."

"Very true."

He laughs, lifting his face from the depths of darkness. When his head falls to the side, his eyes take a moment to follow, but he eventually finds me. "You should leave. Caterina will ruin us both." He twirls his finger around a coil of my hair. "Without you the air cools my skin to ice. Beauty is everywhere but I cannot touch it."

I reach for his scarred hand, curved into an unnatural claw. "Aren't you worn down by her insults? Why let her control you?"

"Because life is all too difficult already." Lucca stares for two long breaths. "I released you. Why would you return?"

I trail my pointer finger along his palm. I need him to trust me. To agree to my plan. "I need you." True enough.

"You have Antonio and his full chest. His masculine hands and his rebellious distaste for convention. What do you need from me?"

"Together, we make beauty, Lucca." So many emotions swirl in my head. Pity, affection, disgust for his weakness. A shadow catches my attention. "Why hasn't Caterina forced me to return?"

His studio is peppered with remnants. Wood shavings and pigment stains. He's fallen deeper into despair after he set the doge's painting on fire and since taking a blade to his own wrist.

"My troubled wife keeps herself busy with *Lord Marco* and their scheming." Lucca frowns as he says Marco's name, his nostrils flared in disgust. He must see the anticipation dangling from my mouth, as he answers the question I came here to ask. "Caterina hopes to throw us all to the Lords of the Night and watch our demise."

The Lords of the Night. Magistrates who lurk at night and conduct punishments under a cloak of secrecy. Of course she wants to report us to them. "How can we take that disgust and make something beautiful with it?" Darkness is the home he knows well. I can always access him there.

A flicker lights his eyes. "Yes." He lifts his hands to the air and casts an invisible shape. "A stone figure of you naked, holding a serpent."

Stone. Serpent. Art has grabbed hold of his soul. It is my job to carry him to the light and lead us both to a better life. I kiss his wrist and place his fingers on my collarbone. "With a serpent?"

"You are the temptation I cannot outrun, ignore, or pray for. My muse, the prostitute who holds my life in her hands."

"You must step away from your wife's abuse. It is time for us both to live." I knead his vulnerability, molding and shaping until he lets me in. In this, I am uniquely skilled.

After a fleeting moment of consideration, he sighs and collapses back to the floor. "It is not possible."

I stand and disrobe, washing my body of Antonio's touch. Playing a role that will lead to everything I need and want.

"Caterina will have you arrested," he says, his eyes lingering on my breasts as I slide my chemise to the floor. "Or force you back to fulfill my every need."

"I no longer take direction from your troubled wife, and neither should you." I reach for a charcoal pen and begin to sketch the outline of myself, holding a snake. Lucca lifts himself to all fours, crawling up behind my naked body.

Ah, the sweet moment of success. Power surges through me as I settle into the knowledge that my body and wits have saved me yet again.

"Tell me your plan." He rests his head on my back and his hand on my bare backside. "You are my compulsion, Sofia Rossi."

"I will help you prepare for Carnival. Together, we will sketch and paint and sculpt, and we will present the buyers with an array of the most intriguing, luscious art they've ever laid eyes on. We take the money and leave Caterina with nothing. Let her live with Marco while we breathe free."

His hold on me softens. Less grip and more of an embrace.

I turn and face him, kneeling to his eye level, knowing he's never seen fury blazing in my eyes. "Marco offers her a new path to the top of the patrician pyramid. She cares nothing for you, your body, or your art."

His eyes fill with tears. Pathetic as they may be, his cries strangle his inspiration. They render him useless. "Every piece I have completed has been to please her. Or you."

As he balances on the tip of my finger, I remember that no wealthy man on the night of Carnival will purchase art from a woman. They may, however, purchase art created by both our hands. I will take half a dream over prison every moment of my life. I slip a lock of his tousled hair behind his ear. "It's our turn,

Lucca." I spin around. Lean my head against his shoulder. "Sofia's serpent will be for us. *The Serpent of Venice*."

"Yes." He reaches around me, laying his spasmed hand on mine as I sketch. "What will I do once you leave me?"

"You will finally find peace. Right now, we can make something beautiful," I say between strokes of charcoal. "A piece that breaks the hearts of every observer will be worth the pain of facing your fears."

I stop drawing, a completed outline of myself staring back at me. "Lucca, I want to be remembered. That is true power." A swift, heartbreaking image of my mother grips me. In her bed, clinging to life, knowing in a matter of hours she would die and no one but I would remember her.

"And what do you wish to do with this power, Sofia?"

"Prevent another woman from a life like mine." I stare at the drawing, Lucca's chin on my shoulder. "I want just one young woman from the Rialto Bridge to choose art over spreading her legs for the highest offer."

"You seemed to enjoy the life of a courtesan," he whispers.

"When there is no world outside your prison cell, you learn to find beauty between the bars."

He wraps me in a surprising hug, childish in its nature. "Together we will sculpt *The Serpent of Venice*."

I stare at what I've done. My body curves in the shape of my initials. S with the serpent, R with my limbs. One way or another, Sofia Rossi will make history.

~

Six hours later, just as the sun illuminates the sea, I climb down the magnolia limbs and land once again under Caterina's window. Through the panes, I see Marco, sleeping soundly, with Caterina nowhere in sight. Subtle clinks and taps catch my attention, so I follow their sounds.

I crawl through the dirt to the window of the studio I once

assumed to be Lucca's but now know is Caterina's. Inside, Caterina sits naked in a chair. Her body doesn't have my curves, yet she stares at herself in a mirror, recreating the arched back and round buttocks I created in this position. She's attempting to be me. The sight erupts my seething hate.

I watch her position her hands on her bony body in an uncomfortable rigidity. Like trying to bend a steel blade. With a huff of frustration, she kicks the easel stands and shoves the chair to the side. She gazes over dozens of smaller art pieces on the workbench. I can't tell the material, even when I press my cheek to the glass.

Suddenly, Marco appears in the doorway, his manhood dangling like a pathetic invitation. "My love," he says.

"Sculpt with me." She extends her hand toward him.

He bares his teeth. Caterina may not notice, but I understand that expression. Marco hungers for fame, for adoration beyond the likes of Raphael and Donatello. His burning desire stops at his fingertips, due to an utter lack of talent. He once attempted to sculpt a lover. Her laughs left her with a bruised eye and bleeding lip.

My talents were nothing but another will for him to break.

Caterina huffs in place, then summons the erotic pose from the chair. Swayed hips and arched low back. I've performed so much, my body moves like this naturally, but she strains and grimaces. She falls into his arms, kissing him wildly. Once recovered from his gripping insecurity, he grabs her, dragging her tall frame back to the bedchamber.

Those pieces. They're sitting there, begging to be seen.

Without hesitation, I slip through the back door from the garden, knowing how the hinge squeaks, sliding the heavy wood while I hold my breath. I remain against the wall, stopping at Caterina's bedchamber.

I peek around the door, eyes locked on the awkward scene. Caterina is on her knees, her arms held behind her by Marco, who thrusts himself like a sweaty rabbit, and yells, "I am the king," between heavy pants and grunts.

Though the whole thing repulses me, I carry on to the studio. Jewelry. Caterina makes jewelry. Agate pendants. Miniature sculptures. Marco spanks Caterina as she moans, but a far more horrifying realization steals my attention.

I recognize these pieces.

She sculpted them from my sketches. Every one of these ideas came from me.

~

I wake Antonio, wild and desperate for answers. He reaches for me to join him in bed, but I resist.

"Please sleep," he mumbles into the bedsheets.

"Caterina's pieces you sold. Were they jewelry?"

"Some, yes." He clears the bedding from over his head and looks up at me with round, glistening eyes. "What happened?"

I peel myself from the dirty, torn clothing and slip into bed next to him. He wraps me in his arms. "I snuck into her studio. It was pendants and rings. Cameos of ivory and agate, all with my likeness."

"How do you know they were you?"

"Because I sketched every one of those ideas."

Antonio knows my work. He sees me sketch and paint and mold at all hours of the day. The figure of a woman is what captures me most.

"Much of what I see is a woman in various moments. Contemplative, angry, determined. Hopeless. I'm not permitted to learn from live models, so I draw what I know. And the figure I know best is me."

Antonio crosses the room to retrieve a paper and red chalk. "I sold a miniature clay bust of a woman with a pearl necklace."

I close my eyes to remember. Under the light of the rich, morning glow, I recreate the sketch I made months ago, while Lucca painted her face on canvas. My knees were bruised from a night of sketching everything in my head. "Was this her?"

Antonio examines the image. "Yes." He props his knee on the bed. "And the figure of a woman with eyes closed, tears on her cheeks?"

I sketch that for proof too, roughly, for time, and tilt it toward him.

"She stole your work," he says.

Many of these sketches never became full sculptures, yet they were mine. My visions and emotions. She may as well have reached into my chest with her bare hands to stop my beating heart. "She's kept everything that looks like me. Her studio is practically a shrine to my face."

Antonio glides my hair from my cheek with the back of his finger. "I understand her obsession." His alluring smile causes my thighs to tighten. "We will make sure she never steals from you again."

"How can we do that?"

"I will handle them." Antonio, in his shining, chiseled face, hides something.

"You can't hurt Lucca."

He pulls away, sliding his hands from mine. He leans to the window, his hair a mess of sleep and worry. "You care for him." He extends his arms, which brace his body on the glass. "I thought he was nothing to you. Just another patron."

I step up behind him and kiss the long, graceful muscles of his back. I run my finger along the curve of his shoulder blade. "These remind me of wings," I say, though he won't be swayed. "Lucca is troubled and dark, yet he sees my talent."

I don't dare reveal the truth that yes, I do care for Lucca. In a twisted way, I both need him and want to be the one to lift him once again to the light. Perhaps then, my art will have meaning in the world.

Antonio sneaks a glance over his shoulder, and I duck under his arm, my back braced against the window. His passionate eyes draw a line to my lips and back to my eyes. "I need to be the only one who holds your heart," he says.

"It has only ever been you. And you it shall always be." I hold his face in my hands, lightly scratching my fingers along his cheeks.

He relents. He presses his forehead to mine. "Tell me why you discarded the piece you've been working on. I pulled it from storage and brought it back to the center of the studio."

I peer down at the floor, tracing the swirled wood grain with my eyes. "It is not enough. My work must stir the soul."

His eye twitches. He wants this piece to live on.

"You've captured us in a passionate embrace." Softness gathers around his eyes. "Please, finish it. For me."

My art, in this moment, has stirred at least one soul besides mine. I love him for helping me feel like an artist. "It isn't good enough."

He lifts my chin by kissing my neck in soft, twirling caresses of his tongue. "What is this need for fame, Sofia?"

"You don't wish to be remembered?"

"Only by those I love," he says.

I curl my fingertips into the flesh of his shoulders. Memories burst in my mind like yeast bubbles. My mother. My insatiable hunger for art as a child. The belief that I would never die a bruised, sick, forgotten prostitute.

"I am deeply, madly in love with you," I say. "Life will never be the same, for you have opened something in me I cannot ignore. A passion buried deep in my soul."

He kisses me softly, caressing his tongue over mine, still holding me close, exhaling a soft cloud of acceptance over my lips. "For you, I will do anything. I will even allow the Armanis to live."

"I promise you, once Carnival has come and gone, you can sweep me away to the sunny gardens of Tuscany, where we will lie naked under the warm summer sun. First, I must take this opportunity. It may be my only chance."

"Sofia Rossi. The great sculptor of Venice."

"Antonio," I ask with an inquisitive smile, "what have you done to keep Caterina away from me?"

"I've promised her my business. Once Carnival has passed, I will hand over my contacts and she may practice in place of me. She will have the entirety of Venice's art world at her grasp. She gets this only by leaving you be."

"You will lose everything for me."

He lifts me against the window and sweeps my legs around his waist. He holds me firm yet gentle, and we make love in the warmth of the morning sunlight. "And I won't regret a thing."

But the ultimate love may come at the cost of all I've ever dreamt of, and everything I wish to be.

Chapter Thirty-One

"Two days, Noah." I pace back and forth on our hotel terrace. "Two days to discover a four-hundred-year-old secret that no one wants us to find. And all I have to go on is hidden initials in a painting, her name mentioned in one tax record, and Paolo's confession to taking a bribe. Holy hell, this got complicated fast."

I knew when I first saw an image of *The Estasi* that she held a story. Her life left breadcrumbs all over this city. I questioned my instincts back in London. Maybe I knew that standing up for what I believed would land me right here, chasing secrets with danger biting at our heels.

Noah steadies my shoulders. "You're doing the right thing."

"But now there are threats and bribes." I shake my head, imagining for just a moment that I could run back to LA, sign the damn press release, and move on with my completely uninspired life.

"Remember what you said? You want the fight the world burned out of you." Sunshine lights the caramel flecks in his dark eyes. "Tell your insecurities to sod off."

"God, even your insults sound polite. You need a few lessons in being truly offensive."

He reaches for my cheek. His soft touch holds me prisoner, gliding his thumb along my jawline. His elbow bends and our mouths move close.

"Aren't you scared?" I ask.

"Bloody terrified." His eyes drop to my mouth then crawl slowly back to my eyes. Noah leans toward me, head tilted. "What do you want?"

A familiar face catches my attention. "My boss."

He freezes, gaze at the wall. "Not exactly what I was getting at."

"No." I push him away. "Right there." We bend over the balcony where Dr. Wright and his new, young, beautiful assistant arrive by water taxi. "What the hell is he doing here?" I shift through every scenario in my mind. He's come with a threat. A bribe. A guilt trip. He's found some loophole in the ethics rules and he's here to kick me off the research.

"He flew to Venice to get your signature? I guess he needs you after all."

I sling my crossbody bag over my shoulder and tuck my contraband—the ring and pendant—inside a zippered pocket. "He has the Italian mob behind him. I can't face him when the only proof I have is my oh-so-reliable female intuition."

"Okay. Let's go."

He stuffs his backpack with his laptop and charger. We open the door and slip into the hallway just as the elevator dings. Noah grabs my arm, yanking me to the terrace at the end of the hallway. Wright and his assistant step out of the elevator just as the door clicks shut behind us. Through the glass, our eyes meet. He pauses, just one beat, to gauge my reaction. When I don't flinch, he stomps toward me, face puffed and glossy red.

"Hurry," I yell.

We fly down the stairs, accidentally shoving two posh ladies out of the way. "I beg your pardon," Noah says.

"Seriously?"

"There's no need to be rude."

With Wright and the girl fast on our heels, we leap to the bottom step and force our way through the café that overlooks the Grand Canal. The sweet roasted garlic doesn't even stop me, nor does the gelato stand that blocks our path. Noah shoves his way through a group of tourists into the tiny space in an alleyway, without so much as a "pardon."

"That's more like it," I say to Noah. "No need to be all Mr. Rogers while we're taking down the patriarchy."

I surmise from his bewildered grimace that he has no clue who Mr. Rogers is. Travesty!

"Mia!" Dr. Wright yells.

We snap right and weave between market stalls of watercolor paintings and evil eye keychains. Noah grasps my hand with such a firm grip, my heart flutters into my throat. With a quick smile, he yanks me into a crowd of American tourists. We watch Wright from the center of the circle as he scans San Marco Square with lips so tight, they've disappeared.

"Will he report you for credit card fraud?"

I shake my head. "No way. He wants this statue to hit the art circuit. He'll keep my secrets to make sure this thing moves forward."

The group begins to move at the behest of a guide speaking of Carnival over the centuries and how Venice stole the body of St. Mark and enshrined him here in this basilica.

"A walking tour," I say with a smirk.

"It's a brilliant cover. Let's go with it." We pass a magazine and newspaper stall as Noah translates the headlines. "'Armani Fever.' This one says 'Bring Us the Dig.'" He picks up a paper. "'People have begun searching for artwork hiding in basements and in canals, metal detecting along the surface of muddy waters. Venetians have been sneaking into houses and digging in gardens under the shroud of night.'" He looks up at me with a devilish grin. "It seems we have competition."

The tour takes us through the Doge's Palace, which allows us to collect our thoughts. While the guide explains the courtyard and significance of a marble staircase and St. Mark's astrological clock, we plot.

"Two statues," I whisper. "One broken and buried in Armani's Garden, another intact in a canal. Both to display a likeness to who we assume is Sofia." We're the only ones who don't believe she is Caterina. And that works to our advantage.

Noah pulls me close as he stares at the bell high above the tower, pretending to follow the guide's storytelling.

"Sofia sculpted *The Estasi* and *The Serpent*. I'm sure of it."

"It makes sense," he says. Our mouths rest near a kiss. His breath warms my lower lip. "Sofia would have access to Armani's supplies. That's why historians think Lucca is the artist. Elements can be traced back to his studio."

That addictive tingle of excitement skips across my skin like a flat rock across a lake. "And Antonio?"

"Antonio commissioned art. He knew everyone in Venice who was creating and buying and would have worked with Lucca. He fell in dangerous love with Sofia."

As history's secrets boil to the surface, I grab Noah by the shirt. "If Lucca took credit for her work, why did it end up at the bottom of the canal and buried under a magnolia tree?"

He searches for answers, but I'm too impatient to wait.

"She would have sculpted herself," I say, my breath speeding up. "Women weren't allowed training in anatomy or models for posing. She sculpted herself in power with a serpent wrapped between her legs and her own body in a moment of passion. That's talent."

"According to the records, Antonio married in 1615 but apparently spoke of his great love and some golden egg." He withholds a growl. "If the bird lady is to be believed, Antonio wanted Sofia to be remembered. He never left Venice."

"He may be the only one who knows what happened to her."

The tour moves us through the doge's apartments and institutional chambers, discussing life as a royal in early modern Venice.

Elaborate frescoes fill every grand room, capped with painted gold plaster detailing. Wealth and excess drip from every corner of this palace.

As the guide leads us over something called the Bridge of Sighs, my stomach tightens. The stone walkways across this bridge tug at my consciousness, as if I've been here before, though I know with certainty I haven't.

"You okay?" Noah asks.

"Yeah." Pressure compresses from the walls and my heartbeat accelerates. A line of tourists holding their cameras glides along this ancient prison to peek into cells and imagine themselves in another life. I don't need to imagine. The anxiety and worry and fear hang in the air, encapsulated in time and waiting for ghost hunters such as myself to step inside and share in their grief.

Dammit, sometimes my paranormal tendencies are more than I can bear.

The guide leads us into a chamber and glides the door shut. Darkness presses down on us, with only scattered light along our feet, a metal grid, thick and rusted, holding us inside its dank walls.

"Imagine life here," the guide says. "Freezing in the winter, roasting hot in the summer. You may live here for months or years, hoping they don't move you to the torture chambers where you'll be hung from your hands bound behind your back."

Noah whispers, "Well, this is unpleasant." He touches my shoulder, but I'm too lost in the energy of the cell. All that fear mixes with something else. Passion and love lost. My right arm burns with heat, buzzes so rapidly I rub it to ensure there's no hidden flame touching my skin.

The guide continues until the group has shifted from fun role-play to subtle concern. He laughs, sliding the grate open, where the tourists resume their boisterous interest in all things Venetian, not a blip of concern that the history of this room practically shouts in your ear. If anyone cares to listen.

As the light filters back in, I examine my arm once more. Though my skin has cooled, something still tugs at me.

Then, I see it.

Without turning my head, I grab Noah's sleeve and drag him next to me. "Look."

He sneaks a glance at the group, who have all moved on to the next cell and the next display of torture devices. "What am I looking at?"

"There." I point to the wall, covered in graffiti, with scratches and drawings from hundreds of years of prisoners. Noah gasps with quiet reserve so only I can hear. Nestled among more prominent, recent words scribbled in the curves of stone rests an image. Faded with time and wear, it would be easy to miss. But not for two historians on the hunt for clues. We see it right away.

A drawing glares back at us. We squint and lean close as I trace the outline of *The Estasi*. Only this drawing is rough, not created by an artist, and obviously drawn from memory. With one very noticeable difference.

"Is that . . ." Noah's voice hitches.

We swallow in tandem. "Yeah," I say. "The entire piece. *Two* figures." The backs of my knees bead with cold sweat. "Who is that other face carved behind Sofia?"

"The hand on her thigh," Noah says in astonished glee. "It isn't hers. It's his."

Chills erupt over every inch of my skin. I grab Noah's sleeve, wondering if realization has hit him yet. "Whoever carved this had seen the original sculpture before it broke. This person had to have known Sofia."

Tourists dip their heads in while we try to act cool, hiding our childlike grins. We stare until they move on. "Didn't Paolo say Lucca was imprisoned here? Maybe he drew this."

Plausible, but something seems off. "He was in Piombi across the bridge. With the lead roof." I look closely, then I remember Sofia Rossi's initials outlined in that photograph.

We can't see when we are too close.

A favorite guidance from teachers in my graduate years. I step back and let the light hit the image from a different angle. "Is that?" I pour from a bottle of water in my bag and rub a faded carving below the image. I outline the grooves with my pointer finger. "A.B."

The veil between myself and the ghosts of this cell has thinned, leaving gaping holes where they reach for my mind. This one tells me he's met me before.

"Antonio Bruni was in this cell," I say. "And *The Estasi* could be what sent him here." I turn on my phone just long enough to snap a few pictures, then shut it down again.

Noah's phone buzzes. He removes it from his pocket and swipes to read a text message, doing his best to hold a firm, unworried gaze.

"What is it?"

Noah shoots me a concerned glance before reading the text aloud. "'Hope you're enjoying the tour. Tick tock goes the clock.'"

I hold firm to my confidence. This is too huge. "They still don't connect Antonio to Sofia and Sofia to Lucca." I look out the door then pretend to be an unaware tourist as what appears to be a docent eyes the prison for any wrongdoings. "We're the only ones who know about Sofia."

"And why did Antonio sweep her away during Carnival then marry someone else?"

"There's one more question we keep forgetting to ask," I say.

Another buzz of Noah's phone makes us both jump. Once again, he taps and swipes. "'We're waiting.'" Then another buzz while in his hand. "'We've reported a stolen cameo to the police. A ring snatched from the Armani house by a crazed historian, out to ruin a legacy and steal Venetian artifacts.'"

"Shit." How do they know I have it?

"We have to get out of here." He leads me down the hall, my hand in his, as we circle the stone square of a prison and dip between people, convinced eyes are on us with every move.

As we emerge from the prison and step into an archway connecting the palace to the basilica, we notice two Italian police meandering in circles, examining the crowd.

"Still in for this ride?" I ask him.

A cheeky smile lights up his face. "We're on the cusp of a history-shattering discovery, Dr. Mia Harding."

"I love when you use my credentials," I say, breathier than I can control.

"You bet your ass I'm in."

My knees practically buckle right there but he catches me, presses my back to the smooth tile wall, and plants a kiss on me the likes of which I've only read about in books. His lips, his scent, the way he grips my arms just hard enough. How his hips press into mine and his hands find their way to my hair. Oh, the danger of it all.

He pulls away. We both gasp for breath as our hearts thump against our chests in tune with each other.

"Okay then, Dr. Noah Beckett. Let's shatter some history."

We dip behind a shaded archway. He holds my hand, bringing me to a halt. "Where do we look next?"

I press against the wall where no one can see me. "Where no one else thought to. We find Caterina."

Chapter Thirty-Two

February 9, 1609

For six weeks, I have let art swallow me whole. It's been glorious. Lucca sends for me while Caterina pleases Lord Marco and escapes in the night to prepare her secret banquet for princes and lords and rulers and kings. He brings me information and Antonio plots our escape. Tonight, I must make sure Lucca is ready to face his greatest fear: selling our work to the highest bidder.

As Lucca and I stare at the completed *Serpent of Venice*, my heart presses with such force my chest nearly bursts open.

"She is stunning," I say.

Lucca still struggles to grasp tools and moves in hitches rather than glides. He can still breathe life into a piece, as if his vision transcends physical restraints. "You made her," Lucca says.

"*We* made her." I glide my hand down the snake's body, textured with hundreds of tiny diamonds. The figure is smoothed to perfection. Curls cascade down her back as they wave in the wind. "The movement makes me want to take flight with her."

"Must we sell her?" His body tenses as his injured arm trembles.

"If we kept our art, she would die with us." I place my hand softly on his, bringing his fingertips to my cheek.

He bites his lip and blinks hard. "You cannot cure me." His voice holds more resolve than usual.

"I do not wish to." I lower his hand to his side and stare into his sea-like eyes. Bright, clear blue waves settle against the shore of his unsettled brow. "I only intend to prevent you from ruining what we've created."

He motions to his own pieces in the back of the room. Unfinished paintings of women in battle, and me draped over a pile of furs near a fire bearing only a look of seduction. "Do you know why those pieces bear no magic?"

"No."

"Neither do I." His shoulders slump, shifting away from me. "When my soul falls away and my heart beats against an empty cavern of darkness, visions rise like the sun."

"I don't understand."

"My darkness is my muse. Much as I wish to find joy and light, those entities aren't accessible." He turns to me, his eyes traveling over my body. "Out of the darkness I find inspiration. And it may be the saddest truth of my life."

He never wanted me. He simply didn't want to be alone in his misery anymore. "Lucca, for all your struggles, you are the first and only patron who has reached my emotions." Good and bad. It's the truest thing about us. "I find you brave for accepting your softness and looking at what most men don't know exists."

"Not like Antonio does." His face doesn't hold jealousy. Admiration, perhaps. He wants to fall in love and wouldn't settle for a beautiful body. He loved the part of me he could, pushing me to create art as only he knows.

I am here to convince him not to ruin everything we've worked for. I rub my thumb over his scar and his tightened fingers. He can still create with his strong hand. "Is this painful?"

"No more than the rest of life." He forces a pained smile. "Come with me now."

He leads me to the corner of the room, behind *The Serpent of Venice*, behind the paintings and busts he has attempted but has never completed.

Sawdust and dried clay fill Lucca's dirty fingernails. He presses his finger to his chin. "I fear you may never forgive me for this."

I imagine something salacious and offensive. What has he done? "Perhaps not. Though I very much wish to see what you've spent your time on."

Lucca forces his gaze tall and his shoulders back. "It is all for you, Sofia. I believe maybe it has always been."

And that may be as close to love as Lucca will ever be. "May I?"

He turns to the window. "I cannot look."

I reach for the canvas, feeling the curve of a head as I gather the material. I slide the fabric away as my heart thunders in my chest.

Stunned into silence, I can't form thoughts, let alone words. I take in the beauty of the form, the overwhelming emotions that patter through my body.

Lucca finally turns. I see him from the corner of my eye, but I can't pull away. My eyes pool with tears and sobs rise to the surface like a grip around my tongue.

"Are you furious with me?" he asks.

I step closer and reach for the figure that is both familiar and better than I could ever imagine. Her look of ecstasy, her back arched and face tangled in the throes of desire. The true beautiful agony of love. Tears stream in thick, constant rivulets down my cheeks and onto my chest.

"This is my work," I say.

Lucca steps to the other side, staring at my tears over the hardened clay figure. "It is. Antonio brought her to me after you discarded it. He is right. This is too magnificent to ignore."

"I couldn't make her sing. Not like you have." I step around all sides, examining everything he's done. "You've added to her. Textured her and made her real."

Behind her seductive clay face is Antonio's. His hand wraps around her belly and between her legs, his mouth savoring her neck. The two figures twist and tangle as if sharing one hammering heart between their bodies.

"Your technique has not reached the pinnacle yet. You are a woman. A courtesan. Opportunities do not exist for you." He forces the slightest hint of a smile. "Despite all that, your work is magical. I completed the portion you've been denied: hands trained in sculpting."

"Caterina has stolen every sketch I've made, and every form I've attempted."

"I gave them to her." Lucca drops his shoulders, facing me in all his brutal honesty. "I did not mean to hurt you."

"Why would you do such a thing?"

He shrugs, staring for a long breath. "I find life in the act of heartbreak."

I don't know that he has a good reason for giving in to Caterina. We all find ways to survive in the prison of what we cannot have. I kiss his cheek, letting my lips linger on his skin as it flushes.

He stares at the sculpture, head tilted. "I will have my workers begin to carve her in marble."

"No," I say. "No stone. I want her just like this; our hands molded every curve. Together."

Lucca seems to understand my plea. "Clay is generally a model for stonework, but I see your love for this piece we've built. I will fire and glaze her, and she will be yours."

"She is called *The Lovers*. And we will sell her for the price of our freedom." Neither of us says what I know we both feel. To pull this off, we must outsmart Caterina and Lucca must believe he deserves more than this shattered life.

He gathers his confidence, which seems to wisp in the air around us, molting along with my rigid anger to the place where only art reaches.

~

One night until our lives change forever. As patricians don their elaborate masks and hooded capes to fill the night with Carnival excitement, Antonio meets me outside Palazzo Armani, extending his hand just as I arrive near the magnolia tree. I intend to enjoy this night, before the risk of tomorrow.

"Lucca completed my piece," I say.

"If anything will make admirers swoon over your name for hundreds of years to come, it will be that sculpture." He runs with me to his gondola, where a couple of gilded masks await. Once inside, he tucks me under the shaded cover of the boat, kneeling at my side. "Are you angry I gave him your work?"

"I should be, but no." I fall to my knees and kiss him as our hands tangle in each other's hair. "Lucca turned my vision into art," I say breathlessly.

Antonio growls as he pulls away, bringing my hands to his lips. "Forget Lucca. Tonight, we will enjoy our city, hidden in the safety of costume. Our plan for tomorrow is set."

Lucca will guide the gondolier to the wrong ship, where Antonio will hold Caterina under lock and key. Lucca and I will present our works together, displaying me as his inspired, creative courtesan who creates sexual art that stirs the soul. A ship awaits to take the three of us, our coins and our freedom, to a new life in Tuscany.

He pushes away from the garden. I watch his handsome form maneuver the oar, his arms rippled with strength and his cheeks glistening under pools of moonlight. He is not a stone piece of art. He is a flawed man who risks everything for the woman he loves.

At Piazza San Marco, he docks the gondola between dozens of others. Like bobbing black swans, their elongated necks curve to the sky. We don our gilded black masks and hoods and he holds my hand to help me ashore. Among hundreds of people, we skip through the night toward the Doge's Palace. A sea of colors hides the identity of every man and woman under those costumes. Carnival is a time where patricians and commoners alike test the limits of hidden desires. Citizens and visitors descend on forbidden spaces to perform forbidden acts.

Antonio holds my hand through the crowds as our shoes crush eggshells from *ovi odoriferi*. The air is soft and floral, filled with perfumed rose water eggs tossed by young romantics.

Laughter fills the night as people flit from one palazzo to the next. Secret celebrations color the city like paint across linen. Caterina chose this time for her dinner for a reason. Dark deeds propel Carnival, frothing us all into the next scandal where our hidden lives explode with abandon.

Antonio leads me by firm handhold into a celebration in Piazza San Marco, where masked individuals sing and dance. Charlatans stand on crates, performing puppetry and magic shows. We know not to give them our coins, though many unknowing travelers here too often revel in the celebrations, hoping for a touch of Venetian magic.

A doctor offers to pull painful teeth for only a small fee. His round spectacles enlarge his eyes, and his neck is adorned with a chain of his work, the old teeth clattering together as he swings his arms. Another waves a snake, promising potions to cure all that ails you.

The movement of a city released from the restraint of law fills me with excitement. I press Antonio to a wall and slip our masks back so I may kiss him in the recesses of the arcade, surrounded by solicitous vendors and clamoring foreigners. He kisses me back, deep and hard, as he squeezes my waist until I moan.

"I never want this night to end," I whisper, running my fingers along his thigh.

"That would mean you would never see your art become famous. And we can't have that now, can we?"

I throw my head back in a laugh, and he yanks me forward toward the Campanile.

We weave between people and past two prostitutes who beckon interested customers with their exposed breasts and disguised faces. A guard smacks their hands with a stick and orders them back to the Castelletto. Those poor girls live by strict rules, relegated to the brothel quarter under complete control of their matron.

"Where are we going?" I ask.

He lifts his finger to his mouth. As we slip through the door, he pulls me close to his back as we climb the dark stairs. Torches burn from sconces embedded in the stone. He lifts the stick to light our way forward as we climb up and up, to what I'm unsure.

"I am not allowed here," I say, tightening my grip on the torch handle. So many rules to serve the pleasure of men.

"Tonight, you are."

We hold our masks at our sides. Antonio reaches around my eyes to cover my sight. "Step forward," he whispers. The air is cold and light, whipping against my cheeks like a tail. I search for the curve of arches to ground myself in place. Antonio breathes in my ear, "Open."

As he drops his hand from my face, the view comes into focus. The Adriatic, like a black diamond shining in the distance, reflects a silver pool of light in a subtle shimmer. The city sprawls out below us in torchlights and bursts of color from delicately stitched masks. Above us, the stars gleam.

"Despite all the things she denies me, I love this Republic," I say. "Serenissima's allure will always impress me." Suddenly, I imagine the quiet of the sunny hills in Tuscany.

Antonio wraps his arms around my shoulders to keep me warm. "I don't know if each star has their own name, but I wanted to feel close to them tonight."

I point to a band of misty purple light spread out like a rainbow above us. "What is that?" I ask.

A voice bellows from behind us. "That is the Milky Way."

We turn to face the older bearded man in a floppy velvet hat with a long feather trailing down the back. "It is made up of thousands of stars." He steps forward. "Would you like to see the moon?"

I nearly laugh, it's so implausible. "I see it right there."

He pulls out a long-handled rod painted with golden scrolls. "This is my telescope."

"What is a telescope?" Antonio asks.

He motions to me, as if asking permission from Antonio, who nods. The man turns me to face the sky and positions this contraption with one end to my eye. My vision turns blurred, and I wobble in place. The man mutters, "Wait," as he twists the tapered end. Suddenly, the moon appears so close I could touch it, its pocks and craters as clear as a drawing.

I pull it away, gasping in delight. "Magnificent."

Antonio takes a turn, stumbling backward once he glimpses the giant moon in front of him. "I do not care for that," he says.

"I suggest you take your leave now. The Lords will be here soon to try out my invention. They won't take kindly to a woman learning astronomy from a forbidden tower."

"You are not bothered by me standing here with you?" I ask.

"Certainly not." He places his telescope in his robe, resting his hand over the fabric to protect his possession. "The Church and I disagree on much, including a woman's right to climb a tower."

Antonio reaches for my hand. "We'll take our leave now. Thank you."

He nods and allows us to pass.

"Who are you, signore?" I ask.

"No one of significance." He examines the view of stars splashed above. "My name is Galileo Galilei."

"Good night, Signore Galilei. Perhaps you'll be known all over the world for your work with the heavens."

"I prefer stars to people, signora. It matters little to me if anyone remembers my name."

"I certainly will." I flash him a smile before Antonio leads me down the stairs and returns the torch to its holder in the stone.

We enter the square just in time as the Lords arrive to enter the Campanile.

"Do you sense that man might be magic?" I ask.

"Probably another charlatan selling lies."

We run hand in hand along the Grand Canal, flipping up masks and sneaking kisses. As the laughter fades, night bobs us along in our gondola back toward Antonio's house, where I will lie in his arms and recount this evening, running in masks and counting stars.

"Not yet," I say as he prepares to push away from the dock. "Lie with me?"

Antonio ducks under our cover and lies with me on a bed of pillows. Sheltered from onlookers, we watch the sky twinkle and glow.

"The Milky Way. Such an odd name," I say. "I've never stopped to notice that crack in the sky." As if someone has torn the black cloth of night and revealed a cluster of gems underneath.

Antonio's eyes remain directly on me. "I already have the most beautiful view in the world right in my arms."

I kiss him. Feel his cheeks with my fingertips. "Promise we will always feel like this?"

"As signora wishes." He lays one soft kiss on my neck. For all the passion and heat that burns between us, this simple kiss breaks me. My limbs grow weak and my stomach flips like an overturned boat. The world seems to crash around our little gondola.

"You are everything, Antonio."

He wraps me in his arms. Somehow, lovemaking would ruin this moment, and he seems to understand that. Rocking together under the moonlight, sharing breath and skin, proves to be the most intimate moment I've ever felt.

Chapter Thirty-Three

February 10, 1609

Sleep has eluded me.

I trace the molding on the ceiling with my finger in the air and one closed eye. Antonio's hand slides across my abdomen. Suddenly, I understand Lucca's fear. By nightfall, I will stand beside my work that may never sell. My art may fail to inspire a single man in the room. "How am I to do this?"

Antonio mumbles into my shoulder, "Are you speaking to me?"

I prop up on my elbow. "I've never been this vulnerable before."

"This is your moment. Vulnerability looks good on you." His sleepy eyes make me want to tear into his body, but fear holds me in place like stone.

"I'm worried. Especially about Caterina." On the bed next to me, I fiddle with our golden egg, turning it in my fingers. "What if Lucca confessed to her? What if he turned on us?"

Antonio sits up, rubbing his sleepy eyes. "She wants power, Sofia. Once I hand her my business and my home, we are free to leave Venice, and your work will travel far and wide, just like your name."

"She despises me."

"Because she can never be you. One more night and she will no longer be a threat."

"Why must my dreams be forbidden?"

He spins the egg in my palm. "We stole this egg and made love in a mansion full of patricians. Everything we do is forbidden." His fingers glide down my neck and sternum, then slip under my shift. "Your vision is bold, and I want to love you for the rest of my days."

With a deep breath, I press into his touch. His palm grasps my breast and his mouth seeks my neck. With warm, soft lips, he explores my body.

I groan and part my knees as his fingertips tickle their way up my inner thigh. The flesh between my legs pulses, begging for his touch. Hungry, I press my pelvis toward his hand, but he grazes me with his finger, teasing me with a grin.

"I need you," I beg.

Just as his fingers slip inside me, a door flies open downstairs. Our mouths part and our bodies turn rigid. Before we can prepare, three men have broken into our bedchamber.

I tuck the egg under the mattress just as our door flies open.

All hands reach for Antonio. He punches one, but the other two restrain him, tie his hands behind his back, and one jams an elbow into his abdomen.

"Let him free."

"Wench," one spits.

As a courtesan, I demand respect. As Antonio's lover, I am merely a woman to be discarded and ignored. Unafraid to show myself in my shift, I stand and let their eyes gloss over me. "This man is my lover. What business do you have with him?"

"That's for the council to determine."

I reach for Antonio, but he shakes his head. "I'll be alright," he says. "Continue on with our plan. I will find a way back to you."

I nod and swallow the fear that grips me.

The men tear him away from me. My body two minutes ago, so hungry for him I could burst, now aches like a black tooth. I look out the window, hands pressed to the glass, choking back a sob.

"Do not fret." Caterina's voice once again ignites a fire I'd like to burn her with.

"He'll never give you his contacts now," I say.

"No, of course he won't." She slides inside the room, attempting to swing her hips. "I have bigger plans to undertake."

I can't imagine what her wicked mind has conjured. "You ugly, horrid woman."

She sighs as if she pities me. "The problem with beauty, you see, is it mesmerizes only until it leaves your body, stolen by age and the worry of life. Once you reach my age and realize men don't care for your looks, that frees you to use them for anything you wish."

"Where did they take him?"

"Oh, do not worry about that, Sofia. He will go before the council to pay for his lies and deceit."

"You profited from those lies, Caterina. And you made money on designs you stole from me."

A wild, feral look bubbles in her eyes. "Do you think you can become a great artist?" She forces a laugh. "You will die in prison for your passionate art. Or worse, in obscurity."

Oh, to know one's greatest fear and wield it like a blade. "What do you want?"

She swivels her hips like a young, impressionable girl, twirling her pearls around her finger. "I want more. Money, power, status. More of everything." She lifts the pearls to her mouth, then runs them along her teeth. "Lucca ruined his arm and you've been helping him sculpt. Now I have what I need to make a name for myself."

I knew I couldn't trust Lucca. My work is in her hands and Antonio is gone.

"Antonio, scoundrel that he is, has bedded half the women in the city looking for hidden artists. You did know this before falling in love with him, didn't you?" She tips her head sideways, feigning sympathy. "None of that matters now. His future involves ropes and screams."

I shudder at the thought of torture. We've all heard that such things happen in the hidden recesses under the Doge's Palace. I have no doubt the council would tear a man's limbs for one drop of power.

She trails her eyes down my torso, gasping with delight. "What a shame to waste such beauty on trust." She bites her teeth together. "I will miss staring at you, Sofia."

"You want only to feel my power over men, and you never will."

"I admit, I want to feel the softness of your skin. I also wish to kill you, devour your soul, and step into your body. Feel what you feel." She parts her lips, breathing in my scent.

"These powerful men tonight will not acknowledge you as anything other than Lucca's wife. They won't let you in the room as they view our art. You need me, the mistress, to sell these pieces."

She snarls at my mention of *our* art. "Your presence would help, yes. But I will perform this on my own. I do not need Lucca or you. Besides, the works speak for themselves. Especially the serpent and Lucca's favorite, the figure of you and Antonio."

"That's mine." Childish, I know, but I'm frantic. I don't know how to stop her.

"No, darling." She reaches for my hair. I lift my hand to slap her, but she shakes her head. A warning. "It is all mine. As of right now, you have nothing." She snaps twice and a line of men raid the studio, taking everything I've created.

"No."

"Don't fret, darling. I won't send you to prison. That is reserved for men like Antonio."

I wrap myself in a bedsheet, unable to tolerate her eyes on me. "Where will I go?"

The men grab me hard enough to bruise my arms. "You will begin your new life, Sofia." She waves the men to carry on. "Take her to the brothel."

Chapter Thirty-Four

I arrive at the steps of a brothel in the Rialto in nothing but my chemise, hair wild and arms bruised. Masked citizens watched these men drag me through the streets. I couldn't bring myself to stare back. Now I present to the matron of the house with only a layer of linen covering my bare, aching body.

"Throw her in," the woman yells.

After I stumble over the threshold, the unkempt matron slams the door. She places her hand on her hip and scowls so intensely, I wonder if she may bite. "The great Sofia Rossi here to earn me a few coins."

The nauseating air fills my nose, thick with sweat and wine, body odor and sex. Threadbare curtains dangle over the windows, accentuating the sickly yellow walls of peeled paint dusted in candle soot.

Matrons always eye the courtesans, waiting for the beautiful women to lose favor and offer their services to their houses of ill repute. "There are hundreds of prostitutes in this city. What do you want with me?"

She turns me to face a mirror. "Look at those big eyes and soft curls. Men will pay me a pretty lira for you."

I shut my eyes, ready to fall against the door, considering how fast I can run.

"Don't think of running away. The custodians know to watch for you. If you leave the district, you'll be whipped and returned to me, you understand?"

I've landed in hell. I can't stay here, but I force a nod. If my work has taught me anything, it's how to keep calm in an unsettling position.

The matron drags me through the entry, into a lounge where bare chested women in skirts straddle men with no teeth. No music, no art studios. No fine linens. Nothing here but used bodies and broken spirits.

"The girls will show you the way. Here." She throws an armful of clothing against me that smells of rotting mushrooms. "The yellow scarf must be worn when in public. Keep the breasts out when in the salon, and nothing shiny." She flicks my hair between her fingers, no doubt considering how much my locks could fetch.

I will not shed tears.

"I know your type. You've already considered how to build back your old life. You can't. Not now. You've been marked with the stink of this house." She laughs. The other girls join in though I'm not convinced they understand what they're laughing at.

"Lucca Armani owns me. He will want me to return to him."

"Ah, you don't know then." She steps close, her breath reeking of wine. "Signora Armani released you from your contract. To keep you from threatening her, signora placed you here. I was more than happy to oblige."

"You cannot keep me against my will."

"Yes, I can." She grabs hold of my sleeve and drags me upstairs to a dingy hallway, throwing me into a room no bigger than a wardrobe. "Get dressed. You start work now."

By the time she slams the door, I can barely breathe. This room smells of dust and sweat. Bloodstains splatter the floor. Antonio has been dragged away to prison for falsifying art documents, while I squander my time here, trading lire for a quick grope.

My mother would cry if she could see me now. From grace and beauty to a brothel in the Rialto. I now face the life that killed her.

I slide open the tattered curtain, but the view is only another wall with a crack of daylight. No escaping through here. I drop my clothes to the mattress on the floor. Lucca would never allow this if he knew.

Caterina still owns me. If I flee, she will have me arrested, and I may never again see Antonio. My mind runs through every possibility, but I see no way to escape the destiny I've tried to outrun.

I am but a body for the taking.

An hour passes while I pace and my airway tightens. Even if I manage to escape, where would I go?

The matron opens the door to find me undressed and unwashed, tears streaking my face.

"Dress."

"I won't do it."

She lifts me by the neck of my chemise, pulling my face toward hers. "You can deal with me, or you can face the men Caterina employs. Now just put on a skirt and spread your knees. You know how to do that."

I shove her away, though she's far stronger. "I don't belong here."

She slaps me hard enough to take my breath away. "Now you belong to me. Start earning your keep." She hands me a skirt and an open swath of fabric to drape around my shoulders.

Through tears and clenched teeth, I do as she demands. She motions to a bucket of water with a film floating on top. "Between clients wash yourself . . . down there."

The foul-smelling liquid is doused with vinegar to limit chances of pregnancy. I shudder to think what else floats in there.

"Even dirty, you're still the nicest thing here." She motions to the door. I leave my pathetic room with bare breasts and a stained skirt. The matron nudges me every time I pause to slow my frantic heart.

Once I arrive in the salon, all eyes turn to me. The women have stringy hair and deadened eyes. One bounces on a man's hips while scratching a rash on her neck. I swallow hard as two men toss women aside and approach me. "I want her," one says.

"I saw her first," the other man says with a nudge.

"She goes to the highest bidder," the matron says, hands out.

I look around at the dark brothel, considering an escape, knowing there is no possibility. The rest of the workers look on, unaffected by my labored, desperate breathing. The first man extends a hand to the matron, filled with coins. She shoves me into him, and his sneer is enough to make me faint. I'll bite his hand off if he dares touch me.

"Go on." She nods to the back hallway. This man wraps his greasy hand around my waist and nibbles on my neck like a rat. I pull away, but that only causes him to grunt and grip me tighter, considering my resistance a naughty game.

The matron points to her eye and then to me. "Close your eyes and pretend he is your lover," she yells. "It will be over before you know it."

The man is not bothered. He drags me into the farthest room and shuts the door. The window overlooks the canal, a flash of life just outside the glass. He approaches, baring his teeth. "You're a fine morsel. Come here."

I shove my hand into his chest. "If you touch me, you will regret it."

"I paid for you, and you will do as I want." He drops his breeches and wags his manhood in my direction. I'm so appalled that I heave. Pale bumpy skin covers a mound of belly.

He approaches me with hands in claws, open and ready to grab my breasts. "You must be mad," I say before he reaches for me. I'd sooner cut my hair at the crown than allow him to touch me. "Prison is preferable to this." I lift my knee and jam it into his crotch as he chokes on a scream. He falls to the floor, in all his naked putridness. "I am not property, and your hands will never touch these glorious breasts."

He growls, reaching for my leg. I kick him away, but still fall to the floor. He crawls to me, managing to bite my ankle. I stifle a scream, knowing that could send the matron running.

I reach to the bedside, searching for anything solid. Just as the man slides his hand up my leg, I thwack his forehead with a brass candleholder.

His eyes seem to spin, then he collapses in an unmoving heap at my feet.

I have one chance to flee. One heartbeat skip later, and I've thrown myself further into danger. All I can do now is run.

Chapter Thirty-Five

Somehow, magically, we bounced safely out of St. Mark's Square in the tourist bustle and now find ourselves squeezed into a merchant's street that sells everything from gaudy jewelry to authentic, shining diamonds. Every other store sells Venetian glass and trinkets with Carnival masks dangling from the window displays.

"Perfect," I say, suddenly aware of the potential.

Once we emerge from the store, we now wear black capes and matching gold and purple masks, the likes of which I've never seen. The owner gave us a history of mask making, called *mascherari*, and encouraged us to do as Venetians always have during Carnival: live the world of the upside down, play a part, and enjoy Venice under cover.

Though Carnival is still a week away, many tourists and artists have begun wearing the costumes, so we will blend right in.

"This street has been here for hundreds of years," I say. "Imagine if any of our cast of characters walked this street and frequented these stores." I look up. "Perhaps Sofia stood here, admiring the blue marble of that sundial clock just as I am now, inhaling Middle Eastern spices."

A policeman approaches under the arch of the clock. Noah turns me to walk the other way. "No time to pontificate." He powers off his phone with a sigh. "We're on our own now."

"Haven't we always been?"

The woman with the sleek bob, dark sunglasses, and deep red lipstick pushes her way through the crowd, heading straight for us.

"Don't react," I mutter. "I bet she can smell fear."

The woman nears, a big brute of a man trailing her every step. My heart leaps to my throat, but she shoves past us, confused by all the costumes and masks floating around.

We move with the tourists, pressed shoulder to shoulder.

"What now?" Noah asks.

Perhaps the upside down of a Carnival mask does inspire one to live the part of who you aren't. Without hesitation, I grab Noah's hand and drag him down an alley, intent on one thing.

"Where are we going?" he asks.

"Back to the archives."

~

Once inside the familiar lobby, it takes no effort at all to summon the character I pretend to play. The fearless courtesan who owns this town.

"We're here to see Paolo."

The guard's face twists into confusion. "Who are you?"

I lift my mask so only he can see. "Dr. Mia Harding and Dr. Noah Beckett. You still have our identification. We got swept up in the new Armani statue earlier."

"Ah, yes. I remember." He stares at our costumes, concern rising in his eyes.

"We're still tourists," I say with a laugh.

"No masks in the archives."

"Of course." We remove the masks but keep our hoods on. This satisfies him, and he allows us to pass.

We know the way to Paolo's office and try not to run. Those documents once again whisper to me, seeming to coax me to their secrets. So many hidden stories to discover. How does one researcher choose from all the history we've never been told?

Noah bursts through Paolo's door. "We're here. We need . . ." He glances at me. "Mia, what's our plan exactly?"

I step inside and lower my hood. "We don't have much time before they come for us. I need everything you think is significant on the Armanis, Antonio, and Sofia Rossi."

Paulo removes his glasses in one swift motion. "Who the hell is Sofia Rossi?"

I slam my hands on his table. "She's the courtesan with all the answers that none of you cared to look for."

He reaches into a cabinet for a giant binder. "This is everything I have." We scan the documents, looking for anything that jumps out. Paolo bites his nails, watching us and the door equally.

"Don't just sit there. Get me a list. Cross check Sofia Rossi and Lucca Armani. See what you find."

Paolo feverishly types on his computer, scrolling the maze that is their online database.

Noah turns the last page of Paolo's binder. "This is nothing new."

"Information is out here. I know it is." I drag my trembling finger down each document, desperate to find something that will take us to the next level of discovery. "Wait, what?" My chest tightens, grabbed with the hooks of a tremendous find. I look up at the men. "The man who took over Armani's palazzo after he disappeared was Lord Marco."

"Yes," Paolo says, "an eccentric patrician. Avid art collector."

"He was Sofia Rossi's benefactor."

"This woman you speak of, she was a courtesan?" Paolo pulls the list of courtesans. "1604 to 1610 records were lost in a fire. Ah, here. One mention in 1603. That's all I have on her."

I clasp my hands together at my chin, weaving my fingers together and squeezing until they ache. "Okay, Paolo, I'm going to hit you with information. You won't want to believe it, but we have no time, and we need help, so shut up and listen."

He nods, presumably terrified I will reveal his bribery secret and probably deep down also ignited with the idea of a rare find.

"Sofia Rossi left Lord Marco and went to work for the Armanis as Lucca's courtesan. Sofia was an artist. She helped Lucca sculpt, and maybe even created these pieces. Meanwhile, she fell in love with Antonio Bruni, the art dealer. He went to prison, possibly for her. They all fell apart, died, or disappeared on February 10, 1609, during Carnival, and now we need to find out where Caterina was in all this and what happened to Sofia." I take a breath as my head swims with more questions than answers.

Noah slams the table next to me. He's playing tough cop. That's cute.

Paolo blinks slowly. "A courtesan carved *The Estasi*?" His voice wiggles at the end like a loose piano key.

"Signs point to yes." I drop my anxiety for just a moment. "We're onto something."

He ponders. "Rumors have been flying that you're angry. All these men will blame your unstable womanly emotions."

"What else is new? I still need proof."

He uncrosses his arms. "My daughter is smart. A math genius. The boys in school sabotaged her work. That's why I took the bribe. She deserves to attend university, even with everything against her."

I exhale, feeling as though we finally have someone in this country on our side. "So, you'll help?"

He begins typing again, glancing at the screen that shows the camera at the front of the archives. "They've offered a reward for you two, and no doubt someone here has already called them. We don't have much time."

We pace and wait.

"Lord Marco took over the Armani household?" I say. "It's too much of a coincidence." The clock ticks from the wall, every second marking a bigger risk.

"Oh." Paolo leans back in his chair, eyes glued to the computer screen. His voice drops an octave. "Oh."

"What is it?" My pulse thumps in my fingertips.

"Antonio Bruni was charged with fraud. The paperwork is faded, but he was accused of selling art under false pretenses. Defrauding the patricians of Venice."

"False pretenses?" I shove Paolo aside and begin to type, scroll, and click as fast as my cramping hands will allow. I've used this antiquated system that organizes documents for years. "You really should update this," I mutter.

Paolo shrugs. "Money, money, money."

I speed read the screen. "Falsify. What do they mean? Was the art not real?"

"Uh, Dr. Harding?" Paolo's voice squeaks. "You have about three minutes to find out."

I don't turn away, but Noah touches my arm. "That woman is outside with several policemen. Your boss is here too. They're all working together now to take you down."

"Shit. Come on, Sofia." I summon her from these ancient records. "Give me something."

Paolo stands at his door, watching the long hallway. "Hurry."

I read pertinent words aloud. "Art dealer. Fraudulent." I halt and lean in to read a passage again that reveals the details of his lies. "Bingo."

"What did you find?" Noah asks.

"Antonio robbed Peter to pay Paul. He sold pieces to patricians, claiming they were made by famous artists."

"Who made them?" Noah asks.

I look up with a smile. "Women artists who couldn't claim their work. Antonio falsified male names so the rich would buy them. Holy hell, this is real."

"Dr. Harding?" Paolo's eyes grow wide. "They're inside the archives."

"Okay. One minute." I keep typing, going back to the search

bar to enter keywords with confusing phrases only those who understand this system would know. Like typing in HTML.

"You only have about thirty seconds before they burst in here." Paolo peeks around the corner.

"Okay, okay." Scroll, look for the highlights. "There! There it is." I email my findings to Paolo and grab my bag just as thundering feet approach.

Paolo points to the door to the document room. "Down the far-right aisle. A doorway leads to a stairwell. From the roof, you'll take the fire escape down."

"Thank you." I attempt a smile, but adrenaline courses through my body and lights movement into my feet.

Paolo whispers, "Go," then shuts the door and knocks into the group, apologizing profusely in Italian. From the window into his office, I lock eyes with Dr. Wright before dashing toward the door. We make it up the stairs and onto the rooftop in the blink of an eye, scrambling over the orange-tiled roofs and sliding down to a metal landing with a thud.

We climb down the escape and land next to the canal, our feet no sooner hitting the ground than we take off in a sprint.

"What did you find?" Noah gasps out between heaving breaths.

"No time." I look all directions and somehow know exactly how to get where I'm going. "We're heading back to our hotel."

"They're waiting for us to return. Why would we go back?"

I brace myself, hands to my knees. "Because that building was once a palazzo that belonged to an eccentric art-loving patrician."

Awareness lights his face. "Our hotel was once Lord Marco's palazzo? Where Sofia Rossi lived for years?"

"Yep." My voice lightens, like life has returned. "And the current owner handed over quite the collection of documents."

We duck under a bridge and lean against the cool, shaded concrete.

"I can't believe that's what you discovered in two minutes," he says.

"Oh no, I found that looking over Paolo's shoulder. Right about now, Paolo will be opening an email with an even more intriguing find."

He dips his chin, eyes wide. "Which is?"

"Multiple artifacts were uncovered from Lord Marco's home during hotel renovations. Most ended up in museums, but there was one document that went unnoticed."

His lips part in anticipation. "What did this document say?"

I lean in, my palms resting on either side of his neck. "In the detailed log of his art collection, he included a note about a piece he pined for but couldn't have. A sculpture of his beautiful courtesan and her lover in flagrante. He called it *The Lovers*."

"No researchers knew *The Estasi* at one time held a second face. They wouldn't know *The Lovers* was actually the most photographed art piece in the world."

Heat grows in my belly. "We only know it's Sofia and Antonio because of that drawing in the prison cell, and no one knew his courtesan moved on to Lucca Armani after him. Of course no one noticed the importance of that document. No one cared to remember Sofia Rossi, but she is the center to this entire story."

He grabs my hands, holding them at his chest. "Wait, so Marco wanted *The Estasi*? How did he know about it?"

I soften into the thrill of the moment. I wish I could bottle this and bathe in it whenever I wanted. A bit of information from the paperwork was so juicy that I kept it to myself until we were alone. "Lord Marco's lover was Caterina Armani."

Chapter Thirty-Six

The window is easy to climb through, but the ledge below is only wide enough to fit the tip of my shoes. Well, the man's shoes. Stealing his clothes was the only way to escape the Rialto at night.

Dressed as a common butcher—I can smell the raw meat—with my hair tucked inside a flat cap, I maneuver along the razor-thin ledge above the canal. With only the wall to pat my hands along, my feet begin to cramp in these too large shoes. A splash in the murky water of the canal would send the guards running.

The cool February night is anything but calm. Between Carnival celebrations and the workers returning home for the evening, this side of town erupts in chaotic rumbles even in the dark.

Just as I near an iron gate, the man I smashed with a candlestick begins to moan loud enough to wake the dead. I keep sliding my feet, though the heels bounce off with every shuffle. The man's moans turn to cries. The matron shoves her face through the open window, shaking her fist and screaming for the custodians.

So close. As my feet cramp and thighs shake, I extend my hand toward the rail. The ledge has ended, but my fingertips barely graze the iron. I shift to the outside of my foot as the skin on my palm stretches to a tearing ache.

My left foot slips.

As I tumble, I grab the rail with both hands. Both feet dangle in the water, which pulls the shoes from my feet. Just as well.

I manage to grab hold of a worn stone with my toes and lift my torso. The matron is now in front of the brothel, screaming for help. I roll my body over the iron fencing onto the walkway. No time to catch my breath as the guards have spotted me. Barefoot, I run over stone pathways, between brothels and along canals.

My feet could be bleeding, and I wouldn't know. I'm so focused on escaping the Castelletto and the matron's clutches, my body turns into an unfeeling instrument meant to flee. Heading west toward San Marco, ducking into *calli* so narrow my shoulders graze the buildings on either side. One man has trailed my path and gains ground, matching me stride for stride through the winding streets of the Rialto.

Screams will do nothing but bring attention and slow me down.

With my gaze set on the wide-open space of the quay between Castello and San Marco, I quicken my speed. The man launches for me, grazing my back. This causes me to stumble to my hands, tangled up by these overly large clothes. I jump up, excess fabric from the breeches balled in my fist.

The custodian grabs me but I duck, leaving my hat in his hand. My hair trails down my back, a mass of wild black curls certain to identify me among a crowd. I run across the cold stones, the man's stolen clothes hanging from my limbs, but I run toward the crowds, over bridges and behind vendors until I finally reach Piazza San Marco.

Women tower under black capes, teetering on their chopines. I hate those lifts and much prefer to cut my bare feet on jagged stones than teeter on those unnatural things. The second custodian catches up with the first, barreling toward me, undeterred by my speed. I split apart two tall women, tipping one over onto a Furlana dancer, clad in a bright saffron skirt, with red roses dotting her hair.

This causes a commotion, so I slide behind a magic lantern. A decorative box that projects light and images similar to Signore Galilei's telescope. A mother holds her young son up to view the landscape, thankfully hiding me behind her layered skirts. I peek out from behind the folds as the custodians throw up their hands. They'll never find me in a sea of costumes. A momentary relief.

The mother notices and swats me away. A woman dressed as a man without shoes would certainly welcome the authorities. A cape hangs on a hook as the owner is dragged along the square by his companion dancer. I slip it off the hook, cover my body and head, and walk, head down, past a mask maker's stall. With one quick swipe, a white Bauta mask is in my hands and under my cape. Chosen from the others for its ability to conceal who is underneath. Another slip of my hand steals a veil of woven lace and a tricorn hat.

I have one day, possibly only a few hours, to rescue Antonio and stop Caterina, so thieving seems a necessary risk. Nothing matters more than helping him escape. Covered in black from head to barefoot toe, I once again find myself in Piazza San Marco, my eye on one target.

The palace.

Chapter Thirty-Seven

Back at our hotel, we're careful to avoid any sign of Dr. Wright or our favorite stalker, Lipstick Lady. Because of the proximity to the Doge's Palace, we aren't the only ones trying out Carnival masks, buying us time to make our next move.

"What an incestuous little group they were," Noah says.

"Draw a line from sex to art, and you'll find a short, twisted web of scandal."

The hotel owner lives in an apartment on the top floor with its own access from the alley, so we sit on a stone bench near the café, eyeing the staircase for any sign. We may only have days or hours to make this discovery before everything implodes.

Noah reads through an Italian newspaper discussing the discovery of the serpent statue. "I thought Venice was sinking. Now there are all these dried canals."

"Global warming doesn't just cause rising sea levels. The unusual heat wave and exceptionally low tides have rattled the delicate waterways. Then you add in prolonged high pressure in the Mediterranean, and the smaller canals take the first hit. Bad for the environment, great for unearthing treasures."

He stares at me, head tilted. "You're a little bit genius, aren't you?"

"I'm just a girl who likes to read." And I have to occupy silent nights somehow.

"And solve riddles." He flashes that glowing smile. "Tell me what you think is going on here."

"Besides the obvious?" We shade our faces when three Italians meander past a little too slowly for my liking. Once they're out of earshot, I lean close and drop my voice to a whisper. "Lucca's art would have been highly coveted. I imagine Caterina wanted her husband working, and she probably bullied the man into producing new commissions."

"Was Sofia a willing participant?"

"I think so. She would have had her hand in everything he made. Maybe sculpting his works in secret." Even now, when a statue appears, the world attributes it to a man without a second thought.

"Then Caterina disappeared." He scratches his temple underneath the cape.

"According to records, she was demanding and very involved in the social scene." I rub my palms together, imagining every piece of information tacked to a giant corkboard with strings between timelines, color coded by person. "One of them was responsible for this theater held on February 10. I bet Caterina was involved."

Noah slides his hand over to mine. "Impressive."

"It's just a theory, isn't it? I mean, my intuition is good, but I can't speak to the dead. I don't really know anything."

"There's an intangible thing with art," he says. "Something mystic and deep, like the piece holds intention in its being. If we can feel the creator's emotions, why can't we feel who they are? You look at *The Estasi* and feel something so strongly you're willing to risk your career for her."

"Yeah." Tears spring to my eyes for some damn reason. *Get it together, Mia.*

Noah's gentle tug at a smile causes me to inhale, sniff, and wipe away my tear-streaked cheeks.

"Someone's home." I grab Noah's hand and cut off whatever he's about to say. I run after a woman I assume is the hotel owner, in a slip dress and sandals.

"*Scusi*," Noah says. We remove our masks and hoods.

She drops her glasses to examine us. "Dr. Harding and friend. Hello."

"Dr. Beckett," Noah says with an awkward grimace.

She knows who we are. Of course she does. Word of the stalled authentication has made it to Italian news. No doubt with the blame squarely on me. "Would you speak with us about what you've found here during renovations?" I ask.

She holds her sunglasses between two fingers, rolling the frames between her thumb and forefinger. "Yes."

That was easier than anticipated.

"My name is Eva. Please, come in." She extends her hand to welcome us inside.

Her golden hair reminds me of a Barbie I once coveted. A girl at school played with the doll on the bus, and I imagined if sunshine had a smell, that doll's hair would be like solar perfume. Eva seems to move with such confidence, she puts me right at ease.

Eva glides past us into one full floor of the hotel, out to her balcony that overlooks the Grand Canal. The iced tea she serves in blown glass tumblers tastes of lemon and elegance.

"You know by now that this hotel once housed Lord Marco?" she asks.

The covered terrace is decorated like a lifestyle spread in a magazine. Moroccan lanterns and silver statues. Not a speck of Italian design. This woman makes her own rules.

"We've discovered that just today," I say between gulps. "Can you tell me more about Marco?"

"Marco Farina was an unusual man. He refused his last name and shunned his family, going only by Lord Marco, though he was nothing of the sort." She crosses her legs and evaluates our attention. "I did extensive research on the man when I inherited this property from my grandparents. He kept a log of art pieces and acquisitions, rating them with his own little scale of importance."

"He sounds eccentric," I say, still sizing her up.

Eva lights a cigarette, quite amused. "You don't believe *The Estasi* is an Armani original. Neither do I."

Despite my best efforts to remain cool and collected, I end up releasing a gasp of excitement. "Who do you think sculpted her?"

"I have a theory."

Noah spins his tumbler in a circle, the condensation dripping over his thumb. "You handed over artifacts. Did you know *The Estasi* was listed on that log as his most coveted piece?"

Eva smirks, pulling her perfectly pink cheeks taut. "Though then it was called *The Lovers*."

Noah leans forward almost in perfect timing with me. We glance at each other then back to Eva, secretly sharing a thrill that someone else knows the real name of the statue. "Why didn't you tell the researchers that?" I ask. She's either scheming her own way through this, or she's just like us.

"I did." Her words are sharp, spoken with the precision of a ballet dancer's lines. "Listen, you're dealing with the most hated family in Venice. They have friends in *polizia* and bribe and thieve their way toward power. And they usually get it."

"But not with you?" I ask.

"I have plenty of money, Dr. Harding." She sucks a drag on her cigarette without even an eye twitch. "They buy researchers. Direct them to eliminate anything that leads them from Armani."

"Why?"

"Because the truth only gets in their way. They want this groundbreaking excavation to move forward without any holdup."

I throw my hands up and scratch my fingers through my hair. "Why do they care so much? Why don't they want the truth?"

"Oh, Dr. Harding. That would ruin their plans. Truth is the enemy of fragile power."

She's sizing me up. Now, I trust her. "What do you know?"

She stubs out her cigarette in a cement ashtray. "Come with me."

In her kitchen she slips on a pair of flats and opens a door to a stairwell. We follow her into what I can only assume is the basement three floors down and ripe with the scent of mold. We step into a dark but cavernous space, a walkway crossing through a reflective pool of lagoon water.

"Much of his prized possessions were found here," Eva says. "Before the rising tides flooded our buildings. Poor Venezia may sink in my lifetime."

"It's hauntingly pretty," Noah says, watching the water undulate against the walls.

"I think so too." Eva points to a wall. "Do you notice there is light in here?"

"Yes." I suddenly realize there are no windows, yet we can see. I follow the source to notice a strip of leaking light where the wall meets the ceiling next to the stairwell.

"Very good." Eva pulls a notch in the tile, where a fairly large door opens that is impossible to see when closed, as the edges appear to line up with the grout of limestone tiles. "Come."

Noah places his hand on my low back, a subtle reassurance as we move to a hidden compartment in the basement of a once famous palazzo with a woman we just met. We step inside a large room removed from the basement and elevated from the gathering water.

Eva crosses her arms. "I have not told anyone about this space. The less the authorities know, the better." She glances at the high, narrow window at street level.

"What did you find here?" Noah asks.

"The rarest pieces from his collection. I handed them over, but here is one I still protect."

Exhilaration powers through me. The surge of a theory about to rise from the depths of history and prove itself at the hands of two secretive women and one adorable Englishman.

"They need *The Estasi* to be Armani. Why?" she asks us.

My mind goes blank. "I can't seem to figure that out."

"That is because you aren't thinking like a thief. Go on."

"Um." I sense the scramble in my brain as words and ideas bounce around, trying to find the light. "They need proof that more Armanis are buried around Italy."

"Yes. Why?"

I shake off the cobwebs of insecurity. "Okay, they want more artifacts so they can steal them."

She sighs. "Close. You're missing something."

"I know that. If I had all the answers, I wouldn't be in this flooded basement with you."

Noah rubs his cheek, scratching his palm over his stubble. "They don't want the artifact; they want the excavations."

"Ah, yes, Dr. Beckett."

A bubble of acknowledgment bursts inside my chest. "If the government initiates searches in Venice, Tuscany, and Verona, this family can have access to everything."

A grin of satisfaction appears on Eva's shining face. "Think. How would they fight historians like you who follow protocol and care about truth?"

I bend and place my hands onto my knees. My breaths shorten. And then, like a slap, it hits me. "Oh god, this isn't about *The Estasi* at all. It's about future digs on protected sites. They plant thieves to pilfer artifacts." Awareness blooms in my chest. "They'll sell them on the black market before proper authorities even know they exist."

Eva smiles, her slow exhale exuding relief that someone other than her understands the stakes. "Whoever sculpted the woman of *The Estasi* left us a clue." She points to a chest, dented and faded with time. Its contents seem to thump against the inside like a heartbeat, begging to be set free.

We hover over the large metal box. Eva opens the lid and carefully unrolls a large canvas, also faded and caked with grime. But behind the dirt and remnants of four hundred forgotten years rests a beautiful picture. I want to cry when I see her face. "That's Sofia Rossi," I say.

"Who is she?" Eva holds up the painting. A woman with blood dripping from her bared teeth, furious after slicing a man's neck in half. Eva points to the lower corner. *SR*.

I hover my hand over the painting, too afraid to leave the oils from my skin on Sofia's surviving work. Anger. Rage. Bloody teeth. This is nothing like the work of the time. This is sheer bravery.

"Sofia Rossi was Marco's courtesan," I tell Eva. "He sold her to Lucca Armani."

Her eyes grow large magically without even a hint of a wrinkle on her forehead. "This courtesan was a brilliant painter." Eva turns over the painting. "Here, she left a suggested title. *The Vengeful Maiden*."

All I can think of is how to preserve this incredible piece of history. "Eva, why are you keeping this in the basement that floods with the tides?"

"I have no choice." She lifts her hand, palm up to the sky. An Italian identifier if there ever was one. "They've raided my house. They own the banks. This is the safest place I can think of."

"And you've waited for someone who will listen."

We all stare down at the canvas.

"A watertight box in this secret room is the best I could do." Eva's pocket buzzes and she lifts her phone to examine the alert.

"Noah, this is huge. We have to report this. It would prove everything. Sofia Rossi. SR. Right there. Our theory is right."

"And we could stop an entire network of art thieves before they pilfer even more history from all over Italy."

On instinct, I kiss him. Firm and passionate, like we're magnetized. "This is it, Noah. We did it."

Eva clicks the lid shut.

"You can't keep this, Eva. We can stop them all if we just get this to the media."

She clears her throat. "It's too late."

"What do you mean? They're all waiting on me, and I'll shout from the rooftops that the artist responsible for the most photographed sculpture in the world is not a man, but a woman who presumably lived so fiercely that history tried to bury her memory." Tears prickle my eyes. "They messed up. They couldn't erase her. This painting is proof that she is real, and I am not wrong."

Eva flashes her phone. I grab it to read a headline:

DIFFICULT RESEARCHER DR. MIA HARDING FINALLY AUTHENTICATES ARMANI STATUE. APOLOGY ISSUED FOR STOLEN ARTIFACTS AND UNNECESSARY CHASE THROUGH VENICE.

"What the hell?" I scan the article that confirms the research indicating Lucca Armani sculpted *The Estasi*, and hypothesizing *The Serpent* was another buried work of his. All this is followed by an apology, citing a stolen ring and cameo pendant to cover my debts to Dr. Wright.

Noah reads over my shoulder. "'I take full responsibility for my actions and will step away from my position as lead researcher. I will then hand myself over to the Italian police. I've been a disgrace to the art world and to Lucca Armani.'" He pauses to swallow. "'We must initiate a full-scale excavation to discover the vast world of missing Armani art.'"

Sickness rolls through me. "I would never say that." We're standing on proof of an earth-shattering, life-altering find that would rock the art world for the better, and I can't do a damn thing.

"This isn't the first time I've been in the path of the Italian Mafia," Eva says. "I have one more thing to show you."

She reaches into the box and comes up with a faded paper inside plastic laminate.

"What are we looking at?" Noah asks.

"That is the other artifact I kept for myself, knowing that someday, someone would arrive to help me use it."

I examine the drawn shapes of X's. "It's a nonsensical map."

"Ah, map yes. Nonsensical, no. Not for the leading researcher in her field."

"They look like riddles," I say, noting what I assume to be Eva's translations. "*Polizia* will hunt me down any minute, Eva. I can't decipher a map from some patrician who deemed himself a lord and hid statues in his basement."

Noah grabs my shoulder. "Mia, this is our last chance. If we don't find proof, we'll both end up in prison, and all these lies will persist forever."

It's impossible. There's no time, and it might lead to a dead end. But Noah stares at me with his hopeful eyes, and I remember, this is all we have. "Fine. Do you think this will lead us to the other half of *The Estasi*?"

"Yes," she says. "And they start here, at the only thing I can make out on that map." Her finger jabs the plastic at a location we all recognize.

Against my racing heart and tightened chest, I manage to say, "The Doge's Palace."

Chapter Thirty-Eight

Doge's Palace, Three Hours Until the Banquet

Hovering two stories over the canal, the Bridge of Sighs connects the palace courtroom to the prisons. Its thick white walls and iron bars hide the view of prisoners. Truthfully, I have never once thought about the people who might walk that bridge. Until today.

With mere hours before Caterina holds a secret banquet with stolen art, time and desperation have forced me to consider the impossible. I must break into the prison and rescue Antonio.

Barefoot on the ancient walkway of the Ponte della Paglia, as the sunbaked limestone warms the soles of my feet, I stare down the serene canal. One woman against an entire prison. *I am strong*, I remind myself. *Capable and cunning. Will that be enough?*

I'm about to find out.

With my artist's eye, I trace the outline like a map. Palace on the left. Prisons on the right. Three stories with multiple entrances, staircases, and arcades that snake through every corner of the square. Rooftops with walkways and windows with open quatrefoils. Antonio could be in either. Interrogated in the palace or left to rot in the wells.

Carnival is my one protector. We are now in the devilish madness of theater, all with our own characters to play. A perfect opportunity to remain invisible.

The women of the night stroll past me, a sea of gondolas bobbing behind us. Each character appears worse than the last. The blanket mask covers a woman head to toe, slipped open only for a sliver of vision, hidden for the sin of fornication. Or the Moretta mask—the mute servant—a black velvet circle held in place by a button in the mouth to keep the woman's hair flowing gold around her shoulders while stifling her voice.

Mocked and shunned. A reminder of my punishments should they catch me.

I tighten my Bauta mask and set my sights on stealing shoes from the cobbler before entering the palace. The *calegheri*'s stall sits in the eastern corner of the square, near the brass flagpole. The flag of Saint Mark whips in the breeze as I consider my options. Nothing but chopines! How I'd imagine a whale's tooth would look braced to the sole of some poor woman. I'd rather take my chances with naked toes. Until I remember stories from Lord Marco of the wells—the lower cells of the prison where men swam in frigid lagoon water full of giant sea rats.

I shudder that image away and weave through the masses, having eyed the best entrance to the palace. Masked citizens linger on the loggia, peering through railings of pointed arches, laughing at the theater below.

Through the space between the basilica and the corner of the rectangle palace, I join dancers through the tunnel and through the ceremonial archway of Istrian stone and red Verona marble that appears more like a silk gown than a building. At the foot of the Giants' Staircase, the lowering sun blasts the steps with light.

Buildings with lace-like stone and pilfered treasures are as false as the façades of pink mosaic that line the waterfront. We live in a world of lies.

I lift my robe, risking the reveal of my bare feet, determined to pass unnoticed between the statues of Poseidon and Mars, naked men whose figures I could mold in the dark. On the loggia floor arcade, I casually pull on every door and peer in every window. Most are dark and locked. I slow my pace and lift my chin when another hooded figure passes, emulating the confidence of a man at home on these patterned stones.

I follow a servant through an opening, up another staircase with a gilded ceiling bright as a smile full of gold teeth. As I leave the protection of the loggia, my heartbeat quickens so much my breath quivers against my lips. The servant nods, assuming that I belong, and motions me ahead as we turn toward the next staircase.

I bend my knees to hide my toes and force myself not to gawk at the gilded panels above me. The moldings and structures have details of such control and beauty, it's as if the paintings were dipped in a vat of magic, doused in pure melted gold, and flung through a dream before landing on the majestic, curved ceilings.

Men, some masked and some scowling, glance up as we enter the most elaborate room I have ever seen. Fine detailing more glorious than any bedchamber and golden panels that glitter brighter than all the platters of every dining room in Venice.

I lower my voice and tell the servant, "I'm looking for a prisoner."

She glances around, eyes narrowed. "The council doesn't want visitors. Leave now, before they throw you in prison with your friend." She motions to a closed door. "The most powerful men in the city rule from that chamber right there."

"Where do they interrogate?"

"I could be killed for telling you that." She squints, briefly glancing over her shoulder. "Who are you?"

I lift my mask just enough for her to look into my eyes. "Have you ever been in love?" I ask.

"Once." She nods. "I was once."

"Would you have lied and thieved your way to save him?"

She considers this. "No."

"Then you haven't been in love."

She examines my face now that the antechamber has cleared. She considers me. "I can't help you."

I place the mask back on when a door clicks open. This girl requires a different approach. "There is a reason these frescoes depict women as godly creatures who must be protected."

"Why is that?" She smooths her hair against her scalp.

"If men didn't protect us poor little things, we would rule them like the feral lions we are." She cracks a smile. I lift her chin to gaze up at my white, linear mask. "We are not theirs, even when laws say we are."

"Your lover, he is the man who sold falsified art to patricians?"

"Yes," I say, working hard to control my excitement. "Antonio Bruni."

She sighs, then holds her empty basket in front of her. "I serve one of the members that live here."

"One of the secret Council of Ten? That's an important position."

"Follow me. And don't let anyone see your hair."

I trail behind her, feigning confidence. We slip through a door in the antechamber, down a long, wood paneled hallway, down a staircase, and through a winding tunnel of darkened corners.

"Stay here."

"In the dark tunnel?" Anything could await us on the other side.

"Yes." She disappears, but a few minutes later opens the door with a pair of court shoes in her hands. "You will not fool anyone with those elegant feet."

"Thank you." I slip them on, grateful for the warmth around my toes.

"Now, to the east wing." Once again, I follow her through hallways of gold light until we arrive at a square atrium decorated with paintings of mythological creatures.

"How do you work around these paintings every day and not swoon?"

"Oh, these?" She looks at the paintings. "I never notice them. Now, listen carefully." She pulls me close by the fabric of my hood. "Inside is a chamber of the three magistrates. In the corner is a wooden cabinet, glossy and large. It is actually a door to the stairwell that leads to the torture chambers."

"Torture?" I gasp.

"Yes. They string them up by a rope with their hands behind their back. Last I heard, they were holding your man near the pulley." She twists her hands as if wringing a towel. "They rip their joints apart to bleed the secrets."

My face flushes hot. I envisioned flirting with a guard to release Antonio, not storming the palace through secret passageways to prevent him being torn into pieces. "How am I to sneak past one of the secret council members?"

"That is for you to find out. Though you better move swiftly." She points out the window to the courtyard. "They're on their way here now."

I inhale, unsure if I should run away while I still can.

The girl straightens. "No one looks at me." She forces her head high. "Thank you, signora." She disappears without another word.

I click the door open to find a quiet, still room. Black and white tiles make the floor appear to move, while the statues of maidens flanking the fireplace cast their disapproval. Yet another gold rimmed fresco takes my breath away, but I force myself to paw at the cabinet, looking for an opening. No handle.

Muffled voices appear outside the door. After a nervous whip of my head to the entrance, I slide my hands frantically over the curved edges. The door opens as men's voices bellow through the chamber. I find the seam, dig my fingernails in, and open the door through a cramping hand.

The men are deep in discussion, and step into the chamber just as I slip into the narrow doorway and shut it. Not before I can sneak a glance.

Three are patricians who have disappeared from the city entirely. No surprise that they are the special three who live here, protecting their fragile identity as traitors to humanity. But the fourth, he laughs nervously, eager to please the trio.

Through the crack of light, I see him. Lord Marco.

Chapter Thirty-Nine

One day later, by late in the afternoon, the sun hovers low in the sky, lighting St. Mark's Square with a glistening burst of saffron light. Eva bought us a change of clothes and hats, so we blend in seamlessly with tourists as they meander through the courtyard of the Doge's Palace.

With the document tucked in the folds of a tourist pamphlet, we orient ourselves. Facing north toward the basilica, we examine the seemingly useless map. The Grand Canal laps behind us carrying taxis and gondolas onto the bustling dock.

"I can't believe my entire future rests on solving some homemade seventeenth century riddle." My heart thumps against my throat. "Eva, what can you tell me?"

"I'm only certain that this X is the Palazzo Ducale." She points to the winged lion offset between the three markers. "Marco's registry of his collection uses a winged lion to denote the pieces taken as castoffs from the palace."

"Okay, good." Not good at all, as this map makes no damn sense. I wonder how long I can feign confidence before I explode, but Noah presses his torso to my shoulder as he examines the map.

"So, the riddles explain where each of the marks are in the city?" he asks.

"I think so." Eva translates. "Three X's, and this first riddle asks the reader to choose between the three. 'A treasure of gold as you wish. One of luster as you have earned, and of metal and all you hold dear.'"

Noah runs his thumb along the corner of the plastic cover. "Gold as you wish. He wanted *The Estasi*. Maybe gold was the Armani Garden?"

"Why does this riddle sound familiar?" I scour my mind for what stands out, before my neck snaps back. "Oh."

"What is it?" Noah asks.

"You don't see it?" He shakes his head. "Lord Marco is quoting Shakespeare. Poorly, I might add."

Noah grimaces.

"How did I recognize a reference to the Bard before a proper Englishman?"

"I am a traitor to my kind." Noah bows.

"It's from *The Merchant of Venice*."

"Apropos," Noah says. "The suitor must choose between caskets of gold, silver, and lead."

"Would Lord Marco have read Shakespeare?" Eva asks.

"*The Merchant of Venice* was published around, what, 1600?" I ask. "Plenty of Englishmen traveled here. He could have heard the riddle and used it by memory, changing gold, silver, and lead to gold, luster, and metal. This entire palace is dipped in gold." I note the presence of lingering policemen through the archway toward the basilica, a subtle yet unmissable presence.

We follow Eva up what she terms the "Giants' Staircase" between statues of Mars and Neptune, to the loggia and through a set of heavy doors. As we weave through the palace, Eva must stop us from gaping at the wall murals, the gilded ceilings, and the art on display at every corner.

"Focus," she says. "Sightseeing comes after we find our treasures."

"What are we looking for?" I ask Noah, but he only shrugs.

Eva dips her head, her eyes level with mine. "This is the treasury. Two books detailing the lives of nobility were kept here, the gold and silver."

Now that perks me up. "Gold and silver?"

"Yes. That's as far as I've ever taken the riddle."

"The answer to Shakespeare's riddle was lead, so we're looking for a lead book?" With no answers in sight, Noah gathers our trio in the corner.

"Eva, it has to be something else." I look around the room, knowing we're wasting time.

She shrugs. "If I knew, I would have followed this trail long ago. You're the expert here."

"I'm an expert in art research, not Venetian narcissists who write nonsensical riddles." I rub my temples, and shuffle through my memories for anything that might jump out. "Noah, when we got caught up in that tourist group and found the Piombi, didn't the tour guide mention something about lead?"

"The rooftops," he says. "'Piombi' means lead in Italian."

"Yes, the roof of the new prison is covered with slabs of lead." Eva directs us through a narrow corridor to the prison, which is nothing more than stone cells and thick doors with metal bolts.

A guard meanders into the hallway, eyeing the tourists and examining faces. "He's standing at the entrance to the bridge," I say. "We can't cross him. He'll recognize us."

Eva nods to follow and we hurry down a long hallway through another door, into an open-air courtyard. "The lead ceiling. This is obviously the right place. Do you see anything?" she asks.

"This square." Noah pulls out a map of Venice and orients himself north to south. "When I draw an X through its corners, look." He overlays Lord Marco's thinned map, which matches perfectly at the northwest angle. The second X lines up with the tip of the Campanile.

I yank at Noah's sleeve, motioning to the guard eyeing us through the window. The man's gaze intensifies, with a sudden recognition and a bolt toward the closest door.

"Run." Eva throws open the door opposite the one we came in.

We run down the corridor toward the stairs, slipping between groups and sliding along the walls, the guard's keys jangling against his hip as he trails us.

We make our way through the exhibition, out to street level, running toward St. Mark's Square. "Come on." I eye a café nearby where we can watch the square from under a large overhang. "The riddle for this second X said something about the cosmos. Eva, what's the translation again?"

She recites from memory, no doubt having spent endless hours pondering the ancient puzzle. "'Stars shine their light on the chosen men of brilliance while traitors die in the dark of night.'"

"This lunatic better lead us to Sofia's art," I say. We all spot the woman with a black bob and red lipstick. "Time to move."

As the sun floods the square, the only three people alive who may find the truth of Sofia Rossi blend into the crowd and slide into the closest alley. We discover a nook, dark and shaded, where we can discuss next moves.

"'Chosen men of brilliance'?" I scoff. "He certainly thought highly of himself."

Noah asks to borrow Eva's phone. He types and scrolls, searching for historical records on the stars and the Campanile.

"Here we go." Noah shows us an article detailing how Galileo demonstrated a new telescope at the top of the tower.

"Lord Marco met with Galileo to learn about the stars?" I pull the other two into the dark alcove as people pass. I grab the phone and keep reading. "Anything else?"

Noah smiles. "Yes."

Eva raises her hands in frustration. "Well?"

"Important men hosted Galileo to learn about his telescope. The only ones with him were Lords of the Night."

The most ridiculous things sometimes help solve a mystery. We know two spots on the map, the Piombi prison and the Campanile, and now we know another piece of the puzzle. "Marco really was a lord."

Chapter Forty

Doge's Palace, One Hour Until the Banquet

As I make my way down the narrow, suffocating stairwell toward the prison, the truth of Lord Marco falls into place.

Marco lost all his money when he bought his way into power. Lords of the Night are magistrates who arrest anyone they deem traitors, torturing and sentencing them at their will. Caterina convinced him to ruin Antonio, toss me in a brothel, and steal enough of my art to fund her lifestyle.

What, I wonder, has she done with Lucca?

Through a corridor and a vestibule, I step into another chamber. So many rooms for this tribunal to hold secret hearings and decide if one will live or die or drown in the wells below the palace.

Another cabinet must hold another staircase.

Thump.

I turn with a gasp, expecting to see a member of the secret council or the senate, but see only an empty room. There's no way out. Something scratches at my neck. I nearly scream as my chest tightens hard enough to squeeze the air right out. On instinct, I fall to the ground in a ball, hiding under my cape and hood.

Something wet and bumpy rubs against my ear. I swat at the offending sensation to find a small gray cat. He meows at me and goes about his business, lurking around the chamber, completely unaware of the masterful art painted all around him.

Another cat sits on the cabinet, cleaning himself. Useful creatures to rid the place of rats who like to nibble on documents, no doubt. I find the seam easily, and step into yet another staircase, but this time with a friend. The gray cat jumps ahead, leading the way.

We hurry down the hall that turns from marble to rigid stone. With one glimpse through the decorative carvings, I know. I'm standing on the Bridge of Sighs.

The cat pounces on a mouse, who wriggles and fights, but it's useless. The cat has already hooked its claws through the mouse's abdomen and sucked its blood splatter. Footsteps approach in the armory. No choice but to move forward into the cold prisons.

Narrow, dark, and silent, save for a few wayward groans. The air rushes through the passageways, sending a chill up my neck. Thick, bolted doors hold in the scent of human waste and sweat, while dimly lit oil lamps blow whispers of light. I pass braided iron grates as dirty fingers crawl out like spiders. One man howls as he manages to grab a lock of my hair.

"Release me," I demand, but the panic in his eyes tells me he hasn't touched anyone for a very long time. He grips tighter, muttering something about family and love. Footsteps thud down the corridor where a shadow appears on the steps. When I glimpse the tips of shoes, I scratch the poor man's hand to release me.

Once free, I run down the icy hall, past the prisoners' whistles and hollers. A guard appears, keys jingling, barking orders for the men to quiet. I climb four steps and round the corner.

"Who's here?" he bellows. "Show yourself!"

The damn court shoes slide out from under me and send me to the slick floor. I push up and gain my footing just as the man climbs the stairs behind me. Though I grip every window grate, nothing budges, so I'm forced to carry on through the hallway, past boarded rooms with the occasional worn hole in the stone for an errant eyeball to frighten me.

The guard moves closer, keys jangling at his hips. So many passageways. A three-way opening sends me into a wide stance and spinning. He launches over the top step, reaching for my robe as he trips. I manage to yank away and duck under a half wall, hoping to find a place to hide until I can sneak my way out of this dungeon. Another hand shoots through an iron window from a blackened room.

I yell and grunt simultaneously, pulling away from a second desperate man, but he grabs harder. "Sofia."

Everything stops. "Antonio?" More keys and feverish footsteps approach. "How do I release you?"

"The keys on the guard," he says. "Run."

"Not without you." Luckily, the guard is frail and wheezy. I remove my cape and throw the mass of velvet under the grate that hangs halfway down from the ceiling.

"Lovely garments," Antonio says.

"Much easier than skirts." I leap for the bottom of the grate, swinging my legs back and forth. Once I pull my feet to the thick rail at the bottom, I loop my knee through the hole and climb up like a trellis to the arched ceiling above, where I cling to the darkness like a bat.

The guard turns the corner, hands braced on his knees to catch his breath. "Where did she go?" Antonio points in the direction of the cape. The man is so focused on an invisible woman on the ground, he fails to see the real one dangling over his head. When he stops to pick up the robe, I hold on through cramping fingers, and swing my feet directly into his back.

He falls face first while I tumble to the stone. No time to consider my scratches and bruises, as I reach for the man's waist and unhook the keys. He grabs my ankle. The poor man is ailing, his lips blue and his breath whistling like a winter wind.

"I'm sorry, signore." Then I kick him square in the chest. When he reaches for his sternum, the keys drop to the floor, and I swipe them before running back under the grate and pulling two pins on each side of the wall. The right peg stubbornly sticks.

The guard stands, gasping for breath, dragging his feet toward me. I brace my foot on the wall and tug until the grate crashes to the ground, nearly slamming into the man's face.

"I . . . I . . ." But he can't complete a sentence.

I run to Antonio's cell, my eyes now adjusted enough to notice his bleeding forehead, swollen lip, and violet patch around his left eye. Although I'm desperate to free him, I can't form thoughts when I see what they've done to him. I stutter out a version of "I'm sorry."

"All is well now, Sofia. You're here."

I fiddle with the keys, attempting one after another, shaking so terribly I drop the set more than once. "We have no time. Caterina is hosting the celebration soon." I work in rhythm to his tapping fingers. Grab, fit, drop. Over and over until . . . *click*.

I throw the door open and rush to his arms. Antonio kisses me with his swollen lip and hugs me with dried blood caked to his bare arms.

"Will there be another guard?" I ask.

"Any moment, yes." He rolls locks of my hair in his hands, staring at my eyes as if we are strolling a garden on a bright day.

"Enough of that." I lower his hand and lead him into the corridor. "How do we escape?"

"You won't like it."

"I don't enjoy one bit of this horrid place. Now speak, where do we go?"

He nods to his left. "Back through the palace."

I want to cry, but I tighten my lips and feign fortitude. Antonio leads me through the maze of corridors, linked into a square. Once we approach the stairwell, another guard appears. Antonio swings at his face, but his injured body doesn't have the power it once did.

A slice of a wooden beam holds open a window, so I dislodge the thick, warped wood and slam it over the guard's head.

Antonio leads me back toward where we came. "Where have you learned all this?"

"Sex and fighting use similar body strengths."

We duck under a tiny opening and into a courtyard in the center of the prison. He finds another door, and by this time we are running down the dark hallways, more than one guard yelling for us to stop. Thankful for men's breeches, I jump and slide in step with Antonio.

"Up one flight," I say. "We need to make our way to the loggia to blend with Carnival."

We climb another staircase and wind through terraces until we discover a narrow, forgotten stairwell to the courtyard.

"Hopefully they will all think us playing a part," he says. "What is Carnival if not to deceive?"

"The sun has set. Have we missed our chance with Caterina?"

Three men with swords barrel out onto the loggia, hanging over the balcony yelling, "Stop!"

Most patricians, dressed in theater attire, don't bother to do much but watch us run. We join the festivities in Piazza San Marco, where boisterous laughter and bursts of colorful costumes provide cover as we head north along Le Mercerie, past merchants who stay open all night. Comfortable among the protective crowd, I notice the sharp tang of nutmeg, mace, and peppercorn hanging in the air as we pass the spice shop, while swaths of bright red Egyptian silks billow from a doorway.

I jump when peacock feathers dangling from a string tickle my neck but recover just as we pass under the blue marble circle above, considering briefly how many women will stop to admire this astronomical clock in the years when I am gone. I count the sun pointer. Out of twenty-four hours, the wavy hand marks seven. "Antonio, Caterina has started. What if we're too late?"

"Foreigners love to drink and talk about their journeys. We have time." He slides his hand into mine with a firm, confident grip.

Venezia devours me in its essence. Its air heady with perfumes and spices and the windows above with flapping red flags of the Republic. Pots of pigments and paints in vibrant colors tease me with things I cannot procure. Not as a woman, and not as a courtesan. Perhaps soon, as an artist.

We turn left over Ponte dei Ferali, then duck between two buildings in dark *calli* so narrow we stand chest to chest, taking in each other's breath. "What happened to you?"

"The council held a hearing. They questioned me, and a few blinks later threw me in a cell and returned to beat names out of me."

"Did you tell them?"

"No. I couldn't report Caterina until you had saved your pieces. I thought you'd be there. Not rescuing me." He slides his palm over my cheek and rubs my skin with his thumb.

"I escaped a brothel for you."

"That must be where you found such lovely breeches." He smiles, washing out the bruised, swollen parts of his face as we hide in this dank alley near the butcher where the air stinks of blood, wanted citizens, and escaped prisoners.

Antonio seems to feel what I feel—that inexplicable moment where the world halts and nothing exists outside our shared gaze and thumping hearts.

"You've lost so much for me."

"I have lost nothing, Signora Rossi. I have only gained the world." Our lips touch in a soft kiss as the evening breeze flutters my hair. "It's time to save your art."

As the city erupts in celebration, I lead Antonio through the limestone streets, past stately homes, and snaking in line with a narrow canal until we reach Lord Marco's palazzo on the Grand Canal. A home I know intimately.

"We couldn't follow through with our original plan, and now we must push our way through. Present my art on my merit. It's terrifying."

Gondolas bob in front of this palace, filling the Grand Canal with visitors from near and far. "We can do this," he says.

"The pieces will be presented in the main entry hall. His crown jewel of frescoes and a vault in the ceiling to let in the light." I glare from the corner of the palazzo, remembering every time Marco refused me access and shooed me from the unused studio.

"Should we try the service entrance?" he asks.

"No. We have one chance here." I head to the street entrance, a detailed façade of pink and white marble. With one deep breath, I burst through the door to the entry, which is empty and still.

I stand in the flood of moonlight, the room lit by candles all around like tiny fires that climb the walls. Lord Marco appears at the top of the staircase. "You've missed your chance. They are sold and gone."

With a thud to the chest, I cannot breathe, cannot feel my feet on the ground. Antonio steps beside me, hand around my waist. "Don't think you have won, Marco," Antonio says.

He laughs, descending the stairwell to join us in the grand marble entryway. "Sofia, you are a mare who needs to be broken." He leans his head to the side, cracks his neck, and grins like a villain in an allegory. "She is broken," he says to Antonio. "Hardened and unfeeling."

"I have not found that at all," Antonio says, pulling me in tight.

"I was only unfeeling with you, as you wept in my lap and demanded that I attend to your every need."

"You were my courtesan."

I shove away from Antonio, needing to face Marco on my own. "And you bought your way into the Lords of the Night." I step close enough to remember his smell. As if cowardice and sweat made a perfume.

"You were a fool then, and you still are." He juts out his chin, forcing himself tall. There's a reason he always stops on the bottom step. "Your grand ideas to become a sculptress should be destroyed."

"I was a fool. I believed that being your prostitute would gift me a life of art and elegance. How wrong I was."

"You wished to be an artist." He snarls, then swipes a cane from the tall vase at the bottom of the stairs. "You, a woman who has spread her legs for a living, thought you could translate the complicated language of sculpture and painting. You know nothing of sacrifice, of the agony of loss."

"I know loss intimately. Agony lives deep in my bones in a way you will never understand. I live and breathe the notion that I am worth nothing in this world. That my thoughts, my body, and my heart serve as mere tokens to men who wish to parade me around as spoils of war."

"What war?"

"The war you will never win. Your useless desire to become a great man."

He cracks his cane on the banister close enough that the disrupted air brushes against my cheek. "You will spoil this important world of art with your dirty morals."

I hold Antonio back. This is my battle. "You will wither to nothing, a nameless man of time gone by, born without the talent to produce anything of his own."

Antonio, though his face is bruised as violets, still intimidates Marco. He yanks the cane from his hand and thwacks the stick against Marco's knee, unbothered by his squeals. "You stole her art and falsified documents for the men Caterina invited, while throwing me in prison for the same crime."

"I am a magistrate. You will pay for assaulting me." He clutches his leg, curled on the step in a writhing mass of bony limbs.

Caterina glides into the entry, unbothered by our presence. Her casual smile sets my instincts ablaze. She's hiding something again. "Oh, my poor Marco. You always cared too much."

I step back when I notice several men behind her. She sways her hips toward us. "I knew Sofia wouldn't last an hour in that brothel, and she would find a way to release you from prison."

I exhale in sudden realization, furious at myself for not seeing it sooner. "You hosted the banquet hours ago, while we were busy trying to save ourselves."

"The palace guards have been distracted for hours searching for you two." Her laugh shoots regret straight through my heart. "Loading your art onto the ships of very rich men proved easier than I anticipated. I don't need your little list of names, Signore Bruni."

"They bought my pieces?" Despite my best efforts, my voice cracks, piercing the air like a pinprick.

She bares her teeth. "They bought *Lucca's* pieces." She throws her hand to the side. "Finally, my husband has served his purpose."

"They're gone," I mutter.

Antonio holds me and whispers in my ear. "You will make more."

I look up at Caterina. "You know he couldn't do it alone. His damaged hand, his erratic moods. They're my work."

Her face tightens, stretched across her reddened cheeks. "They would never sell. Not by a woman. Certainly not by a whore." She reaches for the cane dropped at Marco's feet and crashes it into a bust in a small alcove. He whimpers as shards of dried clay fall in pieces. "Women like you ruin everything I have worked for," she says.

I puff my chest. "You live in delusions."

"I've built Lucca from the poor, lost little boy of the hills into something magnificent. Someone grand and important. He is a renowned artist because of *me*."

"What good is a grand artist who hates himself?"

"I care little about his dark moods." She gathers herself and shakes away her unsteadiness. "You come along and convince him to risk his life for your wild notions. I despise women like you."

"You brought me to fix Lucca's impotent desires. This was what you asked of me." My ribs bind tight against my sides.

Antonio pulls me toward him, inching us away from the men who appear ready to tie our wrists and toss us in the Adriatic.

"I made clear he was mine, and you convinced him to turn on me." Caterina looks me straight in the eyes. "You thought you could outwit me, you miserable waste."

We back away as slight as a shadow. She won't stop at my art. She wants to ruin me.

"Capture them," she says.

We turn to run, but two more men appear. We move closer together, arms wrapped around each other, unwilling to let anyone separate us. Until they rip us apart, cover our mouths, and carry us to a gondola bobbing outside the water door.

I buck like a horse, trying to loosen the binding from my mouth, but nothing moves. Caterina steps inside, close to my face, and motions for the gondolier to sail to a Spaniard's ship.

Caterina sighs, smiling out to the night sky. "Marco served my purpose, just as you have." She kicks Antonio's belly, her steel eyes on mine. "What might it feel like to watch me kill the man you love?"

Too angry to cry, I close my eyes and think, *Caterina, you are already dead.*

Chapter Forty-One

Once the sun has set and darkness provides cover, we slip back into Eva's apartment, where we stare at Lord Marco's map in frustration. A heavy weight presses down on my chest. My career is long gone. So is the fabricated Venice Beach life I've built. My only hope is to grasp my integrity like it's the last thing I have. Because it is.

We're running out of time and options, and by the look in Noah's eyes, he knows it too.

"Nothing from the third riddle?" Eva asks.

"'Out of the eater came something to eat, out of the strong came something sweet.'" Noah throws up his hand. "He's stolen this one from the Bible. The man is just lazy."

"We know this X marks St. Mark's Basilica." I slump against the back of the chair. "But nothing is hidden in Piazza San Marco. Maybe this is all nonsense."

Eva turns the map toward her. "What does it mean, this something sweet?"

"A hero takes down a lion and inside his carcass is a hive of honeybees." Noah looks to me as if I can solve this.

"A prison where a man loses everything but gains love. A view of the stars as taught by Galileo to only the worthy, and a Bible verse where a man defeats a lion and discovers honey." I pinch the bridge of my nose to stave off the headache that knocks at my forehead. "We're missing something."

"It must have something to do with Piazza San Marco. All three riddles take place there."

The fourth riddle has us stumped as there is no X to follow. Noah reads it aloud yet again. "'Into the deep you will go; at the tip of the diamond you will fall with your ruins.'"

I pace the room, hands raking through my hair.

A buzz stops my pacing, and we both look at Eva as she unlocks her phone. "They've called a press conference for eight tomorrow morning. Your boss will announce support for a city-wide exploration for artifacts."

"He knows I have nothing." I drop my head and trace the floor tiles with my shoe. "He has proof I'm a fraud."

Eva looks up through alarmed eyes. "The *carabinieri* will demand the immediate custody of Dr. Mia Harding. A reward will be issued, and the city put on patrol."

Noah sighs. "All for daring to look for the truth."

"What does the truth matter?" I stare out the window at the starry night above. The same stars I watched in Los Angeles just hang over the world, waiting for nightfall so they may shine. "History is a fairy tale told from one perspective. I was foolish to think I could change a damn thing."

Eva stands tall and lights a cigarette. "Do you know why I didn't hand over that map?"

"Because it would fall into the hands of the mob, who would bury it if it didn't serve their purposes."

"Meh." This also seems to be a legitimate word in the Italian vernacular. "I am not that virtuous, Dr. Harding." She pauses to suck on her glowing cigarette. "I am already viewed as a foolish woman who plays dress-up with her family's money. No one talks of how I turned this hotel into the most successful *albergo* in all of Venice. According to them, I am not a savvy businesswoman.

I am frivolous." Her hand waves feverishly now, a trail of smoke twirling from between her fingers. "Everyone underestimates me."

"I know the feeling."

"Imagine," Eva says, her voice resonant and steady. "A silly woman discovers a historic drawing. Luckily, she handed it off to the authorities, men who can handle such an artifact. And any ideas that Lucca Armani is not Venice's greatest artist prove that she cannot be trusted." Another drag. Another sigh. "I've told many city officials my theory, that we have built a god out of a man. We have created a magic story with our chosen hero, a weak man who contributed little to his life. How dare I defame one of our great artists?"

"Wouldn't the map prove your theory?" Noah asks.

We both look at him in pity, and I can't believe he doesn't yet understand. "Women who criticize men are instantly mocked and silenced," I say. "Eva has already been marked by her peers as a threat."

Noah slowly sits. "But they might listen to me?"

"Yes," we say in perfect unison.

"This research was conducted entirely by men," Eva says. "They do not see what they don't know."

Noah's shoulders fall. "And they can't fathom the possibility that a woman may have been Venice's most influential artist."

"Bribes and egos aside, there was no one to offer another perspective because they do not want one." I drop my hands from my neck to my sides, too tired to hold them up. "Dr. Byron's team was entirely men. The research was flawed before it ever began." Physical and emotional exhaustion pull me to the ground like a lead weight around my ankles. I crouch into a ball and lower my forehead to my knees.

The room stills. I'm headed for prison, and we all know it.

Eva swallows loud enough to reverberate through the room. "Well, we still have twelve hours. What can I do?"

"Nothing." I lift my head and smile at her young, enthusiastic face. I'd love if I could inspire something in this moment. Summon some deeper courage. But I'm all out of options.

"I'm not ready to give up," Eva says. "I'll leave you two alone while I go through storage one more time." She stops, as if she wants to say something, but decides to retreat.

Noah lowers to the ground, sitting cross-legged in front of me. "We can still solve this riddle."

I grab the plastic cover and slam it on the ground between us. "Look at this, Noah. The man is an egomaniac. 'I am a Lord of the Night, one of Venice's chosen few. I've met with Galileo and frequented the Basilica. I work in the Doge's Palace, bringing criminals to their knees.'" I rub my eyes with both hands, then bring them to a resting position like a prayer at my lips. "This entire riddle is to celebrate himself."

Noah reaches across to touch my cheek, smiling that dopey, handsome smile of his. In another time and place, this moment would hold me, and I'd wish it would never end. "We aren't done yet," he says.

Despite how I long to curl into his touch, kiss him until it stops hurting, and fall asleep in his arms, I lower his hand from my face. "You don't know what it's like to walk into this world ten steps behind."

"No, I don't."

"I've always been poor. Everyone around me died young or walked the earth in a damaged body with an already departed soul." I meet Noah's eyes, my insides feeling so soft it's like my skin has turned translucent. "I learned and read and worked, determined to fly out of that place and never look back. If I earned scholarships and degrees, I'd be worthy." A stinging sob hitches in my throat. "I could pretend to live among the successful people who bought themselves pearl earrings and a modern studio in the hottest neighborhood. Instead, I buy knockoff pearls, and I felt more at home in my broken-down trailer than I ever have in that cold white shipping container of an apartment."

"Perhaps you were never meant to be one of us."

"Well, yes, that's encouraging."

He sputters out a tiny laugh, then reels it back in. "If you were like every other researcher, you wouldn't have questioned *The Estasi*. An artist named Sofia Rossi would have been forgotten forever, lost to the cruel fates of womankind. Because you aren't one of us, you see things we never could."

A tiny snap of pride pops up inside me like a seedling.

But I'm a researcher still weighed down by the malignant mass of memories from school. How Roman families left newborn girls out in the woods to die. Witches burned for the sin of being outspoken. The image of a scold's bridle to muzzle women who speak out of turn. I salivate, imagining the bit in my mouth and the spike on my tongue.

"There are things none of us can fix, Noah. And most will never understand."

When he meets my eyes, he nods. "Here's the thing, Mia. You've let me into your world. I'm more inspired by your fight than anything school has ever taught me. You've changed me." His voice catches. "Forever."

"Damn you, Noah." I jump in his lap, straddle his hips, and kiss him with a passion I didn't know lived inside me. His hands in my hair and my body pressed to his, I kiss him like I might be in love.

We kiss long enough to help me forget my current state of despair. His passion reaches past my anger and finds my hope. Who knew a kiss could do all that?

He pulls away with a smile, and a look that is neither dopey nor silly. He makes me want to fight until they take everything from me. The moonlight shifts in the sky, landing on Noah's eyes. The moment sparks a thought in my mind.

"Marco is a narcissist, but selfish bastards always leave a blue streak of regret."

"What do you mean?" he asks.

"I've known many in my life. Dated a few." I grimace. "Anyway, they're so blinded by their obsession with other people, they never stop to look at themselves."

"I don't understand."

I pick up the map and examine it with fresh eyes. "In his attempt to wax poetic about himself, he inadvertently tells us about Sofia."

He smiles full on sexy, and it takes massive willpower not to tear off his clothes and enjoy my last night of freedom tangled with his naked body. But Marco tried to bury Sofia, and I owe it to her to fight.

"He mentions a diamond, but there are only three riddles."

He slides his hand along the side of my neck. "How does a diamond help us?"

"Grab your Carnival costume. We're off on one final adventure."

Chapter Forty-Two

My vision returns in a blurry haze of shadows. A shape paces back and forth. The base of my skull pulses with the sharpness of a thousand needles.

"Welcome back."

Caterina's voice could wake me from death for how it grates. I blink until color returns, then the outline of her rigid face. Her sloped nose. "Pity yours is the first face I see," I say.

She smacks me hard. My cheek burns hot as fire.

I suddenly realize my arms are tied to a chair. I search my surroundings but can't place anything.

"Your tall, handsome, thieving lover is safely tucked away with my guards." She softly grazes the cheek she just slapped.

Her caress sickens me. Rocking side to side adds to this uneasiness. Ropes hang from hooks behind her. *Ah, we're on a ship.*

Caterina bends down, hands on my knees. "Why do I both hate you and obsess over your very existence?"

Because you are completely unwell, you beastly rat of a woman. But I know when I'm at a disadvantage, so I keep my mouth shut.

She purses her thin lips. "Lucca, Marco. Your body turned them mad with self-importance." She glides her hand over her waist while eyeing my chest.

"How terribly sad," I say. She drops her arm to her side and waits for my next thought. "You hide your frightened self behind a cloak of perceived invincibility."

She kicks a crate across the room. "I perceive only one thing." She stretches her jaw. "A traitor."

I can't find a soul inside her. My only hope is to keep talking and hope someone arrives to rescue me. "Yes. I convinced Lucca to help me. Together, we could sell our art and begin a new life. But I failed. You no longer need any of us. You've won."

She bares her teeth, her slender neck filling in with throbbing vessels. "I never doubted I would triumph. I have a purse full of coins and the respect of international leaders."

"You do not have my beauty or my power over men. And that turns you wild with jealousy."

A twinge in her eye tells me I've struck her weakness. "You're correct," she says. "To remedy that I shall deal with you in a personal, painful way." She breathes out a smile that sours her entire face. "I want to peel your skin and wear it like a gown."

Her fingers trace my lips. The time for stalling has gone. Now all I have is fight. I clamp down hard on her finger until the tang of metallic blood springs in my mouth and my teeth clatter against her bones.

She wails, removing her hand and recoiling from my lap. Her hand nestled against her chest, she moans, paces, and turns to glare at me. "I will kill Antonio after I show him your dead body."

"He would rather die than bow to you." I lean forward, her blood dripping from my mouth. "Do as you must." I spit on the floor next to my feet.

She keeps her damaged hand against her chest, soaking the fabric with yellowish fluid and deep red blood. With her other, she reaches for an iron rod. As she drags it near me, I stiffen, knowing I only have minutes left to live. "All I wanted was my name on my art," I say.

"Why?" The iron scrapes the ground, bouncing at every plank. "No one would buy from a woman."

"Someday, they will. I see no reason it couldn't start with me."

"You are a whore. A luscious body to conquer." She snickers. "Nothing more."

"You want to believe that because otherwise, I am more than you'll ever be."

She grips the rod tighter, trembling as she lifts it to the air. "Lucca will know I broke you bone by bone. Antonio will know I listened to your screams and did not stop."

I don't look away. Her eyes now flame pink and bloody. "If you kill me, you will have no art to sell."

Her breath now heaves as if pressed through a narrow tube. "Those pieces made me wealthy beyond my imagination. I no longer need any of you." Her bloody hand joins the other as she lifts the rod over her shoulder. "You are nothing special, Sofia. No one will remember you."

My body finally weakens, her words like a knife to my belly. I exhale, slow and accepting, as tears gather in my lower lids. The ship creaks. Years of sculptures hidden in my hands prepare to die with me, evaporated into the darkness of obscurity, where women of all time find their names: discarded and forgotten.

Caterina drops the iron with a clang. Dare I hope for a change of heart?

As she approaches, hate stewing in her gaze, I prepare. Crushing my skull would be too messy. Too uncontrolled. She wants personal. Her bloody hand still holds piercings from my teeth. She reaches for my neck, palms outstretched, thumbs wide, growling and panting. I pull against the rope that binds my wrists, but it only burns my skin raw. Any attempts to buck and drop my head prove fruitless as her fingers press into my flesh.

A mix of panic and resolve sends me to my side, kicking against the rigid restraints of the rope. Caterina turns me to my back and presses her body weight into her straightened arms, hands crushing my windpipe. I thrash against her, fighting a useless fight.

Stinging tightness crushes my throat. Sharp pains erupt in my neck and head.

In the beat of a half second, her hands stop moving, and I wonder if I've died.

Her eyes bulge, her body hunches limp as I cough stinging air back into my throat. She falls to the ground beside me, her bloody eyes frozen, and a blade lodged in her back. I look up, still gasping and crying for the pain of every whoosh of air past my bruised throat. I choke out, "Lucca?"

Chapter Forty-Three

We're hidden under a narrow bridge, waiting nervously as nighttime crowds thump overhead. With Carnival just around the corner, this Friday night absolutely crawls with people. Without the colorful Venetian masks, we would have been spotted instantly. We sent a text to Paolo from a burner phone, and now we wait.

"I'm here," Paolo says as he jumps under the bridge next to us.

My heart nearly stops beating, and I shove him away on instinct, both hands to his chest. "I'm so sorry. I'm jumpy." We help him up.

He wipes his hands on his thighs. "I probably deserved that shove."

Noah pulls him into the shaded protection of the bridge. "You're our only way out of this, friend."

Paolo types in passwords and hands me his phone. "I've done the latest update to my research app. You should have access to every document from the Venetian Archives in there."

"Thank you." I situate myself on the concrete, leaning against the cool stones as the breeze travels through. I begin typing keywords and phrases, using a system of clues I devised since leaving Eva's apartment. "The only way I know how to solve this is in the research."

Paolo rubs his palms on his thighs. "The news," he says. "They fabricated a statement, yes?"

"Yes," I say. We're all in this deep. We've lied, stolen, and cheated. But the three of us now see the same vision, and the truth is our only way out.

"I'll come forward, Dr. Harding." He pauses, as though to gather his conviction. "Once they know about my transgressions, they'll be forced to open an investigation."

I recognize his hesitation. His internal struggles. We justify our mistakes because of the things we believe about the unfair world. This may be as much about letting go as it is about integrity. "Not if they bury the information."

Noah gives him the rundown as I frantically search. About Eva's connections and the mob and how they want to staff looters at dig sites to pilfer artifacts for the black market.

Paolo drops to the ground next to me. "*Porca troia*."

His inflection makes it easy to translate.

"Indeed." I keep scouring. "Paolo, this is so much bigger than Armani now. Lord Marco sold his courtesan to Lucca, took Caterina as a lover, and threw Antonio in prison. There's a story here and we need to discover it."

He nods, squinting to remember something. "Caterina disappeared at 1609 Carnival. After hosting a banquet."

I drop the phone to my lap. "A banquet?"

"Yes." He looks between me and Noah, unaware that he just dropped a potentially major bit of information. "I didn't find it significant, or I would have told you." He scrunches his face in understanding. "The researchers scolded me for frivolous reading. They only wanted information on Lucca."

"Figures." I add "banquet" and the date February 10, 1609, to the search terms. While the men check for policemen and anyone watching, I scour the records for any mention. "Wait."

They crouch next to me. "What have you found?" Noah asks.

"The answer has been here all along."

They drop their gaze, hush, and focus. "Here—"

Before I can explain, a group of teenagers speaking on the steps around the corner discuss the reward for the American researcher. They've decided to search all night, like a scavenger hunt for traitors.

Noah grabs my arm and nods in the opposite direction. We hurry along the canal, casually joining the crowds of night goers and diners out to enjoy the electric air of a city upside down. While all of Venice prepares their costumes and theater, a supposed lying researcher hides in their midst, while the legacy of Lucca Armani hangs in the balance.

"What is it?" Paolo asks.

"Not here." We follow the stream of people through the streets as they sing a drunken tune. I can't say one word that might give us away.

Paolo grabs my arm, and I link hands with Noah. Together, we snake along the canals and find a gondolier whose black lacquered boat is decorated in gold tassels and twinkle lights. Paolo speaks in Italian, rushed and demanding. Then he shuttles us to the back of the gondola and readies himself to hear the big find. "Go."

I lower my mask as I can't breathe in this damn thing. "Under those search terms, I found a Spanish prince who detailed a failed trip to Venice. He corresponded with his lover about how he sailed across the Mediterranean Sea to attend a banquet. He bought her two beautiful art pieces by a Venetian artist with a damaged hand."

Noah lowers his mask too but we're both careful to watch for wandering eyes. "Are you telling me there are Armani sculptures hidden in Spain somewhere?"

"That's where things get interesting. He complained that he paid for two stunning pieces, yet they never made it to the ship."

"Where did they go?" Paolo asks.

"He doesn't know. He considered himself swindled by the woman who organized the banquet for powerful men. Her name was Caterina."

A group screams, and my heart leaps into my throat. Noah reaches for my hand.

"It's only a lively dinner," he says. "Go on."

My heart still thumps into my throat. "Right. Caterina hosted a secret banquet where powerful men from all over the world could buy erotic pieces."

"Secret because of the seductive nature of the art?" Noah asks.

Paolo shakes his finger. "Sumptuary laws of the time banned banquets, lest patricians organize against the rulers."

"This Spanish prince reports someone stole his purchases." I lean forward to whisper. "The pieces were a statue of a man and woman in pleasure and a disturbing painting titled *The Vengeful Maiden*." Just saying this out loud feels like a burst of confetti blasting through my chest.

"Lucca Armani had a damaged hand. There is a second face on *The Estasi*!" Paolo leans his cheek onto his palm, his eyes wide and bright. "How did we not know this?" Paolo asks.

"Why would anyone think to flag this?" I ask. "No one knows about the second form of a man on *The Estasi*, and we only discovered *The Maiden* today. This story develops by the second."

"You discovered another artwork?" Paolo's voice has turned shrill. "What is *The Vengeful Maiden*?"

"Sofia Rossi's painting." The poor man can't digest all this information at once. It's like a firehose of history. He looks to Noah and nods to carry on.

"The painting was kept in secret at Lord Marco's house. It's still there." Noah's words no sooner leave his mouth when the gondolier mutters, "They see you."

A trio of young men points to us while glancing between their phones. The gondolier sways to the other side of the canal, masterfully comes to a firm stop with his oar, and motions for us to run.

Paolo points to a narrow alley. "Through there. Climb the stairwell and follow the potted plants. There's a rooftop I used to watch the city from. You'll be protected."

I squeeze his hand in thanks. That's all we have time for. We do as he instructs, climbing stairs and keeping our heads down past every doorway. We arrive on the terrace, safe from any windows, yet with a full view of Venice's tiled rooftops and flowered terraces. With a few deep breaths, we gather ourselves in the awareness that time is running out, and this may be our last few hours together.

The light in this city glows with an unreal brightness. In shades of marigold, the world seems to burst with blush. Like the heavens chose these islands and canals as a vessel for beauty.

I can't enjoy the view with this looming trouble. "In a matter of hours, they'll hold a press conference and announce a full-scale investigation into Venice with excavations all over the country so looters can steal even more important art."

"We can't let this go," Noah says. "We'll report what Eva told us."

Emotion swells in my throat. He hasn't given up yet. "Who's going to believe us, Noah? I'm a criminal. They've fabricated that press release and set an entire city on watch for the madwoman who dared suggest Armani isn't the genius they all believe him to be."

"Maybe we'll be in jail together."

"No way you're going down with me. This was my hill to die on, and you tried to help me live."

He brings my hand to his mouth. After a soft kiss, he holds my palm against his cheek. "I'm here because I believe in you, and I believe in magic."

Somehow, he always lifts my head to the clouds. "What kind of magic?" I ask.

"The kind where you can feel things other people can't. A room speaks to you and jewelry tells you of its past. The incredible joy of living at a time where people want to rediscover what we've never known." The skin on his neck is warm and inviting. "Magic like falling for a woman who lights a fire in me I never knew was there."

I tuck into his chest, leaning my cheek against his beating heart.

"I don't want to give up either." Why hasn't Sofia spoken to me? I pull the ring and cameo from my pocket and watch them glisten in the cerulean twilight. "These don't give love. They give fight and obsession. I don't think Sofia carved these."

"Marco had an art studio. Maybe he carved them. He certainly sounds obsessive."

I clasp them in my palm and hold them against my chest, asking them to show me something. Anything.

"What's it like to feel history?" Noah asks.

"You know. You've stood at the base of the *David* in awe. You've had your breath taken away by the Sistine Chapel and no doubt been brought to tears by the Duomo in Florence."

"None of those buildings make me feel history though. But there was this one church in Vienna. St. Peter's. Most churches bore me, but this one was different. I stumbled upon it during an evening stroll and felt an inexplicable pull to go inside. A choir lulled me into a calm I've never felt as the gold stucco walls kept me mesmerized. By the time I walked out, it was the magic hour, and the sky was as blue as a globe thistle. The sign revealed that church represents goodness and love. I didn't need the explanation. I felt it. And I've never forgotten it."

"What I experience is no different." When I hold up the ring, my hand buzzes and my shoulder aches. "My mind keeps going back to Palazzo Armani every time I hold this. It's the house."

"What do you see?" he asks.

My mind conjures an image of the palazzo from overhead. A bright red light shines over the room next to Caterina's bedchamber. "Caterina's studio?" I push up and hold the ring between us. I lift the cameo with my other hand. "They both are giving me Caterina energy. What the hell?"

He nods, no doubt excited I haven't given up yet. "Okay, let's put this together."

"Off my wild hunches in a desperate situation?"

He shrugs. "Sure, why not."

"I've got nothing else."

"Okay, Lord Marco was art obsessed. He had a studio in his house that appears to have never been used. His lover was Caterina, who also had her own studio. Antonio loved Sofia and Lucca was in the middle of this hellhole of a triangle."

I nod, waiting for him to make some big reveal.

"The banquet. The riddles." He grimaces. "It all gets so blurry."

I look down at the image in my palm. "What if Caterina crafted these cameos?"

His eyes light up. "Interesting. Why?"

"She needed Lucca to become a famous artist. What little information we have of her paints her as a ruthless social climber, disappointed in her failed husband." I hold them in my open palms and examine Sofia's face. My throat tightens with what feels like obsession and jealousy. "She needed Sofia to fix him. Give him love and affection and help him produce art. She needed Sofia and wanted to ruin her for it."

"Caterina as Sofia's stalker," Noah says, slumping his shoulders. "The internet would go wild with that theory."

Excitement blooms in my chest, the way it always does when I connect with the history of a thing. I've caught the wave of this cameo, and now I glide through her story. "This feels right. Look at the detail in these rings. This isn't any magic. Look how she carved her likeness. No love or admiration, but an almost obsessive detail of her features. Sofia's face is stoic and cold."

"What happened at the banquet?" he asks.

My abilities only take me so far. "Who knows. Obviously, the art was sold, by Caterina and Marco, I assume. Maybe the real artists, Lucca and Sofia, intervened. Or Antonio stole them back for his love. I don't know."

Once again, I sink into the realization that I have nothing. No proof other than a secret painting, my wild notions, and a thinning thread of hope that something will appear in the next few hours.

"What am I doing, Noah?"

He looks in my eyes with such conviction, I gasp. "You're right about Sofia. I know you are."

"Everyone hates me for questioning the great Armani. Whenever someone mentions Einstein, I tell them about his wife Mileva who solved calculations for him and contributed to all his research. They lose their minds when I suggest a woman helped a brilliant man and should get credit for doing so."

"Not everyone." He pulls out his phone and stares.

"What are you doing?"

"A Hail Mary." He presses the phone to unlock, and the lights whir to life.

They could track us now. "Are you going to tell me what's going on?"

"Mia, don't think. Just talk from the heart."

I want to protest, but I have this horrifying feeling that this Hail Mary is all I have left. Besides, the way he looks at me does something to my pride. He makes me believe in myself.

Noah opens TikTok. "I have a few followers."

"How many is a few?"

"Ninety. Thousand."

"What?" Quiet academic Noah is a social media influencer? I almost can't believe it, but his charm is infectious. I bet the world sees it too.

"They're all art nerds. They live for hidden history. We're going live. Get ready."

Instant regret for everything. I don't want this. "Live? What are we doing?"

"We'll only have two minutes before they track my phone. Maybe three. Remember, speak from the heart."

He shoves the phone in front of me. I see my shocked face, my wide eyes and the numbers ticking away. *Sofia*. I have to fight for her.

"Hi." Oh God, I'm really doing this. "My name is Dr. Mia Harding. You might have heard of me. I study art and women's history. If you know my name, you understand my job was to authenticate *The Estasi*. I'm in Venice, and I only have a few minutes. So please listen."

I take one long breath and dive in.

"I didn't authenticate the research because I don't believe Lucca Armani sculpted *The Estasi*." I wait for a collective gasp then I remember, no one can interact with me. "I didn't write that statement, and I did not apologize. My boss, Dr. Wright, is working with Italian criminals to force me to authenticate that statue. They offer bribes and make threats. The research is tainted and can't be trusted."

Noah rubs my hand, smiling confidently as I speak.

"I've made mistakes. Big ones. But who hasn't? I'll take ownership of those, I promise. But right now, I need help."

I turn to stare at Noah, like a touchstone to all this, courageous and good.

"Okay," I say to the phone. "Here's where you need to trust me. I've done my job and researched this statue more than anyone else in the world has. I believe the one who created *The Estasi* and *The Serpent* was not Lucca Armani, but his courtesan, a talented woman named Sofia Rossi."

Time's ticking. I can't help but search my surroundings, expecting the police to run up on us any second.

Speak from the heart.

"Have you ever spent your life believing in something with your whole self, only to discover one day that everyone has been wrong? I have. This trip to Venice has shown me that I am not the voiceless invisible person I've always felt I was. I'm more than a no-name researcher. I'm the one who's going to rock the art world, because it needs to be rocked. It needs to be shaken and woken up to all the dark that thumps through its veins. You've been lied to. All of you."

Noah joins the frame. "Mia has shown me incredible finds I couldn't have discovered on my own. There's so much more to history than we've been told. I want to help her fix this."

"Women, aren't we tired of being erased?" Listeners still. Somehow, I can feel them. "Aren't we tired of being silenced and humiliated for speaking out? I am. I'm fucking tired. Sofia Rossi sculpted and painted with Lucca Armani. Maybe she did everything, or maybe it was collaborative, but I know one thing for sure. Without Sofia, these pieces would never exist."

Footsteps thunder in the distance. "They're coming for us," Noah says.

"Please, listen to me. Lucca's wife Caterina had something to do with the night everything fell apart: February 10, 1609. After hosting a secret banquet to sell forbidden art to foreign dignitaries, Caterina and her lover, a man named Lord Marco, had a fight with Sofia's lover Antonio on the waterfront at Piazza San Marco. I know this sounds like a Greek tragedy but stay with me. There's a record of it. That was the last time Sofia and Caterina were seen. After this, Lucca went off-grid with a badly damaged hand. He languished in obscurity in Florence while Antonio suffered through the rest of his years in love with a woman who history would erase."

"Hurry," Noah says. Footsteps turn from a walk to a run and thump up the stairs surrounding us.

"Hand me the map and a pen." I remain focused, thinking only of Sofia. Noah holds the phone so I can angle the map in the lens. "Lord Marco took over Palazzo Armani after this. I don't know how, but he was involved with their disappearance and the art we are all now obsessed with ending up underground or underwater."

One last breath. "Here." I point the pen to the prison at Palazzo Ducale. "Lord Marco left us a riddle. Our friend Eva will authenticate this. She can produce the map. In this riddle, Marco took us here." I mark an X with a shaking hand. "The next riddle took us here." Another X at the Campanile. "He was a Lord of the Night and had the power to hide things. The third X is here, the Basilica." I draw the third X. "The final riddle said, 'Into the deep you will go; at the tip of the diamond you will fall with your ruins.'" I draw a line between the three points on the map. They form a triangle. When I draw the two remaining sides, the diamond points us to a spot in the water right in front of St. Mark's Square."

An angry group of policemen and people in uniforms blow whistles and run toward us. I see them climb the stairs two flights below, seconds from reaching us.

"Look right here. They will arrest me and silence me. But you can help. Please don't let Sofia Rossi disappear. Please. History has erased us enough."

Noah grabs my hand, but I make one final plea. "They can't ignore us forever."

Click. I close out the app and turn off the phone just as a few men reach the rooftop. We slide off the edge onto a fire escape and run down the stairs so fast we practically slide. By the time we hit the ground, more officers approach from the side of the building. We run down the nearest alley and duck right then left, following a maze of tiny streets and canals.

At the end of an alley, *polizia* spot us. We turn to cross the bridge, but more are coming. We can't backtrack as they're approaching from behind too. With a desperate glance to Noah, he grabs my hand and says, "Jump." He throws his backpack to the ground, and I check my pockets for the cameo and ring, which thankfully are tucked in tight by a zipper. We leap into the canal and swim around the corner, splashing wildly through the icy water. No one jumps after us, but they still fumble around on the alleyway and bridge, yelling to follow us on foot.

"This way." We go through an area where there is only canal and wall. No sidewalk. Under a bridge, we climb out, our bodies heavy and wet. We are out of breath, but not out of fight. Lights turn on ahead as a helicopter circles the area above us. I throw Noah back under the bridge, and we curl up in the dark until the lights scan past us.

"All this for a few researchers with a couple artifacts?" I ask.

"Italy is very serious about their art. And everyone loves a scandal." He guides me out and points to a broken window nearby. "There."

We climb in carefully, though the jagged glass edge still catches my forearm and slices a good gash along my skin. Worth the pain if we buy time to get us out of this mess. Once inside the dank basement, we realize it's flooded. We wade through the frigid water, gasping from the cold. I hold pressure to my arm, but blood gushes through my fingers.

In the corner, we find a dry spot on the stairs leading to a door. We sit and shiver. Noah rips the bottom of his shirt and wraps it around my arm. The white linen fills in with seeped blood, then slows. He moves the wet stringy hair from my forehead and I notice he lost his glasses in the scuffle.

"This has been one hell of an adventure, Mia."

My teeth chatter, mostly from cold, but partly from adrenaline. "Thank you for believing in me."

He kisses my cheek and guides my head to rest on his shoulder. We don't speak but silently watch the helicopter lights flash through the window and listen to the city search for the madwoman who steals art and questions history.

All we have now is the hope that someone heard my pleas and feels the same fire to find the proof I need. The entire world needs it too, they just aren't aware of it yet.

Chapter Forty-Four

Caterina's bulging eyes turn gray. Lucca has untied me and now we stare in shock at the blood that collects at his feet.

"You killed your wife." I didn't think he was capable. I reach for his arm, a small gesture to remind him we're in this together. "Lucca?" I shake his ghostly presence. "We must leave. Now."

He bends down to lower her lids. Still crouched, head hung, and shoulders rounded, he says, "So much blood."

"I'll handle this." I shove him aside. The blade is lodged so firmly in her flesh that it won't budge, so I brace my foot in her shoulder blade, grip the handle with two firm hands, and yank. A thin slice was all it took to kill her while she busied herself attempting to choke the air from my lungs.

A ripped canvas and plenty of rope suffice. In a few minutes, I have Caterina's body wrapped, tied, and ready to be dragged.

Lucca remains still, staring at her blood.

I slap him hard across the cheek. He gasps, the whites of his cheeks instantly flushing pink.

"She's dead," I say. "And if we don't dispose of her body, we will be too."

The poor man only responds to force. Without a word or even the hint of acknowledgment, he lifts her wrapped feet, and I her flopping head.

Luckily, there are no men working the ship. They've all gone ashore for gambling and prostitution. I walk ahead to ensure a clear path to the ladder. Lucca hasn't released his grip on Caterina's feet.

"Your sculptures are on this ship, ready to set sail," he says. "That's how she got aboard." He comes back to life, remembering how wicked his wife was. "She sold you too."

I swallow against the swollen, bruised tightness of my neck. "Sold me?"

"These men bought sensuous, forbidden sculptures, and the prostitute who helped create them. They wanted you too."

Sold me. A sudden realization hits me like a strike to the temple. "She couldn't let them have me. She'd rather see me dead than release me to someone else's ownership."

We drag her long body down the corridor, her ends lifted while her rear end sags in the middle, dragging across the wood planks. I drop my grip as her head thunks to the ground. "You allowed this."

He lowers his head. "I tried to stop her."

"You didn't try hard enough." Once again, his weakness complicates my feelings for him.

"She believed you possess some kind of witchlike power over men. When I saw her hands around your neck, I—" Lucca trembles and closes his mouth, attempting to speak through gathering tears. "My father beat me, and Caterina squeezed the soul from my body. All these years I have tried to love and what was it all for? No one has ever cared for me. Until you."

"Perhaps you've finally found the love you seek. Not in romance, but in creation. We share something special when we sculpt. It's nothing like I've experienced."

He forces a smile. "That will have to be enough."

"What did Caterina do to you tonight?"

Lucca finally drops her feet, staring at her dead form. "She promised me accolades. Approval and admiration. All the things I thought I wanted." He wipes his tear-streaked cheeks with his sleeve. "Then she locked me alone in a room under guard while she sold everything." He gazes up at me, his eyes as red as the blood on his hands. "She would have kept me like a prisoner, if she let me live at all. And I realized something."

"What is that?"

His tears have turned into a glassy sheen. "I retreat from the world, from love and things that are of this earth. I desperately want to feel alive, yet I can't seem to touch what rests just outside my fingertips. This thing I don't understand helps me see emotions others do not."

"Are you afraid that if you lose the darkness, you will also lose the creations inside you?"

"I know I will." He swipes his cheek to catch the gathered tears. "She would only tolerate me if I was someone else entirely. Someone I could never be. So I escaped and came to rescue you."

This man, this incredible artist, thinks he cannot feel love. Despite the serious moment, I break a smile.

With soft indignation, he says, "I find nothing humorous here."

"You risked everything to save me," I say. He knows more love than Caterina ever will.

"My muse." He extends his clawlike hand to me. "I could not let her hurt you."

"The magic of the courtesan is this: Touching my body became a reminder you were alive. I am not your muse, Lucca. I am your friend."

He doesn't hide his twisted face or his tears that flow freely. He lifts the bound feet of his dead wife with a look of determination. "She will spend eternity in the sea."

With great difficulty, we carry her increasingly rigid corpse up a narrow, rickety ladder. Lucca's disfigured hand struggles to grip her weight, so we take several rests. We arrive on an empty deck, where men have abandoned their posts for a night in Carnival.

Through fatigued arms and bloodstained hands, we manage to teeter Caterina's body over the railing and shove her overboard. I glance around to ensure we are still alone. We lean over to watch her splash into the lagoon, where she'll be carried off to disintegrate in the Adriatic Sea.

Lucca chokes back a sob. For everything he lacks, he holds empathy and sorrow even for those who do not deserve it.

I hold his hand. He leads me to a hatch, where a gondola awaits. Inside sits a smiling Antonio, *The Serpent of Venice*, and *The Lovers*. He brought us a way to escape and saved my art. Dreams of a sunlit afternoon warming our bodies in Tuscany seem close enough to touch.

~

I kiss Antonio as if he has returned to life. Through tears, I taste his sweet lips and lean into his soft touch. Lucca checks the sculptures for damage, but I am fully engrossed in the features of Antonio's face. His strong jaw and full lips. His high cheekbones and eyes like flames.

"We've done it," Lucca says. "We've saved them." He smiles brighter than I've ever seen. A toothy beam of relief. A childlike moment of joy. And it's lovely.

"I couldn't allow Venice's greatest works to fall into the hands of some emperor who might shatter them in a fit of rage." Antonio tilts his head, love flooding his eyes. "For you, and that which you love, I will risk my life every second of every day."

The sculpture of myself with a serpent crawling through my legs so clearly forms my initials. The fired clay of Antonio's hands on my neck and breast is more subtle, but the shape of SR is unmistakably mine. "How can I ever thank you?"

"You already have." He presses one soft, deep kiss to the curve of my neck then rests his cheek on my shoulder with an exhale. "You already have, my love."

Lucca clears his throat. He waits for us to look at him and he produces a velvet cinched bag. "I saved more than the sculptures."

I snatch it from him and look inside. It is full of cameos. Agate, ivory, and onyx coins with my likeness. "These sketches were never meant to become jewelry."

"Caterina could carve on a small scale quite well by someone else's vision. It was her only talent." He lifts the pieces and lets them fall through his fingers as they clang back into the bag.

Antonio reaches for a teardrop pendant, running his thumb over my likeness. "This is your gaze. In perfect likeness." He slips it into the inside pocket of his shirt and pats his chest with an adoring smile.

The gondola seems to sink under the weight of the sculptures, slogging through the water. Antonio guides us back through the lagoon toward the Grand Canal. We all know this gondola won't hold for long, and silently we glide back toward the city that may ruin us: Antonio, an escaped prisoner; Lucca, who'll be blamed for stealing money; and the courtesan at the center of the entire saga, whom they see as nothing more than disposable goods.

Lucca sits next to me, our hands resting on the smooth stone of the serpent. "We have riches. The sale of these pieces is enough to fund our lives for years to come. Where will you go?" he asks.

"South. Perhaps Tuscany. Where the sun shines like gold." I trail my finger over the sculpture, along the arm and wrist that form the curve of my hidden S. "And you?"

He looks at the sky with a deep exhale. "I have no family. I will live out my days in solitude, remembering the muse who once danced with me under the stars."

Behind his smile rests a palpable sadness that nearly takes my breath away. "Alone?" I ask.

"It was always meant to be this way." He blinks, holding his eyes closed for several beats before dragging them back open. "I'm sorry, Sofia."

All I can manage is a smile, and a soft touch on his arm.

The gondola creaks and pops as we glide past Dorsoduro and sneak in among the bobbing boats of San Marco, per Lucca's suggestion. "Caterina keeps a boat docked here. It is strong and will carry you south with your treasures. Once docked you can hire a wagon to take you west to Tuscany."

We know the risks. But we hope Carnival will distract from our presence. We approach the square that bursts with celebration as hooded figures stumble from place to place, unconcerned about our trio and our seductive statues.

Antonio dons a cape, and hands us masks. "Wear it so no one recognizes you."

"No one will care about me now that Caterina is gone." I wince a little inside. My work is nothing to anyone but myself.

Lucca rests his hand on my shoulder. "Your work deserves to be celebrated."

"Our work, you mean?"

His face tightens. "No, Sofia. These sculptures came from my hand, but only with your vision. They are yours. Forever."

I turn to bathe in Antonio's smile, to drink his loving gaze, when through the dark, two men shove him to the ground and take turns pummeling him with punches.

I launch for them, knowing it's useless but willing to die for him. One of their hands slaps me back so hard, I crack my head on the dock. As my fuzzy vision focuses, a face appears.

Marco.

He orders his men to lift the serpent statue. "This is now mine."

"It is nothing of the sort." I struggle my way to standing as my woozy head tells me the ground is shifting, though I know that to be false.

He wriggles his way toward me like the worm he is. "I suppose one of you killed Caterina?"

Searing pain shatters through my head like crackling ice. Lucca reaches for my arm as I wobble, but Marco slams his cane on his wrist. Lucca's wail attracts a few partygoers who stop to watch the beating.

Both men lie at my feet. Antonio to my left, Lucca to my right. "You want my art?" I ask Marco.

"What I want means nothing, remember?" Hate spits from his eyes. I could do all he ever asked of me and still, he would ruin me. I should have fought harder. Screamed louder.

The men have stopped punching Antonio, but he isn't moving. I want to scream for him and cradle his head in my hands.

"Don't look at him," Marco orders. "I am the man you must answer to." He presses the flesh below his temple, rubbing out the tension in his jaw. "I made sure to burn every document that mentions you."

Antonio grunts. I'm so relieved he's alive that I throw myself on the ground, reaching for his face. Before my fingertips can touch his bloody jaw, one of Marco's brutes shoves me back again. This time, I know to brace my arms to protect my head from another blow. Marco walks to Lucca, his eyes never leaving mine. "He encouraged your ridiculous notions. Let you break the rules our society thrives on."

"At least he didn't cry every time he climaxed."

If Marco were a stronger man, he would meet my barbs with an even quicker wit. Alas, Marco is not strong in body or in mind. His neck bulges and lips curl so tightly they disappear. "Wench!" Then he whips his hand across my face, where his knuckles clatter against my cheekbones.

He wants me to beg. To apologize. I will do no such thing. He senses my resolve, I'm sure of it. He motions to Lucca. "Break his hands."

One of his brutes stomps his heeled shoe over Lucca's good hand, grinding and crushing through horrific screams. "Stop. You'll ruin his chance to paint and sculpt."

"That's my hope." He reaches for my face. I have a mind to bite his hand to match Caterina's. "I set his art on fire. I hold no hesitation about breaking his bones." Marco spits, "Now his left hand."

As the screams and groans continue, Marco grins, fully aware that Lucca would rather die than live without making art. I resolve right here and now to die with them.

"I have given my body to a great many men, Marco. You have, by far, been the most disappointing."

After a rumbling growl from deep in his gut, a few more people gather to watch the spectacle, laughing as if we are performing a theater. Carnival celebrations drown out most of our battle here on the docks of Piazza San Marco, though a few masked souls watch with intrigue.

Decision made, I embrace that which has been fated in the depths of my soul. "I wanted to believe my role in society would grant me a grander life than my fellow women. Better than the prostitutes of the Castelletto, and certainly better than a wife. How naive I've been." I lift my skirts, ignoring Lucca's cries and choking back tears at Antonio's battered body. "I was no more free than the desperate men you've imprisoned in the wells. I could never sculpt for I have been cursed with breasts, a womb, and a lack of shame over sharing a bed with powerful men."

"It is not your figure that cursed you, Sofia. It is your disrespect."

I press my chest to his, bare my teeth in a wicked grin, and think of all the times men have dismissed me. "I have more talent than you ever will. A deeper desire to create than you could ever dream of. You may steal these sculptures, sell them, and leave me forever forgotten. All your mighty efforts will fail because you will still remain insignificant and incapable of the thing you've most wanted in the world."

"I am an artist, Sofia. You are nothing but a whore."

I laugh, despite the sick fear that crawls up my throat, stalking my every word as it leaves my mouth. "All the wealth and privilege in this world could not make you an artist. It has only made you a coward."

A swift kick to his cockerel grants me a few seconds to run to Antonio. He doesn't move with my touch. His pale face remains hauntingly empty as his breath hitches.

"Please, my love. Wake." My hands bathed in his blood, I grip his clothing and rip his cape to feel the last of his heartbeat. "Come back to me."

The world halts to a frozen second in time as a piercing crack stops me from breathing, from moving or seeing. A sound that can only mean the crack of fired clay. I peer over my shoulder to find Marco, axe in hand, grinning in satisfaction at *The Lovers* in two pieces at his feet. The great sculpture of my love is now nothing more than a severed vision. Two heads untouching, two hearts forever ripped apart.

"This piece sold quickly," Marco says. "A prince in Spain loved the lines and the face of a woman being touched by her lover." He kicks the likeness of Antonio until it clunks and rolls toward the water. "How your hand cups your breast and caresses between your legs. The prince was mesmerized. I, however, am disgusted."

I crawl my way to Lucca, who uses his elbows to maneuver toward the jagged ceramic. Together, we reach for what is left of our masterpiece. Without one, the other is useless. Heartless. Simply a woman in an erotic arch, with no love to balance the heat.

Marco approaches. He lazily kicks the profile of Antonio into the Grand Canal without a beat of hesitation. I collapse into Lucca, cradling his broken fingers in my arms. He rolls to his back, staring at the sky of forever and nothingness, knowing he will never again craft beauty with his hands. Art will die inside him, withering like ripe fruit at the onset of frost, wasted, and shriveled.

I look up at Marco's shadowed eyes of hollow evil. His sunken cheeks and the way his skull puckers his skin, swallowing all life into his aging bones. "You may beat us and kill us, but our hearts you cannot touch." I rest Lucca's hands on his chest, which seems to clunk and shift in such an unnatural way, my stomach clenches at the sound. I stand to face Marco. "Have you won yet?"

He nods to his men. "Leave the young one here to die. The vultures will pick at his remains as a symbol to the city. The older one goes to the Piombi. I will get to him later." He turns to me. "This one is mine."

They grab Lucca, who remains limp and silent, presumably lost in his mind, where the darkness comforts him from the horrors of his broken body. One hollers from behind Marco, "This was tucked in his shirt."

Marco reaches for the velvet bag. He dangles it, shaking to hear its contents. He reaches in and lifts a fistful of cameos, all with my likeness. "Your beauty pains me, Sofia. The kind of goddess-inspired spirit one cannot ever touch for fear it will disappear like smoke." He grips the cameos so tight he could crush them.

"I don't care for those. Break them all."

"Yes, I have already taken what you love. *The Lovers* and the men who inspired such mastery."

My failed attempt to inject my being into memory, into history. My desperation led me here, and here it shall die.

Marco hands the bag off to the last of his men, who carries *The Serpent of Venice*, the broken remains of my face in clay, a satchel of money, and the bag of cameos into the ship Lucca intended to carry us to freedom in. A freedom that will never come.

I lower once more to grasp Antonio's face in my hands and lay a kiss on his unmoving lips. "I will love you, forever." I cannot be certain, though I think I see a tug at the corner of his mouth.

Marco ensures his face is obscured by a hood. He lowers his elaborate gilded leather mask. Then he wraps his arms around my waist to lift me. Of course I fight. I scratch and kick, but Marco's guard holds my ankles. I scream, uselessly I know, so the onlookers may hear something. So they may tell someone the truth of what happened to the masked woman at Carnival.

Marco holds me so tight I can't fight back. Can't reach for something to help me escape. He finally lets me go. My feet don't move when I ask them to. I look down to find a rope binding them together. I look up in just enough time to see Marco smile. With both wicked, bony hands, he shoves me back by the chest.

I crash into the water. Slowly, I hit with a splash, noting the end of the rope tied to a stone block. I have only one breath left. One moment to take in air. I stare up at Galileo's stars that Antonio kissed me under in the Campanile. The diamonds of light that cluster into what I now know as the Milky Way remind me the world goes on.

With one giant swoosh, the stone weight drags me under.

As time fades to a still moment in the space between life and death, I don't think of the saltwater about to rush into my lungs or Antonio's kisses that I'll never again taste. I don't even panic about death's incoming grip. No, the only thing hovering in my mind are Caterina's final words.

You are not special. No one will remember you.

My mind holds a soft image of the girl I once was. Hopeful, and firm in the belief of who I would be. I knew in the very depths of me that time would shift with my name. Wood and clay at my hands would become glorious images that stir the soul. I didn't consider the limits of my womanhood. No, they are strengths. The feminine softness of my touch. The eyes that view the world as the painting it is and not as a society to conquer. I possess a deep, soulful understanding of the wounds handed to me by those who came before. The ability to cry and the ache of understanding why.

All these things lived and breathed inside me without my knowledge, yet I know them, on my skin and in my heart. The joy and heartache of that little girl who could have grown into an astonishingly beautiful artist. I knew then who I was meant to be.

Before the world convinced me that my eyes and body and tears and softness were great disadvantages at best. And at worst, wicked, desperate tools to destroy men and topple republics. How could I be both so powerful and so useless? Not until now, as life leaves my body, do I see the truth that burned inside me all along.

It was I who held the power. The voice inside me that wished to roar was not wrong or evil. She was stolen, beaten, and left for dead.

As bubbles thrash to the surface, carrying the last of my breath, my dreams remain beside me. My hand comes to rest on the ceramic face of Antonio, the missing piece of the greatest art the world will never see. I will never experience my work displayed at a great palace or hear my name spoken in the same breath as Bernini.

Sofia Rossi will forever languish in the Venetian Lagoon, next to the carved likeness of the man who loved her.

Chapter Forty-Five

If ever there was a time to tell someone you love them, this would be it. As the sun rises and shines its glorious Venice light through the broken windows of the flooded basement we hid in all night, I watch Noah admire the light show in a last moment before my world crashes over me.

"It's time," I say.

"We've done everything we can." He holds me and kisses my forehead, and despite the bone-chilling, shake-inducing shivers, I've never felt warmer.

Knowing we have nothing left, we emerge from the basement and enter the streets. I expect someone to grab us, but no one does. Everyone must be glued to their televisions and phones, waiting to hear the press conference that will ruin me forever.

We walk slowly, letting the sun warm us with every step. We notice a few looks, but no one chases us or yells. Eventually, we arrive at the outskirts of St. Mark's Square, watching as a group of Venice officials line up in front of dozens of cameras. Next to them I see Dr. Wright and his young assistant.

Noah holds my hand.

"I won't let you fall with me. I take the hit," I say.

"And let you have all the fun?" He winks and I wonder how he can be so brave.

We walk hand in hand toward the reporters as microphones and speakers blast the voices spoken surprisingly in English.

"We have a thief in our midst. A dangerous, lying woman who wishes to demolish our art world. Miss Mia Harding and her friend have wreaked havoc on our city, and we will not rest until she is apprehended and dealt with appropriately."

"My name is *Doctor* Mia Harding," I yell in my most confident voice. That saying, stand before the people you fear and speak your mind, even if your voice shakes? Yeah, that hits the mark.

The crowd turns to us, more in shock than anything. They stare for a moment before a man says calmly, "Get her."

We don't fight. We hold hands and walk toward them.

"May I speak?" I ask.

All cameras point to me.

"No," the man says. But I already have the attention of reporters and camera crews. I'm the most interesting speaker in this square.

"I may be the only one, but I care about truth. I researched where every man before me refused to go. I listened and looked in places everyone chose to ignore. Lucca Armani didn't sculpt *The Estasi*." There are the gasps I expected. "At least not on his own. The artist that deserves credit for *The Estasi* and *The Serpent* is a woman named Sofia Rossi. She was Lucca's courtesan and his muse. She deserves to be remembered. We've all tried to erase her, and shame on those who never cared to unearth the truth."

"Take her away," a man yells.

Polizia arrive to handcuff both the dangerous historians. We don't resist.

"Her name was Sofia Rossi," I say again.

"She's right." Eva appears, beautiful and brave, holding a scroll. She unrolls the painting and holds it high. "Sofia Rossi painted this. *The Vengeful Maiden*." Eva takes a deep breath and smiles widely, enjoying her moment in the spotlight. "Her initials are right here. Dr. Harding is right."

"Get that thing out of the sun!" Dr. Wright yells.

She hands it off to the authorities and stands in front of us. "I will fight for you both. I promise."

"I didn't steal anything," I yell. "At least, not intentionally. The cameo and ring are in my pocket. The cameo was given to me as a bribe." Heavy eyes and worried looks skitter across the crowd. "The ring was my fault. I needed it for research. I shouldn't have taken it from Palazzo Armani, and I will pay my debt for that. I always intended to give it back."

"We will deal with you later," Dr. Wright yells into the speaker. *Polizia* order the men to take us away.

This is it. I've said what I came here to say, and I've found the truth I set out to find. The rest is out of my hands. They separate me from Noah, which is my first pang of regret this morning.

"Wait!" Eva yells, pointing at the water behind the press conference. Several people in scuba gear rise from the Grand Canal, waving their hands. Everyone moves closer, anticipating something major. Those who hold our handcuffs lead us with the crowd while Noah pushes toward me until our shoulders touch.

As we near the water and push through, still handcuffed, one diver removes their fins and tank and walks forward holding something in their arms.

"It couldn't be," I mutter. Someone heard my pleas.

The diver hands a muddy block of a thing to their fellow diver, who washes away the sand and muck to reveal a carved face. Cameras zoom in and people squeal. Right before our eyes, Antonio Bruni's face comes alive. The other half of *The Estasi* has risen from the depths of the lagoon where he has remained hidden for four hundred years.

The diver removes their hat and mask to reveal long blond curls. A woman found the lost carving. I can't help but smile. Noah leans into my shoulder and whispers in my ear. "I have a feeling Dr. Wright is going to eat a little humble pie this morning."

"Hopefully from the inside of an Italian prison cell."

The woman diver announces loudly, "I found this in the exact location Dr. Harding identified. When I saw her on TikTok Live, I knew I had to help. We've been silenced long enough." She hands the authorities another amazing find from the morning, making sure to catch the cameras when she says, "Something is carved in the bottom. Two initials. SR."

The plaza erupts in cheers. I turn to Noah, face to face and smiling, despite our clasped wrists behind our backs. We kiss simply and honestly, right there among the truth.

"Will this be the beginning of many more amazing finds, Dr. Harding?" he asks.

"Well, Dr. Beckett, they can't ignore us forever."

We lean in to kiss again but we're knocked off balance. "You have been busy."

It takes me a moment to place her. "Gabriella." The bird lady.

She purses her lips. "Remove those things," she yells to the policeman holding my cuffs. He ignores her, but he doesn't drag me away, presumably confused whether he is to arrest me or not. "Go on!"

The man sends his partner to confirm next steps. Gabriella steps next to us, her cockatoo perched on her shoulder. "I added a story to my blog this morning."

"Did it involve the other half of *The Estasi*?" I ask with a grin. "Because that story has broken."

She wriggles her shoulders. "No. Obviously this will be all anyone will talk about. But I have more."

"I can't take much more," Noah says, his cheeks drained of color.

Gabriella reaches into her bag and tucks her hand between us. She turns her hand, palm open, to reveal a golden egg.

"No shit." My head could explode from the shock. "There really was a golden egg?"

"Yes." Gabriella laughs as her mound of wild curls tickles my cheek.

The man holding us unlocks our cuffs. "Don't move. You come in for questioning."

Gabriella elbows past him. "Here." She hands the egg to Noah. "I have no interest in love. Go on."

Noah pries the seams apart with his thumbs, opening the egg on its delicate hinges. "Empty."

"No." Gabriella shakes her head, leaning back with a stifled squeal. "This egg represents the love and connection of Antonio Bruni and Sofia Rossi. You hold that in your hand. Look at Dr. Mia and tell me you haven't fallen in love with her while searching for Sofia."

Noah's cheeks blush again. He smiles and hands Gabriella the egg. "I have." His eyes lock on mine. "Perhaps that's what Antonio meant. Someday, two lost historians will find each other, and they will discover the secret of a woman erased. I do love you, Mia. And I do not need anything more."

"I may have loved you from that first night in the archives, Mr. Purple Jumper." The frenzy fades and all I see are his chin dimple and the most handsome smile in the world. "You've given me a gift even more profound than Sofia Rossi. You helped me see I belong just as I am. A historian on an adventure, finding hidden women the world tried to erase."

"So you plan on more searches for wenches and witches?" He holds my hand and rubs the back of my thumb. "Do you require an assistant on these adventures?"

"*Andiamo*, Noah."

SOFIA

My body crumbled piece by piece in the sand of the Grand Canal as bits of my flesh swelled and softened. But I did not disappear. I remain here in the memory of Venice, not floating as an angel, but present like the air that fills people's lungs. They breathe me without knowing and hear my cries deep in their hearts when they stop to admire the beauty of our most serene Republic.

Sofia Rossi was so much more than a body. More than a courtesan and a woman murdered under the secrecy of a dark night and Carnival costumes. I am hope unrealized and dreams drowned by the weight of an unfair world.

I have watched years unfold and my city change, though time means nothing anymore.

Lord Marco killed me, but he did not just stop me from existing. He systematically erased me through burned documents stored at the palace. He scoured records of my name for years, firm in his belief that I never lived.

I watched him bury *The Serpent* in a drained canal under the light of a full moon. He dumped the bag of cameos off the Rialto Bridge into the canal below, where they fell like raindrops to the silty bottom.

Antonio's sculpted face rested with me under water, yet my likeness remained hidden in Marco's bedchamber, where he would stare at my carving for hours. He held that carving, and at times fell asleep with her. He spent months attempting to recreate *The Lovers* with his own hand. Of course, he never succeeded.

By the time he buried my half of *The Lovers*, Marco had accepted his failures. He understood that his work would never elicit more than a scoff. Though there are no tears in death, somehow I still cried as he wrapped her in linen, enclosed her in a box, and buried her in Lucca's garden under the magnolia tree. He had taken over Palazzo Armani by that time, as Lucca was detained and tortured.

After Lucca admitted his guilt in selling and creating banned sexual artwork, he escaped, wandering the hills outside Siena, penniless and alone. He fled to Tuscany to fulfill the dream I could not. Somehow the seed of freedom grew to fulfill him—released from his art in the saddest way possible.

Antonio awoke on the street the next morning as the sun rose over Venice once again, as it always does, bringing with it a world that did not hold me. Authorities no longer cared about Antonio, and Marco watched him from afar. Antonio fought the urge to kill the man who murdered his great love and retreated to his studio, weeping over memories of our brilliant time together. He never attacked, believing it was more important to keep my memory alive, even if in whispers among his family. Like a lightning bolt, we were a flash of great love, with a burn mark on his heart to remember me by.

He kept the cameo on a teardrop pendant and our golden egg. It hurt to look at me, so he hid the piece in the floorboards, under the place we lay naked and made love by candlelight. He married a kind woman and had three daughters, never allowing them inside the studio. His youngest called it his room of sadness.

I watched the remains of my life fade little by little. Antonio's heart healed, as did Lucca's hands. Lord Marco slept in my old bedchamber, the courtesan's quarters, hoping to feel the muse Lucca spoke of. He even wandered the dome and tunnel at night, placing trinkets around the house to coax my ghost to his lonely, useless hands.

Ghosts don't work like that, I came to realize. We speak in whispers, hoping a mortal soul may hear us from the walls in which we lived and the art we once sculpted.

For one satisfying moment, Antonio held me. As he passed from life to death, from one world to another, I met him with all the love I've ever had for him. He died as an old man, comfortable in his bed, his family at his side. But when he saw me, arms outstretched, ready to welcome him to the place where we no longer exist, he didn't hesitate.

We are the heart of Venice, every one of us who died loving the city that never loved us back. We don't go on together in an afterlife, as we always expected, but float in nothingness.

Even now, as Dr. Mia Harding discovers my secrets, as she finds that Lord Marco erased all memories of me, I know with great gratitude that we are never fully erased. Mia found my memory and brought my art to the world, just as I had always imagined.

Every one of us who died and failed, hearts broken in a thousand pieces, hopes for another Mia Harding to pull us from the ruins of history, where we wait, buried and forgotten.

It is the women who will unearth our secrets and keep our legacy burning.

ACKNOWLEDGMENTS

Writing *The Secret Courtesan* was an experience unlike anything I've felt before. This manuscript unfolded so rapidly, it seemed to write itself. I felt as if Mia and Sofia offered their story in detail and I was merely the audience tasked with bringing their words to the page.

Every book needs a team to help it come to life. This was especially true for this whirlwind of a project. What began as a feverish ride from my manic brain became a finished product with the help of editors Nicole Meier and Jamie McGillen and my always supportive critique partners, Jen Craven, Sayword Eller, Lisa Carnachon, and my friends at The Eleventh Chapter.

Thank you to She Writes for giving this story a home. To Brooke and Addison for helping her come to life, and to Rylee Warner, Hanna Lindsley, and Crystal Patriarche at Booksparks Publicity for giving her a shot in this competitive world of books.

As always, thank you to my husband Mike who nurtures my dreams every day and helps me bring my author visions to life.

I knew from the first page that this story was different. For years, I've been researching and writing about badass women in history. I write articles and short stories on women who made incredible contributions to our world but our patriarchal society all but erased. Sofia became the embodiment of this, and Mia became the voice in my head that burns to right the wrongs of our history books.

I didn't set out to write about the erasure of women in the arts, but this is the story that arose from the anger and sadness of discovering incredible women who should have had their names etched in the narrative of history.

In my research travels, I kept finding stories of women not given access to art materials or being barred from art classes and models. If they did succeed in making art, social biases about women devalued their work. The erasure of women artists is not uncommon. Many misattributions, by artists such as Artemisia Gentileschi and Sofonisba Anguissola, took centuries to correct.

Writing historical fiction has been one of the greatest joys of my life. The women I research change me and empower me every day. It is because of readers like you that I can continue doing what I love and bring more HERstory to the world. Thank you for reading Mia and Sofia's adventures, and thank you for supporting this author's lifelong dream.

ABOUT THE AUTHOR

Kerry Chaput is an award-winning historical fiction author who writes about daring women with loads of adventure and a splash of magic. Kerry's writing has been an Historical Novel Society editor's choice, with *Midwest Book Review* calling her a "Master of the genre." She's also been a finalist for Sarton Women's Book Award and the Chaucer Book Award for early historical fiction. Born in California, she now calls the Pacific Northwest home. Kerry frequents hiking trails, coffee shops, and independent bookstores near her home in Bend, Oregon.

Looking for your next great read?

We can help!

Visit www.shewritespress.com/next-read or scan the QR code below for a list of our recommended titles.

She Writes Press is an award-winning independent publishing company founded to serve women writers everywhere.